SOME D KILL YOU

I never realized a hallucination could seem so real, Massan thought.

This was the environment he had chosen: crushing gravity; killing pressures; oceans of liquid methane and ammonia; "solid ground" consisting of quickly crumbling, eroding ice; darkness; danger; death.

He was encased in a one-man protective outfit that was half armored suit, half vehicle. An internal liquid suspension system kept him tolerably comfortable at four times normal gravity, but still a man could move only very slowly even with the aid of servomotors.

He extended the detector's range to maximum and worked the scanners up the sheer face of the cliff toward the top. There he was! The shadowy outline of a man etched itself on his detector screen. And at the same time, Massan saw a small avalanche of ice tumbling, sliding, growling toward him. *That devil set off a bomb at the top of the cliff!* He toppled off the ledge into the boiling sea. He felt something vibrating on his helmet. The oxygen tubes! They were being disconnected.

He screamed and tried to fight free. No use. The frothing sea filled his view plate. He was being held under. And now the view plate itself was being loosened. The scalding cold methane/ammonia sea seeped through the opening view plate.

"It's only a dream!" Massan shouted to himself. "Only a dream! A dream! A ..."

SOME DREAMS CAN
KILL YOU

BEN BOVA

TEXAS STATE TECH. COLLEGE
LIBRARY-SWEETWATER TX.

THE WATCHMEN

This is a work of fiction. All the characters and events portrayed in this book are fictional, and any resemblance to real people or incidents is purely coincidental.

Star Watchman copyright © 1964 by Ben Bova.
The Dueling Machine copyright © 1969 by Ben Bova.

All rights reserved, including the right to reproduce this book or portions thereof in any form.

A Baen Book

Baen Publishing Enterprises
P.O. Box 1403
Riverdale, N.Y. 10471

ISBN: 0-671-87598-1

Cover art by Darrell K. Sweet

First Baen printing, April 1994

Distributed by
Paramount Publishing
1230 Avenue of the Americas
New York, N.Y. 10020

Printed in the United States of America

Author's Introduction

They say you can't go home again, and as usual, they're wrong.

In re-reading these two tales of the Star Watch some thirty years after I wrote them, all of the passions and motivations that went into the two novels came flooding back into my mind. I was pleasantly surprised to see how well the stories hold up, but struck by a deep sense of sadness to realize that the underlying human problems that form the focus of the novels are not only still with us, but are worse today than they were three decades ago.

Star Watchman was my second novel, and I wrote it at a time when France was deeply enmeshed in colonial wars in Algeria and a place that was then known as Indo-China. *French* Indo-China, at that. Today we call that region Laos, Cambodia, and Vietnam.

The problems of colonial wars, and wars by proxy—where major powers fight "minor" wars in some Third World country—were uppermost in my mind as I wrote *Star Watchman*. Shortly after the novel was first published,

1

010141

in 1964, President Lyndon B. Johnson started the immense American military build-up in Vietnam. Six years later President Richard M. Nixon enlarged the war into Laos and Cambodia. Some fifty thousand young Americans were killed in the fighting.

All through the Vietnam years I kept wondering if I was crazy or if the people running our government were. Before undertaking *Star Watchman* I did a fair amount of research into the history of colonial wars in general (including our own Revolution) and of Algeria and south-east Asia in particular. I began to ask myself, as the Vietnam fighting dragged on year after year: Even if we win, even if Ho Chin Minh surrenders abjectly, what would we gain? I mean, if I could understand that this war was fruitless, why couldn't the men in the White House?

Those of us who love science fiction can't help feeling that, if the politicians and other leaders of society would read SF, maybe we wouldn't stumble into the quagmires that we seem to find with depressing regularity. I don't think that if LBJ or Nixon had read *Star Watchman* either one of them would have changed his policies. But maybe it would have made them at least think a little about what they were doing and where they were heading.

Incidentally, I have not touched a word of either novel. By today's standards, they are not politically correct. Women are called girls, as they were in the Sixties. It's certainly a male chauvinist society out there on the space frontier. If anyone's sensibilities are offended by the implicit attitudes in these novels, they can always go back and re-read Jane Austen.

The Dueling Machine stemmed from an entirely different source. I was working at a high-powered research laboratory in the Boston area in the early Sixties. In those days I was a pretty good fencer; even won the New England saber championship one year (novice class). I helped to organize a fencing club at the lab. On summer evenings we practiced outdoors, on the parking lot. Often our practice was interrupted by the screech of automobile wheels, as drivers passing our lot stared at a bunch of people merrily trying to stab one another, and forgot to watch where they were driving.

Myron Lewis was one of the lab's physicists, and became a good saber fencer. One day, as we were complaining about lawyers (yes, lawyers were not held in high repute even then), I grumbled that Massachusetts had made a mistake when it outlawed dueling. Myron quickly suggested that it would be great if somebody could invent a dueling machine: a device in which two people could fight each other to the death, without being physically harmed.

We had invented Virtual Reality, although neither of us had the sense to pursue the idea except in fiction, and the term would not be coined for another twenty-some years.

I had earlier written a short story, "The Next Logical Step," that John Campbell published in *Analog* in May 1962. It dealt with a computer system for playing war games, in which the player experienced—with all his senses—the battle being fought. Myron and I combined that idea with his to create the dueling machine. We plotted out a novelet, which I wrote. It was the cover story in *Analog*'s May 1963 issue, with a superb cover illustration. That was during the brief era when *Analog* was published in large format, rather than digest-size.

That novelet became the first third of the novel, *The Dueling Machine*, under the sub-title "The Perfect Warrior."

The theme of *The Dueling Machine* is once again about war, and how to avoid or prevent it. It is a thinly-disguised speculation on what would have happened in the late 1930s if doughty Winston Churchill had been Prime Minister of Britain rather than the pacifistic Neville

Chamberlain. Was World War II inevitable? I do not believe any event in human history was inevitable.

Which is one reason why we read science fiction, I think. By looking forward into the possible futures that we may face, we can begin to make decisions about which of those futures we would like to live in, and perhaps even take steps to help that future to come about. The future is no more inevitable than the past. It is created by what we do in the present—and what we fail to do.

So, here are two tales of the future from thirty years ago. I think they still have things to say to today's readers, and I fondly hope that they are as entertaining now as they were when they were first written.

Ben Bova
Naples, Florida

PART I

Star
Watchman

To Mrs. Jaffe, wherever you are

I

Shinar

The Terran Empire stretched over half the Milky Way galaxy, from the lonely fringes of the immense spiral of stars to its richly-packed center. Earth was the capital of this vast Empire, but the planet Mars was headquarters for the Star Watch. The Empire's military arm, the Star Watch had bases on many planets, in all the farthest reaches of the immense Terran domain. But Mars—covered from pole to pole with mighty buildings housing the men and machinery that ran the Star Watch—was headquarters.

In a small office in one of those buildings, a noncom was startled out of his usual routine. His desk communicator lit up, and the dour features of the Chief-of-Staff took form on the screen.

"I want the complete file on Oran VI immediately."

"Yes sir." Before the chief's image had completely faded from the screen, the noncom's fingers were tapping out a message on his desktop keyboard to the mammoth computer that held the Star Watch's master files.

7

He decided to check and make certain that he had requested the correct information from the computer. (The possibility of the computer making an error was unthinkable.) He punched a button on the desk and the communicator screen lit up again.

The screen showed a map of the Milky Way galaxy, with the position of the star Oran marked out. It was on the edge of the Terran Empire, out in one of the farther spiral arms of the galaxy, near the territory of the Komani nation. The map faded, and a block of written data filled the screen:

ORAN: galactic coordinates ZJJ 27458330194126-3232. Eight planets, one terrestrial (Oran VI).

ORAN VI: radius 1.04, density 0.91, gravity 1.025. Atmosphere Earth-normal (0.004 deviation). Three major continents, surface 80% sea-covered. Native human population, 3.4 billion (estimated). Economy: rural agricultural; underdeveloped industrial base. Subject to Imperial Development Plan 400R, priority 3C. Former colony of Masters, incorporated into Empire immediately following Galactic War of last century. Native name for planet: Shinar.

"SHI-NAR!"

The square was thronged with people. Shouting, jumping, dancing people. It was hard to see how so many people could jam into the city square, but still more were pouring in from every avenue. They waved banners and held aloft placards. Several groundcars were overturned and swarmed over. A bonfire glowed near a statue at one end of the square. The people shouted one word, which rose and fell like the endless waves of the sea:

"SHI-NAR! SHEE-*NAR!*"

The Terran governor stood frowning on the balcony of his official residence, at the head of the jam-packed square. He turned to the garrison commander standing beside him. "This has got to be stopped!" The governor had to shout to be heard over the roars of the crowd. "There'll be another riot down there in a few minutes. The native police can't handle that mob."

The commander arched his eyebrows. "Sir, if I send my troops into the square, there may be bloodshed."

"That can't be helped now," the governor said. "Send in the troops.

Star Watch Junior Officer Emil Vorgens sat in his tiny compartment aboard the starship and reread his orders for the tenth time. He found it hard to believe that he was finally a full-fledged officer of the Star Watch. School was finished, his commission was safely tucked away in his travel kit, and here—on plastic film—were the orders for his first official mission.

He slid the tiny film into his pocket viewer again and projected the words onto the bare compartment wall:

"You will proceed to Oran VI and assist the Imperial Governor there in dealing with certain dissident elements of the native population."

Like most Star Watch orders, there was a good deal of meaning in the words that were *not* there. The Star Watch was the Terran Empire's interstellar military arm. In fact, the Star Watch pre-dated the Empire, and existed even back in the old days of the Confederation, more than a century ago.

It had been the Star Watch that fought the successful war against the Masters, the war that had made the Terran Confederation—almost against its own will—the new masters of most of the galaxy. The problems of ruling such a vast territory had been solved only by the creation of the Empire. Now the Star Watch served to control the interstellar space routes. A subsidiary branch, the Imperial Marines, handled any planet-borne fighting that had to be done.

Vorgens sat back in his webbed chair and studied his orders, a worried frown on his face. It was a youthful face, with a high forehead. His skin was a golden brown, his closely cropped hair copperish red, his eyes tawny. Although born into the Terran Empire, and fully human, Vorgens was not an Earth-man, but a native of the Pleiades star cluster.

His orders troubled him. To send a Star Watchman to Oran VI meant that the Empire was considering military action there. "Dissident elements of the native population." That could mean almost anything. It sounded serious.

Just how serious, Vorgens learned a few days later. A coded message from Star Watch headquarters was beamed to the ship for him. When he decoded it, the order stated:

"The Imperial Governor of Oran VI has been murdered. You will assist Brigadier Aikens, 305th Imperial Marines, in restoring order to the planet."

The starship hurtled on toward its destination as Vorgens spent his days fretfully trying to get more information on the situation on Oran VI. Very little could be learned. The Imperial Marines had landed there and the planet was in turmoil. Evidently a band of Komani raiders, sensing a chance for battle and looting, had also landed on Oran VI. A few days before reaching the planet, Vorgens received a final change in orders:

"You will seek out the Komani leader and warn him of the consequences of fighting against the Empire. The Komani raiders are to be offered safe conduct back to their homeworld in return for immediately quitting Oran VI. The Komani leader is to be reminded that all Komani clans have sworn allegiance to the Empire, and he can expect no assistance from the rest of the Komani nation."

Almost before Vorgens had a chance to digest the news that these orders implied, the starship broke out of subspace and entered an orbit around Oran VI. A planetary shuttle brought him down to the major spaceport, heavily guarded by Marines.

The major in charge outlined the situation to him quickly:

"Things are pretty confused here, Watchman. We control the four major cities on the planet, and this spaceport. The Komani raiders have been shooting up the countryside. There are bands of native rebels with them. Brigadier Aikens has the Mobile Force out hunting down the raiders."

Without more ado, the major bundled Vorgens into an aircar and sent the Watchman off, with a Marine pilot and gunner, to find Brigadier Aikens and the Mobile Force.

II
The Valley

Sergeant McIntyre had come a long way in the heat of the afternoon, scrabbling over the broken rocks, half tumbling down the steep slope of the valley, while the big yellow sun of Oran blazed hotter and brighter every minute.

Finally he saw the first outpost of the Mobile Force—a scout car, its turret hatches open, and a few men sitting lazily in the scant slice of shade the car offered.

As he approached, one of the troopers got up slowly, adjusted his glare visor, picked up his weapon and hailed him:

"Who goes?"

"Sergeant McIntyre, K Company, returning from patrol."

McIntyre stopped a few paces before the younger man. He could feel the sweat trickling down his flanks.

"Returning from patrol?" the trooper echoed. "Where's the patrol, Sarge?"

"You're lookin' at it, kid," McIntyre answered. "Are we gonna stand here all day? I'm hot, tired, thirsty and I've gotta make a report to my company commander."

The soldier swallowed his amazement, "Yeah, sure, Sarge. Come on over to the car." He turned and bawled out, "Lieutenant!"

McIntyre trudged over to the shade and squatted down on the bare, dusty ground, leaning his back against the dark, cool metal of the scout car. He took off his helmet, squinted painfully into the shimmering afternoon haze as he mopped his head with a tattered sleeve, then replaced the helmet and slid the glare visor over his eyes again.

One of the men offered him a canteen.

A lean, spotless lieutenant climbed down from the turret and confronted McIntyre.

"Sergeant, are you the man who led this morning's patrol through here and out to the southern edge of the valley?"

"Yes sir," McIntyre said, getting slowly to his feet.

"Where's the rest of your patrol? You had twenty men, didn't you?"

"Yes sir. The others were all killed or captured, sir."

"What? Impossible!"

McIntyre shook his head. "I wish it was impossible, sir. I only wish it was."

Sergeant McIntyre made his report by tri-di beam from the scout car to the communications center of the Mobile Force's main body, camped down in the heart of the valley.

"Sorry we don't have a vehicle for you," the lieutenant said a little stiffly, to hide his embarrassment. "We've been ordered to remain here at the perimeter."

"That's okay, sir," McIntyre answered. Then he added, with just a hint of malice, "I don't mind walkin' back. I'll be going *away* from the Komani for a change."

By the time he reached the main encampment of the

Mobile Force, the hot, yellow sun had sunk behind the hills. The sky overhead was still bright, but the valley itself was now in shadow.

As McIntyre made his way through the maze of land cruisers, dreadnaughts, troop carriers, supply vans and scout cars, it became obvious to him that his own report had been matched by equally bad reports from the other patrols of that morning. None of the guard details took the time to ask his identity. None of the shavetail officers stopped him for a lecture about his no-longer-regulation uniform. They knew where most of his equipment had been left, why he had buckled to his hip an extra sidearm (taken from a dying corporal), whose blood was on his ragged shirt.

The petty routine of military life was finished. They were all too busy with the urgency of self-preservation to bother. They were digging in, all across the valley. The Mobile Force of the 305th Imperial Marines, the military extension of the Terran Empire that ruled most of the galaxy, was threatened with annihilation.

It was cooler now that the sun had dipped behind the western hills. That was one thing to be grateful for, McIntyre thought as he searched out his company commander in the confusion of men and vehicles. The valley was in shadow, but the hills, where the enemy was, were still bright with daylight.

Surrounded, McIntyre thought to himself. *Totally cut off. I wonder how the Brigadier is taking the news?*

"Totally impossible!" snapped Brigadier Aikens.

"I'm afraid not, sir," his executive officer answered quietly. "All the patrols report the same thing—we are surrounded."

Aikens' pinched face, topped by a balding dome, glowered red as he stared at the stereomap on his desktop viewscreen. "Are any of the patrols still out?"

"Only two, sir. It doesn't look as though they're going

to make it back. The other patrols were badly mauled. One of them lost every man except a single sergeant."

Aikens got up from his chair and crossed the tiny compartment in three restless strides. Though the dreadnaught was huge for a land-going vehicle, all the compartments inside had to be as compact as humanly possible.

"Surrounded," he muttered, "trapped in this valley by a horde of barbarians."

"They don't fight like barbarians, sir," the exec murmured.

"What's that?"

The officer flushed. "I only meant, sir, that they have been using modern weapons—very effectively, sir."

Aikens nodded. "I know, I know." He returned to his desk and sat down again. "I've led my men into a trap. Now I've got to lead them out of it." The brigadier stared at the stereomap for a long moment while his aide stood motionless, listening to the faint whir of the air-conditioning system.

The exec was in his prime middle years, tall and dark-haired. A long stretch of desk duty, as part of the original garrison of Oran VI, had filled out his midsection and softened his face somewhat.

Aikens, although older by at least a dozen years, was straight-backed and flat-stomached. The brigadier had picked his aide on the strength of the younger man's first-hand knowledge of the planet.

Finally Aikens looked up. "Well, we'll hold our ground tonight. Double the guard around our perimeter."

"Yes sir."

"They can maul foot patrols, can they?" the brigadier muttered. "Tomorrow morning we'll see what they can do against some solid armor." He looked at the map on his desk again. "All right, you may go. Make certain you get a verbal report from all the company commanders after the guard is changed, and tell my staff I will meet them here in two hours."

"Yes sir."

The exec remained at attention before the desk.

"I said you may go," Aikens repeated.

"There's one more item, sir. That Star Watch officer who joined the Force two days ago. He's still waiting to see you, sir."

Aikens slammed a heavy hand on the desktop. "The situation isn't bad enough! Now I have to put up with shavetails from the Star Watch Academy who want to peep over my shoulder!"

"Sir, he's been waiting two days, and his orders are direct from Star Watch Headquarters."

Aikens fumed silently for a few moments, then said, "All right, get him in here. On the double."

"Very well, sir." The exec saluted, turned, and ducked through the low doorway of Aikens' cubbyhole office.

After a few minutes of searching through the dread-naught's command section, the exec found Vorgens hunched beside a seated technician in the communica-tions compartment, staring intently at a static-streaked viewscreen.

"It's no good, sir," the technician was saying. "The enemy has every frequency jammed. We can't get a word in or out."

Vorgens straightened up. His black-and-silver uniform was in stark contrast to the bright-colored coveralls that identified the crewmen's various jobs aboard the dreadnaught.

"I see," the Watchman said. "Thank you anyway."

"So here's where you've been hiding," the exec called out. "Come on, the brigadier wants to see you right away."

Vorgens stepped out of the communications compart-ment and into the narrow passageway.

"I've been trying to establish contact with the cities or Star Watch Headquarters. No luck," Vorgens said as they started down the passageway.

"They've got us boxed in pretty well," the exec said.

"The reports from the patrols seem to indicate that," Vorgens admitted. "Any chance of signaling to the orbiting ships?"

"What orbiting ships?"

"The transports that brought the Mobile Force here, and their escorts. Perhaps the ships could . . ."

"The ships aren't there, Watchman. They dropped the Mobile Force three weeks ago and left Oran VI immediately. They won't be back until they're called for."

Vorgens blinked in disbelief. "But . . . why?"

"It's a big Empire, son," the exec answered patiently, "and transports are too valuable to be tied up sitting at one planet, empty and useless."

"You mean we couldn't retreat off the planet, even if we wanted to?"

"We could commandeer whatever ships are available on the planet, which wouldn't be enough to carry all the men, let alone the equipment. We could get Star Watch ships in a week or so if we could make contact with somebody outside this blasted valley."

"How in the world did all this come about?" Vorgens wondered out loud.

The exec took him literally and replied, "It started with some protest demonstrations—some farmers complaining about a nutrient-processing center we were building for them. The next thing we knew, there were riots in the cities. Then the Governor was murdered by some fanatic. The Mobile Force landed a week later, and two days after *that* these Komani hordes landed in half a dozen places across the planet and started terrorizing the countryside. So here we are."

The exec stopped walking abruptly, and Vorgens realized he was standing before Brigadier Aikens' door.

"You know what I think," the executive officer stated, rather than asked. "I think the whole mess is a plan by the Komani to take over this planet, and it's just the first step in a much bigger Komani plan."

"But they were our allies against the Masters," Vorgens said.

"That was a hundred years ago, Watchman. Times have changed since then."

Vorgens nodded.

"Well," said the exec, "good luck with the Old Man."

"You're not coming in with me?"

"No, I've got several chores to carry off before I get my supper. *If* I get a chance to eat tonight." He flicked a salute at Vorgens and turned away.

Vorgens automatically returned the salute, then turned and confronted the brigadier's door. After an instant's hesitation, he knocked twice.

"Enter."

He stepped into the compartment, saluted, and stood at ramrod attention. Aikens, sitting behind his desk, regarded the young Watchman for a moment, then indicated with a nod the only other chair in the office. Vorgens sat down.

No two men on Oran VI looked less like each other. Vorgens was small and wiry, and his golden brown skin and coppery hair proclaimed him to be of non-Earthly stock. His thin, fine-boned face, surmounted by a high forehead, gave him a peculiarly babyish look.

Aikens was a typical Terran, towering above Vorgens' height and outweighing him by half again. The brigadier's only sign of encroaching years was his thinning hair and well-creased face. He had made it a point to foster carefully the impression among his men that he was a flamboyant and daring leader. Even now he was wearing the Imperial Marines' semi-dress uniform of green, red and gold, as opposed to Vorgens' standard Star Watch black-and-silver.

"I imagine you realize the situation we're in," Aikens said flatly.

Vorgens nodded. "I have seen the reports of today's patrols."

"This Mobile Force was dispatched to Oran VI to bolster the Imperial garrison and restore order among the native populace. When the Komani raiders landed, we were ordered to induce them to return to their homeworld. 'A demonstration of force': that's how the orders read. Well, for nearly three weeks now we've been trying to pin them down for our little demonstration. Now they've led us into a nasty trap. We're surrounded in this valley, and it looks as though the Komani are perfectly willing and eager to fight a full-scale battle."

"I know," Vorgens said.

"They're well armed with modern weapons, and their tactics so far have been masterful. In short, Vorgens, they've led me around by the nose for three weeks, and they're ready to start slugging."

"Have you any idea of their numbers?"

Aikens shrugged. "We're outnumbered, that much is certain. How badly, I can't tell. But that doesn't worry me. Trained troops can always lick an undisciplined horde of barbarians, no matter how clever the barbarians are. They may have modern weapons, but we have more firepower . . . and armored vehicles."

"They seem to have greater mobility, though," Vorgens observed.

"True enough, and their reconnaissance is much better than ours. What we need is some airpower and a column of reinforcements."

"Reinforcements?"

"Certainly. Oh, I'm positive we could handle this Komani mob with the men we have right here, but once they start taking a beating, the barbarians will melt back into the hills again and we'll lose them." Aikens tapped a forefinger on the stereomap as he spoke. "I want a column of reinforcements, from the city garrisons, with air cover and support, so we can pin down these barbarians from the outside. Then, between our two forces, we can crush them once and for all!"

Vorgens sat in puzzled thought for a moment. Then he said, "Sir, there are two problems on Shinar: the native rebels, and the Komani raiders. If you strip the cities of their garrisons to hit the Komani, you will be giving the cities to the rebels."

Aikens shrugged. "One problem at a time, Watchman. First we crush the Komani. The rebels will be easy to handle after that. Why, we can even show the natives that we helped them get rid of the barbarian invaders. Might win back most of the populace that way."

"But your aide thinks that the rebels are working for the Komani."

"True enough. He's probably right. But the majority of the natives don't know that."

"It's a very mixed-up situation," Vorgens said.

Aikens smiled grimly. "We're going to unmix it and make it perfectly simple. The first step is to get the city garrisons marching toward this valley. I'm certain the Komani won't be able to launch a full-scale attack on us for several days. They've got us pinned down, and they'll want us to run out of food and water before they attack. Attrition tactics."

"Perhaps so," Vorgens said. "Now, brigadier, my orders . . ."

"Yes, your orders, that's why I called you in here." Aikens leaned back in his chair. "I have a copy of your orders here on my desk, but I'd like to hear how you interpret them."

"There's not much to interpret."

"Come now, Watchman," Aikens countered. "You've been with Mobile Force for how long now? Two full days, isn't it? Certainly by now you realize that orders cut and processed at Star Watch Headquarters couldn't possibly foresee all the details of the situation here on Oran VI."

"The orders are quite simple and explicit," Vorgens insisted. "I am instructed to attempt to negotiate with the chief of the Komani raiders. I am to tell him that his people can return peacefully to their homeworld if they stop their raiding on Oran VI immediately. I am also to tell him that the Komani clan chieftains have sworn to the Terran Council that they will remain loyal to the Empire and will not in any way aid or sympathize with this attack on Oran VI. I suppose I should remind the raiders that the Komani were allies of the Terrans during the Galactic War of the last century, and that this attack on Imperial territory is a breach of friendship."

Commander Aikens gazed toward the ceiling as he quietly asked, "And just how do you propose to contact the Komani chief?"

"That's the difficult part," Vorgens admitted. "I had hoped to arrive on this planet before the fighting got so intense that the Komani would refuse to parley. It looks as though I barely made it in time."

"What do you mean by that?"

"Why, simply that the Komani have not really opened battle yet. We might still be able to discuss a truce."

"While we're surrounded?" Aikens shook his head. "You don't understand these barbarians. The only time they're ready to negotiate is when they're taking a beating."

"My orders command me to attempt . . ."

"Your orders," Aikens interrupted, "place you under my command for the duration of your stay on Oran VI. Correct?"

"Yes . . . but with the understanding that as an officer of the Imperial Marines you are subject to the orders of the Star Watch High Command and that you will assist the Star Watch's attempt to bring about a peaceful settlement with the Komani."

Aikens rose from his chair and strode wordlessly across the small compartment. Then he turned and pointed a finger at Vorgens.

"Listen, youngster, I'm just as anxious as you are to talk the Komani out of a bloodletting. Those are *my* men out there, and I'm responsible for their lives—every last one of them. But if we try to parley from our present position—surrounded, cut off, and outnumbered—the Komani will simply take it as a sign of weakness. We'll be encouraging them to attack. We'll be convincing them that they've got us licked."

"It may be entirely unnecessary to fight at all," Vorgens insisted.

The brigadier nodded curtly. "Maybe. We'll see."

Aikens returned to his desk and sat down. Leaning over the stereomap, he said to Vorgens:

"This is what we're going to do. Tomorrow morning, I'll send out more patrols—stronger patrols than today's—with armor. They'll probe the Komani lines and keep the barbarians off balance. Meanwhile, you will take an armored cruiser and a picked detachment of men and break through the Komani lines."

Vorgens' mouth dropped open, but the brigadier waved him down before he could say anything. "You will break through the Komani lines and outrun their communications jammers. Then you will call for reinforcements from the garrisons of the cities we now hold."

"These are your orders?"

"That's right, Watchman. I'll give you two days and two nights to get the reinforcements here. I doubt if the Komani will attack before then. They've got men scattered halfway across the planet, and they'll want to group them together before they tackle us in earnest.

"You'll have to draw every last man you can get. Use your authority as a Star Watchman. I want a strong enough force to smash these marauding barbarians once and for all."

"And the truce negotiations?"

"Let *them* make the request for a truce," Aikens snapped.

"Then you refuse to obey the express orders of the Star Watch High Command?"

Aikens glared at the Watchman. "What are you trying to do, youngster, set me up for a board of inquiry? No, I do not refuse to carry out the High Command's orders. I simply feel that the situation is so precarious at the moment that the orders can't be put into effect. Not at this time and place."

Vorgens stood up. "I suppose it would be pointless to attempt to argue you out of this decision."

"Completely pointless. Good evening."

The young Star Watchman saluted and left the brigadier's compartment. He stood outside the door for a moment after closing it, frowning worriedly. Then he slowly made his way down the narrow passage, past the compact booths of officers' quarters, climbed through a hatch and clambered down the side of the dreadnaught to the ground.

It was not much warmer outside than in, now that Oran had set. But the night was never completely dark, despite the hour. Oran was six times brighter than Sol, and its luminosity was great enough to keep a twilight glow in the air all night long.

Vorgens paced slowly around the mammoth dreadnaught, watching his boots stir up the dust. *The Star Watch orders me to parley; the brigadier orders me to fight*, he thought to himself. *Orders are orders. But which set do I obey?*

III

Father and Son

Halfway across the planet it was still bright daylight.

The home of Clanthas, the merchant, was neither particularly large nor well-adorned. It stood at the crest of a hill, flanked by equally good houses, and overlooked the harbor of the small city of Katan. Unlike the four major cities of Shinar, the port city of Katan was not occupied by a Terran garrison.

Until a year earlier, Clanthas had been distinguished from his fellow merchants only by being a shade quicker-witted and, perhaps, blessed with slightly more than his share of good fortune. In those days, before the rebellion against the Terran Empire, Clanthas could be seen during most sunny afternoons of the warm summer sitting on the balcony that spanned his house, either relaxing or conducting business, as the occasion demanded.

It was about a year ago that the first farmers began to trickle into Katan, complaining that the Terrans had driven them off their own soil, so that the land could be used for factories that made synthetic foodstuffs.

Clanthas, whose business depended on buying and selling the farmers' produce, appealed to the Terran governor. The nutrient processors were necessary, even vital, he was told.

Instead of quietly trying to make the best of the situation, as most of his countrymen did, Clanthas recalled something his son had told him, some quotation from galactic history that the youth was studying at the university:

"A man is free because he has the brains and the courage to stand on his own feet and go his own way. And for a man to remain free, he and his fellow men must be strong enough to resist those who would enslave them."

Those words had been spoken more than a century ago by a Terran, Geoffrey Knowland, the conqueror who defeated the Masters and established the Terrans as rulers over Shinar.

Clanthas decided that the Terran's words made sense, even when applied against the Terrans themselves. So he acted.

He organized the farmers and held a demonstration in Katan. He organized similar demonstrations in the major cities. Inevitably, some of the larger demonstrations developed into riots. Troops were called in; shots were fired. Unarmed civilians were killed. Tempers flared. Violent men took action. The Terran governor was murdered. The Imperial Marines arrived. Komani warriors landed on the planet.

Before he had time to realize it, Clanthas had become the acting leader of his people. He was squarely in an increasingly impossible position. On the one hand stood the Empire-building Terrans, intent on "pacifying" Shinar and returning it to the status of a docile colony. On the other were the fearsome Komani, with plans of their own. Even among his own people, there were hotheads and opportunists over whom Clanthas had no control.

On this particular afternoon, however, he was trying to put aside thoughts of politics and fighting to confront his only son simply as a bewildered and outraged father.

Clanthas sat on the edge of a large, well-padded chair. He watched intently the image of his son on the screen of the tri-di transceiver in the small room that Clanthas used for private conversations. By the standards of his race, the merchant was in prime middle life. His complexion was nut brown, his hair dark, his eyes like coal. He had accumulated weight with his years, so that now he was broad-girthed and puffy-faced, but his eyes were still clear and piercing.

His son, Merdon, showed what the merchant must have looked like in his youth: tall, broad, strong-limbed. The two men shared the same facial characteristics—prominent cheekbones, broad brow, massive, stubborn jaw.

"Merdon, I told you this was raving lunacy when you first revealed your idiotic plans to me," the older man raged. "I was wrong. It's worse. It's doom. It's damnation. It's the ruin of our planet and our people. And my son—my only son—is the ringleader."

Merdon shook his head slowly and waited for his father to go on.

"Why couldn't you have trusted my judgment? You, of all people! You should have remained at my side, and helped me to control your hot-blooded young friends. You should have warned me of the plot against the governor's life. Instead you remained silent. You should have spoken against those who wanted to shoot back at the Terrans. Instead you went even farther."

"I did what I had to do, Father. The Terrans weren't going to be swayed by mere words."

"Oh no, you had to be clever. One step ahead of everyone, including your father. Free the planet! Throw the foreigners out! How? By inviting other foreigners in to fight for us. Barbarians!"

"But it's working," the youth said defensively. "The Komani have beaten the Terran garrison in several engagements."

"Yes, and now the Imperial Marines are here."

"And the Komani have trapped them."

"WHAT?"

"Didn't you know? The Terrans have been trapped in a valley—in the Carmeer district. The Komani have them surrounded. It's only a matter of time. . . ."

Clanthas sank back in his chair. "Only a matter of time," he moaned, "before our planet is completely at the mercy of these barbarians." He looked up at his son. "You're certain of this?"

"Okatar Kang is gathering his men from every corner of the planet. Our own fighting units are joining him. There's even talk of contingents from other Komani clans landing on Shinar to join the battle."

Like vermin attracted to an open wound, thought Clanthas.

Merdon continued, "Okatar wants to be certain of overpowering strength before we attack the Terrans. We'll wipe them out completely!"

"Listen to me," Clanthas commanded. "Keep your men away from that battle. Don't join in it. The Terrans don't realize that we—*you*—invited the Komani to Shinar to fight for us. If they ever find out, they'll never trust any of us again."

"But . . ."

Clanthas waved his son to silence. "If the Komani beat the Terrans, they might be weakened enough for us to overcome them. If the Terrans win, we can say we had no active role in fighting against them. Perhaps we can still escape from this circle of doom in which you've placed us."

"Father, you don't understand. The Komani are our allies. They have come to Shinar because we asked them.

They are fighting for *us*. They are dying to help free us from the Terrans."

The ex-merchant swore under his breath. Aloud, he said, "The Komani are barbarians. They have no allies. Now they are killing Terrans. Next they will kill Shinarians."

"Father, you must learn to trust them."

"I trust them! I trust them to loot this planet when they've finished with the Terrans. I trust them to sack and burn and destroy everything they can't carry away with them, and I trust they'll start just as soon as the Terrans are wiped out."

"No. They've promised they'll loot only the Terrans."

"I suppose the villages that they've raided were populated with Terrans."

Merdon frowned at his father. "That was a misunderstanding. They needed food, and the stupid farmers refused to feed them. Some of the Komani warriors got out of hand, but we've made arrangements that will eliminate that sort of thing in the future."

"Fine. And what will your friend Okatar Kang do when he learns that there are warehouses full of food and an arsenal full of equipment right here in Katan?"

"I will protect you," Merdon said, a slight smile stealing across his face.

Clanthas shook his head. "No you won't. You'll be dead. If you participate in the coming battle against the Terrans trapped in that valley, you will be killed. Either by the Terrans or the Komani."

"Father!"

"Don't be naive. You are one of the principal leaders of the rebels. Alive, you are a stubborn, strong-minded, idealistic, capable leader of all the younger idiots of Shinar. You've turned against the Terrans. Someday you will turn against the Komani. But dead—then you'll be a martyr to the antiTerran cause. The Komani can count on your heroic memory to hold all your rebellious friends in line long past the point where you, yourself, would have broken with them."

"I'm flattered, Father, but you overestimate my importance. The real objective is to free Shinar of the Terrans and their rotten Empire."

"Free us? And leave the Komani on our backs?"

"They'll leave, after the Terrans have been driven off."

"And after we're pillaged."

"No . . ."

"Do you think that the Terrans are going to allow the Komani to escape unpunished? They'll send a stronger force to Shinar. It might even be on its way here at this moment. You're turning your homeworld into a battleground."

Merdon's face went completely blank. "There's no point in continuing this argument, Father. You won't change your mind. But someday you'll be proud of your son and the things he will have done for Shinar."

"I hope so," Clanthas said wearily, "but I doubt it."

The youth said nothing. His body gradually dissolved and disappeared, leaving his father sitting there in silence, staring at the bare screen of the tri-di transceiver.

Merdon also remained sitting before his tri-di set for many minutes after his father's image had faded into nothingness. He frowned moodily, weighing his father's words of warning.

Abruptly, he shook his head and got up from the seat.

"You're a well-meaning old man," Merdon said softly to his unhearing father, "but you're hopelessly wedded to the past. The Terrans became our overlords by driving the Masters out of the Galaxy. It took action, force—not words and demonstrations. To drive the Terrans off Shinar, we must use force." Merdon nodded to himself. He was right, he knew, and his father wrong. And yet . . . Clanthas felt that the Komani could not be trusted. Perhaps there was a kernel of truth there.

The youth stepped away from the tri-di booth and looked around. He was in a deserted factory, one of the few that the Terrans had built before the rebellion had broken out. Long rows of silent machines stood untended in the half-light of evening. Merdon snapped off the lamp that illuminated the tri-di booth and stared briefly at the Terran machinery.

Nutrient processors. His face wrinkled in disgust at them. The Terrans can't grow food from the ground, the way normal human beings do. Too slow. Not enough yield. They must hurry things, take elements directly from the soil and the air and convert them into artificial protein, synthetic foodstuffs. A few chemicals added here and a few enzymes injected there, and the accumulated knowledge of sixty centuries of planting and growing and harvesting is blasted out of existence.

He strode out of the factory, into the cool night air. Shinar had no moon, but the night-long airglow created a shimmering twilight that prevented real darkness.

Merdon looked at the youths lounging in the compound between the massive Terran buildings. These were his fighters, the new heroes of Shinar, he thought. Sons and daughters of farmers and philosophers—and even merchants.

A young girl walked up to him. "There are some new recruits waiting to see you, on the other side of the gates."

"Let them come in, Altai," he said quietly.

She turned and walked toward the gate. Altai was tall for a girl, with a slim athletic build and a natural grace that made watching her a pleasure. She was not particularly beautiful, but she had the knack of looking completely feminine even in slacks, and with an automatic rifle slung over her shoulder. Maybe it was her long, jet-black hair, or her voice.

Merdon found himself smiling as he watched her go

toward the gates. Maybe it was just the way she looked in slacks.

"Merdon, I have the completed tally of the weapons we got from the arsenal. . . ."

He turned and focused his attention on the bookish student who had become his quartermaster. Then a half-dozen of his lieutenants converged on Merdon with questions about rations, ammunition, and the best route to take for joining up with the Komani at the valley at Carmeer.

It was nearly an hour before he could break free and inspect the new recruits. They were a typically mixed bunch: some students, a few adventurers, one boy he recognized to be a distant cousin, and a quartet of farmers, shuffling around, feeling miserably out of place.

Merdon welcomed them all solemnly.

"I want you all to realize," he said as they gathered around him, "that many of us will die before Shinar becomes free. If any of you are reluctant to face death, if any of you belong to families that need you to run their farms, or earn their living, you are free to go now, and no one will think less of you for it. But once you stand with us, you are in an army, and rigid discipline will be enforced."

"May I speak?" one of the students asked.

"Certainly."

"The ground we're standing on now was once my father's farm. The Terrans took it to build their factories."

"What became of your father?"

"Terrans paid him what they said was a fair price for his land. He wasn't permitted to argue. He went to Kolmar City to find a job, but all he knew was farming. He . . . well, he's just a shell of the man he once was."

"I see."

One of the farmers spoke up. "The same thing happened

to us, in our district. I'll die before I see them turn my farm into a factory."

The others nodded agreement.

"I hope that none of us has to die," Merdon said quietly, "but I expect us all to fight until we win."

He turned the group over to one of his lieutenants and walked off toward the far end of the compound. He did not have to look over his shoulder to know that Altai was walking behind him. He slowed down and let her come abreast of him.

"You spoke to your father again?" she asked.

He nodded.

"Do the others know?"

He turned and faced her. "What if they do? He's my father."

She smiled. "So touchy tonight! You get angry and argumentative every time you speak with him. Did you know that?"

"No, I didn't realize it."

Altai put her hand to his cheek. "You mustn't let anyone or anything upset you. Your mind must be clear at all times. You hold our lives in your hands. . . ."

"Your life too?"

"Yes."

"And your heart?"

"Of course."

"That's all I care about."

She shook her head and answered gravely, "You have much more to worry about than me."

"I wish I didn't," he said impulsively. He frowned for a moment, then said:

"Listen. Romal has just made up a tally of the weapons we took from the arsenal last night. I want you to divide that list in half—and tell no one except Romal about it. Then, quietly, with as few men as possible, have half the weapons stored here, and the other half sent along with the new recruits to the Komani camp tomorrow."

"You're keeping half the weapons from the Komani?"

He nodded. "Hide them in the buildings here. Half the ammunition, too."

"But why?"

"I'm not sure. The Komani may be our allies, but I'd feel safer if we had some weapons available that they didn't know about. I don't want to find out some day that we've driven off the Terrans, only to have the barbarians ruling over us."

"Suppose they discover it. . . ."

"They won't."

"But you're supposed to go to their camp tomorrow. You'll be in their midst."

"That's a chance I must take."

"You're playing a dangerous game," Altai said.

"So are we all," Merdon replied.

IV

Prisoners

The sun rose abruptly over the hills, and a wave of heat swept across the valley where the Mobile Force lay huddled.

Sergeant McIntyre stood before a heavy cruiser, shaking his head. "I don't like it one bit, if you'll pardon me for saying so, sir."

Vorgens turned to the sergeant and studied his face for a moment. It was a narrow-eyed, weather-seamed, professional soldier's face: broad and rugged, set on a thick, solid frame. McIntyre was built big, as were all the true Terrans.

"What don't you like, sergeant?" the Star Watchman asked.

"The whole setup, sir. It's goin' to take a lot more'n one heavy cruiser and a detachment of leftovers from yesterday's patrols to break through the Komani lines."

"Would you rather report back to your company commander?"

McIntyre's eyes widened in surprise for just a flash of a second. Then he drew himself up as straight as he could stand. "No sir. I was asked to volunteer and I did. I'll stick it out as long as you do, sir."

Vorgens smiled. "Good. I don't like the setup any more than you do, sergeant, but somebody's got to try it, and I guess we've been nominated. Let's start moving."

They swung up the ladder and ducked into the turret hatch. The cruiser was air-conditioned to Terran standards; the sudden drop of temperature inside made Vorgens shudder involuntarily. He felt more comfortable in the hot sunshine.

The cruiser's blowers whined shrilly and blasted jets of air straight downward. As the shrieking grew higher in pitch, the lumbering behemoth edged higher off the ground, while the air jets scoured dust and rocks from beneath it. Finally the turbos' whining rose past the range audible to the human ear; the cruiser was now a good foot above the ground. She slid forward slowly, hatches open and a knot of footsoldiers riding topside behind the turret.

When they reached the end of the valley floor and rumbled past the last perimeter entrenchment, Vorgens popped out of the turret hatch and told the footmen:

"All right, now—get off and spread out. Keep low and move fast. Stay within sight of the cruiser. Report the slightest sign of movement. Remember, they've been watching us from up in the hills, so we're bound to be attacked."

He dropped back into the bowels of the cruiser and strapped himself into a slightly too-big bucket seat, next to McIntyre. Vorgens turned on the omnidirectional video scanner and donned the communications headset.

Soon they were climbing the first low hills, and the countryside was changing from the bare rockiness of the valley to wide patches of dark grass and ever-thickening bush.

"These cruisers ain't much help in this terrain," McIntyre muttered.

"What's that?" Vorgens asked.

"Cruisers can't take a very steep grade, sir. In climbing terrain like this, we've gotta stick to the gentlest slopes. That means the Komani can plot our course before we can. They know just where we've gotta go."

"Hm. Perhaps so." Vorgens fingered the control dials of the scanner. "No sign of anything so far, though."

After a few minutes of silence, McIntyre said, "Sir?"

"Yes?" Vorgens answered without taking his eyes from the screen.

"How come a Star Watch officer is leadin' this mission? If you don't mind my asking, sir."

Vorgens looked up at him. "Brigadier Aikens is in charge of all Imperial personnel on this planet."

"But ain't the Imperial Marines under the Star Watch's command? I mean, the Marines—this Mobile Force—we're just a branch of the Star Watch."

Vorgens nodded. "Yes. Brigadier Aikens takes orders from the Star Watch High Command. That doesn't mean that a Star Watch junior officer can order around a full brigadier. You know that, sergeant. What are you driving at?"

"Maybe I shouldn't be repeating a rumor, sir," McIntyre said, avoiding Vorgens' eyes, "but—well, is it true that you were supposed to arrange a truce with the Komani?"

So he knows! Vorgens thought. *Probably the word is out to every trooper in the Mobile Force.*

Aloud, he answered, "I was ordered to arrange a truce, when the military situation permits negotiations to be made. Brigadier Aikens must decide when the situation is right for truce talks. I'm responsible to him while I'm here."

"And he ordered you on this breakout mission," McIntyre said.

"Yes."

"That means he don't want a truce ... and he don't expect us back. He's gonna fight the Komani, and he wants us—you, that is—out of his way."

Vorgens stiffened. "Sergeant, our mission is to break through the Komani lines and summon reinforcements to the Mobile Force, not to make half-cocked psycho-analyses of our commanding officer." *No matter how right they may be,* he added silently.

"Yes sir," McIntyre said.

The ground got steeper and more densely covered with foliage as the hours passed. As McIntyre had predicted, the cruiser's pilot had to keep the vehicle gliding along the flattest, easiest slopes. They followed a twisting, meandering path, avoiding the steeper grades and areas that were covered with boulders or large bushes. The sun climbed higher as Vorgens silently watched the seemingly empty countryside unfold on his scanner screen.

There are a thousand places for an ambush along this way, he thought. *But it will take some doing for even Komani warriors to stop a heavy cruiser. It all depends on what kinds of weapons they have; how much equipment. Like the tales of the old ones back home, when the Terrans first proclaimed their Empire ... men against machines.*

"Enemy breastworks at ten o'clock!"

Vorgens snapped his attention to the viewscreen. He twisted a dial and saw the entrenchment, about a hundred fifty yards from the cruiser. He dialed a close-up view. Empty.

"Hey, they're firing from the ridge—three o'clock!" another footman called.

Vorgens dialed the scene. Sporadic small-arms fire was coming from the ridge. Off to one side, he noticed a small clump of trees. He dialed a close-up.

"Enemy troops in those trees at two o'clock," he called into his mouthpiece.

The footmen on the right flank dropped to the ground as McIntyre drove the turret around and swept the trees with ultrasonic beams. Then he swung back and launched a missile toward the ridge.

"They're charging! Ten o'clock!"

Komani warriors were swarming in on one-man flyers, saddlelike machines that gave them terrifying speed and mobility. Vorgens could see them plainly now, huge, humanoid warriors in gleaming battle armor, their arms covered with fuzzy greenish hair, their faces more like cats than men.

McIntyre was blazing away with everything available now and the footmen were laying down a heavy fire. The Komani were being mowed down in the volley, but still more of them came, some of them brandishing their ceremonial broadswords.

Vorgens dialed the other side of the cruiser, and spoke into his mouthpiece, "Keep both our flanks covered, no matter . . ."

The screen exploded in a shower of glass and Vorgens was smashed back in his chair as the whole cruiser lurched violently.

Vorgens shook his head groggily. It was dark inside the turret, and strangely quiet. A surge of panic flashed through the Watchman, but he fought it down automatically. The cruiser was stopped. Power off. *But I'm still in one piece . . . I think.*

Vorgens unbuckled his safety strap and turned around in his seat. His head hurt, a dull, sullen pain. In the dimness he could see McIntyre sprawled unconscious next to him, his left arm twisted grotesquely.

Unconscious or—no, no—he's breathing.

His eyes were getting accustomed to the shadows now. Vorgens could both see and smell a faint acrid smoke drifting through the shattered turret. There were no signs of life from the men below. He realized that his right hand was throbbing. A glass splinter was sticking into the palm and a steady trickle of blood oozed from it.

He pulled it out, wincing, then reached across McIntyre's inert form for the first-aid kit on the turret bulkhead. Clumsily, with his left hand, he swabbed the cut and sprayed a plastic over it. Then he carefully brushed his jacket and pants clean of the other fragments that had showered him.

McIntyre began to moan.

"Easy sergeant. Don't try to move. Your arm's broken."

"What happened?"

"Nuclear grenade, I imagine. They only needed one."

McIntyre closed his eyes and leaned back. "I told you we weren't supposed to come out out of this alive."

"We're not dead yet."

Vorgens rose from his seat gingerly. His knees were a little wobbly, but only a little. He jabbed a sedative into McIntyre's good arm, then decided it was too cramped and dark in the turret to attempt to set the broken bone. He reached up for the overhead hatch, the debris littering the deck crunching under his boots as he moved.

"I'm going to take a look around," he said to McIntyre.

The Watchman climbed up on his chair and pushed open the turret hatch. Cautiously he stuck his head out into the sunshine. The right side of the cruiser was smashed in, the turret itself tilted slightly askew. For a radius of fifty yards around, the ground was scorched black.

At the top of a little hillock, some hundred yards from the cruiser, three figures were moving slowly among the sprawled bodies. Two were Komani warriors, the third a native of Oran VI who wore the flowing white robes of a priest.

Blessing the dead, Vorgens thought.

They saw him, and one of the warriors raised his rifle.

"Don't fire!" Vorgens called out in standard Terran. "There's a wounded man in here."

"Bring him out," the warrior commanded.

"I'll need help."

They consulted among themselves. The warriors seemed apathetic, but the olive-skinned priest evidently persuaded them. One of the Komani came while the other remained with the priest, armed and ready. The warrior literally dwarfed Vorgens. His powerful body looked fully human, but his face was feline—wide-spaced cat's eyes, flat nose, broad slash of a mouth. His ears were a pair of tiny cups atop his skull. The whole face and head was covered with a wiry, greenish fuzz.

With the giant Komani's help, Vorgens pulled McIntyre out of the turret and carried him to the shade of the trees atop the hillock. The native priest set the sergeant's arm while Vorgens applied Terran anesthetics and antibiotics. Together, they put on a plastic splint and binding.

"Are we the only ones left alive?" Vorgens asked the priest in his own language after McIntyre was safely asleep.

"About half the Komani force survived. They have gone elsewhere now, leaving only these two to search for loot and prisoners. There are two others of your footmen nearby, although one is near death from his wounds."

The priest led Vorgens across to the windswept ridge on the other side of the cruiser. They both tried for more than an hour to save the wounded trooper—in vain. Then they started back to the grove of trees where McIntyre was resting. With them came the other Terran prisoner— private Neal Giradaux—tall, lanky, trying hard not to look afraid.

"You speak our tongue," the priest observed as they walked back to the trees.

"It was taught to me before I was sent here," Vorgens said. "Actually, it's not much different from my own native language."

By the time they got back to the grove, McIntyre was

sitting up with his back against a tree, his splinted and bandaged left arm sticking out awkwardly at his side. The two Komani warriors stood some distance away, aloof and impassive.

"By glory, it's Mac!" Giradaux shouted as they approached. "You're alive, sarge!"

"Well, if you made it, soldier," McIntyre shot back, "did you think I wouldn't?"

Giradaux ran up to the sergeant and squatted beside him. "Are you okay, Sarge?"

"Broke my arm when they got the cruiser. How about you?"

"Knocked out by the blast. That's all."

Vorgens joined them as the priest went to the two warriors. "You two are in the same outfit?"

"Not now, sir," McIntyre answered. "But I broke this pup into the service a coupla years ago."

"I see," Vorgens said. "Sergeant, do you feel strong enough to walk? The priest tells me that the Komani want to take us to their headquarters."

McIntyre grunted. "I guess I'll hafta walk, then . . . or be dragged."

"I'll help you, Sarge," Giradaux offered.

"Get your trench-diggin' hands off me!" McIntyre bellowed. "You think a busted arm means I'm helpless?"

"No, Sarge." Giradaux grinned.

McIntyre struggled to his feet and stood at attention. "All right, sir. I'm ready to go."

The sun was nearly at zenith as the little band of men started their journey. The beginning was easy enough—down the reverse slope of the hills they had been in most of the morning. The sun's warmth was tempered by cool breezes and frequent clumps of trees that threw dense shade. They stopped briefly after an hour's march and ate a scant meal: a few dried vegetables, a lump of something like bread, and water from a running stream.

Then came the worst of it—trudging across another dry, rocky valley under the heat of the afternoon sun.

The yellow sun seemed to hang directly overhead, no matter how far or how long they plodded across the barren valley. Twice the size of Sol and six times brighter, Oran beat mercilessly on the bare rocks, withering the scrubby plants, making the air dance with heat currents, wringing streams of sweat from the weary men, roaring in their ears and dazzling their eyes with painful glare.

McIntyre had pulled down the glare visor from his helmet when they started across the valley. But as they struggled through the long afternoon, he saw that Vorgens and Giradaux had neither helmet nor visor.

"Sir," he asked of Vorgens, "would you like my helmet?"

The Star Watchman shook his head. "No thanks, Sergeant."

"I have an extra pair of glare goggles in my pocket, then. They're on this side," he gestured with his bandaged arm, "so you'll hafta get them for yourself."

"I don't need them, McIntyre, thanks. This star is pretty bright, but it's not as brilliant as the one I was born under. What I need more than goggles is a long, cool drink and a fresh breeze."

McIntyre was silent for a moment.

"You might give the goggles to Giradaux. He seems to be having a hard time of it."

McIntyre grinned. "Yes sir. Hey, Gerry!" he called to the trooper, marching a few yards ahead of them.

"Yeah, Sarge?"

"Where's your helmet, trooper?"

Giradaux slackened his pace momentarily, until he was beside the other two. "Gee, Sarge, I dunno where it is. I must've left it on that ridge. . . ."

McIntyre shook his head. "You're expected to give up your weapon when you're taken prisoner, but you don't hafta strip naked! That helmet costs the Empire money."

"I know, Sarge," Giradaux looked miserable, "and I could use the glare visor, too."

"Here, fish in this pocket and get my spare goggles before you go blind ..."

"Thanks, Mac!"

"Think I'm gonna let you charge the Empire for a disability pension because you're careless?"

The going got rougher as the long afternoon wore on. Before they reached high ground again, McIntyre was allowing Giradaux and Vorgens to take turns supporting him. The priest gave them water from a canteen he carried within the folds of his robe. The Komani warriors were impassive, except for insisting that the prisoners maintain the pace of the march.

"How come the Komani don't need glare visors?" Giradaux asked as they struggled up a slope.

"Look at their eyes," McIntyre answered. "They narrow down to slits ... just like a rotten cat's."

Finally they reached the crest of a wooded ridge, and were out of the glaring heat. They rested for a few minutes, then were on their way again—this time along the ridge, under the tall trees.

With McIntyre able to get along by himself again, Vorgens turned his attention to the surroundings. The trees, the grass, the blue sky, the sounds of birds and insects ... it was practically the same as on his homeworld. The leaves were a darker shade of green, the birds were slightly different ... yet not so different after all. And the native priest—he was smaller than Vorgens, his skin slightly darker. No doubt his bones and joints and internal organs were somewhat different, but he was human.

Thousands of parsecs from his homeworld, and even farther from Earth, here was a planet that bore not only Earth-type life, but human life.

Don't get emotional, Vorgens told himself. *Human life is a logical development in the evolution of an Earth-type planet. It happened on your homeworld, it happened on*

Earth, it's happened spontaneously on some fifteen thousand planets within the Empire.

He watched a small, furry animal scurry across the trail up ahead and dash up a tree trunk. *Still*, he thought, *it's not much less than miraculous.*

The priest especially fascinated Vorgens. He was evidently quite old, yet he carried himself with a dignity that forced respect. His skin was a deep brown, his eyes jet black, and what was left of his wispy hair was silverish. His face was spiderwebbed with age, and Vorgens finally realized that this was what intrigued him. He had never seen a really old person before, not face to face. On Plione IX, his homeworld, on Mars, where he received his Star Watch training, on Earth and throughout the Terran Empire, he had never seen a truly old person close up. The physical signs of age had been eliminated by Terran science centuries ago.

Vorgens soon found himself talking with the priest— Sittas was his name—as the little group made its way through the cool woods. They talked of general things, noncommittal things; things that had nothing to do with war and the inevitability of death.

"Tell me of your homeworld," Sittas asked.

"It's a long, long distance from here, even in a starship," Vorgens said. "Plione IX—the ninth planet circling the star that the Terrans call Plione; a giant blue star, much larger and hotter than Oran, although our planet is considerably farther away from Plione than you are from your sun."

"And your homeworld is like our world here?"

Vorgens nodded. "Very much. It's a little smaller than Oran VI. . . ."

"What is Oran VI?"

"Huh? Why, this planet—your world, here."

"Of course, of course," Sittas said, smiling. "That is the Terran name for our world. In the hill villages, where I am from, we see very few Terrans."

"What do you call the planet?"

"Its name is Shinar."

"Shinar," Vorgens repeated. "That means ... um, something to do with home, isn't it?"

The priest nodded. "Home, yes. It also means peace, and life, and many other things besides."

They walked in silence for a few minutes. Then Vorgens said, "I'm surprised to see a native priest with the Komani raiders."

Sittas smiled. "They have souls. I am a priest."

"Yes, but they are looting your people—turning your planet into a battlefield. . . ."

"Does that make them impossible to change? Does that doom them to our everlasting hatred? Were not the Komani of this very clan once the allies of the Terrans?"

"Yes," Vorgens admitted. "The entire Komani nation fought on the side of the Terrans in the Galactic War, but that was a century ago, and now ..."

"And now you kill one another. Does that mean that you cannot stop the killing and live in peace once again?"

"I see," Vorgens said. "I understand." To himself he added, *We have a lot in common, old man. You and I may be the only sane ones on this planet.*

Sittas changed the subject abruptly, and the young Star Watchman told the old priest of many things as they walked through the long afternoon under the cool trees along the nameless ridge. Vorgens found himself talking for the first time in years about his homeworld.

Plione IX, circling the brightest star of the Pleiades, a massive blue giant whose fierce radiation made life impossible on all but its outermost planets.

Plione IX, known as *Bhr'houd'grinr* until the Terrans landed and began to homogenize the local culture into the standard Terran blend and incorporate the planet into the efficient, expanding Empire.

"My people were also allies of the Terrans during the Galactic War," Vorgens said, "but when we were annexed into the Empire, instead of allowed our own government, the people tried to fight. It was hopeless, though.

"My grandfather was one of the few men on our planet to recognize that the Terrans were unbeatable," Vorgens told the receptive Sittas. "As proof of his convictions, he sent his oldest son to join the Terran Star Watch, to be trained and educated by the Terrans—to serve them. By this example, he hoped to prove to his compatriots that life within the Terran Empire was better than a hopeless war of resistance."

"And was he successful?" Sittas asked.

Vorgens shrugged. "He died before the war was finally ended. Assassinated. Plione IX is now a peaceful member of the Empire; its people are prosperous and happy. My father is still in the Star Watch, and he made certain that I became a Watchman, too."

"And you?"

"I'm not very prosperous," Vorgens answered, smiling, "but I was happy enough in the Star Watch—until Oran VI. I mean, Shinar."

Then, quite suddenly, Vorgens had nothing left to say to the priest. They had talked of the past and the present, but neither of them wanted to speak about the future. They moved apart by mutual, unspoken agreement.

Vorgens rejoined McIntyre and Giradaux, who were still slogging along side by side over the steadily-rising ground.

"How's it going?" Vorgens asked the sergeant.

McIntyre shrugged with one shoulder. "Okay. The arm hurts a little, but not much. You know, we've been passin' guard posts for the past hour or so."

"I hadn't noticed," Vorgens blurted.

McIntyre pointed with his eyes. "Up there, sir, there's another one."

Vorgens glanced at a jutting rock off to one side of the trail. A Komani was flattened out on top of it, his

greenish body hair and gray clothing a near-perfect cam-
ouflage in the heavy foliage atop the rock.

"Yes, I see," Vorgens said. "We must be approaching
their headquarters."

"Gerry and I have been takin' bearings as well as we
can, sir," McIntyre said in a lower voice. "I think we'll
be able to spot their headquarters on map coordinates
when we get back to the Mobile Force."

"Fine," Vorgens said absently as he silently changed
McIntyre's *when* to an *if*.

"Sir?" Giradaux asked, and at Vorgens' nod went on,
"How come a native priest is with the Komani? I thought
the barbarians were raiding this planet and the natives
want us to throw 'em out."

"That's what I thought, too," Vorgens said. "But
there's more to this story than the part we know. A lot
more."

V

The Face of
the Enemy

The Komani camp was a shock.

Not only was it bigger and much better equipped than
Vorgens had expected, but there were almost as many
Shinarian natives milling around in it as Komani.

The camp was set on a broad, thinly wooded meadow.
Off to one end were dozens of landing ships, slim,
needle-nosed, erect and gleaming in the slanting rays of
the setting sun. Except for a small blast ring around the
ships, the meadow was covered with Komani bubble-
tents, thousands of them, each brightly colored in a dis-
tinctive family insignia, each housing anywhere from one
warrior to a dozen. Laced between the colorful bubbles
were pennants, ceremonial fires, stacks of equipment and
weapons.

The exact center of the encampment was the site of

the largest tent of all, colored pure gold: the home of the tribal Kang.

"They're pretty brazen, camping in the open," McIntyre growled as they first saw the meadow.

"They've probably got an energy screen that'll protect 'em against missiles and aircraft, Sarge," Giradaux said. "You'd either have to hit 'em with heavy beamguns from a starship, or attack 'em overland. They've got the approaches bottled up pretty tight."

McIntyre muttered to himself.

They were led into the camp, through row after row of gaudy bubble-tents, stared at silently by the solemn Komani warriors, women and children. They stared back intently at this unexpected close-up of their enemy's base.

"What're all the natives doin' here?" McIntyre wondered. "I thought the Komani were raidin' them. Why're they actin' so friendly?"

The Shinarians were there, if not in force, then certainly in numbers. Groups of olive-skinned natives were everywhere in the Komani camp, selling food to Komani women, bargaining over jewelry with Komani nobles, demonstrating mobile energy beam projectors to Komani technicians.

But, worse still, Vorgens saw many of the natives were simply talking—quietly and earnestly—with Komani warriors. And the natives wore weapons.

Finally the Terrans were ushered into a bubble-tent. It was furnished with a single low-slung table; nothing else. The lone doorway was guarded by four heavily armed warriors, the smallest of them a full head taller and seemingly a yard wider than McIntyre.

"The last word in hospitality," Giradaux joked lamely.

McIntyre tapped a heel on the floor of the tent. "Plastisteel, I bet. We won't be diggin' our way out."

"No, we're here to stay," Vorgens admitted, "for awhile."

The last shafts of sunlight were disappearing behind the forest at the edge of the meadow when a Komani youth arrived at the entrance with a tray of food. The youngster hesitated momentarily at the doorway, then walked in, very stiff and grave, placed the tray on the bare table, and half-ran out of the tent.

"Guess he thought we'd eat *him*," McIntyre said.

It was a good-enough meal, although less than would satisfy the Terrans' appetites. By the time they finished eating it was dark. The night-long twilight of Shinar was broken only by the ceremonial campfires that dotted the camp.

McIntyre rose from his cross-legged squat at the table, stretched as well as he could with his bandaged arm, and said, "I'm gonna grab some sack time. With your permission, sir."

"It's not my permission that counts," Vorgens murmured.

"Sir?"

"Nothing, sergeant. Go on, have a good sleep. We can skip the formalities for the time being."

"Okay, sir. If you want me, just holler."

With a nod of his head, McIntyre made it clear to Giradaux that he should sleep, too.

Vorgens left them alone and stepped out to the doorway of the tent. He could sense the Komani guards tighten a fraction as he appeared in the flickering firelight. He stopped just outside the doorway. The guards said nothing.

Vorgens stood there looking out across the bizarre camp, etched in firelight. A chilling night breeze moaned by, and then, mixed with it, came a low, plaintive chant from somewhere near the center of the meadow.

He listened as the slow, melancholy sound of women's voices drifted through the night. A *funeral dirge*, he realized finally. *A dirge for the men who were killed today. For the men we killed today.*

The Star Watchman remained motionless as he listened to the weird, haunting music. But his mind was churning endlessly and again he saw the charging Komani warriors, heard the shouted orders, the blasts of weapons, the screams of men in battle. Now he realized that these warriors—these men—were also sons and fathers who feared death as much as anyone. What was it the old priest had said? *They have souls.*

The dirge ended at last, and one of the campfires suddenly blazed into a huge pyre. Vorgens watched as the flames soared skyward and then, slowly, slowly, died down into nothingness. After the funeral pyre had faded completely, Vorgens found himself looking up at the stars overhead. The airglow and the glare of the campfires made it impossible to see any but the nearest, brightest stars. Vorgens knew that the Pleiades were too far away to be seen, and then he realized, with a sudden shock, that he did not even know just where in the skies of Shinar they would appear.

"Can you see your home star?"

Vorgens turned to find Sittas standing beside him. "No," he answered. "I don't even know where to look for it."

"Are your men comfortable?"

"They've eaten and now they're asleep."

Sittas nodded. "Would you like to talk? I have many questions on my mind. Or perhaps you are tired from today's—events."

"No, I couldn't sleep if I tried. I have some questions, too."

"Good, we can talk." The old priest turned to the guards and said a few words to them in their own language, then led Vorgens away from the tent.

"I find that walking stimulates my conversation," Sittas said. "Walking and conversation are the only vices left to one of my age."

Vorgens studied the old man's face in the flickering

firelight. On another world, at another time, Sittas might have been a teacher, or a physician, or even a planetary governor. His face had the natural dignity, the touch of good humor at the corners of the mouth, the impression of wisdom in the silver hair and wrinkled brow. But deep in his eyes was a sadness born of many years and long experience of the failure of man's grandest dreams.

"I was surprised," Vorgens said finally, "to see so many Shinarians in camp."

Sittas said nothing.

"I had thought . . . that is, Terran intelligence believes, that the Komani raiders have landed on your planet while you are in rebellion against the Empire—taking advantage of the confused situation to loot your people."

"There *was* some looting," Sittas agreed noncommittally.

"I don't understand."

Sittas stopped walking and looked up at the young Watchman. "Perhaps it is not me you should speak with, but Merdon."

"Who is Merdon?"

"A youth—very much like yourself. And yet, very unlike you."

Vorgens shrugged. "All right, let's talk to Merdon."

Sittas led him through a maze of tents, and finally left him standing in front of one of the smaller bubbles. After a few minutes, the old priest reappeared at the doorway and gestured Vorgens inside.

The tent was sparsely furnished with three cots, a table, a pair of chests, a few stools, and a single globular lamp overhead. Seated behind the table was Merdon, poring over a big paper map and a pile of reports; a miniature tri-di transceiver held down one corner of the map, and a beam pistol rested on the opposite corner.

Merdon looked up as Sittas said, "This is the Star Watchman I told you about."

"*Vhro'rgyns* is my name. The Terrans find it easier to say Vorgens."

Merdon looked into the Watchman's tawny eyes and smiled. "In this case, I find myself forced to agree with the Terrans. I am Merdon—in Terran as well as Shinarian."

Merdon gestured to the stools before the table, and Vorgens and Sittas sat down.

"Sittas tells me," Merdon said, "that you can't understand why so many Shinarians are here in the Komani encampment. The answer is simple: the Komani are here in Shinar because we invited them here. They are our guests, our allies. They are helping us to fight against the Terrans."

Vorgens felt his breath catch in amazement. "You . . . *invited* the Komani? As mercenary troops?"

"As allies. Oh, I know what the Terran commanders think. They believe that we on Shinar are acting as unwitting pawns for some deep, dark Komani plan of conquest. The truth is exactly the opposite. The Komani are working for us."

"Why?"

Merdon snapped, "Why? Why do you think? Because we want to be rid of the Terrans and their blasted Empire!"

"But why should the Komani help you? What do they gain by going against the Empire?"

Merdon's brows knitted thoughtfully for a moment. Then he replied, "The Komani are born fighters. The smell of battle, a chance of loot—that's all they want."

"You make it sound very simple," Vorgens said quietly.

"No, it's the Terrans who oversimplify everything. They think that because our culture is a peaceful, agricultural society that we are a simple, stupid people. That is a mistake. We are as complex in our desires, in our fears, in our loves and hates, as any Terran—or any other human."

"All right," Vorgens agreed, "but what's that got to do with——"

"Your Terran officials think that we Shinarians are all sheep. Well, perhaps many of us are. But not all of us."

"So you decided to resist the Empire."

"A few of us did, yes. Some tried to resist with words, with protests, with street demonstrations. The Terrans' answer was force. Well, now we are meeting force with force. We will fight and die and fight again until the Terrans are no longer willing to pay the price for Shinar. Until they leave us in freedom."

"And the Komani are helping you in this struggle."

"The Komani—and any other recruits we can find," Merdon said, looking straight at Vorgens.

"Any other recruits?"" the Watchman echoed.

Merdon leaned across the table. "You are not a Terran. Sittas tells me that your own people fought against the Empire. Join us! Help us to free Shinar! Perhaps someday we can destroy this evil Empire altogether, and free your own people."

Vorgens blinked, and turned toward Sittas. The priest shrugged his bony shoulders to indicate that the idea was Merdon's alone.

"I am not a native Terran, that is true," Vorgens said, "but I am a citizen of the Empire. My people did fight against the Terrans, once, a long time ago. But today they are so much a part of the Empire that they could not establish an independent nation if they wanted to— which they don't. I am a sworn officer of the Star Watch. I cannot turn my back on my own word, and fight against the men with whom I have served."

"You hide behind your duty," Merdon snapped.

Vorgens' face tightened. "Perhaps so. But listen to me. No matter what the Empire has done on Shinar, the peoples ruled by the Terrans would be plunged into chaos and starvation if the Empire were destroyed. The Terrans may seem evil and arbitrary to you—perhaps they are, in many cases—but they are also the carriers of law, of stability, of commerce and order, throughout more than half the galaxy. Their job is not an easy one. Here on Shinar they may have failed, but you cannot destroy the Empire unless you replace it with something better . . . not unless you are an unthinking barbarian, as the Komani are."

"You *are* a Terran, after all," Merdon growled.

"I am an officer of the Star Watch," Vorgens said, his voice rising. "I was sent to Shinar to try to arrange a truce that will end this bloodshed. I can offer you the same terms I offer the Komani: lay down yours arms and return to your homes. Otherwise the Empire will be forced to crush you."

"Get out!" Merdon shouted. "Take your truce terms and go back to your tent and wait for the Komani to deal with you. Star Watchman, truce-bearer—you're a prisoner, a Komani prisoner, and before long you'll be dead!"

Vorgens rose and strode from the tent. Sittas hurried out after him.

"He had no excuse for speaking to you like that," the priest said. "I am ashamed for him."

"He lost his temper," Vorgens said, calmer now in the open air. "I know I lost mine. We see the world through different eyes. . . . And he's right, you know. I am a prisoner. I'm not in a position to offer anyone anything."

"Still, Merdon's behavior was inexcusable."

"He just doesn't understand the reason for the Empire."

"I must confess," Sittas said softly, "that I, myself, do not see why the Empire must have this particular planet, when there are so many . . ."

Vorgens thought it over for a moment, then answered, "I suppose the answer is that, if Shinar were allowed to quit the Empire, others would want to leave it, also. It's the first step on the road to chaos.

"The Terrans didn't want an Empire. No one planned it this way. At one moment, the Terran Confederation was fighting for its life against the Masters. A moment later, the Masters were utterly defeated, and their empire fell to the Terrans. Suddenly the Terrans found themselves responsible for administering, feeding, governing, half the galaxy. They tried to get various star systems to govern themselves, but it didn't work out. The Empire was needed. The Terrans had no choice."

"Regardless of the cost," Sittas said.

"The cost?"

"Yes. In maintaining the Empire of the Masters and making it their own, the Terrans have obliterated the individual cultures of their member planets. Their effort to turn Shinar into a Terran-type food-manufacturing world has touched off this war. You, yourself, told me how your native culture has been submerged by the Terrans."

Vorgens nodded. "That's right. My people are almost exactly like all the other people in the Empire. The old customs, the old beliefs—they're only for teachers of ancient history, or museum keepers. I—I suppose it was inevitable. Unavoidable."

"Was it?" Sittas asked.

"Yes," Vorgens replied. "There are reasons . . ."

"Reasons?"

Vorgens looked at the old priest for a long moment. Then he began to explain to him what every servant of the Empire was expressly forbidden to tell a native.

He told Sittas of the Terrans' gradual realization that, a million years earlier, a race of Terrans had reached into space, met a powerful alien race, and been smashed in a devastating war. He told the priest of the discovery of the ruins on Mars, of the machinery that had produced the Ice Ages that was found on Titan, of the remnants of the crumbled First Empire that the Terrans had found as they expanded into the stars once again.

"They are building their new Empire as solidly as they can," Vorgens finished, "because they know that somewhere among the stars—perhaps in another galaxy, even—the Others still exist. They nearly exterminated the Terrans once, a million years ago. The Terrans are building an Empire that can exterminate the Others, if they show up again."

"And for this reason Shinar must become a cog in their Imperial machine?"

Vorgens nodded.

"Are we not men? Would we not help to fight the Others?"

"I know," the Star Watchman said. "My own people would, too. They wouldn't have to be regimented by the Terrans. But now my homeworld is a planet of mines and factories. There are ten times more people there than we could possibly feed with our own resources. If, for some reason, the Empire should break down, nine people of every ten would starve."

"Yet you fight for the Terrans."

Vorgens shrugged. "I fight for what I believe. The Empire is not the best way, but it's the only way we have. Its laws are just. I know that what's happening to your planet is hard to accept, but there is no alternative. I don't like to fight against your people, but your people started the fighting."

Sittas agreed with a nod. "Yet, who is without blame in a war?"

"It's no longer a matter of blame," Vorgens said. "Now we must decide where we go from here."

They found themselves back at Vorgens' tent, with its quadruple guard.

"You have answered my questions quite frankly," Sittas said, "for which I thank you. Now tell me, what questions can I answer for you?"

Vorgens immediately asked, "How many Komani warriors are on Shinar?"

"I don't really know," the priest said. "An entire clan has landed here, as you can see. I suppose there must be something like fifteen thousand fighting men."

"An entire clan," Vorgens repeated. "And who is their chief?"

"Okatar Kang."

"Could you arrange an audience with him for me? Tomorrow, as early as possible?"

Sittas shook his head. "That I cannot do. The Kang does not usually see prisoners, unless they are remarkable in some respect—a general, or a renowned warrior. I have no influence whatsoever over Okatar and his Elders. Merdon might have arranged such a meeting, but . . ." Sittas's voice trailed off.

"I see," Vorgens said. "Well, thank you anyway. I'm sorry the meeting with Merdon wasn't more fruitful."

Sittas nodded silently.

"Good night," Vorgens said.

"Good fortune to you, my friend."

Vorgens watched the old man disappear among the tents, and slowly realized that it was the first time since he had left the Star Watch Academy that someone had called him "friend."

Inside the tent, he found McIntyre and Giradaux awake, talking quietly while squatting as far from the entrance—and the guards—as they could.

Vorgens told them what he had learned from Sittas.

"So it seems that we are facing not just the Komani," he concluded, "but a well-armed and very determined band of rebels, as well."

"It's a dirty business," McIntyre grumbled. "Fighting these barbarians is bad enough, but half the planet might be up in arms against us."

Vorgens nodded. "Under any circumstances, it means that the forces holding down the Mobile Force could be two or even three times larger than Brigadier Aikens believes them to be."

"We've gotta get back to the Force tonight," McIntyre said, "and let them know what they're up against."

"Right," Vorgens said.

"The Sarge and I were talking over our chances of breaking outta here," Giradaux said.

"And?"

McIntyre answered, "There's four guards against the three of us. They're armed. Gerry was frisked good when they captured him. He's clean. I managed to sneak a stinger under my belt before they took us." He pulled out a slim rod. "It won't kill anybody, but it'll put him outta commission for a few hours."

Vorgens grinned. "Good. And I fixed that cast of yours so that it ought to be as hard as plastisteel by now."

McIntyre looked surprised. He tapped the cast on the floor. It sounded good. He ran a hand over the innocent-looking bandages. "By Pluto, this'll break any bone in the galaxy. Did you bring anything from the cruiser, sir?"

"Just something from the medical kit. It's not a weapon, but it could be just as important to us."

He pulled a small bottle of pills from his jacket pocket. "These are mescal capsules," Vorgens explained, opening the bottle and handing them out. "They speed up your perceptions, temporarily, so that everything around you seems to be moving very slowly. If we're going to depend on surprise, it might be useful to be able to see the enemy's reactions in slow motion. It would give you time to think about your next move—in the middle of a hand-to-hand fight!"

McIntyre popped a capsule into his mouth, swallowed hard, then grinned. "I'm glad we've got a Star Watchman with us, sir. Us poor footsloggers wouldn't think to look for weapons in the infirmary."

"Coming from you, sergeant, that's a real compliment."

They discussed tactics for a few minutes, while

allowing the mescal to take effect. As a test, Vorgens took McIntyre's stinger and dropped it to the floor. It floated down like a feather and bounced lazily for what seemed like several minutes. They were ready.

Their plan was simple, based on speed and surprise.

Giradaux was lead man. He came bombing out of the tent at top speed, diving straight into one of the guards. The big Komani, half asleep, toppled over and Giradaux started to spin free of him. As the other three guards turned to face the Terran, drawing their weapons, Vorgens and McIntyre entered the fight.

It all seemed like a dream to Vorgens, under the effect of the mescal. Every move they made—friend and foe alike—had that underwater languor about it. He saw the Komani drawing their sidearms, saw Gerry slowly rising to his feet.

Then the nearest Komani began to turn toward him. Vorgens raised the stinger (it seemed an eternity to lift it) and touched it to the warrior's chest. He froze for an instant, then began slumping toward the ground.

Vorgens turned to see McIntyre swinging his arm-cast into the face of a startled Komani. Another was already on the way down, his head split and bleeding. Giradaux chopped artfully at the neck of the warrior he had toppled, and the fight was abruptly finished. Vorgens' stunned victim finally hit the ground, as if to punctuate the end of it.

They took the Komani sidearms and made a cautious retreat to the edge of the camp. It was late, and the camp was quiet. No one seemed to be stirring.

Vorgens whispered an order to set the captured handguns to stun, rather than on killing power. McIntyre grumbled something about "fighting tomorrow the enemies we don't kill tonight," but a quick glance at the Star Watchman showed that he was not going to argue the point.

Their first trouble came at the outer guard perimeter.

A Komani warrior spotted them and let out a warning yelp before McIntyre's shot knocked him unconscious.

Then it was an agonizing race in slow motion for the edge of the meadow. Beacon flares began to pop around them, and although Vorgens knew that the three of them were dashing for the thick foliage at the meadow's edge, the mescal made it seem as though they were suspended in mid-flight while the whole Komani camp had plenty of time to take leisurely aim at them.

"They ain't set to stun!" McIntyre yelled as energy beams sizzled past them.

They zigzagged the last few yards to the meadow's edge and plunged down the steep slope, stumbling and falling in the darkness. They made their way toward the thick brush, where they would be safe from the Komani—temporarily.

After a few minutes' thrashing through the foliage, they found a gulley that led away from the camp. They flopped down, bellies in the dirt, and gasped for breath.

"Everyone okay?" Vorgens asked.

Two grunts answered him. Through the foliage, he could see lights swinging back and forth.

"Sergeant, can you find your way back to the Mobile Force from here?"

"I think so, sir," McIntyre said.

"Can you evade those guard posts we saw on the way up here?"

"Yes sir."

They could hear shouts now, and the sounds of men probing through the brush.

"All right, Sergeant," Vorgens said. "You and Giradaux make a break for it. I'll scuttle off in another direction, making enough noise for the Komani to spot me. I'll lead them on as long as I can. You two make certain to get back to Brigadier Aikens."

"But, sir . . ."

"You tell Brigadier Aikens—personally—that he's facing

a whole Komani clan, not just a few raiders, plus a large number of native rebels. They've got modern weapons of every type."

"Yes sir."

"All right—now get going."

"But—they're shootin' to kill. You can't . . ."

"Sergeant, are you a soldier or a lawyer?"

Vorgens could sense McIntyre's face going red. "Yes sir."

"Now get moving. Don't worry about me. I've got something else in mind. Good luck to you both."

"Luck to you, sir."

They scrambled off down the gulley. Vorgens waited a moment, then headed across the gulley and up the other side. Once there, he started diagonally away from the spot where he had left McIntyre and Giradaux, toward the oncoming Komani.

As he scuttled through the foliage, he spotted three Komani warriors groping cautiously through the twilight haze. *The effect of the mescal's worn off*, he realized as he stopped to watch them.

Vorgens edged carefully off to one side of the approaching Komani, working his way to a position as far as possible from the direction the Terrans had taken. Another flare burst overhead, and in its sudden light Vorgens saw another trio of warriors moving slowly through the brush toward him. *Now is the time*, he said to himself.

He fired at the first group of Komani, hit two of them and left the third to scream for aid. Then he swung around and fired quickly at the other trio. He dropped one of them and got a sizzling blast by his ear in return.

Ducking into the deeper brush as the flare petered out, Vorgens crawled farther away from the Komani searchers, always leading them—he hoped—away from the escaping Terrans.

Twice more flares bloomed overhead, and twice Vorgens

stopped to hit-and-run, making certain that the Komani knew from which direction he was firing.

Then for a long stretch there was dark silence. Vorgens squatted in the foliage and waited, straining his senses for some hint of what they were doing. He began to realize how a mouse might feel, if a pack of cats were quietly stalking it.

I wonder if they have infrared snoopers? Then they wouldn't need flares. His answer was a sudden, searing flash, and a long, long fall into oblivion.

VI
Okatar

The darkness lifted slowly, and Vorgens gradually became aware that he was lying in a cot. There was no pain, no feeling whatsoever. He was aware that his eyes were open, but he was unable to focus them. The world was a gray blur. He tried to move, but found he could not. The effort was too great. He lapsed back into unconsciousness.

He awoke again. This time he could see. Things were still blurry, smeared at the edges, but he could see.

A girl was sitting by his cot, watching him, completely unaware that he was conscious and his eyes could function again. Her face was a curious mixture of anxiety and interest, as though she were looking into a mirror to find some flaw in herself. She was young and slim, with jet-black hair falling to her shoulders and wide, dark eyes.

Gradually, the girl's image became indistinct, and his head began throbbing painfully. Vorgens found himself slipping back into darkness again.

Then he heard voices. There were two of them, speaking a language he either did not understand or could not grasp through the ache in his head. Slowly his eyes focused on the glowing roof of the Komani bubble-tent. Vorgens found that he could turn his head slightly. He saw Sittas, deep in conversation with the Shinarian girl, who was standing now near the entrance to the tent. They were speaking something close to the Shinarian language he had been taught, Vorgens finally realized, probably an up-country dialect.

Vorgens closed his eyes, momentarily, he thought, but when he opened them again, the girl was gone and Sittas was standing alone by his cot.

"What time is it?" the Star Watchman asked.

The priest smiled. "Past midday. You have been unconscious all night and morning."

"What are you grinning at?"

"Your Terran training. Only a Terran would awake from many hours of unconsciousness and ask what time of day it is."

Vorgens propped himself up on an elbow. "Time is getting to be important . . ."

"How do you feel?" the priest asked.

"Not bad. My head hurts a bit. How seriously was I hit?"

"You took a strong bolt from a sonic gun. I have no way of knowing how seriously the shock might have affected your nervous system."

"There's one way to find out," Vorgens said. He pushed himself up to a sitting position, and with Sittas' help got to his feet. "A little wobbly," he said, walking slowly across the tent with the old man at his elbow, "but I think I'm all right."

"You should try to eat," the priest said, gesturing to a tray of food on the small table in the middle of the tent.

Vorgens nodded. "How about the other two? Did they get away safely?"

"Yes," Sittas answered. He hesitated for a moment, then said, "Perhaps it is not proper for me to ask, but I do not understand how they escaped successfully and you did not."

Vorgens sat down on a stool, next to the table.

"I didn't want to escape," the Watchman said.

Sittas' mouth formed an unspoken *why*?

"It was necessary for someone to get back to the Mobile Force and warn Brigadier Aikens of the odds he's facing," Vorgens explained. "McIntyre can do that. Giradaux is better off with the sergeant than here. But I have a mission to carry out—a mission that calls for me to see Okatar Kang. You said he would not see an ordinary officer, only someone of high rank or great fighting ability."

"That is true."

"Please tell him, then," Vorgens said, "that the Star Watchman who engineered the escape of the two prisoners last night from under his nose has a message for him from the Commander-in-Chief of the Terran Imperial Star Watch."

Sittas' weathered old face slowly unfolded into a broad grin. "It might work."

The priest left to try to reach Okatar and arrange a meeting. Vorgens sat alone at the tiny table and nibbled on some of the meat and fruit from the tray.

He smiled wryly at the irony of the situation: *Brigadier Aikens tries to prevent me from negotiating with the Komani, and his very orders bring me almost face-to-face with the Komani chieftain.*

After a few minutes the Watchman got up and returned to his cot. The ache in his head was nearly gone, and the food had refreshed him. He stretched out on the cot, not to rest, but to think.

Vorgens tried to push every unwanted thought out of his mind, to reach back to his classes at the Academy, to remember what he had been taught about the

Komani. He pictured in his mind the stereocast lecture he had sat through.

"A nation of warriors, consisting of nomadic clans that fight each other almost as often as they raid their neighbors. Their culture is feudal, their energies directed toward battle and loot. Komani warriors are disdainful of civilized values. . . ."

Yet through it all Vorgens heard in the back of his mind the keening funeral dirge of the women; the solemn, frightened-yet-brave face of the youth who had brought them food the night before; the calm, firm insistence of Sittas that despite politics and wars, the Komani had souls.

How to appeal to them? That was the question. How to present the Star Watch's demands in a way that they could understand and accept? Vorgens thought about it, and tried to frame the words he would use with Okatar.

At length, Sittas returned to the tent. He stood silently at the entrance for several minutes before the Watchman noticed him there.

"Well?"

The old priest looked into Vorgens' eyes. "You asked me to arrange a meeting with Okatar Kang."

"That's right."

"He wants to see you immediately."

Vorgens jumped to his feet. "Good!"

"No, my friend, not good," Sittas murmured slowly. "He wishes to see you merely to pronounce a death sentence over you."

Vorgens was escorted to Okatar Kang's huge golden bubble-tent by a half-dozen warriors. Sittas walked at his side as they tramped through the encampment. The sun was high, the skies cloudless. The Watchman could not help but notice that there was much more bustle and activity in the Komani camp than there had been the previous afternoon.

They're pulling in their men from all over the planet, Vorgens said to himself. *They're getting ready for a major attack on the Mobile Force.*

He had expected the Kang's tent to be crowded with people, but instead it was nearly empty. A small group of Komani and Shinarians were sitting at a low-slung table off to one side of the tent. The guards marched Vorgens to the middle of the tent, then turned to face the table. Sittas remained just inside the doorway.

Vorgens guessed that the second Komani from the right was Okatar. He was no bigger or more impressive physically than the rest, but his head was held a trifle higher, his back was a shade stiffer, and his yellow cat's eyes gave an impression of unquestioned authority. Komani faces gave Vorgens a feeling of fierceness. He almost expected them to have saber-like fangs jutting from their lips.

Vorgens recognized Merdon among the Shinarians. The young rebel was going over a long list with Okatar while the others at the table listened in silence. For several minutes, Vorgens and his six guards stood in the middle of the tent, while Okatar carefully ignored them.

Finally he put the list down on the table and turned to face Vorgens.

"I am Okatar Kang," he said, in standard Terran, "and you are the Terran prisoner who tried to escape last night. Prisoners who spurn our hospitality are traditionally executed. Therefore . . ."

"Before you go any farther . . ." Vorgens began.

"Silence!" roared one of the Komani nobles.

Okatar glanced at the roarer, then returned to Vorgens. "Pleas for mercy will not avail you."

"I am not pleading for mercy," Vorgens said, "and I did not try to escape from your camp last night. If I had wanted to escape, I could have done so easily with my two fellow prisoners."

"You aided their escape," said another Komani noble, "so the death penalty still holds."

Sittas interrupted. "He is not a true Terran," the old priest said, walking up from the doorway toward the table, "and has never been in contact with the Komani before. Your customs and laws are probably strange to him . . ."

Vorgens disagreed. "I am familiar with your customs. I helped the two Terrans escape because I knew they would be put to death ultimately by you. Which of you would have done less for his own men?"

Okatar gave a grunt of grudging approval. "And why did you not escape with them?"

"Because I have come to this planet to see you, Okatar. I have been sent by the Star Watch to offer you peace."

"You were taken prisoner in a skirmish that cost us a score of lives," one of the Komani countered. "You were fighting from within an armored cruiser. What kind of peace offer is that?"

"My mission to this planet is to discuss a truce with you," Vorgens insisted, talking straight to the Kang. "Last night, we could have killed many more of your men. Instead we merely stunned them. I am not here to kill, but to save lives."

Okatar glanced at Merdon, then, smiling grimly, said, "I have heard of the peace offer you made to the Shinarian fighters. Do you presume to offer the same terms to the clan of Okatar?"

"If you leave Shinar at once and return to your homeworld without further bloodshed," Vorgens said, "the Star Watch will take no punitive action against you."

"And if we do not leave Shinar immediately?"

"You will be destroyed by the forces of the Terran Empire."

Dead silence filled the room for a moment. Vorgens added, "The Empire has half a galaxy of resources to pit against you ... powerful armies and fleets. You cannot hope to overcome them all."

"No, not by ourselves," Okatar said quietly.

"I have also been instructed to inform you that the other Komani clan chiefs have sworn to the Empire that they will remain loyal and will not assist you, regardless of what you do."

The slightest trace of a smile flickered across Okatar's grim face.

"I see," he replied. "Our choice is to return meekly home, or suffer complete destruction. Now then, about this destruction, where are the Imperial forces that will accomplish this mighty victory? Your Mobile Force is trapped and living on borrowed time. Your vaunted Star Watch fleets are nowhere near Shinar, and cannot get here within a month, at least."

How does he know that? Vorgens wondered.

The Kang continued, "Your mighty Empire has no military arm that can withstand the Komani peoples. One small clan of us has humbled your Mobile Force and planetary garrison. By this time tomorrow the word will be spreading through the galaxy that the Komani are on the march. Shinar is the beginning. The other clans will join us. In fact," Okatar leaned forward and lowered his voice, conspiratorially, "how can you be sure that *all* the warriors on Shinar are really members of my clan?"

Vorgens felt as though he had been shot again. Slowly, he answered, "What you are saying is that you propose to cause a galactic war between the Komani clans and the Terran Empire. You cannot win such a war. The Empire has resources that will crush you; it will only be a matter of time—and lives."

Okatar waved down the Star Watchman. "No, my naive Terran. Not at all. Your Empire is crumbling already. If you had the strength to crush us, you would do it now, here, on this planet. Instead you send a small Mobile Force that will be extinguished in another day.

"The people of Shinar do not want your Empire. The people of the galaxy have learned to hate the Terrans. How do you think the Terrans gained control of their Empire? By taking it from the Masters. Now the Komani will take it from the Terrans. For too long now the Komani have fought each other, while the Terrans gained strength from our weakness. But that time is drawing to a close. When the other Komani clans see that the Terrans can be humbled in battle, they will join the clan of Okatar. Your Empire is ripe for picking."

"You are going to plunge the galaxy into hell all over again," Vorgens said, "and you will not live to see the end of the chaos you cause."

"Perhaps," the Kang retorted, "but certainly you will not live to see even the beginning. Unfortunately, we do not have the time to enjoy the ceremonial execution that bearers of ultimatums are traditionally given. Therefore, you shall be shot, before the sun sets."

With that, Okatar nodded to the guards. One of them seized Vorgens' arm and turned him around. They marched out of the tent.

Vorgens walked blindly, numbly, seeing nothing and hearing nothing, his mind in a dizzying whirl that pulled in tighter and tighter on itself.

The Komani aren't interested in a peaceful settlement. They want only war. Aikens was right. He was right! This battle, here on this minor planet, is only the opening skirmish in a war that will engulf the whole galaxy. The Empire is in danger. Humankind is in danger. If the Empire crumbles, nine people out of every ten will starve. If the Komani have their way, the whole fabric of civilization will be destroyed.

They want to destroy, to kill. They want to kill me. I will be executed. Shot. Killed. Dead.

VII

Altai

Merdon sat at the low-slung table, feeling slightly uncomfortable in the overlarge Komani chair, and watched Vorgens walk numbly out of the tent, escorted by the six guards. Sittas remained at the doorway for a moment, and Merdon's eyes met the old priest's and held there. Sittas' face was expressionless, but Merdon knew what was in his mind.

The Shinarian youth turned away and glanced at Romal and his other lieutenants, sitting at the table with him. When he looked back at the doorway, Sittas had gone.

"To return to these tallies of weapons . . ." Okatar said.

Merdon focused his attention on the Kang. "One moment. I have never heard you talk before about this plan for conquering the entire Terran Empire. I would

72

like to hear exactly how you propose to do it, and how your plans affect Shinar."

Okatar smiled. "In a few days—a few weeks, at most—the Komani will have left Shinar. The Terrans will be wiped out, and before they can bring more troops to your planet, we will have struck somewhere else, closer to the heart of their Empire. When we leave you, Shinar will be free of the Terrans for all time, never fear."

Merdon said, "But you are using Shinar as a stepping-stone in your plans against the Empire."

"Of course. What of it? We will free Shinar of the Terrans. Our motives are inconsequential."

"But do you really believe that you can defeat the Empire? With all their resources and manpower, the Terrans . . ."

Okatar's smile vanished. "The resources and manpower of the Terrans come from worlds like your own. They are stolen from peoples who will gladly rise up against the Terrans, as they rose against the Masters a century ago. All they need is a leader, and an army to join. The Komani will be that army, and I will be that leader."

"After you've defeated the Empire, what then? Will the Komani become the new masters of the galaxy?"

"In a sense, yes. But we will not become like the Terrans. We are fighters, not governors. The Komani will live on tribute, freely given by the peoples we liberate from the Terrans. We shall leave all peoples in peace, and fight against only those who work for the Terrans, or who oppose us."

Merdon nodded. "I see." But in his mind he saw his father's worried face, and heard his words of warning.

"Now then," Okatar resumed, "about these tallies of weapons. I had assumed that there would be more weapons available. This list seems too short."

Merdon could sense Romal, sitting next to him, tense at the Komani's question. He answered calmly:

"My quartermaster has prepared very accurate tallies. Remember that we took those weapons from small garrison posts among the outlying towns. The Terrans kept most of their weapons in the major arsenals in the four cities that they still hold."

Okatar nodded. "I understand that there are good-sized arsenals in some of the smaller cities. The port of Katan, for instance."

"There is an arsenal there, yes," Merdon agreed. "But it is relatively small and nearly empty. Besides, Katan is a long distance from here. We could never get the weapons from the arsenal to our troops in time for tomorrow morning's attack on the Mobile Force."

"Sound logic," Okatar said. "In any event, we have more than enough weapons for tomorrow's attack." His lips parted in a smile, but his yellow eyes were cold.

"I have the latest information about food deliveries," Romal said, changing the subject. His voice, always high-pitched, nearly cracked from nervousness.

They discussed the questions of provisions and other logistics problems for another hour. Neither Okatar nor Merdon mentioned the weapons again, or the arsenal in Katan. But both knew that the other was thinking hard about the matter.

When Merdon finally left Okatar's tent, he started back toward his own quarters, with his four top lieutenants accompanying him. As they made their way through the Komani bubble-tents, Altai came up and joined them.

"My uncle would like to speak with you," she said, striding along beside Merdon.

"It will have to wait. There are other things to do."

She looked up at him. "I heard that Okatar made a speech."

Merdon grinned humorlessly. "Several of them. He announced his plans for crushing the Empire, told us that he will expect us to support him by paying his clan tribute, and showed quite a bit of suspicion about the weapons tallies."

"He knows that we're keeping back some weapons?"

"He suspects."

"What are you going to do?" Altai asked.

"I'm going to hold a conference with my four best men, and we'll decide on what to do."

"A conference? In your tent?"

"No," Merdon said, shaking his head. "Right out here, in the open. We're going to stroll around the camp and talk. I don't want to go to the tent ... too much of a chance that a microphone might be hidden there."

Altai nodded in agreement. "All right. I'll wait for you at your tent."

"No. Stay with us. We might look a little less as though we're plotting something if there's a girl with us."

"A girl?" Altai repeated. "Just any old girl? Just someone to make the Komani think you couldn't possibly be talking about anything serious?"

"Now don't be silly," Merdon said, taking her hand in his. "Of all the girls on the planet of Shinar, there is none that I would rather have standing here beside me, dazzling the Komani with her radiant beauty, more than you. There, are you happy now?"

Altai shrugged noncommittally. "May I join the discussion, or must I merely listen?"

Merdon glanced at the other four. They were grinning broadly.

"You may speak," he said, "if you have something serious to say. This is a serious matter."

"Yes I know," Altai countered. "But it's good to see you all smiling again. You looked so solemn a minute ago."

"For good reason," Merdon said.

"Okatar Kang thinks that the Komani can conquer the whole Terran Empire. Shinar is just the first step in his plan," Romal said, his voice squeaking in excitement.

"We face the prospect," Merdon said calmly, "of having the Komani as overlords after the Terrans have been driven away."

Altai shuddered involuntarily. "They wouldn't even try to govern us. They would take whatever they wanted by force."

The others murmured agreement.

"Don't be so sure," Merdon argued. "If the Komani are going to tackle the whole Terran Empire, they won't want to be bothered by uprisings in their rear. If they act belligerently toward us, we can fight. Okatar knows that."

"Yes, and he knows his warriors can whip us," said Tarat, the lanky son of a farmer, who now served as Merdon's chief tactician. "Our men are willing fighters, but—I hate to admit it—we're just not strong enough or experienced enough to stop the Komani."

"The Komani could whip us," Merdon agreed. "But not if they were fighting the Terrans at the same time."

"You're walking out on a slender branch," Tarat said.

"Without a safety field to catch you if you slip," Altai added.

Merdon stopped walking and looked at them. They had reached the edge of the encampment, and were near a clump of tall trees. Beyond the grove shimmered the barely visible energy screen that protected the camp from missiles and force beams.

"Let's consider the basic things first," Merdon said. "Are we agreed that we want to be rid of the Terrans?"

"Not if it means living under the Komani," Romal said stubbornly.

"Of course not," Merdon said. "But if we can be free, should we fight for freedom, or remain under the Empire?"

"Freedom!" snapped Tarat. "Freedom or death. We've come too far to turn back now."

"Right," Merdon agreed. "Even if we wanted to return

to the Empire, the Terrans would never trust us again. We would all end up in exile, or worse."

"No," Altai said. "Uncle Sittas said that the Terran Watchman . . ."

Merdon's scowl silenced her. "The Watchman brought us an ultimatum—stop fighting or be wiped out by the Imperial troops. He never said what would happen after we stopped fighting. You can guess at what the Terrans would do."

Altai stared at the rebel leader, her face set in a perplexed frown.

Merdon went on, as they resumed walking, "At the moment, the Komani have the same aim that we do—to drive the Terrans off Shinar. Good. We can work together toward that goal."

"And afterward?" Romal piped.

"Afterward, the Komani will want to attack another planet of the Empire. Again good. We will help them. We will provide them with all the food we can gather. We will give them ships, and clothing, and any equipment we have."

"Weapons?"

"We will give them weapons, too. Half of all the weapons taken from the arsenals at the four major cities. The other half we will keep. All the other weapons we are now holding on to—including the arsenal in Katan—we shall keep."

"And if Okatar finds out?" Altai asked softly.

"It will be no secret. We will tell him that we are keeping these weapons in case we are attacked. We have a right to defend ourselves, if we are free."

Tarat grunted in sudden understanding. "Woof. You'll be telling Okatar that if he tries to take anything else from Shinar, we'll fight him."

"That's right," Merdon said. "We'll be perfectly willing to have him fight the Terrans elsewhere, and leave Shinar in peace."

"You're gambling," Tarat said, "that Okatar will prefer to fight the Terrans rather than us."

"He'll have more to gain fighting the Empire. There's no profit—and no glory for him—in staying here and crushing us."

The four lieutenants muttered among themselves.

"I know this is a hard decision to make," Merdon said. "We're running a terrible risk. If things don't work out well, we'll see our world turned into a blood-soaked shambles. We will be killed, no doubt. But if we're smart enough, and strong enough . . . we can achieve freedom. Is it worth the risk or not?"

"It is!" Tarat said.

Romal nodded unhappily. "I guess there's no other way."

The others agreed.

Altai remained silent. But Merdon could read the question in her eyes: *Is there no other way? Is there absolutely no other possible way?*

In a small chamber within his main tent, Okatar Kang watched the six young Shinarian rebels on a tabletop viewscreen as they walked back from the trees at the edge of the camp and returned to their own tents.

"The remote receptor picks up their every word, does it not, my lord?" asked the Komani noble at his elbow.

"Indeed so," Okatar said. "My compliments to the technicians."

"You have seen enough?"

Okatar nodded. "Yes. Quite enough."

The four lieutenants scattered to their private tents, while Altai accompanied Merdon back to his own quarters. Inside the plastic bubble, Sittas was sitting quietly, his eyes closed. The old priest looked up as the two youngsters entered.

"Were you sleeping or praying?" Merdon asked jokingly.

"A little of both, I fear."

Merdon sat on a corner of the table and faced the priest. Altai stood beside her uncle's chair.

"You want to talk to me about the Watchman."

Sittas nodded. "You must ask Okatar to pardon him. Keep him a prisoner if you must, but a cold-blooded execution . . ."

Merdon held up three fingers. "First, Okatar would not pardon a man he has sentenced to death. The Komani aren't interested in clemency. Secondly, the Watchman has killed Komani warriors, and can hardly be treated as an innocent ambassador of goodwill. Thirdly, if he got back to the Terrans he would end up by killing our own people. So how can you ask for mercy?"

"This Watchman is not an ordinary Terran," Sittas began.

"I know," Merdon interrupted. "He's worse. He knows the Terrans conquered his nation, and yet he fights for the Terrans. He's an enemy—by his own choice and his own admission."

"A very unusual enemy," Sittas countered. "On the whole planet of Shinar, this youth is the only one who has mentioned the word peace in seriousness since the rebellion began. I believe that he holds the key to peace on Shinar."

"Peace under the Empire? Never. That would merely be returning to the situation that caused the rebellion in the first place."

"It doesn't have to be that way, Merdon," Altai said.

"It doesn't? Why not? Because we don't want things to be that way? Because we dream of a world ruled by our own people, without the Terrans or anyone else standing on our necks? Well how is this wonderful world

going to come about? By prayer? By dreaming? By long-
ing for peace, at any price?"

Merdon pounded a fist onto his open palm. "We must
fight for freedom! The Terrans will not give us freedom
for the asking. The Komani will not leave us alone unless
we are strong enough to discourage them from attacking
us. Is peace worth slavery? Is life so precious that we
would place our worthless hides above freedom for our
people, above freedom for the generations that haven't
even been born? No. We will fight, and keep fighting,
until we have our freedom. Then peace will come, and
we will welcome it as men, not as spineless dogs."

Sittas smiled and nodded. "Fine oratory. It will sound
stirring in the history books, but I am not convinced that
unending warfare will bring peace to Shinar—or freedom. This Star Watchman, Vorgens, might possibly turn
the trick for you. In the vast Terran Empire, there must
be officials who would be willing to listen to our cause,
and work out some solution satisfactory to all of us."

"No such Terran has ever taken an interest in Shinar.
I doubt that such a Terran exists."

"Perhaps the Watchman could help us to find the right
officials."

"The Watchman is a prisoner and sentenced to die,"
Merdon repeated doggedly. "Your dreams of finding
peace are nothing but wishful thinking. The Watchman
is only a junior officer. Do you think he could actually
command a truce here on Shinar? Do you think the
commander of the Imperial Marines takes orders from a
junior officer? The Watchman has no power, no authority. His life is worthless."

The old priest slowly rose, trembling, from his chair.
"The strain of your duties has taken its toll on your good
sense, Merdon, and on your heart. Never in my life
would I have expected you to say what you did a moment
ago. A human life—worthless? You had better examine

your conscience, my son. You are beginning to enjoy this war too much."

Merdon started to reply, thought better of it, and simply sat there on the edge of the table, his eyes meeting the priest's. Finally Sittas turned and silently walked out of the tent.

"The old fool," Merdon grumbled. "He knows I didn't mean it that way."

Altai asked, "How did you mean it?"

"Now don't you start arguing against me!"

She looked at Merdon's strong, stubborn face for a moment, then turned her eyes away and said, "Merdon— many people have died since this fight began. My own village has been nearly wiped out, first by the Terrans and then by the Komani."

"That raid was a misunderstanding."

"Yes, I know. But many people were killed anyway. Dozens of our classmates were killed in the fighting at the university . . ."

"I remember. And you fought by my side during those early days."

"Early days," Altai mused. "A few weeks ago. It seems like a lifetime has passed since then."

"A lifetime has passed," Merdon said. "None of us is the same person he was before this began. We can never go back to those days, Altai. Never."

"Merdon, listen to me. Please. Don't let this Watchman be killed. I don't know why, but I can't just stand back and allow a man to be executed. This war has already killed many, many good people. But they were killed in battle. Now—now you're going to let them come in and shoot him. You can't let it happen!"

The young rebel shook his head. "Altai, it has to be this way. There's no other way. He's a Komani prisoner, not ours. We can't set him free. We can't help him escape."

"You mean you won't try to help him."

"I can't."

She drew herself up to her full height. Merdon smiled inwardly at her, trying to be as tall as a man.

"You can't help him," Altai said, "but there are others who can."

Instantly, Merdon's amusement vanished. "What do you mean by that?"

She started for the doorway. "You'll see."

"Altai! Don't do anything foolish. The Komani wouldn't hesitate to shoot a girl—or a priest."

VIII

Through the Flames

Vorgens sat in stunned silence in the tent to which the guards had brought him. The Komani warriors loitered outside while the young Star Watchman stared at the blank wall of the tent.

The touch of a hand on his shoulder startled him. He looked up and saw Sittas standing beside him.

"Have courage," the priest said quietly.

"Does it show? The fear?"

"Not much."

Vorgens ran a hand through his close-cropped hair. "You heard what Okatar said. The other Komani clans are in league with him. This is the beginning of a galaxy-wide war."

Sittas shook his head. "Not necessarily. The other clans may be giving him some aid, and no doubt they are giving him considerable encouragement, but they will not move in force until it becomes clear that the Empire is too weak to stop them."

83

"If the Mobile Force is wiped out, that would be their signal, wouldn't it?"

"It could be."

"They'll attack tomorrow morning, for certain," Vorgens said. "They've got more men and equipment than Aikens dreams they have. If he stands and fights in that valley, we'll lose Shinar and the whole Komani nation will begin to march against the Empire."

But Sittas was no longer listening. He was standing at the doorway of the tent, looking out. The late afternoon sun slanting through the doorway touched his wispy hair and gave him a modest halo.

Vorgens stood up. "Well, when is the firing squad coming? Or do they like to let their victims dangle for a few hours?"

"Death comes to us all, my friend," Sittas murmured, still gazing intently outward.

"It's odd," Vorgens said, pacing across the tent floor, "I never thought about how I would die. I've been aboard starships that have run into trouble—real trouble. And yesterday, in battle, and last night, helping McIntyre and Giradaux to escape, I was frightened, all right, but the thought of death—my death—it just never entered my mind. But now ... I never thought I would die before a firing squad—on a planet I didn't even know existed until a few weeks ago."

"If we knew the time and place of the end of our lives," Sittas said, glancing at the Watchman, "we would hardly find life interesting enough to go through with it."

"That's not much help."

The old priest smiled. "Then perhaps your next visitor will have better words for you."

Puzzled, Vorgens stepped over to the entrance of the tent, where Sittas was still standing. Walking through the Komani encampment toward them was a Shinarian girl. Vorgens recognized her as the girl he had seen while he was still half-unconscious after being shot.

"So she's not a dream," he muttered.

"Altai? She is my niece. We are from the same village. She joined the rebel forces at the university, where she met Merdon."

Vorgens frowned. "One of Merdon's rebels. So she hates the Terrans, too. And me. Just as Okatar said they all do."

"She is too young to hate," Sittas said.

They stepped back from the entryway as Altai walked into the tent. The girl looked at Vorgens for a moment, then turned to her uncle and nodded silently.

Sittas said, to no one in particular, "Let us pray for guidance."

The old man stood a few paces from the entrance, and began chanting. But his eyes were on Vorgens, and he gestured with one hand, first pointing to his ear, then to the guards outside.

Vorgens smiled in understanding. Altai pulled a low bench up to the table in the middle of the room and sat down. Vorgens sat next to her. She took a thin slip of plastifilm and a stylus from the waistband of her slacks and began drawing as Vorgens watched.

Altai sketched the tent they were in, and a dozen nearby tents. In two of the circles she drew she wrote a single word: *ammunition*. Then she put down a pair of wavy lines, running parallel from Vorgens' tent outward to the edge of the film. Within the lines she wrote *safe lane*; outside the lines, on both sides, she wrote *fire*. She looked up at Vorgens to see if he understood. Vorgens nodded, and noticed that her eyes were as black and deep as space itself.

While Sittas continued to chant, Altai gestured toward the wall of the tent. Then she touched the stylus on the word *fire*.

Vorgens shook his head and whispered, "Nonflammable. Will not burn."

Altai smiled and whispered back, "Thermal grenade. It will burn."

Vorgens grinned at her. "How soon?"

"As quickly as possible," she answered, rolling up the film and tucking it back into her waistband.

They stood up together. Altai was nearly Vorgens' own height. Sittas finished his chant.

"I hope our prayers are answered," the priest said.

Vorgens watched the two of them leave the tent. He stood at the entrance as the old man and the girl walked slowly away and finally disappeared behind some of the gaudy Komani bubble-tents.

The Watchman stepped back toward the middle of the tent. *Now it's a race to see who is ready first: Sittas and his niece, or Okatar's execution detail.*

His answer—several minutes later—was a dull booming sound and the jarring smack of a concussion wave that jolted everything in the tent. Another explosion, ear-splitting, knocked Vorgens off his feet and toppled the table next to him. A Komani warrior stuck his head through the entrance as Vorgens was climbing to his feet. Shouts and screams were mixing with a series of explosions and the peculiar *whoosh* sound of huge sheets of flame leaping skyward. Vorgens could hear men running outside, and saw behind his guard's back the eery, flickering light that could only be coming from a huge blaze.

The warrior ducked through the entryway and motioned to Vorgens with a huge, pawlike hand.

"Out. Danger. Fire."

Vorgens stalled. "You mean you're worried about me?"

The Komani took another step toward Vorgens, and fingered the pistol on his hip.

The whole far end of the tent suddenly dissolved into flames. The Komani gave an involuntary shriek and leaped for the entrance. Vorgens, without time to think about it, dived straight into the burning plastic wall.

He jumped headfirst, as hard and as far as his legs

could catapult him. He landed, hands down on cool moist grass, and somersaulted. Getting to his feet, Vorgens saw that Altai's plan was working just as her sketch had shown.

The dome of the tent behind him was engulfed in fire. Flaming tents stretched off on either side of him, but the ground between them was clear. The heat was intense though. Not even the grass would last long at this rate.

Vorgens took off at top speed, straight down the alley of fire, legs pumping as hard as they could, lungs sucking in searing, spark-filled air. Smoke burned at his eyes and he could feel that parts of his face and hands were scorched.

Finally he was free of the flames and stumbling down the shrub-choked slope that marked the edge of the meadow and the end of the Komani camp. Gasping for breath, exhausted and riddled with pain, he sprawled in the bushes.

For several minutes he lay there, chest heaving, legs aching, watching the heavy black smoke, occasionally mixed with tongues of flame, billowing from the Komani camp.

"Are you all right?"

Startled, he turned to see Altai kneeling beside him.

"Yes. I'll be fine as soon as I catch my breath."

"The Komani will have the fire out soon," she said. "We'd better move quickly."

Vorgens scrambled to his feet. "I'm ready."

Silently she led him deeper into the brush, past a clump of tall trees. Beyond the trees stood Sittas, his robes tinged red by the last rays of the sinking sun.

"I took the liberty," Altai said as they approached the priest, "of borrowing three flyers from one of the Komani tents that I had to set on fire. They will never miss them."

"*You* set on fire? You mean you did all that . . . yourself?"

She nodded and tried not to look smug, but Vorgens could see that she was proud of herself. "It wasn't too difficult. None of the tents was occupied. The Komani used them for storing ammunition and equipment. All it took was a couple of small grenades to set off everything."

"And a lot of courage," Vorgens added.

By this time they were close enough for Sittas to join the conversation. "You made it safely," the old priest said.

"A few singes here and there, but I'm still alive."

"It'll be dark soon," Altai said. "We'd better wait for a while before trying to take off on the flyers."

They spent the last few minutes of daylight examining the saddle-like, one-man Komani flyers. None of them had ridden one before, but after a few tests of the controls, Vorgens showed them how to handle it.

Night finally came, softened by the ever-present airglow. A flicker of fire still rose from the Komani camp.

Vorgens straddled his flyer and touched the buttons on the pummel that activated the machine. The flyer seemed to pulse into life. It stirred and vibrated, as though waiting for a command to action. He glanced at Sittas and Altai. They both seemed ready to go, although Vorgens worried about the priest's ability to handle the machine.

At a nod from Altai they started off, keeping low and sticking as much as possible to the shadows until they were well away from the Komani camp. Then they soared above treetop level and made better time.

As they skimmed along, Vorgens allowed Sittas to set the pace for them. The old man had some difficulty managing the flyer, but with Vorgens and Altai staying side by side with him, they got along without any real trouble.

They flew toward the valley where the Mobile Force

was encamped, and landed on a hillside nearby, after less than an hour's flight. They edged the flyers into the bushes, where they would be reasonably safe from discovery.

"I'll go the rest of the way on foot," Vorgens said. "If I tried flying over the guard posts at night they'd shoot me down automatically."

Sittas nodded. "What will you do after you get there?"

"I've got to convince Brigadier Aikens to break out of this valley. He's hopelessly outnumbered if he sits there and tries to battle it out. There'll be a slaughter . . . on both sides."

"If you do get the Terran forces out of this trap, what then?"

Vorgens shook his head. "I don't know. We'll be buying time. We'll be saving lives. That's enough for now."

"Okatar plans to attack at dawn," Altai said, "from the side of the valley that will give him the sun at his back."

"I expected that," Vorgens said. "Where will Merdon's forces be? I'd rather avoid firing on Shinarians, if it can be helped."

In the semi-darkness, Vorgens could not see Altai's eyes widen in surprise and joy. There was a moment's hesitation before she answered.

"Our people will be directly on Okatar's left flank, and one thing more, the Komani are pulling back most of their men from this end of the valley, so that they can mount a stronger attack at sunrise. There will be only a thin screen of warriors in this area."

"Then we could break through," Vorgens said, "if we hit them with everything we have."

"Yes," Altai agreed, "and without firing on Shinarians."

"You must tell your commander," Sittas reminded, "that a defeat here may well touch off a galactic war."

"I know. I know."

Sittas looked up at the sky. "You have only until dawn. You must move quickly."

"I . . . there are no words to thank you enough," Vorgens said, "not just for your help—but for my life."

The priest smiled and put a hand on his shoulder. "Go quickly. And good fortune to you."

"What about you and Altai?"

"We will be safe enough. This is our homeworld, remember."

Vorgens nodded. He turned to Altai. "Thank you, too. I hope that the fighting is ended quickly."

He wanted to say more, then decided against it. He turned away from them and started down the grassy slope of the hill toward the Mobile Force.

Okatar Kang stood watching the smoldering ruins of the tents, with several of his nobles beside him. His face was an impassive mask as Komani warriors sprayed and beat out the last glowing embers.

Merdon walked up slowly, alone except for a single Komani escort.

"It was a stubborn fire," Merdon said.

Okatar looked down at the young rebel. Though tall for a Shinarian, Merdon barely stood as high as the Komani Kang's shoulder.

"Several cases of Terran thermal grenades made the fire difficult to fight," Okatar said.

"This was an unfortunate time for such an accident," Merdon said. "With the attack . . . ."

Okatar cut him short. "This fire will have no effect on our attack. And it was no accident. It was deliberate sabotage."

"Deliberate? You can't mean it."

Okatar said nothing.

"But who would do such a thing?" Merdon asked.

"I was hoping you might be able to tell me. Obviously no Komani would destroy his own tents and some of his precious ammunition."

Merdon nodded and remained silent for a few

moments, his mind racing. Then he asked, "Wasn't the Watchman quartered near here?"

"Yes," Okatar said, gesturing toward a patch of charred earth. "That was where his tent stood."

"Where is he now?"

Okatar shrugged. "We have found no sign of him."

"Then it must have been him! He knew he was going to be executed, so he somehow set this fire, trying to cause damage to us. He probably died in his own flames."

Okatar's yellow eyes flickered with amusement. "An engaging theory. However, there are three flaws in it. First, we have not found his remains among the ruins."

"His body could have been totally consumed . . ."

"Second," Okatar continued, ignoring Merdon, "one of my warriors saw the Watchman inside his own tent *after* the first explosions. The fire had already started."

"Could he have—"

"And finally," Okatar went on, relentlessly, "we have the very curious pattern of the fire itself."

Okatar pointed to one of the warriors standing nearby, and the Komani switched in a huge floodlight that bathed the whole area in brightness.

"Look carefully at the scene of the fire," Okatar said to Merdon. "Tell me what you see."

Merdon said, "Blackened ground where the flames were burning. Some withered grass nearby. What else?"

"Starting here, where the Watchman's tent stood," Okatar said, striding to the scorched oval, "and looking outward toward the edge of the camp—what do you see?"

Merdon looked out along the direction indicated by the Kang's outstretched arm. The evidence was clear: two lanes of fire-blacked ground, and between them, a path of safety that led to the edge of the camp.

"I see," Merdon said at last.

"Yes," Okatar answered. "Now I ask you—who would

have done this? Who would have committed this sabotage, and rescued the Watchman? One of my men, or one of yours?"

Merdon looked directly into the Komani chieftain's eyes. "Perhaps neither," he said evenly. "Perhaps it was the two Terrans who had escaped. They might have returned to free their fellow prisoner."

"How would they know where he was being held?"

Merdon stroked his jaw for a moment. "They could have been watching the camp from those trees. Or the Watchman might have had some sort of miniature signaling device hidden on him."

Okatar nodded. "Perhaps so. I had not considered that possibility."

"My people have been fighting shoulder to shoulder with your warriors," Merdon added. "There is no reason to think that they would have aided the Watchman, and done this damage to our cause."

"Perhaps," Okatar muttered. "Perhaps."

"Still," Merdon said, "I will check with my people to see if they can shed any light on this."

"Good."

"The attack is still set for dawn?"

Okatar nodded.

"All right. I'd better get down there with my men."

Merdon turned away and left the scene of the fire. Okatar gestured to the warrior at the light, and the Komani turned it off.

"Do you believe him?" asked one of the nobles.

"Of course not," Okatar replied. "There were six Shinarians present when I sentenced the Watchman to death: Merdon, his four underlings, and that priest. Send a man to check on each of them. If any one of them is missing, your man is to find him—no matter where on Shinar he may be, and when he finds him—kill him."

"It shall be done."

IX

The Hours
Before Dawn

Brigadier Aikens sat in frowning silence for a moment as the Star Watchman stood before him. Vorgens looked bedraggled and utterly worn. His uniform was torn and grimy. There was an angry red burn on his right cheek.

Finally the brigadier hunched over his desk and jabbed a finger at Vorgens. "Do you seriously expect me to believe this story?"

"Sir, if my word is not—"

"I don't doubt your word, Watchman. It's your judgment." Aikens grinned humorlessly. "Befriended by a native priest. Rescued from a firing squad. Tipped off to the Komani strategy and shown a route by which we can escape. Use your head, boy! You've been hoodwinked."

"I can't believe that, sir," Vorgens said quietly. "I know what I saw."

Aikens ran a hand over his balding dome. "All right, what did you see? That the barbarians have more men and equipment than we thought? That some of the natives are on their side? That we can't count on reinforcements from the city garrisons? So what? It makes no difference on the military situation here."

"But that's the whole point, sir," Vorgens insisted, his voice still soft. "The tactical situation here is overshadowed by the strategic importance of your decision. If the defeat of the Mobile Force is to be the signal for a general uprising of the Komani clans, then *strategically* you must withdraw and decline combat. You can't afford running the risk of a defeat at this time and place."

"Are you lecturing me on military concepts?" Aikens got up slowly from his chair and his voice rose in pitch. "My men can whip any horde of undisciplined barbarians, I don't care what their numbers are!"

"But the Komani are not undisciplined. They're as well trained as any troops in the galaxy. And the odds are overwhelmingly against you. If you fight here you will be wiped out. Your defeat will touch off a war of terrible proportions."

Aikens thundered, "I've served this Empire for more years than you've known, and on more planets than I care to remember, and I've never heard such panicked, sickening, fear-ridden talk in my life. If you think for one minute that I'll be scared into a withdrawal that'll be, at best, a humiliation to our uniforms, and might possibly lead to a well-planned ambush . . ."

"But, sir—"

"But nothing!" Aikens slammed a fist on his desk. "Wake up, Watchman! Just because you're racially closer to these natives than to real Terrans doesn't mean that you have to swallow everything they tell you. They've fed you a fairy tale. There's nothing those savages would like better than to see my Force trying to sneak out of this valley. They'd cut us to ribbons between here and the next range of hills. That priest, and that girl you seem so entranced with—they're probably waiting for us up in those hills, with guns in their hands, waiting for us and laughing at you! It's a trap, Watchman. A trap set for a gullible young fool."

Vorgens sucked in his breath. "Sir, I cannot stand by and—"

"Just get out of my sight, mister, and stay out of my way."

Aikens sat down again and turned his attention to the pile of reports on his desk.

"Brigadier Aikens, you don't realize what you're—"

"Dismissed."

"But, sir—"

"*Dismissed!*"

Vorgens left the brigadier's office and walked blindly down the narrow passageway to the outer hatch. He climbed down to the ground and stood for a moment next to the mammoth dreadnaught, looking at the maze of vehicles spread across the valley floor, waiting for the dawn. Most of the men were sleeping, he knew—or trying to.

Can Aikens be right? Vorgens wondered. *What makes me so certain that I'm not wrong? He was right about Okatar Kang's reaction to the truce offer. It could be a trap. Sittas lying? Altai working for the Komani? Leading me and the whole Mobile Force into a slaughter? And yet . . . I went across those hills tonight. The Komani really have pulled most of their men away. Can that be part of the trap? Whose judgment can I trust: my own, or Aikens'?*

He began to walk away from the dreadnaught, looking for the cruiser in which he had been quartered. As he walked, he continued to question himself.

How long has Aikens been on Shinar?

A few weeks.

Has he met any of the native rebel leaders?

No.

Has he seen any of the Komani?

Only in battle.

What does he know about the situation on Shinar?

Only what he tells himself.

Then why was he right about Okatar's refusal of the truce?

Vorgens stopped for a moment and puzzled over that one. *He knew what Okatar would do,* the Watchman realized suddenly, *because that is exactly what Aikens himself would have done if he had been in Okatar's place.*

Aikens and Okatar! The same personality, really, when you strip away the differences in race and cultural background. Both warriors. Both impatient with anything less than battle. Both eager to fight it out, here in this valley.

Aikens doesn't want to retreat from the valley because he's anxious to meet Okatar in battle. His fear of a trap is just an excuse. Probably he doesn't realize it himself, but it's only an excuse. He *wants* to fight Okatar!

Vorgens frowned. *Or do I merely want to believe it, because I think Aikens is wrong?*

There was a way to verify his idea, Vorgens suddenly remembered. He turned back and half ran toward the dreadnaught. He clambered inside and made his way to the main computer. A dreadnaught's computer served an amazing variety of functions, from directing fire control to making statistical predictions of an enemy's intent. Vorgens was interested in the personnel records stored in the memory banks. The records were carried to allow officers to pick particularly qualified men for any given task. As a matter of course, the brigadier's battle history would be there.

The computer control center was a tiny compartment, consisting of a desk-console with its control keyboard, and a readout viewscreen. The cramped compartment was unattended at this hour.

It took Vorgens a few minutes to figure out the coding

system that unlocked the computer's memory banks, but finally he had Brigadier Aikens' battle record on the viewscreen.

Vorgens tensed in sudden shock as he read about Aikens' first major battle. It was in the Pleiades Uprising, the rebellion in which Vorgens' own grandfather had been killed.

So Aikens fought against my people, Vorgens said to himself.

The Star Watchman read the details of the record. Aikens was a junior officer then, and he did not see action on the planet where Vorgens' family lived.

Still, he doesn't think very highly of my people.

Vorgens read on. There were two other major battles in Aikens' record. His first action as a senior commander was a daring attack on the capital planet of the Saurian Federation. Vorgens recalled from his history courses that the Saurians had attempted to withdraw from the Terran Empire. Aikens' raid on their capital was the blow that collapsed them.

Vorgens scanned past scores of minor skirmishes, and then found the third major battle on the brigadier's record. It was against a Komani clan that was raiding a Terran planet. Aikens was in charge of the garrison. He had been awarded the Legion of Courage medal for his successful defense of the planet.

The citation that accompanied the medal read, in part, "For heroically standing his ground in the face of overwhelming enemy superiority in numbers . . ."

So that's what he's up to, Vorgens thought. *He wants to repeat the tactics that won the medal.*

Vorgens flicked off the computer and leaned back in the chair before the control console. The record had made many things clear—Aikens' immediate dislike of Vorgens, and the brigadier's stubborn insistence on standing his ground and facing his enemies, no matter what their number and advantage.

Only one thing was not clear: what could Star Watch Junior Officer Vorgens do to correct the situation?

Impulsively, Vorgens tapped out another set of instructions on the computer keyboard. He spent a few more minutes reading very carefully the Star Watch regulations that appeared on the viewscreen in answer to his request.

Vorgens nodded to himself. He turned off the computer once again and stepped out of the tiny compartment into the passageway. At one end of the passageway was an open hatch, and Vorgens could see the sky beginning to pale.

The Watchman made his way to the dreadnaught's dispensary. A sleepy-eyed medic, gray-haired and sour-faced, was sitting next to the diagnostic booth, checking his inventory of supplies.

"I'll need some energy capsules that will keep me going at top efficiency for the next day."

The medic looked up at him. "When's the last time you slept?"

Vorgens had to think a moment. "Night before last—until about noon."

"Pills are no substitute for sleep."

"Doctor, I have no time to argue."

The medic got up from his chair and went to a cabinet. "All right. But I want your name. I'll have to check on you. I don't want anybody living on pills."

Vorgens grinned. "Doctor, if we're both alive by the end of this day, you can check on me as much as you like."

The medic handed him three orange capsules. "That should keep you going for a whole day. Take one now, the others when you feel you need 'em."

"Thank you. My name is Vorgens. Star Watch Junior Officer."

Vorgens left the dreadnaught and trotted toward the cruiser where his quarters were. His thoughts were racing even faster than his body, though.

You know what you think and what you believe. Do you have the nerve to act on it? Do you have the strength to make a decision that will mean life or death for all the men in this valley? Can you shoulder that much responsibility?

He knew that, in reality, it did not matter whether he wanted to take the responsibility or not. It was his, and he could not escape it.

While Vorgens was arguing with Brigadier Aikens, Merdon was striding along the narrow crest of a ridge overlooking the valley where the Mobile Force lay huddled and waiting for the dawn.

The young Shinarian was inspecting his troops in the final hours before battle. In the softly lit night, he watched his rebels—students, farmers, young workers from the cities—as they cleaned their guns, checked their ammunition, went over their assignments with their squad leaders.

Tarat, walking beside Merdon, said, "They're ready. They're primed and ready for the battle."

Merdon nodded. As he stepped along the ridge, the young fighters—girls as well as men—recognized him and waved or grinned in greeting.

Beyond the crest of the ridge the ground sloped away toward the valley floor. The Terran forces there were hidden in shadow, but Merdon could sense their presence.

"Any activity tonight?" he asked Tarat, pointing a thumb toward the darkened valley floor.

The lanky tactician shook his head. "They've been very quiet. A few patrols this morning, but they withdrew as soon as we offered some opposition. Since then, nothing."

"H'm. Where are Romal and the others?"

"A little further down the line. They're waiting for you."

"Good."

"Say, have you told Altai to stay away from the battle?"

Merdon's head jerked upward involuntarily. "Why . . . what makes you ask?"

"She hasn't been here all night. We thought she'd be coming with you, but she didn't. She's always been in the thick of everything—ever since the first fights at the university."

"She'll be here," Merdon said flatly.

"When? I mean, what's keeping her? She's our good luck charm."

"She'll be here!"

Tarat stared at his chief for a moment, then decided to drop the subject. "I've set up the command post up there," he pointed, "on that little knoll. Gives us a good view of the ridge and the whole valley."

"Good."

They climbed up the side of the knoll and stepped into the dugout that had been cut into its crest. It had a bare, earthen floor and walls, and was roofless. Merdon glanced up at the sky. A few clouds were scudding across the stars.

"It's not going to rain, is it?"

Romal answered, "We made a radio contact with our underground forces in Capital City. Their meteorologist predicts some cloudiness here for tomorrow, but no rain."

Merdon turned from the little quartermaster to another of his lieutenants. "Ron, you're a farmer. Will it rain tomorrow?"

Ron scratched his head. "Shouldn't. But we might get a shower towards sundown."

"So much for meteorology," Merdon muttered.

He turned and surveyed the dugout. Portable communications equipment stood along one wall, with a table full of maps alongside it. Merdon went to the table and half sat against it.

"I assume everyone is ready for the attack, and you all know exactly what you're expected to do."

They murmured agreement.

"I just want to call your attention to the basic job we've got to do. The Komani will be mounted on their flyers. They'll be the shock troops. Their mission is to hit the Terrans with beamguns and missiles, and knock out or neutralize the Terran armored vehicles.

"We'll be the infantry. We move in behind the Komani attack waves and mop up. We're the ones who'll actually board the Terran vehicles and smoke out their crews. It'll be tough, unspectacular, dangerous work. Our casualties will probably be high. But at the end of this day— before the showers that Ron predicts—the Terran Mobile Force will be wiped out. Within a week, the garrisons of the four cities either will have surrendered or been destroyed. Shinar will be free."

None of the young leaders cheered, but Merdon could see the eagerness and determination in their eyes.

"Is this meeting for men only, or can a lowly female come in?" Altai asked, and without waiting for an answer she stepped into the command post. A beamgun was buckled at her hip, and a bandolier of grenades slung over one shoulder.

Merdon grinned at her. "I was beginning to wonder what was keeping you."

"You didn't think I'd stay away, did you?"

Their eyes met and locked for a long, wordless moment.

Romal broke the silence. "Did you see the fire in the Komani camp?" he squealed. "It took them hours to get it out. Six tents full of stores and ammunition, up in smoke."

"Yes," Altai answered with a slight smile, "I saw the fire."

"And where is your uncle?" Merdon asked.

"He wanted to come, but I thought it would be better

TEXAS STATE TECH. COLLEGE
LIBRARY-SWEETWATER TX

if he remained further back in the hills. The front line is no place for a man of his years."

"True enough."

"I'm not in the way, am I?" Altai asked. "Did I interrupt?"

"No," Tarat said, "We were just leaving. There's nothing remaining to be done now except wait for the dawn's first light."

"Good luck then," Altai said to the four lieutenants as they filed out of the dugout.

When the last of them was out of earshot, Merdon took both her hands in his and said, "I'm glad you came. I was worried about you."

"We saw the Watchman back safely to the Terran forces."

"It was a foolish thing for you to do. Foolish and futile."

"Perhaps," she answered. "But I had to do it."

"And yet you came back to fight against him."

"Not against him, Merdon. For Shinar. No matter how much we differ about the Watchman, we are still together on the basic fact—Shinar will be free."

While Merdon and Altai talked away the final hour before dawn, six Komani warriors huddled together in a trench not far from the Shinarian command post.

"Every one of the Shinarians is here except the old priest," said one of the warriors.

Another of the warriors nodded. "I cannot find him anywhere."

"Then according to Lord Okatar's command," said the first, "he is the one responsible for the fire at camp."

"Yes. I must find him, wherever he is hiding, and kill him."

The six huge, cat-faced warriors agreed with solemn nods.

"I will miss the battle, then," said the Komani.

"Better to miss the battle than to disobey the orders of your Kang."

"True. Still, it is hard to turn one's back on a battle."

"Lord Okatar will reward you greatly for your faithfulness."

"If I find the priest."

"There is no alternative. You may not return to our tents until you have carried out the Kang's command. The priest must die."

"Yes."

The warriors stood up and began to exchange farewells when, involuntarily, their ears pricked up.

"Listen?"

"What is it?"

A faint, far-off whining. A distant, high-pitched shrill.

"I know that sound," said one of the Komani. "It comes from Terran engines. They are starting up their cruisers and dreadnaughts. The battle is about to begin."

X

Time of Decision

Vorgens reached his cruiser at about the same time Merdon met his lieutenants in the dugout command post.

The Watchman spent only a few minutes in the cramped cubicle of his quarters. He stripped off his ragged clothes, ducked into the lav-stall for an automatic shower and air-blown drying, changed into a clean uniform and strapped on a sidearm. Then he left the cruiser and began to hunt for McIntyre.

The effect of the stimulant had reached its full force now, and would sustain Vorgens for several hours more. He felt strong and buoyant, his head was clear. He knew what he had to do, and although he was not particularly happy with the task ahead, he realized that it was the best possible alternative, under the circumstances.

As he searched through the welter of vehicles and equipment that comprised the Mobile Force, Vorgens could see that the men were ready for an attack at dawn. Hardly anyone was alseep. They were checking their weapons, taking stock of their supplies, making last-minute mechanical repairs on their battlewagons. Even the few that were stretched out on the decks and turrets mostly wide-eyed and sleepless.

McIntyre was sitting in front of a cruiser, carefully adjusting the firing sight of a one-man missile launcher. He had to work with one hand, since his injured arm was still in the cast.

"Good morning, Sergeant."

McIntyre looked up, then leaped to his feet, knocking the tubular missile launcher off its tripod.

"Sir! You made it back!"

Vorgens nodded curtly. "I don't have much time for talking, Sergeant. I need volunteers—real volunteers."

McIntyre's eyes widened as Vorgens explained what he intended to do, and the Star Watch regulations covering such situations.

"I'll need a dozen men. They should all be experienced, and they should be told exactly what they're getting into. Can you get me that many men in fifteen minutes?"

For the first time since Vorgens had known him, McIntyre seemed uncertain of himself. "I can sure try, sir. I can sure try."

It took closer to twenty minutes, but finally McIntyre had assembled a dozen men, noncoms and troopers, all of them. Vorgens looked them over as they lined up before the battle cruiser. They were a hard-faced, veteran crew.

"The sergeant has explained what this is about," Vorgens told them. "Although I am taking full responsibility for this action, there is a chance that your own records may receive a damaging report because of your help to me. If there is any man here who is afraid to run the risk of hurting his service record, he is free to fall out."

None of the twelve moved. In fact, an extra man

stepped out of the shadows and joined the tail end of the line.

"Giradaux!" McIntyre roared. "Get outta there."

The trooper's lean face twisted into a frown. "Sarge, if you're in this, I want to be in on it, too. By glory, I'm a soldier, same as you."

McIntyre stood before the youngster, his tall, thickset form looming over Giradaux's lanky frame. "You're a soldier, all right, and when the wind's behind you, you're a bloody expedition. But this ain't soldiering, sonny, it's politics, and I'm gonna have enough to do without worryin' about you. Now fall out! *Move!*"

Giradaux stepped out of line, his face miserable. Vorgens walked over to him.

"I don't have time to explain," the Watchman said, "but the sergeant is trying to do you a favor. Don't feel disappointed."

Without further ado, Vorgens marched his tiny contingent straight to Brigadier Aikens' dreadnaught. The sky was beginning to turn noticeably pink. There was precious little time left.

At the main hatch, Vorgens split up his men: "You two take the communications center. You two, the engine compartment. Three of you take charge of the control center; three more, take the main turret. The remaining two will stay here at the hatch. Let no one in or out. Sergeant, you come with me."

"You three headin' for the control center," McIntyre instructed, "make sure that all the other outside hatches are shut off."

They clambered in through the hatch and hurried off to their assigned positions. Most of the dreadnaught's crew were in their bunks, and only a skeleton force was on hand to oppose Vorgens' armed men.

While the troopers seized control of the giant fighting vehicle, Vorgens and McIntyre marched to the exec's compartment. Vorgens knocked once and entered.

The exec was sitting on his bunk, with a writing table pulled across his lap. He looked up from the letter he was dictating into the audioprinter.

"What's wrong, Watchman?"

"Get your jacket on and come with me," Vorgens ordered.

"What?"

"I don't have time for arguing. We're going to see the brigadier."

"He'll throw you out . . ."

"No he won't. Put on your jacket and come. I'm sure the brigadier will want you as a witness."

The exec pushed the writing table away and stood up. "Witness? To what? What's going on here, Watchman?"

"You'll see soon enough. Come on."

The exec grabbed his jacket from the rack over his bunk, then looked down at his bare feet.

"No time for putting on boots," Vorgens said. "Let's move."

With a helpless shrug, the exec padded out into the passageway behind Vorgens, pulling on his jacket and buttoning it as they advanced to Brigadier Aikens' compartment.

Aikens, in full-dress uniform, was buckling a pair of ornate pistols across his middle when the door to his compartment abruptly opened. Vorgens and the exec stepped in. McIntyre remained out in the passageway.

"What on earth do you think you're doing?" Aikens bellowed. "I told you to stay out of my sight, Watchman. What's the meaning of breaking in here like this? And you," he turned to the exec, "where are your boots?"

Vorgens said quietly, "Brigadier Aikens, you are hereby relieved of duty. I am assuming command of the Mobile Force."

Aikens' mouth popped open, but for once in his life he was speechless. He simply stood there, his lips pursed into a silent, *Oh*.

"I realize that this is an unusual circumstance," Vorgens continued, "but the standard regulations clearly point out that all Imperial Marine personnel are subject to Star Watch jurisdiction."

"But a junior officer can't assume command from a full brigadier." the exec protested.

Vorgens smiled tightly. "The regulations have no provision in them that prohibits such an action. I am the only Star Watch officer on this planet. I represent Star Watch Headquarters. I am not satisfied with Brigadier Aikens' handling of the situation, therefore, I must relieve him of duty. There is no one else to place in command but myself."

"You're taking command of my Force?" Aikens rasped, finding his voice at last.

"This is not a decision I arrived at lightly, I assure you," Vorgens said to the brigadier. "I can see no alternative. I know this is unpleasant for you. It is equally unpleasant for me."

"Unpleasant!" Aikens screamed. "By all the gods of war, I'll have you shot before the sun comes up!" He began punching buttons on his desktop communicator.

Vorgens shook his head. "I'm afraid that you'll find the dreadnaught is already under my command. I would appreciate it if you'd take off those guns and hand them over to me."

For a stunned instant, Aikens stood frozen behind the desk. Then he slowly unbuckled the gunbelt and tossed it on the floor at Vorgens' feet. Vorgens waited for another explosion from the brigadier. Instead, the older man seemed more bewildered and uncomprehending than anything else. He sank down in his chair and stared ahead blankly.

Vorgens turned to the exec. "We're going to break out of this valley. Inform all the officers that we will regroup immediately in Standard Formation 014. The breakout will be made in sectors W5 and W6. I want all units ready to move as soon as the sun clears the hills."

The exec gasped. "That's only ten or fifteen minutes from now."

"Then you'll have to hurry."

"Yes sir!"

The exec scampered out of the compartment, past McIntyre, headed for the communications center.

Vorgens turned back to the brigadier. "I'm sorry it had to happen this way, sir. But I really have no other choice. I was sent to Shinar to try to arrange a truce. Now it is apparent that my first job is to prevent the Komani from destroying this Force, because if they are successful against us, a new galactic war will be triggered. That must be avoided at all costs. Surely you can see that."

"I can see that you're trying to ruin me," Aikens said dully. "You're trying to destroy a record of fifty-five years of service with your own half-cocked dreams of glory."

"That's not true at all," Vorgens countered. "Ever since I came to Shinar, I've been shunted around from place to place by you, by the Komani, by some of the Shinarians. I've been pushed into killing some of the people with whom I came to negotiate. I've been turned into a messenger boy. I've been taken prisoner, and had a death sentence read over me. I've been rescued from a firing squad by an old man and a girl, because they saw in me what I had almost forgotten was there—a chance to bring peace to Shinar, to prevent this war from starting.

"Now I've stopped playing messenger. I'm a Star Watch officer, and I'm going to take the responsibility that goes with the uniform. I've seen the enemy face to face, and I've seen the rebels, too. Fighting, killing, destroying—that's not going to bring peace to this planet. I've got to convince the rebels of this."

Aikens grunted. "And the Komani? Are you going to talk them out of their plans of conquest?"

"No, I'm afraid not. They will pay attention only to force. But when we fight them, I want it to be on *my* terms, at a time and place that *I* chose, not at Okatar's convenience."

Aikens' eyes glittered with rage. "If—I say, *if*, Watchman—if we both live through this, I'm going to see you before the highest military tribunal in the Empire, stripped of rank and uniform, and sentenced to the worst penalty they can mete out."

"Perhaps," Vorgens said, "Perhaps." Then he added softly, "But the first thing we must do is live through today, isn't it?"

Vorgens dropped to one knee and picked up the brigadier's pistol belt. Then the Watchman straightened to attention and made a formal salute to Aikens. The older man did not return the salute, but merely sat behind his desk, glaring at Vorgens.

The Star Watchman left the compartment. McIntyre was still standing out in the passageway.

"Get one of your men," Vorgens said, as he shut the brigadier's door, "to stand watch at this post. Then join me at the control center."

"Yes sir," McIntyre said, with a salute. Then he relaxed for a moment and said, with a grin, "Congratulations, sir. And good luck."

Vorgens returned the smile. "Thank you, sergeant. We'll need all the luck we can get."

The control center was a half-level above the officers' quarters, and just under the dreadnaught's main turret. Like every compartment in the mammoth groundcar, the control deck was cramped and low-ceilinged. In addition, it was crammed with computer units, communications equipment, and a tight semicircle of control desks, where tech-specialists could keep in constant touch with every part of the vehicle, and with every vehicle in the Mobile Force.

Vorgens climbed up the ladder from the level below,

and silently took the commander's seat at the half-circle of control desks. In the dim, greenish light from the viewscreens he could see that most of the crew was uncertain, anxious. The battle was about to begin, and a new, totally untried commander was in charge.

"I want my instructions processed automatically by the master computer and relayed immediately to the rest of the Force," Vorgens said quietly.

The computer and communications men nodded and began setting up their instruments to carry out the Star Watchman's commands.

"Computer ready, sir," called out the tech-specialist.

"Communications ready, sir."

Vorgens nodded. On the desk before him, he could see a pair of green lights signaling what the men had just told him.

For a moment, he hesitated. Looking up at the men around him—all of them staring back at him—Vorgens suddenly realized that every one of them was a complete stranger. Even McIntyre he had known for less than a week.

With an abrupt shake of his head, Vorgens put such thoughts aside. He began dictating his instructions.

Deep in the bowels of the dreadnaught, the master computer translated the Star Watchman's words into electromagnetic pulses and began sorting them out with the speed of light. Automatically, the computer processed the instructions into a separate set of orders for each of the three hundred individual vehicles in the Mobile Force.

Automatically, each set of orders was relayed to the communications transmitter and beamed to each individual dreadnaught, cruiser, scoutcar, troopcarrier, supply van. On three hundred separate vehicles, communications receivers relayed the messages to computers. On three hundred vehicles, computers suddenly chugged to life and busily rattled off detailed orders. As the tapes wormed out of the printers three hundred skippers read the orders and began barking commands. The sum total of all these individual messages was Vorgens' plan for breaking out of the Komani trap.

Scoutcars and troopcarriers were to speed to the slopes where the Komani had thinned out their forces—Sectors W5 and W6 on the Terran maps. The troopers were to seize those two sectors and hold them, with the scoutcars neutralizing any pockets of enemy resistance. Light cruisers, slower and less maneuverable than the smaller vehicles, would follow up the first assault and provide extra firepower.

As the troopers gained command of the slopes, engineers' vans were to immediately begin grading the territory, using force beams and explosives. The objective was to gouge out a broad, easy slope with no major obstructions, so that the larger vehicles of the Mobile Force could skim up the slopes and out of the valley as quickly as possible. Vorgens remembered how his battle cruiser was forced to crawl along the twisting, narrow trail up the slopes. He wanted no more of that. If the entire Mobile Force had to file out of the valley like that, they would never escape alive.

While the troopers were holding open the escape route and the engineers were making it ready to handle the main body of the Mobile Force, the rest of the Force was to fall back slowly toward the escape slopes. A special task unit of ten dreadnaughts, including Vorgens' flagship, was to form a rear guard, and to keep the Komani attack stalled and off balance until the final dash for freedom.

"That's the plan," Vorgens muttered to himself as he watched the computer's steady stream of orders flash across the viewscreen at his elbow. "Now to see if it will work."

XI

Breakout

Okatar Kang stood at the crest of a hill with the first rays of the rising sun at his back. Below him, the valley floor was still cloaked in darkness, but the Komani technicians had set up a battery of viewscreens that showed the Mobile Force.

The Kang paced restlessly behind the technicians, who were seated before their mobile viewscreens. The high-pitched shriek of Terran engines was wafting up from the valley.

"What are they doing?" Okatar demanded of no one in particular.

One of his nobles, pacing alongside him, answered, "They are preparing for the battle, starting their engines."

The viewscreens suddenly went blank. Before Okatar could say anything, the technicians had readjusted them, and the pictures of the sprawling Terran armored Force reappeared.

"They've put up an energy shield," one of the technicians said.

"We expected that," said the noble at Okatar's elbow. "It cannot be a very powerful shield, since its generating equipment must be small and mobile. An hour's worth of force beams should saturate it."

"What about missiles?" Okatar snapped.

"The Terran shield will probably stop some of them, but not all. Their shield could not possibly be as strong as the screen we have around our camp. Of course, our warriors will be able to penetrate the shield with ease. Not even the Terrans have been able to devise an energy screen so solid that a man cannot step through it."

Okatar nodded. "How much longer before the signal?"

The noble glanced at the watch set into his jeweled wristband. "The signal should be given—*now*."

A hundred beams of light lanced out of the hills down toward the still-shadowy valley floor and splashed into blinding brilliance against the Terran energy shield. Missiles roared through the morning mists and exploded in flashes of flame. Through the noise of the explosion rose a mighty shout as Komani warriors charged down from the hilltops, riding their one-man flyers straight toward the Terrans.

Okatar stood riveted before the viewscreens, his nobles clustered about him. They watched the Terran armored vehicles shift positions as they awaited the onslaught of the Komani. Here and there, missiles penetrated the Mobile Force's energy shield and blasted into the ground. One of them hit a cruiser, and Okatar could not restrain an exultant laugh. The force beams, though, were stopped completely by the shield.

"What are they up to?" Okatar wondered aloud as he watched the screens.

The smallest Terran vehicles—scoutcars and troop carriers —seemed headed for the rear, while the big dreadnaughts and battle cruisers were moving up to face the Komani attack.

"They're moving their lightly armored vehicles away from our missile barrage," one of the nobles said.

Okatar looked up from the screen. It was light enough now to see the valley floor clearly. The Komani warriors were halfway down the hills, halfway to the valley floor. But his attack was not interesting Okatar as much as the Terrans' moves toward the rear.

"Why are they pulling their troops away from the fighting? Do they expect to face my warriors with their armored vehicles alone, without infantry support?"

"The Terrans have no stomach for facing our warriors man to man," said a noble. "They are too cowardly to fight, except from within an armored vehicle."

Okatar nodded, but his face was still frowning in puzzlement.

At his slot in the control center, Vorgens watched the viewscreen before him, his high forehead puckered into worried wrinkles.

Someone slid into the empty seat next to him. Vorgens looked up. It was the exec.

The older officer smiled, "Reports from Sectors W5 and 6 sound pretty smooth so far. Everything progressing according to plan. Light resistance."

"Are the engineers ready to go?" Vorgens asked. "That's the most critical part of the operation."

"Ready and anxious. As soon as you give the word."

Vorgens nodded. "Where's Sergeant McIntyre?"

"I believe he went out with the other troopers in the vans."

"Yes, that sounds like him."

The Star Watchman returned his attention to the viewscreen. It was bright daylight now, so that the infrared scanners were no longer necessary. The screen showed the hills before them, with the glaring, yellow Oran automatically filtered out. Flashes from force beams blazed almost continuously against the energy shield now, and explosions churned up the valley floor. The mammoth dreadnaughts and battle cruisers were weaving back and forth in an intricate, computer-controlled dance that had so far kept the Komani missiles limited to two damaging hits and a half-dozen minor ones. Anti-missiles were picking off a good many incoming missiles, as well. So far the Komani had not used nuclear warheads. Probably they only had a few and were saving them for an emergency, Vorgens thought, or for the moment when the energy screen collapsed.

The Watchman's attention was focused on the Komani warriors making their way on their one-man flyers down the broken, tumbled rocks toward the valley floor. They were about halfway between the crest of the hills and the bottom.

"They're sticking pretty close to cover," the exec observed.

"Yes, but the cover thins out rather quickly as they approach the valley floor," Vorgens said. "I think we can hold our fire for another few minutes, and then hit them with a massed barrage."

The exec nodded agreement. "We might try peppering the hilltops with missiles, too. The Komani probably have their second and third waves up there."

Vorgens thought a moment. "I'd rather wait until I see some definite targets. No sense wasting ammunition on probabilities."

"As you wish."

And no sense bombarding the Shinarian rebels, Vorgens thought to himself, *if we can avoid getting them into combat altogether.* "What's the latest word from W5 and 6?" the Watchman asked.

The exec flicked a switch on his desk communicator, and scanned the report that flashed across its tiny viewscreen. "The troopers have advanced about halfway up

the slopes. Their perimeter is almost exactly as planned—
the outer edges of the two sectors. Looks good."

"Start the engineers to work."

"Yes sir." The exec pressed a stud on the communicator.

"Are all the units in the forward battle line ready to
fire?" Vorgens asked.

"All units report fire control tracking and standing by,"
answered the communications tech.

Vorgens took a last look at the viewscreen before him.
The Komani warriors were nearing the base of the hills.

"Commence firing."

The Terran battle line let loose a devastating hail of
beams and missiles that caught the advanced elements
of the Komani attackers in an inescapable deluge of fire.
The force beams sprayed back and forth across the lines
of warriors and their little flyers. Men and machines were
sliced apart, brush and grass set ablaze, rocks and earth
vaporized by the intense beams of light. Anti-personnel
missiles exploded overhead, showering the area with
deadly shrapnel.

The spearhead of the Komani attack was shattered.
The Terran curtain of fire began to creep up the face of
the hills, catching the Komani warriors further back. The
Komani advance halted and the warriors took whatever
cover they could find among the sparse bushes and jagged rocks of the hillsides.

"We stopped them!" the exec marveled. "Stopped
them cold."

"Too easily," Vorgens countered.

"We could counterattack; move up those hills and mop
them up."

Vorgens shook his head. "Perhaps that's what they
expect us to do. No, instead of attacking, we're moving
back. Pass the word—all units to fall back slowly half a
mile."

"But that will give us less room for maneuvering—make us a more compact target."

"Yes, and it will also make a greater open space between us and the enemy; an open space almost completely without cover. This is a rear guard action, remember. We're trying to avoid major contact with the enemy."

The exec nodded, then began giving out the necessary orders on his communicator.

Slowly, the ponderous dreadnaughts and cruisers and their escorting vehicles began to withdraw from their positions. The battlewagons on the flanks pulled back first, then those in the center joined in the movement. A huge bowed line, spreading nearly the width of the valley floor, edged backward, away from the still-rising sun.

They were in the midst of the maneuver when the *real* Komani attack came howling out of the hills on both their flanks. Thousands of warriors swarmed down on both sides of the Terran line and began pouring fire into the armored vehicles.

"This is it," Vorgens muttered as he watched his viewscreen. The hills, even the sky, seemed black with charging Komani.

"Good grief, look at them," the exec said. "It's a lucky thing we didn't advance when I wanted to. We'd have been surrounded."

"Let's get to work," Vorgens said.

The Watchman began dictating a steady stream of orders. In response, the Terran battle line continued to edge backward, and bowed even more, with the battlewagons on both flanks pulling back further and facing outward to meet the double attack of the Komani.

A sudden hail of missiles and force beams, including a few nuclear missiles, smashed into the Terran forces. One of the nuclear warheads got through and vaporized a dreadnaught. Vorgens' own vehicle, a few stations up the line, bucked and rattled when the concussion wave blew past.

As abruptly as it came, the Komani barrage ended, and the flying warriors swarmed into the massed Terran vehicles. Vorgens met them with concentrated fire, his dreadnaughts and cruisers sweeping the sky with force beams.

Despite frightful losses, the warriors continued to bore in. They penetrated the energy shield, and began attacking individual vehicles with grenades and missile-guns. Vorgens ordered his vehicles to "pop hatches" and allow the crews to meet the attackers with handguns and rifles—much more effective now than the powerful, long-range weapons in the turrets.

The main batteries of the dreadnaughts and cruisers, at Vorgens' orders, kept up a constant rain of fire on the slopes of the hills, in an effort to prevent the Komani from reinforcing their first wave of attackers.

The battle line of Terran armor was enveloped in a wild, confused struggle of men and machines. Komani warriors swooped everywhere, shooting and bombing as they flew. Terran Marines crouched in their hatches and fought back with force beams and anti-personnel missiles and grenades. The big turrets spat their beams of death toward the hills, while the smaller gun batteries aboard the battlewagons spun and fired at the darting Komani warriors. Dust and smoke, explosions and flame, enveloped everyone and everything.

Deep within his dreadnaught, at the control center, Vorgens could hear the muffled explosions as his eyes watched the battle shift back and forth, on the viewscreen.

"We've got to disengage from the warriors," he muttered to himself. "We've got to scrape them off our backs ... otherwise the whole plan will fail."

Okatar Kang stood under the cloudless sky and watched the raging battle on the valley floor. He ignored the viewscreens set up before him, and instead held a pair of molectronic binoculars to his eyes. When he put them down, his face was set in a grim mask of anger.

One of the nobles standing beside him said, "The warriors have penetrated the Terran energy shield on both flanks. It is only a matter of time now. Shall I have the Shinarians join the attack?"

"They have no transport. It will take them the better part of an hour before they can reach the fighting," Okatar grumbled.

"Then we had better start them now."

"Yes, send them off." Okatar paced along the crest of the hill. The breeze was blowing down from the higher hills toward the valley floor, so that the smoke and noise of the battle was carried away from him.

"Why did they retreat?" Okatar demanded. "The frontal attack did not fool them. They did not hold their ground. They retreated. Why? Did they know that we would attack their flanks? If they had advanced, or even held their ground, our double flank attack would have overwhelmed them. Now—the issue is in doubt."

"Their commander made a lucky guess," one of the nobles answered. "Our men will still prevail over them."

"But at what cost? Our losses will be very heavy."

"For every man who falls today," another noble predicted, "a hundred Komani warriors will join your standards tomorrow. This victory will establish you as the leader of all the clans, everywhere."

Okatar looked hard at the noble. "If we have a victory today."

"Surely you don't think that the Terrans could defeat us!"

"Not of themselves," Okatar replied. "But we have traitors in our camp. Men in whom our trust is misplaced. Perhaps . . ."

A communications technician jumped up from his field table and dashed over to the Kang.

"What is it?" Okatar demanded.

The tech bowed quickly and answered, "Reports from our men holding the far hills, on the other side of the valley, sire. They have been under attack since the sun rose, and steadily forced back. If they are not reinforced, the Terrans will drive them from their positions and open an escape lane out of the valley."

Okatar snapped his binoculars to his eyes. "By the blood of our forefathers," he thundered, "the smoke is covering the area completely."

A noble shrugged at the news. "A Terran diversion. They cannot possibly get those lumbering vehicles of theirs across the hills in any time less than a day. There are no roads, and no trails wider than—"

"Sire, the Terran engineers are blasting out roadbeds through the area that our warriors have been driven from."

Okatar roared something unintelligible and thrust the startled technician aside. He strode to the communications table and talked directly to the leader of the Komani under attack.

When Okatar straightened up and faced his nobles, his face was furious. "They're seizing the hills and building an escape road through them. If we don't stop them, they'll be out of this valley before nightfall."

"But how . . ."

"How did they know that those particular hills were held with only a skeleton force? Who told them?"

"Sire, we can find the traitors later. At the moment we must prevent the Terrans from escaping."

"Contact the second and third waves of our attacking forces and order them to close the gap in our lines in those hills."

"But—what about the main attack?"

"The first wave alone will have to do as much damage to the Terrans as it can," Okatar said. "Have the warriors who made the original frontal attack join them."

"What about the Shinarians?"

"Get them into the battle as quickly as they can get there. But I doubt that they will be in time."

The oldest noble of the group, his facial hair grizzled and his back bent with years, spoke up. "Sire, you are condemning the brave warriors of the first attacking wave to certain death. They cannot destroy the Terran forces by themselves, without support."

Okatar nodded curtly. "They will buy time for us, while we sew up the trap again. The Terrans must not escape, no matter what the price. That is my command!"

As he sat in the control center, watching the progress of the seesaw battle over his armored vehicles, Vorgens felt a cold, hard knot forming in his stomach. He had taken the responsibility of command, and now the anxiety and tension of that burden were making themselves felt.

"What time is it?" he asked.

"Almost noon," the exec replied.

"It's not going too well, is it?"

"We're holding our own."

"But we've got to disengage from this attack. We can't retreat, or try to support the troopers up in the hills, while the Komani are on top of us."

The exec rubbed his jaw for a moment. "Listen," he said, "each vehicle has a complement of armored flying suits. Why don't we form a reserve brigade and throw them at the Komani? Maybe we could clear them off."

Vorgens nodded. "It's worth a try."

As the exec began rattling off the orders to form a flying reserve brigade, Vorgens suddenly felt the strength ebbing out of him. His head began to throb, it was an effort to raise his arm and rub his forehead, even his vision seemed to be going blurry.

Energy capsule, he said to himself, as he fumbled with his tunic pocket. *Need another booster.*

He pulled the two remaining pills from the pocket and

stared at them in the palm of his hand for a blank moment. Then he realized a noncom was at his elbow with a cup of water.

"Thank you," Vorgens mumbled, and he took one of the capsules.

"Anything else, sir?" the noncom asked.

Vorgens looked up at the Terran. He was as young as the Watchman himself, pink-cheeked, bright-eyed, without the weight of the galaxy's peace on his shoulders.

"No, that's all, thanks ... Or wait—remind me in six hours to take the other pill."

"Certainly, sir."

Vorgens focused his attention back on the viewscreen. The battle was still raging outside the dreadnaught. Several vehicles were ablaze now, and the ground between them was bomb-pitted and littered with dead and dying men, both Terran and Komani.

"The flying squads are ready to go, sir."

Vorgens squeezed his eyes shut and tried to think. "It would probably be better if they massed at one spot, and then hit the Komani as a solid unit. Don't you think so?"

The exec nodded. "Exactly. I've given them the word to group first at battle cruiser J-7"—he pointed to the stereomap on the desktop before him—"in the middle of our battle line."

"Good. Have them sweep to the far side of the valley first, and once that flank is cleared, they can come back this way."

"Right." The exec flicked a switch on his communicator and gave the orders.

From every vehicle of the embattled Terran group, a half-dozen or so men emerged, clad in armored suits with jetbelts on their backs. Some of them never cleared the hatches: Komani warriors cut them down. But most of them fought their way toward the rendezvous point over a flame-blackened, battered cruiser, and then wheeled as a unit and began advancing on the milling, free-wheeling Komani attackers.

The Komani warriors fought mostly as single units. That was their glory and their strength. Their tactics were chaos and confusion. They merely blackened the sky and hit their enemy from every direction at once.

But the Terran flying brigade had the solidity and firepower of an airborne dreadnaught. Like a mammoth cloud of death, the Terrans began sweeping the sky clean of the Komani.

Vorgens watched the progress of the aerial battle. But a corner of his mind refused to devote itself to the struggle overhead. Something was out of place. Something had changed in the picture on his viewscreen. What was it?

The main batteries of the dreadnaughts and cruisers were no longer firing into the hills, as he had ordered! But some of the battlewagons were shooting missiles and force beams across the valley floor, in the direction where the first attack had come from, at sunrise.

What's going on? Vorgens wondered.

The Star Watchman began twisting the control knobs of his viewscreen, in an effort to get a panoramic view of all the action.

Komani warriors were advancing along the valley floor, from the same spot where the sunrise attack had started.

But that was just a holding attack, meant to draw us into the trap on our flanks.

And on those flanks, where the Komani should be pouring wave after wave of attackers—nothing. Silence. No enemy action.

The main attack was coming from our flanks, Vorgens reasoned. *Now Okatar has stopped that attack. He's left his men here over our vehicles, with no further support.*

The answer flashed into his mind with blinding clarity. At the same moment, a trio of nuclear explosions rocked the summit of the hills where the Terran troopers and engineers were struggling to open up an escape route.

"The enemy has broken off his attack on us," Vorgens shouted into the exec's ear. "They're trying to recapture Sectors W5 and 6!"

The exec arched his eyebrows and punched a button on his communicator. A report lit up on his viewscreen.

"The troopers have taken the crest of the hills. The engineers have blasted out a passable grade about a third of the way up to the top. . . . Hold on, there's more. The troopers are under bombardment. Looks as though a major counterattack is on the way."

"Get every cruiser out of this battle line and up those hills as fast as possible," Vorgens snapped. "Put every available man from the dreadnaughts into flying suits and clear the attackers off our decks. I want nothing but skeleton crews aboard the dreadnaughts. We've got an escape route open. Now it's going to be a race to hold it!"

Sergeant McIntyre wormed through the brush, a pistol in his good hand, and took a careful look out over the edge of the ridge. Down below, a hundred yards or so, a squad of Komani were setting up a heavy beamgun to spray the ridge where McIntyre's men had dug in.

The Terran troopers had won that ridge in midmorning against stiff Komani resistance, and had held it against three counterattacks of steadily increasing fury.

The Terrans had dug in and waited for the engineers, and finally the main body of the Mobile Force, to reach them. But now, late in the afternoon, they had seen nothing but enemy warriors.

A missile shrieked by. McIntyre instinctively dug his face into the grassy ground. The blinding flash, instantly followed by an ear-splitting explosion, told him that another nuclear warhead had been fired at them. Fully half the men he had started out with were already dead or wounded, but that particular missile, McIntyre knew, was off target. It plowed up some ground, knocked down trees for a square mile around, and sent up an ugly mushroom cloud, but it hadn't hit any of his men. If anything, it had merely made the engineers' job a little easier by clearing some more of the hilly country for them.

Patiently, McIntyre waited until the Komani squad had put their beamgun together. Then he tossed a pair of grenades at them, in rapid succession. The explosions were sharp but unspectacular. When the smoke cleared, the beamgun was a shambles and the Komani killed. With a grim smile of satisfaction, McIntyre edged back to the slit trench where Giradaux and the rest of his men were waiting.

Another strong attack'll finish us, the sergeant knew. *And th' Komani are gettin' set for a big one. Pretty soon now. Plenty of movement down in that brush. They're just about set to wipe us up.*

Someone was rushing toward him, racing as fast as he could while doubled over so that one hand nearly touched the ground. McIntyre pointed his pistol at the lanky, awkward form, then recognized Giradaux.

"I thought I told you to stay with the others," the sergeant growled as Giradaux flopped belly down beside him.

"We got a visitor back at the trench, Sarge. An engineer." Giradaux's lean, angular face was split by a big toothy grin. "Say's he's got a couple of cruisers crawling up right behind him, and the dreadnaughts are on their way, too!"

McIntyre looked at the grinning trooper, then suddenly scrambled to his feet. Standing bolt upright, he stared down toward the valley floor.

About twenty Terran vehicles were scattered across the valley, smoking and inert. The rest of the Mobile Force was streaming up the hillsides, along paths of raw earth gouged out by the engineers and the Komani bombardment, toward the crest of the hills—toward freedom.

Giradaux and the sergeant scampered back to the slit trench. A battle-scarred cruiser was already there, and the troopers were clambering aboard its rear deck.

"He did it!" McIntyre shouted to the young trooper. "That Star Watchman has pulled us outta the trap. We're gettin' outta this valley—alive!"

The engineer, grimy and hollow-eyed, called from his one-man scoutcar, "No time for celebration, sergeant. Let's get out of here before the Komani try to hit us again."

McIntyre grabbed a handhold on the cruiser's side and hoisted himself upwards.

"They ain't gonna try anything now," he answered, over his shoulder. "They've lost this battle, and they know it."

The cruiser whined into life, lifted off the ground by about a foot, and rumbled off with the battered, jubilant troopers aboard. The engineer gunned his little scrambler and scooted up alongside, placing the crusier between himself and the Komani.

Half a mile away, a Komani officer stood under a cloudy, smoke-filled sky and spoke into his wrist communicator:

"The main body of the Terran forces has reached the summit of the hills. We will attack again if you order us to, but my company is down to less than half its original strength. The Terrans have the advantage of massed firepower, and their armored vehicles are faster than our flyers, once they are in open country."

After a long wait, an utterly exhausted voice sounded from the communicator, "Break off contact with the enemy. Regroup your men. The battle is over."

XII

Sittas

It showered briefly at sunset, as the Mobile Force streamed out to the rolling, open countryside. Then all through the night clouds piled up thicker and darker until, by dawn, it began to rain steadily.

Sittas heard the first drops strike the roof over his head. The old priest was standing by a window on the upper floor of the town hall of Matara, a tiny farming village a few miles from the valley of Carmeer.

He had turned the town hall—the only two-story building in the village—into an emergency hospital. Terrans, Komani, and the few Shinarians who had been wounded in the battle were being brought in. Sittas stood by the window after a full night of dressing wounds and blessing the dead, and watched the maimed and shattered men still being brought through the muddy, rain-spattered morning into the makeshift infirmary. When would the pitiful parade end? Sittas had gathered every doctor and every available boy and woman from miles

128

around. But they were few, terribly few, for this horrible toll.

"It's not a very pretty sight, is it?"

Sittas turned and saw Altai at the door, a raincape over her shoulders, her hair glistening wet.

"You are ... all right?"

She nodded. "The Watchman kept his word. The Terrans avoided firing on us. Only Merdon and his best three squads got into the fighting, and they had to ride piggyback on Komani flyers to reach the Terrans. Merdon could have stayed out of it altogether. The Watchman gave us that opportunity."

"Well, thank heaven that you are safe, and that more of our people were not involved in the battle. Merdon was not hurt, was he?"

"No, he's all right."

"Good."

Altai stepped over to the window and looked at the steady line of wounded coming into the building.

"It was an awful battle, though. Even if our people didn't have much to do with it."

"I know," the priest said. "Unless we can bring peace to Shinar quickly, this will be only the first of many, many battles, and our people will be fully involved in the next ones."

"What do you intend to do?" she asked.

Sittas shook his head. "I'm not certain. That's the terrible part of it. I don't know what to do next."

"You're tired," Altai said. "We all are. Time to sleep now."

"But the wounded need help. . . ."

She took him by the arm and steered him to a couch along the far wall of the room. "The wounded don't need someone who's about to fall asleep on them. Sleep now, and you'll be much better able to help them when you awake."

The old man sat on the edge of the couch. "You

remind me very much of my sister . . . your mother. She was very domineering, too, despite being much younger than I."

Altai smiled at him. "Enough talking. Sleep," she said firmly.

With a resigned shrug, Sittas kicked off his sandals and stretched out on the couch. Altai put her raincape over him, and walked softly out of the room. The lights went off as she closed the door.

Squatting outside the pelting rain, a Komani warrior eyed the town-hall-turned-hospital with the patient cunning of a stalking panther. The old man is in there, the warrior knew. Only the wounded, or Shinarian doctors and helpers, were allowed inside. Sooner or later the old man would come out. Then the warrior would kill him. Time did not matter. The reason behind the warrior's orders did not matter. All the warrior knew was that Sittas must die. There was no other purpose for the Komani's existence but to carry out the order of death. Silently he sat in the rain, his chin cupped in his massive hands, and waited.

Sittas was awakened by the sounds of three Shinarian youths trying to place a wounded Komani on a makeshift pallet of blankets and coats. The town hall was overflowing. The rain had stopped, and a late afternoon sun was slanting through the windows. Outside, Sittas could see that more wounded had been left on litters in the town square.

The old priest immediately went downstairs, into the welter of cots and pallets and doctors and weary, busy women and boys who were attending the injured men. Altai was among them.

"Here," Sittas said to his niece, as she tried to wrap a bandage over a young Terran's arm. "I'll do that. You find the town mayor and bring him here immediately."

The mayor was short, round and bland-faced. He listened patiently as Sittas explained what he wanted to do, then replied with a shrug:

"The people probably won't want to bring wounded foreigners into their homes, but I shall tell them that you have asked them to do so. We shall see how they react."

The reaction was startling, even to Sittas. Nearly every family in the tiny village showed up at the town square and took at least one of the wounded men lying out on the worn old paving stones. The casualties were all safely indoors before night fell.

The mayor was amazed. "These people revere you, Sittas."

The priest shook his head. "It is not me. They are good-hearted people. I only pointed out how they could help."

All through the night, with only an hour or so of rest, Sittas attended "his" patients. Near dawn, one of the doctors reported worriedly:

"We have just about stripped the entire district clean of medical supplies. There's practically nothing left to go on."

Altai, standing nearby her uncle, said, "Perhaps I can get more."

As she went off toward the building's only tri-di transceiver, a Komani officer strode into the main entrance. He looked across the sea of bedridden men that filled the entryway and stretched on into the other rooms.

"Which of you is in charge here?" he demanded of the Shinarians.

Everyone turned toward Sittas.

"I am Sittas," the priest said, making his way toward the Komani. He saw a trio of warriors standing just outside the doorway.

The Komani officer said, "In the name of Okatar Kang, I claim the Terrans sheltered here as prisoners . . ."

"Never!" Sittas snapped, with a vehemence that surprised them all.

The old man walked up to the Komani, and, standing barely as tall as the officer's breastbone, said furiously, "This place is sanctuary for wounded men. Do you understand? Sanctuary. Neither Okatar Kang nor the Terran commander has any right to claim prisoners here. The men here are no longer warriors—not until they are well enough to rejoin their companions. In this town the war does not exist. Isn't it enough that you have killed and crippled so many? Get out of here—you smell of death. Out!"

The Komani officer was forced back a step. Uncertainly, he mumbled, "Well, if it's sanctuary . . . we have no quarrel with your religious feelings." He turned and walked out. The three warriors followed him.

Outside, the Komani warrior who had been silently waiting for almost three days, sat immobile and watched the entrance to the town hall. For an instant Sittas was framed in the doorway, and the warrior's hand slid to the butt of his pistol, but then the priest turned away and went back inside the building. The warrior grunted to himself and relaxed. He did not stop watching.

News of sporadic fighting between the Terrans and Komani trickled into the hospital that morning. The Mobile Force was in the open country, and a few of their scoutcars had brushed briefly with Komani patrols.

Near noontime a Terran supply van rumbled through the dusty main street of Matara and stopped before the town hall. A white flag flew from its whip antenna. A lieutenant and five other Marines got out of the cab and entered the building, looking for Sittas.

"We have a van full of medical supplies, sir," the lieutenant told the priest. "Compliments of the Terran Imperial Star Watch and Marine Corps."

As the Terrans, with a dozen Shinarian youths helping them, unloaded the supplies, Sittas found Altai and said:

"I know this is your doing. But how did you accomplish it?"

She smiled at her uncle. "I phoned our people in Capital City. They saw to it that the Terran garrison there learned of your need for medical help. The garrison informed the Star Watchman, I suppose, and he sent the supplies."

Sittas shook his head. "Lines of communication become very strange in wartime."

Before the Terran van was unloaded completely, a small civilian groundcar pulled up beside it. The driver hopped out lightly, trotted around to the passenger's side, and opened the door. A tall, broad-girthed, balding Shinarian stepped out—Clanthas.

He cocked an eye at the Terran vehicle, then walked into the town hall. For several minutes he spoke to no one, but merely paced slowly through the improvised hospital, watching Shinarians tending the wounded Terrans and Komani. He nodded to a few of the doctors, grinned at the women and youths assisting them.

Finally, Clanthas spotted Sittas. The old priest was standing on the balcony that ran around three sides of the large, ground-level room that had been the town hall's main auditorium. Clanthas climbed the stairs slowly, yet he was still puffing a bit when he reached the top.

Sittas was locked in a discussion with one of the doctors.

"All right, they're well enough to leave and rejoin the rest of the Terrans," the doctor was saying. "But how do you get them back to their own men safely, without the Komani stopping them?"

"We can put them on the Terran van, outside," Sittas replied.

"And what about tomorrow, or the day after?"

"We can ask the Terrans leaving today to have their commander keep in touch with us by tri-di. When we are ready to release more of them, they can send another vehicle, under a truce flag."

"And you expect the Komani to honor the flag of truce?"

Sittas nodded. "They know that their own wounded are being tended here. If they do anything to disrupt our work, their own men will suffer for it."

The doctor shrugged. "I hope you're right. . . . Very well. I'll tell the Terran lieutenant that we'll have a few men for him to take back with him."

"Good."

As the doctor turned to find the lieutenant, Clanthas stepped up to the old priest.

"You do not know me. My name is Clanthas."

Sittas' wrinkled face broke into a smile. "Clanthas of Katan? The merchant who organized the first protests and demonstrations against the Terrans?"

Clanthas nodded, with a rueful grin. "I did help to get the movement started; it has gone much farther than I expected."

"Yes. But your aims and ideals were good ones. I am honored to meet you."

"Thank you."

"You are looking for your son, Merdon? He is not here, but he is well and happy."

"Yes, I know. I spoke with Merdon on tri-di last night. Actually, I came here to see you, and this hospital. News of what you have done is spreading all over Shinar. You have become a national hero, Sittas."

"Me?" Sittas laughed. "An unlikely hero, I must say. I have done practically nothing. It is the doctors, and the good people of this town. And the Terran commander, too; he sent us a van-load of medical supplies."

"Yes, I know. My driver parked next to the Terran van. Fortunately, they don't know who I am."

Altai hurried up the stairs to her uncle. "Excuse me.

The Terrans have finished unloading. Their lieutenant wants to speak with you."

"Ah yes; and there are several things I want to talk over with him." Sittas turned back to Clanthas. "Will you pardon me for a moment?"

"Certainly."

The priest gestured toward the girl. "My niece, Altai, will be glad to show you around the building and to answer any questions you may have. Altai, this is Clanthas of Katan, Merdon's father."

"Merdon's father?" Altai gasped as Sittas started down the stairs. Her hands flew to her hair. "I. . . . I must look terrible. These slacks and this old blouse . . . you must excuse my appearance, I had no idea . . ."

Clanthas chuckled at her. "I wasn't expecting to find you in a ball gown. Merdon has told me quite a bit about you. You are as lovely as he said you were."

"Oh . . . thank you."

They began to talk, mostly about Merdon, and were deep in conversation when Sittas returned.

"I have decided to accompany the Terrans back to the Mobile Force," the old man said. "The lieutenant has told me that the Star Watchman has assumed command of all Terran units on Shinar. He has asked to see me, and I believe it might be helpful to go to him, now that he has such power in his hands."

"I've heard some rumors about a Watchman on the planet," Clanthas said. "You know him?"

Sittas nodded. "Altai can tell you about it. I must hurry off, the Terrans are anxious to leave."

The old priest, flanked by the Terran lieutenant and five troopers left, the building and climbed into the cab of the bulky supply van. The Komani warrior who had been waiting in the town square watched with helpless fury. He could not get a good shot at the old man with six Terrans surrounding him, and he could not get close enough to use a grenade without the Terrans stopping him.

As the supply van whined to life and lifted off the pavement, the Komani wearily trudged back to his own flyer, resting in an alley off the square. Perhaps he could catch up with the van in the open country. If the Terrans were not alert, he could execute the old man, and get a half-dozen Terrans in the bargain.

XIII

Vorgens

Sittas eyed the Star Watchman critically as they sat in the tiny compartment aboard the dreadnaught. The priest had never before been inside a vehicle of such size, yet he was most amazed at how much the Terrans were able to squeeze into the big groundcar.

Vorgens' quarters, where they were sitting, was typical. The bunk was folded into the bulkhead; the webbed chairs and table had been slid out of the same opening that the bunk fitted into. The short side of the compartment was taken up with a translucent viewscreen, another wall had a stereomap scanner built into it. The furniture was stored in the third wall, and the fourth was barely wide enough to accommodate the door that led into the passageway. The ceiling was covered with light-panels. There must have been a clothes closet in the compartment, but Sittas could not determine where it might be.

His inspection of the compact room took only a

moment. As he shook hands with Vorgens and they both sat down facing each other, Sittas could see that the Watchman had changed.

It was nothing obvious, but Vorgens looked somehow different. He seemed well and hearty enough, but there were tiny lines around his eyes, and his face was slightly thinner, tauter. There was a different air about him. The Watchman was no longer a troubled, bewildered youth thrown into the middle of a world he could not understand. He was a Star Watch officer, in command of the Terran forces on this planet. He had accepted the responsibility of command, and had discovered at last that he could, to a degree, take that world into his own hands and begin to shape it for himself.

"I hear you were attacked on your way to join us," Vorgens said, hunching forward slightly in the webbed chair.

Sittas shook his head. "You could hardly call it an attack. Your troopers discovered a lone Komani warrior following our van. They fired a few beams at him, and he shot a small missile at us, which a trooper disposed of with another beamgun. Then the Komani dropped out of range."

"But he continued to follow you?"

"Yes. Until we reached the scoutcars at the perimeter of your encampment."

Vorgens laughed. "We're not camped here, Sittas, we're merely stopped for a few hours. I've been keeping the Mobile Force on the move constantly since we broke out of the valley."

"Then it is true that you have assumed command."

"I had to," the Watchman answered, serious now. "Aikens would not listen to reason. There was no one else to whom I could turn. I decided that I had more information about the situation than anyone else, so I took charge."

"A Star Watch officer has such authority?"

"I do, now. Whether or not I had the right to take such authority into my own hands is a matter that will be settled by a Star Watch court, sometime in the future."

Sittas leaned back in his webbed chair. "The lieutenant you sent to Matara with the medical supplies said that you wanted to see me."

"That's right," Vorgens replied. "First, I want to thank you again for your part in saving my life—and the lives of all the men in this Mobile Force. Nothing that we could do can ever repay the debt we all owe you."

Sittas waved a hand of protest. "That is all in the past. It is tomorrow that interests me—and you, I should judge."

"Yes, tomorrow, and all the days that come after," Vorgens agreed. He hesitated for a moment, framing the right words in his mind, then asked, "If I invited the leaders of the Shinarian rebel movement to a truce conference here, would they come?"

The old priest shook his head. "No, I doubt that they would."

"Suppose I went to Capital City and asked them to meet with me there?"

"They would still smell a trap," Sittas answered. "They realize perfectly well that you do not know who they are. Why should they expose themselves?"

"I know Merdon."

"Everyone on the planet knows Merdon. But he is only one of the leaders. He commands the youngest, and the most aggressive of the rebels, but there are many other groups—in the cities, in the hills, among the farming villages. They do not make up an army, as Merdon's people do, but they will fight in their own ways for Shinar's freedom. These are the people you must reach, and these are the leaders you do not know."

"Then help me to meet them," Vorgens pleaded earnestly. "They trust you. Tell them that I want to discuss a peace settlement with them. Tell them that I'll meet them in Capital City, if they like, and they'll be guaranteed freedom from arrest."

Sittas stroked his chin thoughtfully. "They will still be revealing themselves to you. What's to stop you from having them arrested after the conference?"

"My word," Vorgens replied, "and your trust in me."

"You are putting it up to me to bring the rebel leaders to your conference table," the old man mused.

"You're the one man on this planet that both sides can trust."

"That is very flattering."

"And very true."

Sittas shrugged. "I suppose you have the right idea. We can lose nothing by trying."

"Good!" Vorgens grinned broadly. "You have the Mobile Force's communications equipment at your disposal."

"Yes, using the tri-di would be faster than contacting each man in person. If they are not afraid to appear on tri-di and run the risk of having you Terrans trace their whereabouts."

Vorgens shook his head. "They have to take some risks. Peace isn't built on flowers and handshakes alone."

It took four days to arrange the conference. Four days in which the Mobile Force, spread across the countryside like a moving cloud of giant insects, covered more than three hundred miles and fought six skirmishes with Komani attackers.

One of the clashes was fairly serious. A full battalion of Komani swooped down on a temporarily disabled light cruiser and two repair vans, just as dawn was breaking. The cruiser and her escorts were in the rear of the Terran formation, separated from the rest of the Mobile Force by a broad, swift-running river with thick woods on the far bank. The Komani reasoned that they could overwhelm the stragglers before any other Terran vehicles could get back to help.

The Komani warriors slashed across the sky with the sun at their backs and caught the surprised Terrans in the open. Before they could scramble into their vehicles, half the Terrans were killed or wounded, and one of the repair vans was in flames. The men aboard the cruiser quickly started to fight back, though, and frantically called for help.

The cruiser was being pounded by grenades, and the second repair van was badly damaged, when the Komani attackers were startled by movements in the woods across the river.

Trees seemed to be toppling, bursting into flame, exploding. As the turmoil approached the river bank, the Komani could see that a pair of battle cruisers was smashing through the woods, using their force beams to destroy the trees in front of them.

Finally the cruisers burst through the woods and started down the bank of the river. They did not pause a moment at the water, but skimmed right across, completely indifferent to the material underneath them.

As the Komani started to face the counterattack, another pair of Terran cruisers fell on them from the flank. The attackers were decimated; only a handful escaped the Terran envelopment.

Attacks on straggling vehicles ceased after that action.

The conference room that Sittas had picked was actually part of a church building. The room, warmly appointed in polished Shinarian wood, stood off to one side of the main chapel. It was a small chamber, with a central oblong table surrounded by leather-padded, high-backed chairs.

Vorgens sat at one side of the table, flanked by Sergeant McIntyre—whom the Watchman had made his personal aide—and Sittas. The priest introduced the eight Shinarians who sat across the table.

"And the spokesmen for all the groups represented at this meeting," Sittas concluded, "is Clanthas of Katan."

Clanthas nodded pleasantly.

"You are Merdon's father?" Vorgens asked.

"Yes, I am."

"I can see the family resemblance. The commander of the city garrison has told me quite a bit about you."

Clanthas answered evenly, "I could tell you quite a bit about the commander."

"I imagine you could," Vorgens said, grinning.

"We are ready to begin," Clanthas said, "if you are."

"Is Merdon going to be here, or are you representing him?"

Clanthas' broad face clouded over. "I do not know if Merdon intends to join this conference or not. No one here represents him, or his group."

"I will represent Merdon."

Vorgens turned round in his chair and saw Altai standing in the arched doorway of the conference room. She was still wearing a "field uniform" of slacks and tunic, but somehow she looked more feminine than Vorgens had ever seen her to be.

The men rose from their seats. Altai went to the chair next to her uncle's and Sergeant McIntyre stepped over and held the chair as she sat down.

"I believe, then," Vorgens said, "that all the factions on Shinar are represented—with the exception of the Komani, who are not noticeably enthusiastic about truce conferences."

They all murmured agreement.

"The purpose of this meeting is quite simple," the Watchman began. "Everyone here, I think, wants peace for Shinar. The question is: what is the cost of peace?"

"Merdon's price for peace is well known," Altai said.

"He has instructed me to tell you that he will stop fighting when the Terrans leave Shinar. Freedom is his price."

Vorgens nodded. "And the official Terran price for peace is submission to the Empire. The Marines were sent to this planet to smash the rebellion and restore order under Terran terms."

One of the Shinarians protested, "Surely you cannot have called us here merely to tell us this!"

"Of course not," Vorgens replied. "I'm only trying to show that inflexibility on either side will only prolong the fighting." Turning to Altai, he asked, "Doesn't Merdon realize by now that if the Terrans should leave Shinar, your planet would become a prize for the Komani?"

Altai glanced at her uncle, then answered, "Merdon believes that once the Terrans are driven off Shinar, Okatar Kang will want to attack the Empire somewhere else. He believes that we can be strong enough to prevent the Komani from overpowering us."

"You know the rebel situation as well as Merdon does. Do you believe this too?"

"Merdon is our chief. He knows better than I."

"But do you agree with him?" Vorgens asked.

After a long pause, she said, "I'm only a girl. My opinion counts for very little."

Clanthas broke into the conversation. "Perhaps I should recapitulate the history of this rebellion. It started when the Empire began installing nutrient processing plants and uprooting our farmers. We appealed to the Terran governor, to no avail. We organized demonstrations, and the governor used troops to suppress us. Riots broke out. Many of the younger people—my son among them—decided to fight force with force. The governor was assassinated. The Marines were called in. The younger rebels asked the Komani to help us. . . ."

"And here we are," Sittas murmured.

"Exactly," Clanthas said. "The situation is completely out of control. All we want is for Shinar to be left in peace. We do not want to become a cog in your Empire. Neither do we want to become vassals of the Komani. Yet the Terrans and the Komani are fighting over us, turning our own world into a battleground. No matter who wins, we will lose."

"All we want is to be left alone," said another Shinarian.

Vorgens answered, quietly and patiently, "That is a dream that will not come to pass in my lifetime or in yours. Shinar will not be left alone. It can't be left alone, no matter how much you wish it to be. If the Terrans don't make you part of their Empire, the Komani or someone else will. The simple truth is that Shinar is not powerful enough to remain completely independent. You never were. Before the Terrans, you were ruled by the Masters, remember. You were never alone. No nation is. Or could be."

"Then what choice do we have?" a Shinarian blurted miserably. "Must we stand meekly by and watch you and the Komani rip our world to pieces in a battle to see which of you will be our overlord?"

"Your choice," Vorgens reasoned, "is one of degree. It may be possible, I think, for you to work out some system of self-government within the Terran Empire. I know that other nations have done this. I can't see why Shinar couldn't—in time. Within the Empire, there is the hope of eventual self-government. Not the total freedom that Merdon wants, perhaps, but a good part of it. Under the Komani, you have nothing to look forward to except destruction and death."

Sittas countered. "The Terrans have never permitted us the luxury of hoping for self-government before."

"I know, and you have no official promise of it now, only my own feeling that, if we can act boldly and successfully in the next few weeks, the Empire might be more favorably disposed to hear your case."

Clanthas' eyes narrowed. "What are you suggesting?"

"Simply this. The Mobile Force can't defeat the Komani here on Shinar by itself. We can defend ourselves, and that's about all. Reinforcements are on their way, but Okatar Kang could ravage this planet quite thoroughly before they get here. If you want to prevent the Komani from destroying your world, you must help me to fight against them.

"Okatar has one weakness. He must win, here on Shinar. He must win quickly and decisively. If he can be held at bay, frustrated, kept off balance, then his dream of glory will soon fade. The other Komani clans will not ally themselves with him. Perhaps even his own people will become tired of fighting a fruitless war. Then, when the Star Watch reinforcements arrive, you, yourselves, will have achieved already a large part of the victory.

"The choice is yours to make. Either you fight for your own world, with the Terrans and against the Komani, or you allow the Komani to take over your planet, and you give them the springboard they want to touch off a galactic war."

One of the Shinarians asked, "Do you think that, if we help your troops fight the Komani, the Empire will look with favor on your request to govern ourselves?"

"I think they might, but I can't guarantee it."

"You ask us to risk much for only the hope of freedom," Clanthas said.

"Men have risked everything time and again," Vorgens shot back, "for the hope of freedom. It's the only hope you have."

Altai laughed softly. "What you're saying is that the threat of the Komani will force the Terrans to treat us with respect."

"I am saying," Vorgens answered firmly, "that your own courage and self-respect are the only tools you have for achieving freedom. It's your choice. You must decide."

"May I point out," Sittas said, "that we have here an

official of the Terran Empire telling us to make our own decision about our own fate. That in itself is a milestone."

The little group remained silent for a moment.

Finally Clanthas said, "You are right, Watchman. It is a decision we must make for ourselves. Such a decision is not easily arrived at. We must have time to think. To discuss. You understand that?"

"Of course," Vorgens said. "But you must understand that time is precious, to all of us."

Clanthas nodded. He rose from his chair, and everyone else got up.

"We will give you our answer within a few days."

"Good enough," Vorgens said.

More than an hour later, as their speedy little skimmer raced across the grassy countryside back to the main body of the Mobile Force, McIntyre said:

"I just hope that Star Watch Headquarters really does decide to send the reinforcements you told the natives we were gettin'."

"So do I, Sergeant," Vorgens answered fervently. "So do I."

XIV

Poles Apart

The yellow sun of Shinar glittered brazenly on the sea and pressed its warmth into the long, curving, white beach. But the six young Shinarians trudging slowly along the sand paid no attention to the brilliant sun, nor to the steady, stiff breeze coming off the water, and the crashing surf that it propelled.

"And that's all that the Watchman had to say?" Merdon asked, rhetorically.

Altai nodded. "It seemed to be a good beginning."

"Beginning?" Merdon laughed. "He's just asking us to go right back to where we started."

"How did the other leaders take to his proposal?" Tarat asked.

"They seemed"—she hunted for the right word—"impressed."

"When you boil down to essentials," Merdon said, "the Watchman is asking us to help the Empire fight off the Komani. In return for this, he promises to do his best to get the Imperial bureaucracy to consider—consider, mind you—giving us some measure of freedom in the undetermined future."

"What more can he do for us?" Altai asked.

"More? He hasn't done anything. Not a thing. The conference was a farce."

"Well, maybe not," Romal piped. "The Watchman is giving us a chance to prove to the Terrans that we can take care of ourselves. After all, wouldn't the Empire be indebted to us if we helped to stop the Komani threat?"

Merdon glared down at his little quartermaster.

"What other choices do we have?" Altai insisted. "The Komani haven't crushed the Mobile Force. The chances are that the war will go on for some time—until either the Terrans or the Komani bring enough reinforcements to Shinar to overpower the other. If we wait until that happens, we'll be at the mercy of the winner, whichever it may be."

"Not if we help the Komani to smash the Terrans."

Tarat objected, "But the Empire is probably sending more troops here. We can't fight the whole Star Watch!"

"There are no reinforcements on their way here," Merdon answered flatly. "Okatar Kang is certain of that, and so am I."

"How do you know?"

"He has his ways of finding out. Shinar is just a tiny pebble to the Terrans. They won't risk more men here until they realize that there's much more than our single planet involved. By the time they make up their minds, it'll be too late."

"All this might have been true," Altai said, "if we had beaten the Mobile Force in the valley of Carmeer. But we haven't. The Mobile Force is still here, as strong as ever. The Watchman can fight the Komani indefinitely, if he has to."

"Thanks to you," Merdon snapped.

Altai stared at him, stunned.

"Well, you let him escape from the Komani. We had the Terrans boxed in, but he pulled them out of the trap. We had a chance to get rid of the Terrans, and you worked for them, instead of for us."

For several moments, no one spoke.

Finally Altai replied, in a voice trembling with pain and anger, "If I hadn't helped the Watchman, if we had fought the battle that you were hoping to fight, most of us would be dead right now, and Okatar would be ruling this planet."

"Shinar would be free, you mean."

"No, Merdon, you're wrong. If we must choose between the Terrans and the Komani, I will go with the Terrans."

"What about freedom for Shinar?"

"There are more ways to obtain freedom than with a gun," she said.

Merdon looked at the four youths, watching them waiting for his next reaction.

"All right, then," he said, with a deadly calm, "you can go with the Terrans if you like. I won't stop you."

Without another word, Altai turned her back on Merdon and walked away. In shocked silence, the others watched her stride up the beach, toward the groundcars parked on the grassy dunes above.

"If any of the rest of you feel the same way, now's the time to say it."

The four young lieutenants glanced uneasily at each other. Ron shuffled his weight from one foot to the other, then blurted out, "I'm sorry, Merdon. She's right and you're not. I'm going with her."

He broke into a run, following Altai's footsteps.

Tarat shook his head. "There'll be others joining them when they hear about this."

"Let them go," growled Merdon, furious, "They'll crawl back to us when we've freed Shinar."

Altai climbed up the dune and reached the groundcar without noticing Ron following her. She opened the door of the little bubble-topped car and dropped into the driver's seat. Only then did she allow herself to break into the tears that she had been holding back.

Okatar Kang paced his tent like a caged jungle beast, while his council of nobles sat passively at their long table and watched their chieftain.

"So the Terrans have been talking with the native leaders, have they? These spineless Shinarians blow with the wind. When we had the Terrans trapped, they were pleased with us. Now that there is more fighting to be done, they're not so sure."

"The natives are no immediate threat to us, Lord Okatar," said one of the nobles. "It is the Terrans."

"The Terrans!" Okatar spat. "They're lucky to be alive, and they know it. They are merely trying to protect themselves; they are no danger."

"But still, they have a powerful force."

"I wish they would offer us battle," Okatar said. "We would overwhelm them, once and for all. But, no, instead they retreat, they flee from us. Very well. Let them run."

"What have you in mind?"

Okatar stopped his pacing and faced the council table. "We are going to make this planet feel the full might of the Komani. Until now we have attempted to deal with the Shinarians as allies. But they have betrayed us. Now we shall treat them as subjects. This planet is ours for the taking, and I intend to take what we want from it."

"What about the Shinarian forces still allied to us?"

"They have plotted against us. Merdon and his children's army have hoped that we would drive off the Terrans, and then be so weakened that they could drive us off."

"Do you intend to force Merdon to join the Terrans?"

"That, he will never do. No, I intend to offer him a bargain—a bargain on Komani terms. He can still serve with us, but as a subject, not an ally. When we are finished with Shinar, he can take control of the planet, but he will be our subject."

"If he refuses this bargain?"

"He will die."

"And the Terrans?"

Okatar smiled fiercely. "We shall start a campaign of terror and looting that will turn this planet upside-down. We shall take what we need and what we want from the Shinarian countryside and the towns that have no Terran garrison. Sooner or later, the Terrans will be forced to offer us battle. They will stop running and try to attack our forces; possibly they will attempt to attack this camp. When they mass, we will mass. When they attempt to strike at us, we will destroy them!"

"In the meantime, we will be gathering supplies and equipment from the natives."

"Exactly so," Okatar said. "With every day, our strength will grow, and the Shinarians' dread of our power will grow equally. With every day, the Terrans will become weaker."

As the exec sat in Vorgens' quarters and listened to what the Star Watchman was telling him, his eyes widened more and more, until white showed almost all the way around them.

"I—I can't believe you mean what you're saying," the exec protested.

Sergeant McIntyre, standing at the doorway to the tiny cubicle, nodded grimly. "Neither could I, when he told me, sir. Can't you talk him outta doin' it?"

Vorgens half turned in his webbed chair and surveyed the sergeant with a wry smile. "My aide, here," he said to the exec, "said he thinks the idea is crazy."

"It's certainly . . . unusual," the exec said, lamely.

The smile faded from Vorgens' face. "Unusual or not, do you think the idea is sound?"

"From a military point of view, yes sir, I do," the

exec admitted, nodding. "But from your own personal point—"

"That's *my* problem," Vorgens said, abruptly getting up from the webbed chair. "All right, if it's sound militarily, we've got to do it. Let's go."

"Now?" McIntyre asked.

"Right now, and I want the two of you along as witnesses."

With a frown on his beefy face, McIntyre led the way down the narrow passage to Brigadier Aikens' quarters. When the sergeant hesitated at the door, Vorgens knocked.

"Come."

McIntyre opened the door, and the three of them stepped in. Aikens was lying in his bunk, reading a report projected overhead.

The brigadier cocked an eye at Vorgens, then swung up to a sitting position. The projector automatically shut off.

"To what do I owe this honor?"

"Was that the Officer of the Day's report you were scanning?" Vorgens asked.

"That's right. I like to keep up on what you're doing with my men. Any objections?"

"No. None at all. . . . May we come in?"

Aikens gestured to the unfolded writing desk and the pair of webbed chairs flanking it. "Make yourself at home. You're in command, aren't you?"

McIntyre could see Vorgens' whole body stiffen at the brigadier's sarcasm. The Watchman took one of the chairs. The exec and the sergeant remained standing.

"I trust you've been physically comfortable," Vorgens said.

"Don't play games with me, Watchman. You're up to something. Now what is it?"

"You've been keeping track of the Mobile Force's actions." It was a statement, not a question.

"Yes, of course."

"Good. I've been thinking over the situation for the past two days, and I've come to a decision . . ."

"And you expect me to give you advice? Don't waste your time."

Vorgens clenched his fists. For a moment, he said nothing. Then, with a visible effort to remain calm, he resumed, "I'm not looking for advice, but I do have a question to ask you. Your answer will affect the lives of the men of this Mobile Force, and the lives of every man, woman and child on Shinar."

For the first time, Aikens looked directly at the Watchman. "Well?"

"I want to know if you're willing to resume command of the Mobile Force."

Aikens' eyes flashed for an instant. Then he asked slowly, "Resume command? What brought you to that decision? You made it pretty clear that I'm unfit to command."

"Brigadier, don't make this any harder than it has to be. I assumed command because I represent the authority of Star Watch Headquarters, and you were unwilling to follow the policies expressed by my orders."

Aikens glared at the Watchman, but said nothing.

"It's quite obvious," Vorgens went on, "that my training as a Star Watch officer can never match your experience as a commander in the field. I took over the command of this Force because it was the only way to get us out of the Komani trap. But I have no delusions about my ability to direct a full-scale planetary action. The situation calls for an able, experienced field commander. Are you willing to resume command, or not?"

The brigadier grinned humorlessly. "I knew you'd be handing the ball back to me sooner or later. You haven't got the backbone for this kind of responsibility."

Strangely, Vorgens smiled back at the older man. "Perhaps you don't understand me," he said. "I want you to resume command of the Mobile Force ... *under my authority.* I am in charge of all Terran forces on Shinar, and until a higher-ranking Watchman reaches the planet, I shall remain in command. I'm offering you tactical control of the Mobile Force; strategic decisions will be made by me."

"You ... you ..." Aikens' face glowered red, and the rage seemed to well up in his throat, choking him. "You're offering me—tactical command—under your authority! I—I'll ..."

"Before you say anything else," Vorgens warned, his voice suddenly as sharp as a cutting beam, "I'll be forced to turn over the job to the executive officer, if you don't accept the command."

Aikens half rose off the edge of the bunk, then sat down again. His face turned a mottled purplish color.

"I'm sorry that it has to be this way," Vorgens said, more gently, "but I can't see any other way."

"All right, Watchman," Aikens said, after several moments' silence, "I'll resume command of the Mobile Force. I'll pull your little carcass out of the fire ... and when we've settled this business on Shinar, I'll call for a court-martial so fast your head will swim."

Vorgens nodded. "I'm sure a court of inquiry will be necessary to straighten out our differences. But, for the moment, let's hope we can both rise above our personal feelings."

"I'm a soldier, youngster; I know how to keep my feelings to myself when it's for the good of the men. But don't have any illusions. We're poles apart, you and me. Now and always. Understand?"

"Perfectly."

Vorgens walked back to the dreadnaught's control center in silence. His face was immobile. He felt empty and drained of emotion.

It was a complete surprise to see Altai sitting at an

untended control desk. The trooper on watch said to Vorgens:

"She just showed up at one of the scoutcars on the perimeter and said she wanted to see you, sir. Wouldn't talk to anyone else."

The Watchman went to her. Altai's face was outwardly calm, but Vorgens could sense the tenseness within her. Her dark eyes showed no trace of the tears she had been shedding.

"You wanted to see me?" he asked, sitting down next to her.

"I've left Merdon," she said quietly. "Several squads of our fighters have decided to join you and fight against the Komani. They are waiting for your orders."

"I see. And Merdon?"

"He . . ." For just an instant it seemed her self-control would crack. "He refuses to change his mind. He will fight against you, he says, until Shinar is free."

"I'm sorry to hear that," Vorgens replied, "and sorrier still to see you so—upset. He means very much to you, doesn't he?"

"Once he did," she said. "Now, we couldn't be farther apart if we were on opposite ends of the world."

Vorgens smiled at her.

"What's so funny?"

"It's not funny, merely an odd coincidence. Someone just told me that I was poles apart from him."

"You? You're among your own men, why should you worry about one person?"

"He's a very important person. And as far as being among my own men . . . I'm among strangers. With the exception of two or three people, I've known you and your uncle longer than any of the men here."

"You're as alone as I am," Altai said.

"Yes," Vorgens agreed. "That's right."

XV

Choices and Plans

The Komani warrior sat under a tree at the crest of a hill overlooking Shinar's Capital City. He had lost track of the days since he had first started hunting the old priest, first at the town of Matara, then along the road to the Mobile Force's camp, and finally here at the city.

He could not follow his prey into the city, of course. The Terran garrison would shoot him on sight. So he waited, living off terrified farmers and villagers nearby, sleeping in the open, waiting with remorseless patience. Sooner or later, the priest would leave the city, and he could be attacked or killed.

As he sat with his broad back against the sturdy shade tree, the warrior studied the city spread out on the plain below. It was the biggest collection of buildings he had ever seen, even larger than the rare clan gatherings of the Komani, which covered whole valleys with bubble-tents.

A thought drifted across his mind like a dark cloud:

156

What if the priest left the city by a road other than the one he came in on? There were many roads into and out of the city. What if the priest was no longer there, and had escaped?

The warrior pondered over the matter. The priest did not know he was being stalked. There was no reason for him to leave the city stealthily. On the other hand, there was no reason for him to choose the road the Komani was watching.

After a long struggle with the problem, the warrior finally made a decision. He would return to Matara. If the priest left the city, he was bound to turn up at the hospital again, sooner or later. Time was of no importance. And, besides, at Matara there were many other Komani available for companionship.

The warrior rose, took a last look at Capital City, and turned toward Matara.

Vorgens sat at the command desk in the deserted control center and sifted through the morning's reports. The Komani were stepping up their activities; strikes against the perimeter of the Mobile Force, raids against isolated villages and farms, even a hit-and-run attack on one of the larger cities. They were spreading terror and destruction all around Shinar.

As he read through the reports, Vorgens' mind kept turning over other problems. Aikens had not come out of his quarters since their conversation, three days ago. If the brigadier was willing to take tactical command of the Mobile Force, he had yet to show it. The rebels still had not contacted him, even though more than a week had gone by since their conference in Capital City.

Altai stepped through one of the hatches and entered the control center.

"Are you busy?" she asked.

"Not terribly. Have your people found adequate quarters?"

She nodded as she made her way through the compact maze of desks and consoles and sat down beside the Watchman. "Yes, there's an old monastery nearby. Once the monks learned that Sittas is my uncle, they allowed us to stay. The boys sleep in the cellar, the girls in the barn."

Vorgens grinned. "Sounds charming. But, you know, we won't be in this area much longer. Do you intend to follow us, or stay here?"

"I think we'll stay here for the time being—until we decide on what to do."

"We've all got some decisions to make, and not much more time to waste before we make them. The Komani are beginning to run wild all over the planet."

"I know," she said. "Have you received any further word from Star Watch Headquarters about reinforcements?"

"Nothing definite," Vorgens admitted. "Reinforcements are being prepared, but I can't get firm word on how much and how soon."

The desktop viewscreen at his elbow chimed softly. Vorgens touched the control stud.

"Message for you, sir. From Capital City."

"Is it the garrison commander?"

"Relayed through his office, sir. But the message is from a native. Clanthas . . ."

"Put him through!"

Vorgens glanced at Altai as the viewscreen began to glow with color. She looked as excited as he felt.

Clanthas' broad, slightly jowly face filled the screen. "A good day to you, Watchman. And to you, Altai."

"And the same to you," Vorgens replied. "I've been waiting for your call."

The merchant assumed a slightly apologetic expression. "It took somewhat longer than I expected, but I think you'll find my news worth the waiting." He paused dramatically. "The other leaders and I have decided to take you at your word. We will help you and work against the Komani in whatever way possible."

Only now did Vorgens realize he had been holding his breath. He exhaled slowly and murmured, "You did it."

"Don't overestimate my powers of persuasion," Clanthas said. "Most of the leaders were dead set against working with the Empire. Even now the best that can be said is that they are going ahead with grave misgivings, but with the Komani killing and looting everywhere . . . we really have no choice."

"Except surrendering to the Komani."

"We discussed that possibility," Clanthas admitted cheerfully, "and rejected it. We will help you—or allow you to help us, depending on how you look at the matter."

"We will work together to defeat the Komani and bring peace to Shinar," Vorgens said, firmly.

"And then what?" Altai asked.

Vorgens turned to her. "Then we will work together just as hard to give your people the freedom for which they are fighting."

"Amen to that," Clanthas said. "Well . . . now that we're at your disposal, what are your plans for us? Most of my people are not organized into fighting groups, the way Merdon's units are. But they can help to defend themselves, if you'll show them what to do, and give them some weapons."

Vorgens nodded. "Our plans haven't crystallized yet. But your decision should certainly clarify our thinking. I'll call you back as soon as we have drawn up a comprehensive picture. Will you remain in Capital City?"

"I think not," Clanthas said. "I'm going back to Katan."

"Is my uncle still with you?"

"He was, until this morning. Helped tremendously in convincing the other leaders that you were trustworthy, too. He started back to the hospital at Matara this morning. Should be there by nightfall."

The three of them chatted for a few minutes longer.

When Clanthas' image had faded from the viewscreen, Vorgens touched a button and called for McIntyre.

The Sergeant's face took form on the screen.

"Please give my compliments to Brigadier Aikens and ask him to meet me in the control center as soon as possible. Tell him that the native leaders have decided to work with us, and we must draw up a battle plan immediately."

"Yes sir," said the sergeant.

Within a half an hour, Aikens, the executive officer, and the top officers of the Mobile Force's staff were crowding the control center. Vorgens was still at the command desk, with Altai beside him and McIntyre standing behind.

"I have already drawn up two tactical plans," Aikens said, with a slightly malicious emphasis on the word *tactical*. He dropped two thick notebooks on Vorgens' desk.

"One of the plans is based on the assumption that the natives will not aid us, and I assume that such an assumption is now outdated."

"That's right," Vorgens said.

"Very well then." Aikens tapped on the cover of one of the notebooks. "This is the plan to use, in that case."

Vorgens opened the book and thumbed through it. "Very detailed," he said. Then looking up at the brigadier, he asked, "Would you care to give me a brief rundown on the main features of the plan?"

"It's quite simple," the brigadier said. "Have you ever seen what happens when you put a drop of ink into a glass of clear water?"

Vorgens' eyebrows arched, and his forehead wrinkled. "Why . . . the color spreads through the whole glass."

"Exactly. Now suppose that the glass of water is a certain district of this planet, open to attack by the Komani. And the drop of ink—"

"The drop of ink would be a unit of Marines," Vorgens said.

"Very good, Watchman! You're quite astute today."

Vorgens' eyes flashed angrily for a moment, then he regained his self-control and answered, "I have my moments. Evidently what you're proposing to do is to split up the Mobile Force into small units and spread them through Shinar."

"Right," Aikens said. "Each unit will be strong enough to fend off a Komani raiding party, and the units will be spaced close enough together so that one group could come to the aid of another, in case the Komani mount an unusually heavy attack."

"And what if the Komani mass a really large force, such as they did in Carmeer?"

It was Aikens' turn to flush with anger. For a moment he said nothing. Then, finally, "We will depend to some extent on the natives for intelligence reports. If we learn that the Komani are massing for a full-scale battle, we will also mass our forces."

"Fine," Vorgens said. "Now, how much territory can we protect in this manner?"

Aikens took up the notebook from Vorgens' desk and rifled to a page toward the back. "We analyzed the cruising speed of our vehicles, the logistics problem, our response time to an attack-alert, and other factors ... the computer came up with an answer." He showed the page of computations to the Watchman. "We can cover roughly half the populated area of the planet."

"And the other half?"

Aikens shrugged his shoulders.

"Have you assumed that the natives would be armed?"

"No."

"Suppose we armed them and trained them ... couldn't we gradually extend our protection to the whole planet, then?"

Aikens hesitated a moment, then, looking at Altai, he answered, "We could arm the natives and train them briefly. But could we trust them?"

Vorgens replied instantly, "They're trusting us, brigadier. So I guess we'll have to trust them."

"I see."

"It's a good plan," Vorgens said. "Please take the necessary steps to put it into operation immediately, and contact the garrison commanders at the four cities we now hold. Tell them that you'll be taking some of the stocks from their arsenals to give to the natives."

Aikens glowered. "I will do so only under protest."

"Do it any way you like," Vorgens said. "But do it."

After Aikens and his staff had cleared out of the control center, Altai said, "I would like to go to Matara briefly and see my uncle once more. It looks as though we'll be fighting again soon, and I'd like to visit him while I can."

"All right," Vorgens said. "I'd like to see him, too. Sergeant, how long would it take us to drive over to Matara?"

McIntyre thought for a moment. "I could get you there on a scrambler before nightfall."

The farmer's truck was ancient and slow. Sittas, already bone-weary from a solid week of pleading and cajoling with the rebel leaders at Capital City, was even too tired to pay attention to the flaming colors of the sky as Oran dipped behind the hills that surrounded Matara. Soon they would be back at the hospital, and he could rest. The farmer, sitting in the driver's seat, was too awed by his unexpected guest to utter a word throughout the long, hot, dusty trip.

It was dusk when the truck finally pulled into the town square of Matara. The normally placid air of the place was still banished by the bustle of activity connected with the hospital. A Komani litter, buoyed by four of the versatile one-man flyers, hovered at the bottom of the town hall's steps. Evidently more wounded warriors had just arrived. Merchants and farmers had set up stalls along one side of the square, to supply the makeshift hospital with the goods (and a few luxuries) that it required. People of all descriptions were coming and going through the square. Even a Terran scrambler was parked in front of the hospital, Sittas noticed.

He climbed down stiffly from the truck and started toward the steps that led into the town-hall-turned-hospital.

Altai appeared at the door, atop the steps, and ran down to meet him.

"So here you are!" she said. "Clanthas told us you were coming here. We got here before you."

"We?" the old man asked, slightly puzzled.

"The Watchman and his aide and I. We came to see you. Vorgens and the sergeant are inside. He's amazed with the hospital."

"I see . . ."

A Komani warrior, dusty and travel-stained, advanced on them. "You are the one called Sittas?"

The old man turned to face the Komani. "Yes, I am Sittas."

The warrior drew his ceremonial sword. "In the name of Lord Okatar, I must take your life."

Everyone froze. The square, pulsating with life an instant earlier, became as still as death. No one moved, even the breeze seemed to die, as the Komani held his sword before him, pointed directly at the old priest.

It was Altai who broke the spell. She stepped in front of Sittas and said, "You cannot kill him!"

"You are a woman, and unarmed. Stand aside."

"You'll have to kill me first."

Before the warrior could reply, the farmer who had driven the truck rushed up and stood beside the girl. "And me too!"

Immediately, everyone in the square began to throng around the warrior. There was not a weapon on any of them, but they stood there, unmoving, as the Komani watched them through his unblinking, yellow cat's eyes.

With his free hand, the warrior reached for the pistol on his belt. Before he could grasp it, a beam lanced through his shoulder. The warrior sagged to the ground. His sword clattered on the paving stones.

Everyone turned, and saw Vorgens and McIntyre at the top of the town hall steps. The sergeant held a gun in his massive fist.

Vorgens dashed down the steps, with McIntyre at his heels. The crowd opened a lane for them.

"He was going to kill us!" Altai sobbed.

Vorgens put his arm around her. "It's all right. It's all right."

The warrior painfully climbed to his knees and began to reach for the sword that he had dropped.

McIntyre stamped a heavy boot on the sword and put his gun to the Komani's head.

"Don't kill him!" Sittas cried. "He was only following the orders of Okatar."

Without taking his eyes from the warrior, McIntyre said, "I know how they think. As long as this one lives, he'll have nothin' else on his mind but killin' you."

"Does that mean that I must have him killed?" Sittas asked.

"Take the gun away from him and place him under guard," Vorgens ordered.

"It is fortunate that you came when you did," Sittas said to the Watchman.

Vorgens looked around at the crowd. "It looks to me as though you had quite a bit of help without us."

It was late at night when Vorgens and McIntyre returned to the Mobile Force. Most of the dreadnaught's crewmen were asleep. Altai had stayed at Matara, and the Komani warrior had been placed under Shinarian custody.

A yellow light flashing at the command desk told Vorgens that a message was waiting for him. He activated the viewscreen and scanned the words printed on it.

"Is it from Star Watch Headquarters?" McIntyre asked eagerly.

Vorgens slumped into his seat. "Yes, it is."

McIntyre stepped over beside the Watchman to read the screen:

MINIMAL RELIEF FLEET OF THREE STARSHIPS AND NORMAL COMPLEMENT OF MARINES WILL ARRIVE AT SHINAR IN SIX WEEKS. SWHQ.

"Three ships," McIntyre said, stunned. "Three lousy ships."

"A token force," Vorgens said. "I suppose that they feel we're not worth risking more men and ships."

"But that ain't gonna do us any good at all!"

"I know. It will prove what Okatar's been saying all along—that the Empire isn't able to meet the strength of the combined Komani clans. It would've been better if they had decided not to send any reinforcements at all."

XVI

"Shinar Has Been Conquered"

Merdon gnawed fretfully on his lower lip as he sat before the blank viewscreen. Standing outside the tri-di booth were Tarat and Romal. The trio were in the abandoned nutrient-processing plant where Merdon had hidden a cache of weapons.

"Is he going to speak to you or not?" Romal asked nervously.

"He'll come on," Merdon said. "He'd better."

As if in answer to the young rebel leader, the viewscreen seemed to dissolve and the powerful form of Okatar took shape. The Komani Kang was seated in his tent. Although no one else was in the line-of-view, Merdon sensed that Okatar was far from alone.

"I have asked you to come to my camp," Okatar said. "Why do you refuse, and attempt to speak through the tri-di? It is difficult to confer fully with you in this manner."

Merdon sat without answering for a moment, and the two stared at each other, face to face. Finally Merdon said, "Shall I be frank?"

"By all means."

"I was going to visit your camp, but my lieutenants asked me not to, for two reasons. First, they feel that you have broken the bonds of friendship and common purpose that we once had between us. Second, they fear that I might never leave your camp—alive."

"You have suspicious friends," Okatar said impassively.

"They value my life more than I do, perhaps. But I agree with them on the first point—your raids on our people are not the works of an ally."

Okatar nodded. "Correct. I have learned that your people are no longer allies of the Komani. They were friendly with us only when it seemed that the Terrans would be wiped out in the valley of Carmeer. Now that there is the prospect of continued fighting before us, your people have meekly returned to the Terrans and asked to be forgiven for their audacious dreams of freedom."

"And because they are weak you attack them," Merdon snapped.

"The Komani take what they want. If your people resist, we use force. The time for wheedling and coaxing is past. If we fail on Shinar, everything fails, and I will not see the Komani conquest of the Terran Empire thwarted by a herd of self-pitying sheep!"

"We can fight!" Merdon shouted. "We've shown that we can. We've stood up to the Terrans before. It's *you* who has driven my people back into the arms of the Terrans."

Okatar raised a massive hand. "The time for discussion and argument is past. To all intents and purposes, Shinar has been conquered. The Terrans are content to huddle within their cities or inside the armored vehicles of their Mobile Force. These raids on your people have shown that the Terrans will not fight for Shinarians, but only to save themselves. Shinar is ours. Those who resist us will be crushed."

"And you'll take what you want from us," Merdon said dully.

"Exactly so."

"Suppose . . . suppose you drew up a list of the supplies and equipment you need. Suppose I could convince my people to give you what you require. Would you leave Shinar in peace then?"

The faintest hint of a smile flickered across Okatar's face. "If such a bargain could be arranged, I would consider striking at the next Terran target."

"And leave Shinar?"

"Yes, I would leave Shinar. . . . Of course, one of my nobles would remain behind as governor of this planet. He would see to it that you continued to honor my requirements for supplies."

"And the Terrans?"

"The Terrans on Shinar would be forced to withdraw when I struck the next planet, or else their lines of supply with the rest of the Empire would be cut."

Merdon nodded. "Yes, and Shinar would be free of them."

"Shinar would be a vassal of the Komani," Okatar said. "In return for our protection, we would expect tribute."

"Tribute," Merdon echoed, "and the first payment would be the list of supplies and equipment you'd need to attack the next Terran planet."

"Correct," said Okatar.

Merdon glanced at his two lieutenants, outside the tri-di booth. They both seemed to be in an agony of impatience.

"I must discuss this with my people," Merdon told Okatar. "I will call you again, shortly."

"Very well," Okatar replied. The viewscreen went blank.

As Merdon stepped out of the booth, Romal yelped, "Do you realize what you're saying? Okatar will demand everything his men can carry ... he'll strip us bare!"

"You can't be serious about this," Tarat added. "We can't ask our people to give the Komani whatever they want."

Merdon folded his arms across his chest and stared them both into silence. "I don't see that we have any choice in the matter," he said firmly.

Clanthas basked in the warm sunshine flooding the broad veranda that surrounded the upper floor of his house in Katan. Beyond the railing of the veranda, the flat white roofs of other houses marched down the sloping hillside to the bright blue waters of the harbor. Across the harbor was the busy port of Katan, where the farm produce from a thousand miles around was gathered together and loaded on the big sea-going transports which skimmed across Shinar's oceans and lands with equal ease.

Seemingly sitting across the veranda from the merchant was the tri-di image of Vorgens. The Star Watchman had been explaining, for the past half-hour, the Terran plan of action which Brigadier Aikens had drawn up.

"Let me see if I understand this correctly," Clanthas said. "The Marines will set up small task units—based on your armored vehicles—in the villages, towns, and cities. They will give arms to the people and teach them how to fight. They will patrol the farmlands until the people themselves are able to guard their own land. Then they will move on to another district and repeat the same procedure."

Vorgens nodded. "That's right. The ultimate goal is to have the entire planet covered by either Terran Marines or your own people. We want to deny the use of your land to the Komani—to fence them in, so to speak."

"Suppose the Komani mass for a major attack?" Clanthas asked. "They still outnumber your Mobile Force by a great margin."

"If they mass, we'll have to face them. I hope that we'll have enough time to train a good number of your people, and that they will be fighting alongside us, in the event of a major battle."

Clanthas murmured agreement.

"What we're trying to do," Vorgens went on, "is to throttle down the Komani raids on your people. We're trying to keep the skirmishes and fighting down as much as possible."

"I understand. Still, it appears that there is no end to the fighting in sight."

"True enough," Vorgens admitted.

Clanthas suddenly shifted the subject. "Do you know why this rebellion began? I mean, the real reason?"

"I think I do," Vorgens said, "but I'd like to hear your opinion."

"The reason goes back more than a century, to the time when we were still dominated by the Masters. You see, the Masters saw to it that we remained a static nation. Our population was fixed at about 500 million, and we never rose much above that figure."

"Yes, I know," Vorgens said.

"In those days," Clanthas went on, "Shinar fed not only itself, but all the worlds within fifteen light-years of our planet. We were not prosperous, of course, but we were in equilibrium with the rest of the Masters' domain. We knew what to expect, from one day to the next."

"And then the Terrans came."

"Yes. The Terrans crushed the Masters and liberated Shinar. We were suddenly thrown on our own devices. For a while, everything continued as it had always gone. But something important had changed. Slowly, at first, and then with explosive speed, our population began to grow. When I was Merdon's age, Shinar had two billion people; now we have three billion."

"And it is difficult for you to feed yourselves," Vorgens said.

"Not yet difficult, but that day is fast approaching. However, we must use all the food we produce to feed ourselves. Practically nothing is left for export. Our trade with the other worlds around us is dying, and we are becoming a bankrupt nation. *That* is the underlying reason behind the people's resentment of the Empire. The installation of the food processing plants was merely the trigger. They already hated the Terrans, because they were becoming overcrowded and pauperized, under the Empire."

"But couldn't they see that the nutrient plants were the answer to their problem?" Vorgens asked. "Didn't the governor explain that the processing plants would enable you to multiply your output of foodstuffs many times over, and reopen your trade with the other planets?"

Clanthas shrugged. "A proclamation of that sort was issued, but very little effort was made to explain things to the farmers. All they knew was that they were being moved off their farms to make room for the Terran factories."

Vorgens shook his head. "I was afraid that this was the case. Evidently the Terran governor didn't realize that people can't change their whole way of living overnight—even when it's extremely necessary for them to do so."

"It may be necessary," Clanthas answered, "but hardly desirable."

"I realize that, but the planets that depended on your food a few decades ago are now going hungry, to a large extent. From the Empire's point of view, the problem of Shinar affects all of Shinar's neighbors. If we can't solve your problem, and solve it soon, rebellion against the

Empire might well break out elsewhere. That's what I fear most," Vorgens said worriedly, "that this movement against the Empire will spread to other planets. If it does—or if the Komani decide to attack another Empire planet—then there'll be no way to stop a general war from developing. We've got to keep this problem confined to Shinar, and solve it here. Otherwise we've lost."

The argument had raged hotly while Merdon, Tarat, and Romal paced the length and breadth of the idle nutrient-processing plant.

"You're going to ask our people to strip their homes, their farms, their cities, and give everything to the Komani. They won't do it!" Tarat bellowed.

"They'll have to," Merdon said evenly. "The Komani will just take it anyway."

"No, no, no," Romal said, his round face flushed with agitation. "The people are willing to fight the Komani."

Merdon laughed bitterly. "Then the Komani will take what they want and kill our people, too."

Tarat shook his head. "I never thought I'd see you give up."

Anger flashed in Merdon's eyes. Then he replied quietly, "Can we beat the Komani?"

"No, but ..."

"Do we want them off Shinar?"

"Of course."

"Will their attack on another planet force the Terrans to leave Shinar?"

"Probably it will," Tarat admitted.

"Then I don't see that we have any choice," Merdon said. "I don't like it any more than you do, but if it will get rid of both the Terrans and the Komani ..."

"How do you know it'll work out that way?" Tarat said. "There's only one chance in a million."

"Then I'll take that one chance!" Merdon snapped.

"But it's so dangerous, Merdon," Romal pleaded. "Maybe the best thing to do, after all, would be to put in with the Terrans. At least they're not as bad as the Komani, and the Watchman said . . ."

"It would be safer to join the Terrans," Merdon said softly. Then, his voice rising, he continued, "It would have been safer still never to have tried to rebel against them, but we weren't interested in safety then. We wanted freedom! Now that things look black, are we going to turn our backs on our hopes, our dreams? Are we going to tell our people: 'Go on back home, the whole thing was a big mistake. Go home and ask the Terrans to forgive you'? Well, are we?"

"What else can we do, Merdon?" Tarat asked. "Let the Komani rule us in the Terrans' place?"

"No! I'll tell you what we can do. We can dare! We can take that one chance in a million and make it work for us—or die trying. As long as there is that one chance—no matter how slim it might be—we've got to risk everything for it. Do you understand? *We've got to*. Otherwise everything we've done so far is wasted. The men who've died for our cause, died for nothing. The people who believe that we will fight to the last drop of sweat and blood to make Shinar free, will have been hoodwinked.

"I know how hard it will be to fill the Komani's demands. I'm not sure that we can convince the people to make this sacrifice, even for their own eventual freedom, but I'm going to try! Who will follow me?"

Tarat scratched nervously at his cheek, glanced at little Romal, and then said softly, "Well, if you think there's really a chance that we can get rid of both the Terrans and the Komani . . ."

"We won't be rid of the Komani," Romal argued. "You heard what Okatar said. There'll be a Komani governor over us."

"We had a Terran governor over us once. Where is he now?"

Romal blinked. "He's—he was—assassinated."

"And what's to stop us from driving off a Komani governor, after the warriors have left Shinar? What would the Komani governor have to back up his word, except our own fear of Okatar?"

"That would be enough," Tarat said. "If we didn't behave, Okatar could have the whole Komani nation on our backs in no time flat."

"Not if they're fighting the whole Terran Empire. Shinar could still become free while the Terrans and the Komani exhaust themselves in their war."

Romal shook his head. "That's an awfully long gamble to take."

"But if it works . . ."

"Fine, if it works," Tarat said. "But what if it doesn't?"

"It'll work," Merdon said stubbornly. "It's *got* to."

Within a few minutes, the Shinarian youth sat facing Okatar on the viewscreen while his lieutenants stood uneasily off to one side.

"Draw up your list," Merdon said firmly, "and I'll try to get my people to meet your needs. But the list must be kept to essentials. We don't intend to supply tribute. Shinar is a poor planet. There'll be plenty of booty for you elsewhere in the Empire."

"True enough," Okatar said, noncommittally. "I will instruct my seneschal to prepare the list."

"Very well."

"Oh yes, there is one other item which I want to make clear to you," Okatar said. "I have sent a column of warriors to investigate rumors about a well-stocked arsenal, and warehouses filled with food, in the city of Katan. I intend that they should carry through this investigation, even if they must use force. I don't want to have the feeling that anyone—including you—might be hiding things from me."

Abruptly, the viewscreen went blank.

XVII

Merdon

Vorgens perched atop the cab of a troop carrier and watched the Marines working with the farmers under the bright, hot sun of Shinar. The meadow spread out before him was dotted with groups of men and machines. The Terrans, in their bright uniforms, helmets and glare visors towered impressively over the indifferently dressed, dark-skinned little farmers.

One knot of men was clustered around a dismantled heavy beamgun. The Shinarians were learning how to put it back together. Another group was tinkering with field communications helmets. Close by the troop carrier, a young captain was lecturing the village elders on modern theories of defense in depth against flying Komani attacks. Farther off, near the edge of the meadow, a platoon of youngsters was peppering a grove of trees with small arms fire.

This had been the first day, the first experiment in the joint Terran-Shinarian defense system that Aikens and

Vorgens had worked out. The Star Watchman smiled to himself. Both sides had been somewhat wary at the beginning, early in the morning, but now they seemed immersed in the problem. The Shinarians appeared especially impressed with the idea that they could defend themselves; no Terran had ever granted them that much before.

A communications tech popped his head up from the open hatch beside Vorgens.

"Message for you, sir."

"What is it?"

"From the main body of the Force, sir. One of the natives was looking for you—that girl, the one that was with the priest."

"Altai?"

"The exec spoke with her a few minutes ago. She seemed very agitated, he said, and was coming over here to see you. She's flying on a Komani vehicle, sir."

Vorgens nodded absent-mindedly. What was wrong with Altai? Suddenly the tech's last words made an impression on him:

"Alert everyone in the area that a single Komani flyer will be coming in. I don't want anyone firing at it . . . especially those eager recruits down by the woods."

The tech arched his eyebrows and nodded. "Yes sir." He disappeared inside the hatch.

Vorgens' face knitted into a frown. Something was wrong. *Altai isn't the type that panics—but she's flying here to see me—instead of using the tri-di. Something is very wrong.*

Yet, strangely, he felt pleased that she was coming to him. No matter what the trouble was, he would be glad to see her.

About a half-hour later, a lone Komani flyer whizzed over the meadow, then slowed and spiraled down lower. Vorgens could see Altai's hair streaming in the wind. She spotted the Watchman, and put the flyer down beside the troop carrier.

Vorgens clambered down from the groundcar as she ran up toward him.

"It's Merdon," she said breathlessly, before he could ask anything. "He's gone wild. Okatar is sending a column of troops to sack Katan—where his father lives. Merdon is gathering up as many men as he can to attack Okatar's main camp and kill him."

It took Vorgens a moment to digest the news. "But that's insane," he said finally. "The camp is too heavily guarded for him to get through. It's a suicide mission, and it won't help his father in Katan."

Altai nodded. "Katan is too far away to be reached in time. The Komani troops will be there tomorrow morning, at the latest. Even if Merdon had enough groundcars for his men, he couldn't be there until late in the afternoon. What can we do? He'll kill himself!"

Vorgens looked at her. Altai's lovely face was twisted with worry over Merdon.

"Has he at least told his father about the attack?"

"I—I think so. Oh, he was so furious! He was raging. I've never seen him like this before."

"It's all right. He has a temper and he uses it. It saves strain on his nervous system."

"But what are we going to do?" she pleaded. "What can we do?"

Vorgens grinned at her. "First, we can calm down and try to think straight. Second, can that flying machine carry the two of us?"

"Um . . . yes, I imagine so. It's built to carry Komani warriors, and neither of us is much more than half their weight."

"Good. Let's go back to my headquarters. We've got work to do."

"And that's the way I see it, brigadier," Vorgens said.

Aikens was sitting across the table from the Watchman, in the dreadnaught's officers' wardroom. A pair of majors and the exec were also at the table. Steaming coffee mugs stood before each man.

Aikens had listened in dour silence to Vorgens' analysis of the situation. Now, he hunched forward in his chair and leaned his elbows on the green tabletop.

"Let me understand you clearly. You want to dispatch troops to Katan to beat off the Komani attack, and you expect me to devise a tactical plan of battle." As usual, he placed a slight, sullen accent on the word *tactical*.

"First of all," Vorgens answered, "I want your opinion on whether we can beat off the Komani attack. I don't want to waste troops on a meaningless gesture."

Aikens nodded. "That's sensible. Based on what the observation planes from Capital City have reported, the Komani column should be at Katan by mid-morning tomorrow. The earliest we could get there would be mid-afternoon. So we can't stop their attack."

"That's what I was afraid of."

"But we can," Aikens went on, with a curious crooked smile, "smash that column of savages just the same. Let them hit the city. Let them wreck it. Then we'll hit them when they're totally disorganized and unprepared for fighting."

"But there wouldn't be much left of the city when we got through."

Aikens shrugged. "Perhaps the citizens could hold off the attackers for a few hours. You claim they're fighters."

Vorgens let the brigadier's sarcasm slide past him. "That might work. I'll get in touch with Clanthas and see what he can organize in the way of a defense. In the meantime, your staff should draw up detailed battle plans. Determine how many troops you'll need and how much transport. Also, I'm going to dispatch a transport group for some of the natives who're willing to fight in defense of Katan."

Aikens grunted noncommittally. "I'll keep the few planes we have at Capital City in the air to watch the Komani."

"Should you have them try to bomb the column—slow it down?"

The brigadier shook his head. "No, the Komani are too spread out for nuclear weapons, and trying to go low and hit them with beams or missiles will just get the planes shot up. If we had more planes, or if these backward natives had some . . ."

"They're not backward. They just don't need aircraft," Vorgens said. "Groundcars can go almost as fast as subsonic planes, and they can carry considerably more payload. With groundcars, and tri-di communications, these people simply don't need fleets of fast aircraft."

"Well, backward or not, they don't have what it takes," Aikens said acidly. "Now, if you'll excuse us, we have work to do."

"Yes," Vorgens said, rising from his chair, "so do I."

The Star Watchman hurried through the narrow passageways to the dreadnaught's communications center—that compact jumble of molectronic transceivers, coders, viewscreens and recorders. Altai was there, talking quietly with the two technicians on duty. The techs seemed happily amazed at the chance to talk to a young, good-looking girl. As Vorgens stepped through the open hatch, though, they both shot out of their seats and stood at ramrod attention.

"Stand easy," Vorgens said. Then, he asked Altai, "Did you reach Clanthas?"

"Yes. Merdon had already called him, and advised him to abandon the city. Clanthas refused. He's organizing the people of Katan. They're going to fight for their city."

"Good, we're going to help them."

"What . . . what about Merdon?" she asked.

"Can he be reached by tri-di?"

Altai shook her head. "I tried a few minutes ago. He's left the factory, where he had set up headquarters."

Vorgens rubbed his temple thoughtfully. "In that case," he said, "we'll have to go out and find him." He turned to the techs. "Get Sergeant McIntyre and tell him to have an aircar ready for us in ten minutes."

"Yes sir."

The Mobile Force had three aircars, used mainly for scouting. They took off vertically on jets of air blasted straight downward—somewhat similar to the method used to raise the groundcars above ground level. The aircars lifted for several hundred feet, though, and then the jet engines swiveled and moved the craft forward. Stubby wings provided all the necessary lift, and the craft could sprint at twice the speed of sound, when required.

"There they are, sir," said the Marine pilot as they flew over Merdon's forces.

McIntyre, sitting in the gunner's seat, grunted. "Not much of a force t' tackle th' whole Komani camp."

Vorgens and Altai looked through the plastic bubble window as the pilot banked. Several hundred young men and girls were gathered on the grassy field below. Some were in trucks and small groundcars, most were afoot. They had plenty of small arms, but practically no heavy equipment. At the head of the loosely organized column was a light Terran armored groundcar.

"We captured that in the first battle at the university," Altai explained. "It is Merdon's prize possession."

"Put us down in front of the armored car," Vorgens told the pilot.

The aircar settled down swiftly, on screaming jets. As it touched the grass with its landing wheels, the armored car pulled up and stopped. The rest of the Shinarians slowly began to gather around, as Vorgens and Altai stepped down from the aircar, and Merdon, Tarat and Romal got out of the armored vehicle.

"We meet again," Vorgens said.

"What are you doing here?" asked Merdon.

"I want to talk with you."

"The time for talking is finished. Get out of our way. We have work to do."

They stood face to face—the young, slim foreigner in his Star Watch uniform, and the equally young, slightly bigger native. They were nearly the same height, and almost the same complexion. From a distance, where you could not see the difference in clothing, they might seem to be brothers.

"Your mission can wait a few minutes, can't it?" Vorgens insisted. "What I have to say is vitally important to all of us, including your father."

The tenseness in Merdon's face relaxed a bit. "All right. A few minutes."

Vorgens looked around at the crowd that had gathered about them.

"Perhaps we could talk better up there." He pointed to a little knoll.

Merdon shrugged.

"We're going for a walk, sergeant," Vorgens told McIntyre, "and I don't want to be disturbed."

Merdon said much the same to Tarat. Then they started walking, in silence.

But as they reached the foot of the knoll and began climbing its gentle slope, Merdon asked: "You talked with my father?"

"Altai did. He's organizing a defense of the city."

"He'll get himself killed."

"What are you going to do to help save him?"

Merdon glanced at the Watchman. "There's nothing I can do. You know that. Katan is too far away, even for the fastest groundcars. The Komani will be there before we can get to the city."

"So?"

Merdon stopped walking. "So I'm going to hit the

Komani where it will hurt the most. I'm going to kill Okatar."

Vorgens pursed his lips thoughtfully. Then he said, "That won't save your father."

"He could save himself if he'd abandon the city."

"Would you run away, if you were in his place?"

Merdon opened his mouth to answer, but no words came out.

"You may have heard," Vorgens said, resuming his climb toward the top of the knoll, "that my personal situation has changed somewhat since our last meeting."

Merdon, striding swiftly to catch up with the Watchman, could not help grinning. "I've heard."

"I'm no longer a prisoner, and while my rank is still that of a junior officer, I am the Star Watch officer in command of Shinar."

"I—I apologize for the way I treated you on our first meeting. I lost my temper."

Vorgens plucked a leafy twig from the shrubbery. "I accept your apology . . . under one condition. I want you to hear me out."

"I'm listening."

"There are only three points I want to make. First: the Empire has not treated Shinar well. This is not because of Terran maliciousness; it's just an accidental by-product of the Imperial system. You could be treated much better under the Empire. Other worlds are.

"Second: Shinar is too small a world, and too weak militarily, to stand alone. If Imperial troops were not here fighting for your people—don't frown, that's what they're doing—if they weren't here to fight for your people, the Komani would be ruling you with a whip and a gun.

"Finally: Shinar can achieve its own internal freedom under the Empire. I'm saying *can*, not *will*. Other planets have done it. Perhaps yours can, too. It's something worth working toward, worth risking a lot for—it's even worth fighting for—because it's the only way you'll ever gain freedom."

"What kind of freedom would it be?" Merdon asked, with quiet bitterness. "The Terrans would still control us. They'd own our souls."

"Don't be dramatic," Vorgens said. "The usual arrangement is to allow the planet complete internal freedom. You can rule yourselves in any way you see fit. The Empire would reserve the right to regulate your commercial treaties with other planets, but once a treaty is made, it's binding on the Empire as well as you. The Empire is ruled by law. You'd have all the legal rights that any other self-governing planet of the Empire enjoys."

"You make it sound like Sittas' dreams of heaven."

Vorgens laughed. "No, it won't be heaven. While the Empire is ruled by law, it is still governed by men. There'll always be differences of opinion, problems, arguments. But you'd have as much of a chance to get your own way as anyone else would."

They had reached the top of the knoll, and stood in knee-deep scrubgrass. A soft breeze moderated the heat of the sun. The deep blue, nearly violet, sky stood sparkling and cloudless all around them.

Vorgens stretched an arm toward the horizon. "This is a good world, Merdon. A green world, filled with people who deserve a chance to live in peace."

"They deserve freedom!" Merdon insisted. "And they're willing to fight for it."

Vorgens stepped over to the slightly taller Shinarian and grabbed him by the shoulders. "Don't you understand, you hothead? I want them to be free! I want them to live their lives the way they want; to reach in any direction they choose; to be free from all outside domination."

Merdon took a step backward, and Vorgens let his hands drop to his sides. Then he went on, "They can do

this under the Empire. It won't happen overnight, but
they can achieve this freedom. Peacefully! What alternative to the Empire do you have? The Komani? Nonsense.
Complete independence? You'd be swallowed up by more
powerful neighbors within a year. Fine words and brave
sentiments are perfectly good in their place, Merdon, but
it takes more than that to achieve freedom. You must
look at the real world, as it actually exists—not the world
you would like to see, not your own dreams. In this real
world, you must work for solutions that can be achieved.

"You can't solve all your problems with a wave of the
hand," Vorgens went on. "You tried to do that by bringing the Komani to Shinar. What's happened? Chaos. No
one's going to come to Shinar and grant you complete
independence at a stroke, but under the Empire you
have a better chance to achieve more freedom than any
other way offers."

Merdon scratched his head. "Maybe you're right," he
admitted. "I—I told Okatar he could name his own price
if he would just leave Shinar and attack another Empire
planet. Anything—all the equipment, food, ammunition
he wanted—just to leave Shinar. It was a stupid thing to
do. A wrong thing. His answer was—to take the offer,
and at the same time attack Katan."

"He wants to show you that you've been conquered,"
Vorgens said.

"Right. To Okatar, we're already slaves. He'll take what
he wants from us."

"Unless we stop him."

"And that's what I'm going to do," Merdon concluded
grimly.

"Not by attacking his camp," Vorgens countered. "All
you'd accomplish there is your own death."

"I've got to try!"

"Then try this: join us in the defense of Katan. Your
father's organizing the citizens of the city. If he can hold

out for a few hours, we can bring up Terran Marines, and your own forces, and crush the attackers."

Merdon shook his head. "Don't you think I've thought of that? I just don't have enough groundcars to get to Katan that quickly."

Vorgens grinned. "Don't *you* think *I've* thought of that? I can have a squadron of vans and troop carriers here within the hour."

Merdon was silent for a moment. Then, looking straight into the Watchman's eyes, he said, "I've been terribly wrong about a lot of things, but most of all about you. I'm going to tell my people to follow your orders. I'll stay behind—unless you—unless you're willing to have me fight alongside you."

Vorgens said nothing, but put his hand out toward Merdon. The Shinarian smiled broadly, and took the Watchman's hand in a firm grasp. Then they went down, side by side, to the waiting people.

Clanthas was sitting out on the veranda again, watching the sun go down. For the first time in his life, he felt fear at the approach of night. Somewhere off in the rolling countryside, he knew, a column of Komani warriors was advancing on his city.

A Terran jet flew overhead, its engines barely audible at the great altitude it held, its contrail of "frozen lightning" picking up the reddish glow of the dying sun. There was no airfield at Katan. The busy port city depended on groundcars and the huge, ocean-spanning transports that skimmed over land and sea with equal ease.

That was a Terran jet overhead. Strangely, it seemed to comfort the merchant. The Terrans were active. They were coming to the aid of Katan. But would they come soon enough? That was the question.

XVIII

The Race to Katan

Through the long night the people of Katan prepared for the oncoming Komani. The arsenal was opened and every citizen—male or female—old enough and strong enough to handle a weapon was issued one. The city's lights burned all night long as, building by building, block by block, people huddled together to make plans, to pick the best windows and rooftops to mount guns, to pray.

By dawn, they were ready. The usual early-morning bustle of commerce was replaced by a deadly, calm, quiet. Shops and offices were closed. Windows and doors bolted. The streets were empty, except for a few patrolling policemen. The hot, yellow sun rose, the sparkling water lapped the harbor docks and seawalls, the morning breeze blew in from the ocean, but the citizens of Katan were not out of doors to see. They waited indoors, grimly checking their weapons and ammunition.

The city lay curving around its crescent-shaped harbor. A small river cut through the heart of Katan, dividing it into two unequal segments, called the Lesser City and the Greater City. Beyond the outskirts of the city, beyond the parks and playgrounds and occasional suburban estates, were the rolling, wooded hills that masked the approach of the Komani.

The lulling calm of the morning was shattered by the scream of an aircar streaking fast and low over the buildings. The plane circled twice, then made a vertical descent into a deserted public park in the residential section of the city.

A handful of policemen ran to the aircar as its jets whined to a stop. Guns poked out ominously from dozens of windows and rooftops. Vorgens, Aikens, McIntyre, and two of the brigadier's staff officers climbed out. The Shinarians relaxed. A groundcar slid up to the Terrans, and they were whisked to Clanthas' home.

Clanthas had turned his veranda into a battle headquarters. The town council, the mayor, the police chief and several other community leaders were there to greet the Terrans. Vorgens quickly introduced Brigadier Aikens, Sergeant McIntyre, and the brigadier's two aides.

"We passed over the Komani column," the Watchman said before Clanthas could say anything. "They're about two hours away—perhaps a little less."

"And your troops?" the mayor asked.

"They're moving up in land cruisers," Brigadier Aikens said, stepping between Vorgens and the mayor. "Won't be here until noon, at the earliest. You must defend the city as best as possible until then."

The mayor exchanged worried glances with the others.

"The brigadier has drawn up a plan of action," Vorgens said.

"Do you have a map of the city?" Aikens asked Clanthas.

The merchant smiled. "Better than that . . . I have the city itself."

Clanthas led them around the veranda to the side that faced away from the harbor. The entire group clustered around Aikens as he looked out over the rooftops of Katan.

"I see what you mean," the brigadier said. "An excellent view. Now then, that large square building down there, across the river . . ." He pointed. "That's the arsenal, isn't it?"

Clanthas nodded.

Aikens turned and leaned slightly over the railing. "And down on this side . . . those are the warehouses?"

"Yes, along the waterfront of the Lesser City."

Aikens grunted with satisfaction. "All right. Now, the arsenal and the warehouses will be the two principal objectives of the Komani."

"The arsenal will be practically useless to them," Clanthas said, "since we have distributed almost all the weapons and ammunition to our people."

"Good! I was counting on that. We'll let the Komani spend some time and effort taking the arsenal, but we won't defend that end of the city very strongly. Evacuate your people and leave only a thin screen of men; fight a rear guard action."

The mayor gasped. "You mean that we should allow them to take half the Greater City? But the factories, the business district, the homes . . ."

"They have no military value," Aikens snapped. "You're fighting for time, with untrained rabble facing tough, battle-tested troops. You can't hold the entire city. You've got to pick out the part that you *must* defend, and let the Komani have the rest, temporarily."

"But they'll loot it . . . destroy everything."

Aikens planted his fists on his hips. "Listen! I'm here to save your necks and to defeat the Komani. I'm not going to worry about real estate values."

Vorgens added, more softly, "If all goes well, the Komani won't have much time for looting. Besides, the buildings would be damaged much more severely if heavy fighting took place in them."

The mayor shook his head. "I suppose so."

"All right then," Aikens resumed, turning slightly away from the Watchman. "The warehouses will be defended. We'll set up a firm line of resistance a few blocks in front of them. And we'll also set up a flanking line along the river."

"The river is no barrier to Komani mounted on flyers," Vorgens pointed out.

Aikens smiled icily, and with an obvious patience, explained, "No, but it's a moderately wide open space, with no buildings to provide shelter. If they try to fly across the river, they'll be putting themselves in the middle of a firing range."

"Good," Clanthas said, sensing the hostility between the two men and trying to change the subject before it broke out into the open. "What else?"

"Three companies of Imperial Marines are being flown here by jet. They should arrive momentarily."

"But we have no airfield."

"They'll jump from the planes and come down on jet-belts. When our task unit from the Mobile Force arrives, we'll be able to drive the Komani out of the city—if all goes well this morning."

"Very well," Clanthas said. He turned to the mayor, "We must inform our people about this plan of battle. We have to move swiftly."

Within a moment, the veranda was deserted, except for the Terrans.

"They seemed to accept your plan," Vorgens said to the brigadier.

"They'd better."

Sergeant McIntyre asked the Watchman, "Sir, when the airborne troops get here, they'll need somebody t' show 'em where they're supposed t' set up . . . won't they?"

"Very well, Sergeant," Vorgens said, "you may report to the brigade commander. I didn't think I'd be able to keep you out of the fighting."

McIntyre saluted briskly. "Thank you, sir!"

Aikens said, "If you're going back to the Mobile Force, Watchman, you'd better start off right away. There's not much time left before the shooting starts."

Vorgens met the older man's eyes. "When are you leaving?"

"When the battle's done."

"Then I'll stay too, if you don't mind."

They stood facing each other in silence for a moment. Then Aikens turned away.

"Look!" shouted one of the brigadier's aides. "The jets."

They could see three fine, white contrails hurrying across the morning sky. Within minutes, the planes had come low enough to flood the city with the thunder of their engines. Tiny figures began to jump from them, with crisp military precision, and float slowly downward.

Vorgens turned away and looked at the hills. Wordlessly, he reached out and tapped Aikens' shoulder. The brigadier turned and stared in the direction of Vorgens' gaze.

Coming over the hills, like a dark cloud of angry locusts, was the swarm of Komani flyers.

It was not pretty to watch a city being destroyed.

Vorgens stood at his post on the veranda, within earshot of the communications center that Aikens had set up, and saw the battle unfold.

The Komani split into two columns. One bore straight down on the Lesser City, driving for the warehouses by the waterfront. The other swung wide across the open suburban greenery and attacked the Greater City, aiming for the arsenal.

By noontime, the bright sunshine was blotted out by a pall of smoke rising from dozens of fires raging through Katan. Vorgens could see that most of the Greater City was a shambles. The Komani had slashed their way easily to the arsenal, and when they found it nearly empty, had turned their frustrated rage to the building itself. They set it ablaze, and then fanned out through the Greater City, looting, burning destroying. Now the arsenal was a blackened, gutted shell, and the buildings around it smoldered also.

But all this was secondary to the fierce battle flaring through the streets of the Lesser City.

The Komani column driving toward the warehouses had met stiff resistance from the citizens of Katan and from the hastily assembled brigade of Marines. Aikens' defensive perimeter, drawn up a few blocks in front of the warehouses and swinging around to follow the riverside flank, had temporarily stopped the Komani onslaught.

The fighting had slowed down to a bitter, house-to-house, man-to-man struggle. Most of the Komani had dismounted from their flyers and fought now on foot. A few still remained aloft, though, to pepper rooftops and windows. Clanthas' veranda had been buzzed several times. Vorgens now held a beam pistol in his hand.

Although they were outnumbered, the Komani were relentlessly pressing their attack home. They had quickly learned to stay out of the buildings, where a dozen Shinarians could surprise a lone invader. Now they were boring through the streets and over the rooftops, routing the city's defenders with superior discipline and the dispassionate courage that comes from long experience in battle.

Three times Aikens had to move his core of Imperial Marines backwards, because the Komani had penetrated the streets on their flanks and threatened to surround them. Now they were fighting in the square that opened onto the warehouse district.

Vorgens could see, too, that the Komani sacking the Greater City must have received word of the heavy fighting going on near the warehouses. They had stopped their senseless looting and burning, and were forming up in the streets.

The Watchman ducked around a corner of the veranda to Aikens at his makeshift communications center. The brigadier had taken one side of the veranda and filled it with technicians, aides, and equipment.

He was leaning over one of the techs, barking orders into a viewscreen. Vorgens touched his arm. The brigadier straightened and turned to the Watchman.

"In another moment or two," Vorgens said, "the warriors from the Greater City will be flying here to help their friends."

"I know!" Aikens snapped. "What do you think I'm trying to do here, organize a tea party? I'm setting up a lane of fire on both sides of the river. We'll cut down as many of 'em as possible before they can join the attack here."

"What about our task unit from the Mobile Force?" Vorgens asked.

"They're on their way."

It was almost two hours more before the Terrans finally arrived.

The three companies of air-dropped Marines had been whittled down to a stubborn handful, fighting tenaciously at the steps of the warehouses they were defending. Shinarians—old men, boys, women among them—fought and died alongside the Imperial troops.

All along the river Komani warriors were darting wildly on their utterly maneuverable flyers, trying to avoid the withering fire coming up from both banks. Some of the flyers got through, and went on to join the attack on the warehouses. Most of the others had turned back though, and were blasting the buildings from which the Shinarians fired.

A squad of flying Komani warriors had fought its way to the roof of one warehouse when Vorgens saw the first

Terran troop carriers racing over the final row of hills before the city.

The Watchman turned to Aikens, and saw that the brigadier was still immersed in crackling out orders to his men. Beyond the brigadier's shoulder, Vorgens could see more battle cruisers skimming over the harbor water, heading for the warehouses at top speed. Only then did he realize that the vehicles coming in from the hills carried Merdon's men, not Marines.

The Komani were caught in a vise.

Aikens' Marines, in battle cruisers and armored cars, drove up the streets between the warehouses, crushing the Komani attack with massed firepower. The invading warriors fell back, slowly at first, but when they tried to regroup, they found Terran armored vehicles boring down on them. The Komani fled for the city's outskirts, only to be met by Merdon's vengeful fighters.

By nightfall it was ended. A few of the attackers had escaped—very few. Merdon and the exhausted citizens of Katan rejoiced by torchlight through the blackened, rubble-strewn streets.

Vorgens remained at the railing of the veranda, watching the celebration, in the dark. The city's electrical power generators had been heavily damaged.

"Sir."

He turned, and in the flickering shadows saw McIntyre, grimy and tired, but alive. "You've—done a good day's work, Sergeant."

A satisfied grin broke across McIntyre's beefy face. "Thank you sir. Uh—we're just about ready t' leave. The brigadier has already gone back t' the Mobile Force. All other troops have pulled out."

"All right," Vorgens said quietly. "I suppose there's no sense in my staying any longer."

McIntyre peered out over the railing. "They're havin' some time down there—celebratin' their victory. I—uh, don't suppose we could stay a bit longer and join 'em?"

"Victory?" the Watchman echoed. "What victory? Look at this city. It's smashed to pieces. Who won?"

McIntyre shrugged. "They seem t' think *they* won, sir. They're already talkin' about how they're gonna rebuild the damaged sections of town."

Vorgens did not answer. He started toward the stairs that led down to the courtyard before Clanthas' home and the aircar waiting there. Someone was coming up the steps. Altai.

"Here you are!" she said to Vorgens.

"I'm on my way back to the Mobile Force," he said.

"Leaving? But why?"

"Why not? The battle's over. Your people want to celebrate. You'll want to get back to Merdon and the others."

She smiled and stepped closer to him. "I haven't said more than six words to Merdon since yesterday, and I'm not joining the celebration until you come with me. They're celebrating their freedom, and you're the man responsible for it. You're coming with me!"

"I . . ."

Devilishly, she added, "You wouldn't want Merdon to get *all* the credit, would you? Come on!"

Vorgens grinned back at her. "All right, you win. Sergeant, I guess we'll be staying awhile longer."

"Yes *sir*," McIntyre said happily.

XIX

Attrition

The celebration at Katan was followed by six weeks of virtually uninterrupted battle flaming across the breadth of Shinar. Okatar Kang had decided to sack the planet, relentlessly raiding every district, every town, systematically taking all the food, weapons, equipment and ammunition he desired.

Opposed to the Komani plan stood Vorgens and his concept of Shinarian self-defense, directed and keystoned by the Terrans.

It was a peculiar battle in many ways. Instead of large masses of troops and weapons clashing head-on, there were skirmishes, maneuverings, feints, sudden vicious attacks, ambushes—few single actions involved more than a battalion of men.

Vorgens worked constantly, almost without rest, living on stimulants, cajoling Aikens, persuading the Shinarians to trust the Terrans.

With the Shinarians taking over a good part of their

own defense, and with Merdon's fighters providing reconnaissance and intelligence, the Terrans were able to meet the Komani on their own terms. When a Komani raiding party headed for a town, it would be intercepted by a fast, strong squadron of battle cruisers. Farming villages became little fortresses dotting the countryside, often with a Terran dreadnaught camped in the village square. Komani columns were ambushed. When Okatar massed his strength and tried to force a pitched battle, he found that the Terrans could also disperse and disappear into the countryside.

The Komani still outnumbered the Imperial troops on Shinar. But whenever the Terrans struck, they usually had superior strength at that particular place for that brief time.

It was a war of attrition, with fatigue and hunger and mechanical breakdown playing as important a role as weapons.

"We're failing," Vorgens said tiredly. "We're failing miserably."

He was sitting at the head of the green-covered table in the officers' wardroom of the command dreadnaught. Grouped around the table were Merdon, Brigadier Aikens, the exec, Sergeant McIntyre, and a few other officers.

"I wouldn't say that, Watchman," the brigadier objected. "We're holding our own against the barbarians."

"We've beaten off most of their attacks. The people are learning to defend themselves," Merdon agreed.

Vorgens shook his head. "The best we can say is that we've accomplished a stalemate. Our objective is peace. We have perpetual fighting. That's failure."

"What do you propose?" the exec asked.

"That's the worst part of it—I can't see any clear way out," Vorgens admitted. "Either the Komani will remain here until one side or the other collapses from exhaustion, or—worse still—Okatar will pull his clan off Shinar and attack another planet. Then the whole bloody business will be repeated again."

"What about the reinforcements on their way here?" Aikens asked.

"They won't be enough to make much difference," Vorgens said. "In fact, just because they're so few, they'll verify Okatar's claim that the Empire can't defend Shinar adequately. Those reinforcements might lead to strengthening Okatar's hand! Other Komani clans might be tempted to join him when they see how weak the Empire's response is."

A gloomy silence settled over them.

Finally, Merdon said, "I know a way of breaking this deadlock."

Everyone turned to him.

"Kill Okatar," Merdon said simply. "Decapitate the Komani clan."

Aikens grunted. "You'd never be able to get to him."

"It would just make the Komani fight harder," the exec said.

"That would be barbaric," Vorgens said. "To deliberately plan a man's death. . . ."

"This is war," Aikens snapped. "Every one of us runs the risk of being killed."

"In battle, yes," Vorgens countered. "But not in bed. No, I can't condone assassination."

"But if it were done," Merdon insisted, "it would break the stalemate, wouldn't it?"

"Possibly. I don't know. It would certainly throw the Komani into confusion, at least temporarily. Perhaps then they might be willing to talk about peace. . . ."

Merdon changed the subject then, and the conference droned on for another fruitless hour. No decision was reached. The Terrans and Shinarians would continue to fight as they had been fighting for more than six weeks. The war of attrition would go on.

In the passageway outside the wardroom, Merdon grasped Sergeant McIntyre's arm and asked, "Can we talk for a moment?"

The sergeant nodded, and the two of them walked slowly down the passageway. McIntyre loomed bulkily next to the slim Shinarian youth.

"What do you think about the chances of getting to Okatar?" Merdon asked in a half-whisper.

McIntyre shrugged. "It's a big camp—hard t' get into. And even harder t' get out of."

"Listen," Merdon whispered, suddenly intense, "I know every blade of grass in the camp. I can get six men through the guards and into Okatar's tent. I've been planning this for weeks, and I know it can be done!"

The sergeant rubbed his massive jaw. "How d' you get 'em away afterwards?"

"Jetbelts."

"Might work."

"I need six men trained in silent night fighting."

"Five, countin' me," said Sergeant McIntyre.

Three nights later, they made their try.

McIntyre had recruited five Marines, including Giradaux. The lanky young trooper had sensed that the sergeant was up to something, and had forced McIntyre to take him along, as the price of silence.

A driving rainstorm had blown up from the south, predicted by the Terran meteorologists. Merdon was counting on the storm to provide a cover of darkness against the usual twilight glow of the Shinarian night.

They commandeered a scoutcar and started off cross-country, guided by the car's infrared lamps. Ordinary lights would have been detected too easily, both by the Komani and the occasional Terran patrols.

McIntyre drove, with Merdon in the skipper's seat directing him. The five troopers sat in dark silence amidst their jetbelts, guns and grenades, listening to the whine of the car's engine and the rain pelting the armored roof just above their helmets.

"There's the forest coming up," Merdon said, pointing into the viewscreen in front of McIntyre. "You won't be able to take the car very deep into it."

McIntyre nodded as he eased up on the throttle. "I'll put 'er in a little ways, so she'll be under cover."

Within a few minutes, the seven of them were slogging through the rain-soaked woods.

It took nearly two hours of steady marching through the angry rain before they cleared the forest and saw the edge of the Komani camp.

Crouching in the bushes at the forest's edge, Merdon scanned the camp with infrared binoculars.

"Only a few guards," he muttered, "and plenty of open space between them. The camp is almost completely blacked out. The rain has even put out the ceremonial fires."

"Don't they have automatic detection equipment that sets off an alarm as soon as somebody crosses th' energy screen?" McIntyre asked.

"No. That's a Terran refinement that the Komani don't have. Guards with snooperscopes ... that's what they use. Believe me, it'll be tough enough to get through them."

They skirted along the edge of the encampment, looking for their best opening. At last they found a spot where the foliage nearly reached the energy screen. There were only about twenty yards of open space between the forest shrubbery and the nearest Komani tents.

They waited for the guard to make a couple of rounds, so they could time his approach. Then they started crawling—two at a time—for the tents. McIntyre and Giradaux were the first pair to start. The rain had slackened a little but was still heavy enough to be troublesome. For what seemed like hours, the two Marines inched along on their stomachs, while the others covered them with their guns.

Merdon was the last to go across. He pulled himself along the wet, slippery grass and mud, his vision restricted to the same view of the world that a worm might have.

Suddenly he heard McIntyre's harsh whisper in his helmet earphones. "Freeze!"

Merdon stopped dead and buried his face in his arms. He was wearing a black uniform and equipment, as the Marines were. But still it seemed his heart was pounding loud enough to be heard all over the camp.

Finally McIntyre whispered, "Okay."

The young Shinarian slithered across the last remaining yards and joined the others in the relative safety behind the tents.

"What happened?" he asked as they helped him to his feet.

"Changing of the guard," McIntyre answered. "Two of 'em walked right out in fronta you. Lucky they didn't look your way."

Merdon grinned. "Well let's get moving while our luck still holds."

They made their way as quickly as possible toward the center of the camp. Merdon pointed the way, and McIntyre directed their movements. The seven of them fanned out slightly, but still kept within sight of each other. One man would move ahead the distance of a single tent, make certain the way was clear, then signal the next man to move up. They kept to the shadows, and their guns were always in their hands, ready to fire.

Four times they had to stop, as guards crossed their path, treading sleepily through the darkened camp. Once a guard started to walk directly toward a pair of Marines, crouching alongside a tent. McIntyre sprang at the Komani's back and felled him with a savage chop at the neck.

"Is he dead?" Merdon whispered.

"Dunno . . . but he'll be out for a good long time, at least."

"Come on," Merdon said. "The rain's slackening. It's starting to brighten up a little."

Finally they reached Okatar's golden dome. Light was streaming from the main entrance.

"There are two other entrances, on the other side of the tent," Merdon said.

McIntyre nodded to his men. "Two of you take each entrance. Gerry, you and Merdon come with me, through the main gate. Now get this straight, all of you: no Komani leaves that tent alive. Understand?"

They nodded.

The four Marines disappeared into the shadows. McIntyre hunched down into a squat and surveyed the tent's main entrance. A pair of guards stood tiredly leaning on their rifles.

"How many Komani will be inside?" the sergeant asked.

Merdon shrugged. "It depends. If Okatar has his full council in there, it might be twenty-five or thirty men."

The Marines at the other two entrances signaled through their helmet radios that they were ready.

"Okay," McIntyre whispered. "*Now!*"

He got both the guards with a single sweeping blast from his beam rifle as they dashed out of the shadows and toward the entrance.

Inside, the tent suddenly looked deserted—a single large area, richly decorated and furnished—but empty of Komani. Then a grenade went off, somewhere on the other side of the tent.

"The council chamber," Merdon shouted as he ran toward the far end of the room.

Before they could get to the doorway, a trio of Komani nobles bolted through it and faced them. Merdon cut them down with his beam pistol before they could change the surprised expressions on their faces.

Inside the council chamber, one of the Marines was sprawled limply over an ornate chair, while another was kneeling beside him, firing at five Komani who had taken shelter behind the massive council table. The farther end of the table was splintered and blackened from a grenade's blast. McIntyre pushed behind a chair and up to the table itself, then sprayed the length of it with the highest-power beam he could get from his rifle. The table flashed into flames, forcing the Komani back away from it. Within less than a minute they were all mowed down.

"Okatar's not here," Merdon shouted. "Come on, we've got to find him."

They dashed through several other rooms, while the three surviving Marines took up defensive stations at each of the three entrances to the tent.

The rooms were empty. Smoke was starting to crawl ominously around them.

"The whole camp'll be in here in a minute!" McIntyre shouted.

Merdon said, "He's got to be ... LOOK OUT!"

Nearly a dozen Komani burst out of a doorway off to their right. Their first shots knocked down both McIntyre and Merdon, but Giradaux hurled a grenade into them before ducking behind a low-slung table. The concussion flattened everything in the room.

McIntyre was the first to recover. He rolled over onto his stomach and pulled the pistol from his belt. But none of the Komani were moving. Merdon climbed stiffly to his feet, the right side of his tunic showing a spreading stain of blood.

He pointed with his pistol. "This one—here in the middle—that was Okatar."

McIntyre pulled himself up. There was an ugly gash

along the side of his head. "Okay," he said. "Let's get outta here."

The tent was filling with smoke now, and they could hear the shouts of fighting men approaching. The three Marines were still at the entrance, but two of them obviously were badly wounded.

"I'll get 'em," Giradaux said. He touched the control stud at his waist that activated his jetbelt and rocketed across the room to the first of the wounded men. The trooper hurled his last grenade at the oncoming Komani, then took off on his own jetbelt and started toward McIntyre.

The sergeant and Merdon had joined the one unhurt Marine, at the entrance he was holding. Flames were licking up the side of the tent, and the Komani were beginning to organize their frantic, helter-skelter attempts to recapture the tent.

Before Giradaux could reach the other wounded Marine, the trooper keeled over and a horde of Komani boiled into the room.

Without an instant's hesitation, Giradaux jetted straight upward, sliced open the tent's dome with his beamgun as he flew, and disappeared through the roof.

Merdon took off at the same instant, leaping through the entrance and spiralling up around the tent's curving dome. McIntyre grabbed the wounded Marine and started to follow the Shinarian, but the trooper had collapsed and could not control his jetbelt. McIntyre hesitated for a moment—just long enough for a Komani warrior to reach him with a ceremonial broadsword gleaming wickedly in his upraised hand.

XX

The Boldest Step

Vorgens did not notice that McIntyre was missing until the following morning. It took a little while for him to discover that the sergeant was nowhere in the Mobile Force, that Merdon and a few Marines were also gone, and that a scout car had disappeared.

The Watchman summoned Brigadier Aikens to the dreadnaught's wardroom. In cold fury, Vorgens explained the situation to him.

"I have only one question," Vorgens concluded, barely able to keep his voice calm. "Did you authorize this raid in which they must be engaged?"

"Raid?" Aikens asked.

"On the Komani camp," Vorgens snapped. "Did you authorize it?"

Aikens laughed. "Until just now I didn't even know about it."

"I see ..."

The wall communicator chimed, and a trooper's face

took form on the viewscreen. "Sir, there's a trooper here at hatch four who demands to see you. Name of Giradaux. He says . . ."

"Send him here at once," Vorgens said.

It took a minute for Giradaux to get from the outside hatch to the wardroom. He stepped wearily through the doorway, ducking his head to get his tall, lanky frame through. He looked utterly bedraggled. His uniform was caked with mud. His face was hollow-eyed and grimy. His shoulders slumped dejectedly. He didn't bother to salute. "We got him for you," he said to Vorgens.

"Got him?"

"Okatar. He's dead. I hope that makes you happy."

"What are you . . ."

"We got Okatar," the trooper said, his eyes filling with tears, "and they got th' Sarge. Four killed, one wounded—sir. Trooper Martinis and I weren't touched. It's a big victory for you—sir. A big victory."

"McIntyre was killed?"

"That's right," Giradaux answered, his voice rising. "Did you expect any of us to come back alive?"

"I didn't even know . . ."

"You knew he'd try it. You must have knowm. He's dead, and you—"

"That's *enough*!" Aikens bellowed.

Giradaux snapped to attention.

"Get to your quarters, trooper. And don't budge a toe out of them until you're told to. *Move.*"

With deliberate care, Giradaux made a letter-perfect salute. Aikens returned it, and the trooper pivoted on his heel and left the wardroom. But Vorgens could still feel the pain that he felt, and sensed the anger within him.

"Whatever possessed a veteran like McIntyre to—to ignore my wishes, to go dashing off on his own?"

Aikens smiled grimly. "An army is built on discipline, Watchman. McIntyre saw that discipline shattered the day you took over command. He was simply following the example you set—and you see where it leads."

Vorgens sat in stunned silence as Aikens got up from his chair and strode out of the wardroom. He remained there, alone, heedless of time, staring at the bare, metal wall with unseeing eyes. Officers and orderlies would open the door to the wardroom from time to time, and, seeing him there and the expression on his face, would silently shut the door and leave Vorgens to himself.

Finally, the exec stepped in, hesitated a moment at the door, then walked to the chair next to Vorgens and sat down. He placed a yellow dispatch film on the table-top before the Watchman.

"The ships from Star Watch Headquarters have arrived and taken up a parking orbit around the planet. When do you want the troops to land?"

Vorgens blinked, and focused his thoughts on the exec's question with an obvious effort.

"Tonight," he said at last. "Tell them to land under cover of darkness. I don't want the Komani to see how few they are."

The exec nodded. "Sir—I've been thinking. We could run the landing ships up and down as many times as you wish. They don't have to have a full load of troops on board. They can just shuttle back and forth between the starships and the planet all day long, if you like. The Komani won't know."

"That would only fool them temporarily," Vorgens said.

"Yes, I suppose so."

"Is there anything else?"

"That—uh, that girl, sir. Altai. She's been waiting to see you."

"No, I don't want to see anyone."

"Sir, she's been waiting almost all day."

"Oh? What time is it?"

"Nearly dark, sir."

"I—I didn't realize that I'd been here so long." He ran a weary hand across his eyes. "All right, I suppose I'll have to see her sooner or later. Send her in."

"Yes sir."

"Oh . . . and release Trooper Giradaux from his quarters," Vorgens called out as the exec headed for the door. "He's to resume his normal duties."

"Very well, sir."

The exec opened the door, stepped through, and held it open for Altai. Vorgens rose and stood at the head of the table as she walked across the compact little room to him.

"I—I just realized that I don't know if Merdon's dead or alive," the Watchman said.

"He's in the infirmary," Altai said, sitting down next to Vorgens. "He lost quite a bit of blood, but otherwise he's not in serious condition."

Vorgens sat down and said nothing.

"Merdon told me that the plan was his," she went on. "He takes full responsibility for it."

The Watchman shook his head. "No. I'm in command. Whatever happens is my responsibility."

"But you didn't know."

"I should have. I might have guessed at it. I know Merdon doesn't give up an idea so easily. I gave McIntyre the impression that only Okatar's death could save us from continual fighting. He gave up his life at my suggestion, not Merdon's."

"But you can't blame yourself for everything that happens on Shinar. That's wrong!"

"I blame myself for what happened last night, and for a lot more, besides. As I look back on it, I realize how foolish I've been. I was going to bring peace to Shinar—single-handedly, if necessary! What a joke. All I've brought is pain and death and unending fighting." He ran a hand over his close-cropped hair. There were hollows under his eyes, and his voice sounded husky.

"But you—I . . ." Suddenly Altai was tongue-tied. "Do you have a first name?" she blurted. "I can't call you Vorgens, or Watchman."

In spite of himself, he smiled. *"Ehml'n*, in my native language. The Terrans find it easier to say Emil."

"All right—Emil. Don't you realize how much you've done for Shinar—for all of us?"

He shook his head.

"You're blaming yourself for all the killing that's taken place here. That's wrong! Thanks to you, the men who've died have put a meaning to the deaths. They're accomplishing something that only you have allowed them to do."

"Yes," Vorgens replied. "Only me."

She reached out and grasped his hands on the table-top. "You've given us something to fight for—not the dream of complete freedom that Merdon wanted. Most of the people never believed that such a dream was possible. That's why Merdon's followers were only among the young. You've taught us that we may be able to gain real freedom within the Empire."

"That might be an even wilder dream than Merdon's," Vorgens said.

She smiled at him. "You don't believe that, and neither do I. You've shown us that Terrans and Shinarians can work together. You've proved to us that we can think and act for ourselves, that we can defend our homes when necessary. Not by calling in warriors from another land—but by ourselves.

"And you've shown me," she said more softly, "that a man who hates fighting is a much better man to follow than someone who has learned to enjoy it."

"That's—very kind of you," he said, looking into her deep, dark eyes. "In all the bitterness and bloodshed of these past months, the only touch of warmth and bright-ness has been you. Knowing you was almost worth all the rest."

"Was?"

"I've decided to leave Shinar. There are Star Watch officers aboard the ships carrying our reinforcements. Any one of them would be much better qualified to command the Imperial forces here than I am."

"No! You can't. They wouldn't know the situation here the way you do. And how can our people trust a total stranger?"

"What else can I do?"

"Finish the work that you started out to do! You're the only man who has the grasp and the courage to try. Don't give up now. Keep working to bring peace to Shinar. Finish the work that we've all given so much to—especially your sergeant."

"Do you really think it might be possible?"

"It has to be," Altai insisted. "With Okatar gone now, who knows what will happen next?"

"The next step," Vorgens muttered, half to himself, "probably depends on us."

She said nothing, but sat back and watched his face as he thought over the alternatives.

Suddenly Vorgens got up from his chair and strode to the communicator on the wall near the door. He punched out a call number on the directory buttons. The exec's face showed up on the viewscreen.

"Please send my compliments to the commander of the relief ships in orbit," the Watchman said, "and ask him to delay landing the troops until full daylight at Capital City. The troops are to be landed just outside the city. And your idea about running the shuttles an extra few times to impress the Komani sounds good. Keep the landing ships running all day."

"Yes *sir*," the exec replied, grinning.

"And another thing—I want an aircar for tomorrow morning, with a volunteer pilot. The car must be painted white."

Thus the boldest step of all in the struggle for Shinar was begun.

Vorgens should have been surprised to see Giradaux standing at attention beside the white-painted aircar, but somehow he was not.

"You volunteered to pilot me?" the Watchman asked as he stepped up to the craft. He spoke softly enough so that the officers and men standing nearby would not overhear.

"Yes sir," Giradaux answered, looking straight ahead. "I wanted to—well—to make up for what I said yesterday, sir."

Vorgens nodded. "I understand."

Brigadier Aikens joined them. "If this pilot isn't satisfactory . . ."

"He'll do," Vorgens said.

"You're still determined to go through with this?"

The Watchman nodded. "Military action has taken us about as far as we can expect. It's time to try a political stroke."

Aikens frowned distastefully. "You probably won't get through this alive."

"Perhaps," Vorgens admitted cheerfully, "but that would be no great loss to you, would it?"

Before the brigadier could reply, Vorgens swung up the access ladder and climbed into the aircar's open cabin. Giradaux trotted around to the other side, got in, and pulled down the plastic bubble top. The turbines growled into life, spraying dust around the base of the little craft. Aikens and the other men backed away as the car climbed slowly, its engines rising in pitch as its altitude increased. Finally the engines tilted forward, and the aircar shot ahead through the morning sky.

Aikens shook his head as the car disappeared from sight. "We'll never see them again," he said to the exec.

*   *   *

Vorgens spent most of the time aloft looking at the tri-di viewscreen on the control panel before him. He was watching the Imperial reinforcements land, just outside Capital City. A half-dozen needle-sleek, silvery landing ships were sitting tail-down on the plain and disgorging Marines. As he watched, two more settled down slowly, making the ground beneath them shimmer in the haze of their gray fields. Another ship took off, rising slowly, catching the morning sun on her gleaming hull.

It was an impressive sight, even though the actual number of Marines was quite small.

Finally Giradaux touched his arm and said, "There it is, sir."

Vorgens followed the trooper's gaze and saw the Komani camp.

A ring of ceremonial fires, spaced every fifty yards or so, circled the perimeter of the vast encampment. The gaudy domed tents were decked with blood-red drapings. Long processions of men, women and children were filing among the tents, heading for the center, where the dead Kang lay.

In the place where Okatar's golden tent had stood there now rose a tall pyre, unlit as yet. Heaped atop it were piles of offerings—weapons, ornaments, warriors' trappings, personal treasures—glittering in the sunshine. Vorgens could see the processions of Komani all converged on this pyre. Each person, no matter how young or old, handed something to the warriors who were stacking the offerings on the wooden structure that held the dead Kang's coffin.

Suddenly the sky around them was black with Komani flyers, buzzing angrily all around. Vorgens held up his hands in the sign of peace.

One of the Komani pulled up close enough to touch the aircar, and for several moments they flew side by side, staring at each other. Finally the warrior touched a jeweled band at his throat and then pointed to his lips.

"Try the radio," Vorgens said to Giradaux.

"Leave here at once," the warrior was snarling, "and be grateful that we do not kill on a day of mourning. Only our ancient custom has saved your lives today."

Vorgens replied evenly, "I have come to pay my respects to your chieftain. I would like to land in your camp, and do him what little honor I can."

The warrior looked thunderstruck. "You dare to suggest that you should be allowed to—to . . ." He sputtered with rage.

"Do you dare," Vorgens asked calmly, "to refuse an honor to your Kang? How many chieftains have had an enemy leader ask to see their pyre?"

The warrior hesitated. Finally he said. "This is not for me to decide. The council must make the choice."

For nearly an hour, the Terran aircar circled slowly over the camp, with its sullen escort of Komani flyers.

"You're depending on an awful lot on their customs, ain't-cha, sir?" Giradaux asked.

"They're ruled by custom," the Watchman replied. *At least, that's what they told us at the Academy.*

At last the warrior told them to follow him to a landing. They put down in a cleared area near the edge of the camp. A knot of elders stood there, solemn and hostile, as Vorgens climbed down from the aircar.

"I am Lensor," said one of the Komani, a grizzled, wrinkled nobleman, slightly stooped with age. Still he towered above the Watchman. "Until a new Kang is chosen, I am leader of the council. By what right do you presume to interrupt our sacred funeral ceremony?"

Vorgens said, "I have come to express my sorrow at Okatar's death."

"Sorrow?"

"His death was not by my order. I did not know of it

until after the assassination took place. I did not wish to have him killed."

"Yet you are the leader of his enemies."

"Yes," Vorgens admitted, "but this battle has gone beyond my control—beyond anyone's control. The war on Shinar has lost its meaning. We are fighting each other now simply for the sake of fighting."

The Komani said nothing.

"I don't have much in the way of personal possessions to add to the pyre," Vorgens went on, "but I do want to give these, as a token of my regret." He unpinned the diamond insignia clips from the collar of his tunic and handed them to the nobleman.

For a moment, Lensor stood frozen, immobile. Then slowly he extended his massive hand and accepted Vorgens' offering.

"I shall place them on the pyre myself," he said.

"Thank you. May I stay to witness the ceremony? I could remain at this spot, if you wish."

The nobleman turned to his fellow council members. None of them objected.

"Very well, you may remain. And—after the ceremony, you will accept our hospitality."

"Agreed," Vorgens said. "Perhaps then we can talk of ways to stop this killing."

"Yes, perhaps the time has come to talk of peace."

XXI

A Better Man

Sittas sat in Vorgens' tiny compartment aboard the dreadnaught while the Star Watchman packed his few belongings in a travel kit.

"This court-martial that you must face," the old priest asked, "is it serious?"

"More than serious," Vorgens said. "I may be lucky just to remain in the Star Watch."

"Even though you have stopped the fighting? Even though the Komani have left Shinar?"

"That will have very little to do with it, I'm afraid. The charges filed by Brigadier Aikens concern insubordination, armed mutiny, personal malice, and a few other items."

"But the Imperial Senate wants you to report to them, to present the case for Shinar's self-government."

Vorgens looked up from the travel kit, which was resting on his bunk. "Yes, I've been ordered to appear before the Senate, together with Clanthas and some of the other

Shinarian leaders, but that's got nothing to do with the court-martial."

"Still, I doubt that you have much to fear," Sittas said hopefully.

Vorgens shook his head. "I'd like to stay in the Star Watch . . . but—I'd do it all over again, if I had to!"

"You were right, and the brigadier was wrong," Sittas said.

"I was lucky."

"The Komani have gone. Shinar is at peace."

"More luck than skill," Vorgens insisted. "Okatar's death took most of the fight out of them. The way your own people were fighting helped to make them realize they had no glory to gain here. I guess that handful of reinforcements was the last straw. So the Komani nobles blamed everything on Okatar and went back home."

"Of course, your hint that more Terran reinforcements might arrive at any time helped to push them in the right direction."

Vorgens nodded. "I wanted to make certain that they knew the Empire was ready and able to defend itself. They took the bait and accepted a path to peace that wouldn't shame them."

"Therefore, the court-martial must acquit you," Sittas concluded. "None of this would have come to pass if Brigadier Aikens had remained in charge."

"I wish you would be sitting on the bench at the trial," Vorgens answered, laughing. "I don't know. Nothing is definitely settled yet. Suppose the Senate decides not to allow Shinar any measure of self-government? Then the court-martial could add treason and sedition to its list of charges."

He looked around the compartment, satisfied himself that he had everything he wanted, and snapped the kit shut. He opened the door to the passageway.

"Do you seriously believe," Sittas asked, rising to join him, "that the Empire will refuse our modest request?"

Vorgens grinned. "I think they'll listen to Clanthas and agree with him. If they're wise, old friend, you have nothing to fear."

"Yes," the priest agreed. "Sooner or later, wisdom wins through."

"Sooner or later," Vorgens agreed. "But in the meantime a terrible toll of bloodshed can take place. A lot of men—good men—can be sacrificed."

"The violent ones have had their day on Shinar," Sittas said. "Now it is time for a wiser man, a better man, to hold sway."

"I hope so," the Watchman said.

They reached the outer hatch and swung it open. The bright, yellow sun sent a shaft of warmth into the passageway. Outside, Vorgens could see the landing ship waiting to take him up to an orbiting starship and then back to Earth. Clanthas and several others were clustered by the base of the ship.

Vorgens clambered down the ladder to the ground, then helped Sittas navigate the metal rungs. He turned around to pick up his travel kit, and found Altai standing beside him. For the first time since he had met her, she was wearing a dress—simple, feminine, beautiful.

"I—I was wondering if I'd—get to see you," Vorgens said.

Sittas cleared his throat and announced, "I believe I'll chat with Clanthas for a moment. You two can join me there."

"Did you think I wouldn't come to see you off?" Altai asked, with a touch of mischief in the corners of her mouth.

"I wasn't certain if you'd get a chance to."

"I won't say goodbye," she said, "because I expect you to return to Shinar before the year is out."

"That might not be possible," Vorgens said quietly. "At any rate, you'll soon have other things to occupy your mind, without worrying about me. Merdon will be out of the hospital soon. By the end of the year, you might even be married."

"I don't think so," she said.

"We hardly know each other."

"We'll have a lot to talk about."

He grinned at her. "Yes, I suppose so. All right, I'll be back, then. One way or another."

They walked together toward the men at the ship. Within a few minutes Vorgens, Clanthas, and the others had boarded. Altai and Sittas stepped back and watched as the ship reverberated with power, took off majestically, and disappeared into the distant sky.

PART II

The Dueling
Machine

To Myron R. Lewis—Scholar, swordsman, friend and inventor of the dueling machine

I

The Perfect Warrior

Dulaq rode the slide to the upper pedestrian level, stepped off, and walked over to the railing. The city stretched out all around him—broad avenues thronged with busy people, pedestrian walks, vehicle thorough-fares, air cars gliding between the gleaming, towering buildings.

And somewhere in this vast city was the man he must kill. The man who would kill him, perhaps.

It all seemed so real! The noise of the streets, the odors of the perfumed trees lining the walks, even the warmth of the reddish sun on his back as he scanned the scene before him.

It is an illusion, Dulaq reminded himself. *A clever, man-made hallucination. A figment of my own imagina-tion amplified by a machine.*

But it seemed so very real.

Real or not, he had to find Odal before the sun set. Find him and kill him. Those were the terms of the duel.

He fingered the stubby, cylindrical stat-wand in his tunic pocket. That was the weapon that he had chosen, his weapon, his own invention. And this was the environment he had picked: his city, busy, noisy, crowded. The metropolis Dulaq had known and loved since childhood.

Dulaq turned and glanced at the sun. It was halfway down toward the horizon. He had about three hours to find Odal. And when he did—kill or be killed.

Of course no one is actually hurt. That is the beauty of the machine. It allows one to settle a score, to work out aggressive feelings, without either mental or physical harm.

Dulaq shrugged. He was a roundish figure, moon-faced, slightly stoop-shouldered. He had work to do. Unpleasant work for a civilized man, but the future of the Acquataine Cluster and the entire alliance of neighboring star systems could well depend on the outcome of this electronically synthesized dream.

He turned and walked down the elevated avenue, marveling at the sharp sensation of solidity that met each footstep on the paving. Children dashed by and rushed up to a toyshop window. Men of commerce strode along purposefully, but without missing a chance to eye the girls sauntering by.

I must have a marvelous imagination. Dulaq smiled to himself.

Then he thought of Odal, the blond, icy professional he was pitted against. Odal was an expert at all the weapons, a man of strength and cool precision, an emotionless tool in the hands of a ruthless politician. But how expert could he be with a stat-wand, when the first time he saw one was the moment before the duel began? And how well acquainted could he be with the metropolis, when he had spent most of his life in the military camps on the dreary planets of Kerak, sixty light-years from Acquatainia?

No, Odal would be helpless and lost in this situation.

He would attempt to hide among the throngs of people. All Dulaq had to do was to find him.

The terms of the duel limited both men to the pedestrian walks of the commercial quarter of the city. Dulaq knew this area intimately, and he began a methodical search through the crowds for the tall, fair-haired, blue-eyed Odal.

And he saw him! After only a few minutes of walking down the major thoroughfare, he spotted his opponent, strolling calmly along a cross walk, at the level below. Dulaq hurried down the ramp, worked his way through the crowd, and saw the man again, tall and blond, unmistakable. Dulaq edged along behind him quietly, easily. No disturbance. No pushing. Plenty of time. They walked down the street for a quarter-hour while the distance between them slowly shrank from fifty meters to five.

Finally Dulaq was directly behind him, within arm's reach. He grasped the stat-wand and pulled it from his tunic. With one quick motion he touched it to the base of the man's skull and started to thumb the button that would release a killing bolt of energy.

The man turned suddenly. It wasn't Odal!

Dulaq jerked back in surprise. It couldn't be. He had seen his face. It was Odal ... and yet this man was a stranger. Dulaq felt the man's eyes on him as he turned and walked away quickly.

A mistake, he told himself. You were overanxious. A good thing this is a hallucination, or the autopolice would be taking you in by now.

And yet ... he had been so certain that it was Odal. A chill shuddered through him. He looked up, and there was his antagonist, on the thoroughfare above, at the precise spot where he himself had been a few minutes earlier. Their eyes met, and Odal's lips parted in a cold smile.

Dulaq hurried up the ramp. Odal was gone by the

time he reached the upper level. *He couldn't have gotten far.*

Slowly, but very surely, Dulaq's hallucination crumbled into a nightmare. He'd spot Odal in the crowd, only to have him melt away. He'd find him again, but when he'd get closer, it would turn out to be another stranger. He felt the chill of the duelist's ice-blue eyes on him again and again, but when he turned there was no one there except the impersonal crowd.

Odal's face appeared again and again. Dulaq struggled through the throngs to find his opponent, only to have him vanish. The crowd seemed to be filled with tall blond men crisscrossing before Dulaq's dismayed eyes.

The shadows lengthened. The sun was setting. Dulaq could feel his heart pounding within him, and perspiration pouring from every square centimeter of his skin.

There he is! Yes, that is him. Definitely, positively him! Dulaq pushed through the homeward-bound crowds toward the figure of a tall blond man leaning casually against the safety railing of the city's main thoroughfare. It was Odal, the damned smiling confident Odal.

Dulaq pulled the wand from his tunic and battled across the surging crowd to the spot where Odal stood motionless, hands in pockets, watching him dispassionately. Dulaq came within arm's reach. . . .

"TIME, GENTLEMEN. TIME IS UP. THE DUEL IS ENDED."

The Acquataine Cluster was a rich jewel box of some three hundred stars, just outside the borders of the Terran Commonwealth. More than a thousand inhabited planets circled those stars. The capital planet— Acquatainia—held the Cluster's largest city. In this city was the Cluster's oldest university. And in the university stood the dueling machine.

High above the floor of the antiseptic-white chamber that housed the dueling machine was a narrow gallery.

Before the machine had been installed, the chamber had been a lecture hall in the university. Now the rows of students' seats, the lecturer's dais and rostrum were gone. The room held only the machine, a grotesque collection of consoles, control desks, power units, association circuits, and the two booths where the duelists sat.

In the gallery—empty during ordinary duels—sat a privileged handful of newsmen.

"Time limit's up," one of them said. "Dulaq didn't get him."

"Yeah, but he didn't get Dulaq either."

The first one shrugged. "Now he'll have to fight Odal on *his* terms."

"Wait, they're coming out."

Down on the floor below, Dulaq and his opponent emerged from their enclosed booths.

One of the newsmen whistled softly. "Look at Dulaq's face . . . it's positively gray."

"I've never seen the Prime Minister so shaken."

"And take a look at Kanus' hired assassin." The newsmen turned toward Odal, who stood before his booth, quietly chatting with his seconds.

"Hmp. There's a bucket of frozen ammonia for you."

"He's enjoying this."

One of the newsmen stood up. "I've got a deadline to meet. Save my seat."

He made his way past the guarded door, down the rampway circling the outer wall of the building, to the portable tri-di camera unit that the Acquatainian government had permitted for the newsmen to make their reports.

The newsman huddled with his technicians for a few minutes, then stepped before the camera.

"Emile Dulaq, Prime Minister of the Acquataine Cluster and acknowledged leader of the coalition against Chancellor Kanus of the Kerak Worlds, has failed in the first part of his psychonic duel against Major Par Odal of Kerak. The two antagonists are now undergoing the routine medical and psychological checks before renewing their duel. . . ."

By the time the newsman returned to his gallery seat, the duel was almost ready to begin again.

Dulaq stood in the midst of his group of advisers before the looming impersonality of the machine. Across the way, Odal remained with his two seconds.

"You needn't go through with the next phase of the duel immediately," one of the Prime Minister's advisers was saying. "Wait until tomorrow. Rest and calm yourself."

Dulaq's round face puckered into a frown. He cocked an eye at the chief meditech, hovering on the edge of the little group.

The meditech, one of the staff that ran the dueling machine, pointed out, "The Prime Minister has passed the examinations. He is capable, within the rules of the duel, of resuming."

"But he has the option of retiring for the day, doesn't he?"

"If Major Odal agrees."

Dulaq shook his head impatiently. "No. I shall go through with it. Now."

"But. . . ."

The Prime Minister's expression hardened. His advisers lapsed into a respectful silence. The chief meditech ushered Dulaq back into his booth. On the other side of the machine, Odal glanced at the Acquatainians, grinned humorlessly, and strode into his own booth.

Dulaq sat and tried to blank out his mind while the meditechs adjusted the neurocontacts to his head and torso. They finished and withdrew. He was alone in the booth now, looking at the dead-white walls, completely bare except for the large viewscreen before his eyes. The screen began to glow slightly, then brightened into a series of shifting colors. The colors merged and changed, swirling across his field of view. Dulaq felt himself being drawn into them, gradually, compellingly, completely immersed in them. . . .

The mists slowly vanished and Dulaq found himself standing on an immense and totally barren plain. Not a tree, not a blade of grass; nothing but bare, rocky ground stretching in all directions to the horizon and a disturbingly harsh yellow sky. He looked down at his feet and saw the weapon that Odal had chosen. A primitive club.

With a sense of dread, Dulaq picked up the club and hefted it in his hand. He scanned the plain. Nothing. No hills or trees or bushes to hide in. No place to run to.

And off on the horizon he could see a tall, lithe figure holding a similar club walking slowly and deliberately toward him.

The press gallery was practically empty. The duel had more than an hour to run, and most of the newsmen were outside, broadcasting their hastily drawn guesses about Dulaq's failure to win with his own choice of weapons and environment.

Then a curious thing happened.

On the master control panel of the dueling machine, a single light flashed red. The chief meditech blinked at it in surprise, then pressed a series of buttons on his board. More red lights appeared. The chief meditech reached out and flipped a single switch.

One of the newsmen turned to his partner. "What's going on down there?"

"I think it's all over. . . . Yeah, look, they're opening up the booths. Somebody's scored a win."

"But who?"

They watched intently while the other newsmen quickly filed back into the gallery.

"There's Odal. He looks happy."

"Guess that means. . . ."

."Good lord! Look at Dulaq!"

More than two thousand light-years from Acquatainia was the star cluster called Carinae. Although it was an even greater distance away from Earth, Carinae was still well within the confines of the mammoth Terran Commonwealth. Dr. Leoh, inventor of the dueling machine, was lecturing at the Carinae University when the news of Dulaq's duel reached him. An assistant professor perpetrated the unthinkable breach of interrupting the lecture to whisper the news in his ear.

Leoh nodded grimly, hurriedly finished his lecture, and then accompanied the assistant professor to the university president's office. They stood in silence as the slideway whisked them through the strolling students and blossoming greenery of the quietly busy campus.

Leoh was balding and jowly, the oldest man at the university. The oldest man anyone in the university knew, for that matter. But his face was creased from a smile that was almost habitual, and his eyes were active and alert. He wasn't smiling, though, as they left the slideway and entered the administration building.

They rode the lift tube to the president's office. Leoh asked the assistant professor as they stepped through the president's open doorway, "You say he was in a state of catatonic shock when they removed him from the machine?"

"He still is," the president answered from his desk. "Completely withdrawn from the real world. Cannot speak, hear, or even see. A living vegetable."

Leoh plopped down in the nearest chair and ran a hand across his fleshy face. "I don't understand it. Nothing like this has ever happened in a dueling machine before."

The president said, "I don't understand it either. But, this is your business." He put a slight emphasis on the last word, unconsciously perhaps.

"Well, at least this won't reflect on the university. That's why I formed Psychonics as a separate business enterprise." Then Leoh grinned and added, "The money, of course, was only a secondary consideration."

The president managed a smile. "Of course."

"I suppose the Acquatainians want to talk to me?" Leoh asked academically.

"They're on tri-di now, waiting for you."

"They're holding a transmission frequency open over two thousand light-years?" Leoh looked impressed.

"You're the inventor of the dueling machine and the head of Psychonics, Incorporated. You're the only man who can tell them what went wrong."

"Well, I suppose I shouldn't keep them waiting."

"You can take the call here," the president said, starting to get up from his chair.

"No, no, stay at your desk," Leoh insisted. "There's no need for you to leave. Or you either," he added to the assistant professor.

The president touched a button on his desk communicator. The far wall of the office glowed momentarily, then seemed to dissolve. They were looking into another office, this one in distant Acquatainia. It was crowded with nervous-looking men in business clothes and military uniforms.

"Gentlemen," Dr. Leoh said.

Several of the Acquatainians tried to answer him at once. After a few seconds of talking simultaneously, they all looked toward one of their members—a tall, determined, shrewd-looking civilian who bore a neatly trimmed black beard.

"I am Fernd Massan, the Acting Prime Minister of Acquatainia. You realize, of course, the crisis that has been precipitated in my government because of this duel?"

Leoh blinked. "I realize that there's apparently been

some difficulty with one of the dueling machines installed in your cluster. Political crises are not in my field."

"But your dueling machine had incapacitated the Prime Minister," one of the generals bellowed.

"And at this particular moment," a minister added, "in the midst of our difficulties with the Kerak Worlds."

Massan gestured them to silence.

"The dueling machine," Leoh said calmly, "is nothing more than a psychonic device . . . it's no more dangerous than a tri-di communicator. It merely allows two men to share a dream world that they create together. They can do anything they want to in their dream world—settle an argument as violently as they wish, and neither of them is physically hurt any more than a normal dream can hurt you physically. Men can use the dueling machine as an outlet for their aggressive feelings, for their tensions and hatreds, without hurting themselves or their society.

"Your own government tested one of the machines and approved its use on Acquatainia more than three years ago. I see several of you who were among those to whom I personally demonstrated the machine. Dueling machines are becoming commonplace through wide portions of the Terran Commonwealth, and neighboring nations such as Acquatainia. I'm sure that many of you have used the machine yourselves. You have, General, I'm certain."

The general flustered. "That has nothing to do with the matter at hand!"

"Admittedly," Leoh conceded. "But I don't understand how a therapeutic machine can possibly become entangled in a political crisis."

Massan said, "Allow me to explain. Our government has been conducting extremely delicate negotiations with the governments of our neighboring star-nations. These negotiations concern the rearmament of the Kerak Worlds. You have heard of Kanus of Kerak?"

"Vaguely," Leoh said. "He's a political leader of some sort."

"Of the worst sort. He has acquired complete dictatorship of the Kerak Worlds and is now attempting to rearm them for war. This is in direct contravention of the Treaty of Acquatainia, signed only thirty Terran years ago."

"I see. The treaty was signed at the end of the Acquataine-Kerak War, wasn't it?"

"A war that we won," the general pointed out.

"And now the Kerak Worlds want to rearm and try again," Leoh said.

"Precisely."

Leoh shrugged. "Why not call in the Star Watch? This is their type of police activity. And what has all this to do with the dueling machine?"

"Let me explain," Massan said patiently. He gestured to an aide, and on the wall behind him a huge tri-di star map glowed into life.

Leoh recognized it immediately: the swirling spiral of the Milky Way galaxy. From the rim of the galaxy, where the Sun and Earth were, in toward the star-rich heart of the Milky Way, stretched the Terran Commonwealth—thousands of stars and myriads of planets. On Massan's map the Commonwealth territory was shaded a delicate green. Just beyond its border was the golden cluster of Acquatainia. Around it were names that Leoh knew only vaguely: Safad, Szarno, Etra, and a pinpoint marked Kerak.

"Neither the Acquataine Cluster nor our neighboring nations," said Massan, "have ever joined the Terran Commonwealth. Nor has Kerak, for that matter. Therefore the Star Watch can intervene only if all the nations concerned agree to intervention. Naturally Kanus would never accept the Star Watch. He *wants* to rearm."

Leoh shook his head.

"As for the dueling machine," Massan went on, "Kanus has turned it into a political weapon. . . ."

"But that's impossible. Your government passed strict laws concerning the use of the machines. The dueling machine may be used only for personal grievances. It's strictly outside the realm of politics."

Massan shook his head sadly. "My dear Professor, laws are one thing, people are another. And politics consists of people, not words on tape."

"I don't understand," said Leoh.

"A little more than one Terran year ago, Kanus picked a quarrel with a neighboring nation—the Safad Federation. He wanted an especially favorable trade agreement with them. Their minister of trade objected most strenuously. One of the Kerak negotiators—a certain Major Odal—got into a personal argument with the minister. Before anyone knew what had happened, they had challenged each other to a duel. Odal won the duel, and the minister resigned his post. He said he could no longer fight against the will of Odal and Kerak . . . he was psychologically incapable of it. Two weeks later he was dead—apparently a suicide, although I have my doubts."

"That's . . . extremely interesting," Leoh said.

"Three days ago," Massan continued, "the same Major Odal engaged Prime Minister Dulaq in a bitter personal argument. Odal is now a military attache of the Kerak embassy here on Acquatainia. The argument grew so loud before a large group at an embassy party that the prime minister had no alternative but to challenge Odal. And now. . . ."

"And now Dulaq is in a state of shock, and your government is tottering."

Massan's back stiffened. "Our government will not fall, nor shall the Acquataine Cluster acquiesce to the rearmament of the Kerak Worlds. But . . ." his voice lowered, "without Dulaq, our alliances with neighboring nations may dissolve. All our allies are smaller and weaker than

Acquatainia. Kanus could pressure each one individually and make certain that they won't take steps to prevent his rearming Kerak. Alone, Acquatainia cannot stop Kanus."

"But if Kerak attacks you, surely you could ask the Star Watch for help and. . . ."

"It won't be that simple or clear-cut. Kanus will nibble off one small nation at a time. He can strike a blow and conquer a nation before the Star Watch can be summoned. Finally he'll have us cut off completely, without a single ally. Then he'll strike Acquatainia, or perhaps even try to subvert us from within. If he takes Acquatainia, he'll have whetted his appetite for bigger game: he'll want to conquer the Terran Commonwealth next. He'll stop at nothing."

"And he's using the dueling machines to further his ambitions," Leoh mused. "Well, gentlemen, it seems I have no alternative but to travel to the Acquataine Cluster. The dueling machine is my responsibility, and if there's something wrong with it, or with the use of it, I'll do my best to correct the situation."

"That is all we ask," Massan said. "Thank you."

The Acquatainian scene faded away, and the three men in the president's office found themselves looking at a solid wall once again.

"Well," Leoh said, turning to the president, "it seems that I must request an indefinite leave of absence."

The president frowned. "And it seems that I must grant it—even though the year isn't even half-finished."

"I regret the necessity," said Leoh. Then, with a broad grin, he added, "My assistant, here, can handle my courses for the remainder of the year quite easily. Perhaps he'll even be able to deliver his lectures without being interrupted."

The assistant professor turned red from collar to scalp.

"Now then," Leoh muttered to himself, "who is this Kanus, and why is he trying to turn the Kerak Worlds into an arsenal?"

*   *   *

Chancellor Kanus, Supreme Leader of the Kerak Worlds, stood at the edge of the balcony and looked across the wild, tumbling gorge to the rugged mountains beyond.

"These are the forces that mold men's actions," he said to his small audience of officials and advisers. "The howling winds, the mighty mountains, the open sky, and the dark powers of the clouds."

The men nodded and made murmurs of agreement.

"Just as the mountains thrust up from the pettiness of the lands below, so shall we rise above the common walk of men," Kanus said. "Just as a thunderstorm terrifies them, we will make them cower and bend to our will."

"We will destroy the past," said one of the ministers.

"And avenge the memory of defeat," Kanus added. He turned and looked at the little group of men. Kanus was the smallest man on the balcony: short, spare, sallow-faced. His gaudy military uniform looked out of place on him, too big and heavy, too loaded with braid and medals. But he possessed piercing dark eyes and a strong voice that commanded attention.

He walked through the knot of men and stopped before a tall, lean, blond youth in a light-blue military uniform. "And you, Major Odal, will be a primary instrument in the first steps of conquest."

Odal bowed stiffly. "I only hope to serve my Leader and my Worlds."

"You shall. And you already have," Kanus said, beaming. "Already the Acquatainians are thrashing about like a snake whose head has been cut off. Without Dulaq, they have no brain to direct them. For your part in this triumph . . ." Kanus snapped his fingers, and one of his advisers quickly stepped to his side and handed him a small ebony box, "I present you with this token of the esteem of the Kerak Worlds, and of my personal high regard."

He handed the box to Odal, who opened it and took out a small jeweled pin.

"The Star of Kerak," Kanus announced. "This is the first time it has been awarded to anyone except a warrior on the battlefield. But, then, we have turned their so-called civilized dueling machine into our own battlefield, eh?"

Odal smiled. "Yes, sir, we have. Thank you very much, sir. This is the supreme moment of my life."

"To date, Major. Only to date. There will be other moments, even higher ones. Come inside. We have many plans to discuss . . . more duels . . . more triumphs."

They all filed into Kanus' huge, elaborate office. The Leader walked across the plushly ornate room and sat at the elevated desk, while his followers arranged themselves on the chairs and couches placed about the floor. Odal remained standing, near the doorway.

Kanus let his fingers flick across a small control board set into his desk top, and a tri-dimensional star map appeared on the far wall. At its center were the eleven stars of the Kerak Worlds. Off to one side of the map was the Acquataine Cluster—wealthy, powerful, the most important political and economic power in this section of the galaxy. Farther away from Kerak, the slimmest edge of the Terran Commonwealth showed; to put the entire Commonwealth on the map would have dwarfed Acquatainia and made Kerak microscopic.

Pointing at the map, Kanus began one of his inevitable harangues. Objectives, political and military. Already the Kerak Worlds were unified under his dominant will. The people would follow wherever he led. Already the political alliances built up by Acquatainian diplomacy since the last war were tottering, now that Dulaq was out of the picture. Kerak was beginning to rearm. A political blow *here*, at the Szarno Confederacy, to bring them and their armaments industries into line with Kerak. Then a diplomatic alliance with the Etra Domain, which stood between the Acquataine Cluster and the Terran

Commonwealth, to isolate the Acquatainians. Then, finally, the military blow against Acquatainia.

"A sudden strike, a quick, decisive series of blows, and the Acquatainians will collapse like a house of paper. Even if the Star Watch wanted to interfere, we would be victorious before they could bring help to the Acquataine Cluster. And with the resources of Acquatainia to draw on, we can challenge any force in the galaxy—even the Terran Commonwealth itself!"

The men in the room nodded and smiled.

They've heard this story many times, Odal thought. This was the first time he had been privileged to listen to it. If you closed your eyes, or looked only at the star map, the plan sounded bizarre, extreme, even impossible. But if you watched Kanus and let those piercing, almost hypnotic eyes fasten on yours, then the Leader's wildest dreams sounded not only exciting, but inevitable.

Odal leaned a shoulder against the paneled wall and looked at the other men in the room.

There was fat Greber, the Vice Chancellor, fighting desperately to stay awake after drinking too much wine during luncheon and afterward. And Modal, sitting on the couch next to him, was bright-eyed and alert, thinking only of how much money and power would come to him as Minister of Industry once the rearmament program went into full speed.

Sitting alone on another couch was Kor, the quiet one, the head of Intelligence and—technically—Odal's superior. Silent Kor, whose few words were usually charged with terror for those whom he spoke against. Kor had an unfathomed capacity for cruelty.

Marshal Lugal looked bored when Kanus spoke of politics, but his face changed when military matters came up. The Marshal lived for only one purpose: to avenge his army's humiliating defeat in the war against Acquatainia. What he didn't realize, Odal knew, was that as soon as he had reorganized the army and re-equipped it,

Kanus planned to retire him and place younger men in charge. Men whose only loyalty was not to the army, nor even to the Kerak Worlds and their people, but to the Leader himself.

Eagerly following every syllable, every gesture of the Leader, was little Tinth. Born to the nobility, trained in the arts, a student of philosophy, Tinth had deserted his heritage to join the forces of Kanus. His reward was the Ministry of Education. Many teachers had suffered under him.

And finally there was Romis, the Minister of Foreign Affairs. A professional diplomat, one of the few men in government before Kanus' sweep to power who had survived this long. It was clear that Romis hated the Chancellor. But he served the Kerak Worlds well. The diplomatic corps was flawless in their handling of the Safad trade treaty, although they would have gotten nowhere without Odal's own work in the dueling machine. It was only a matter of time, Odal knew, before one of them—Romis or Kanus—killed the other.

The rest of Kanus' audience consisted of political hacks, roughnecks-turned-bodyguards, and a few other hangers-on who had been with Kanus since the days when he held his political monologues in cellars and haunted the alleys to avoid the police. Kanus had come a long way: from the blackness of oblivion to the dazzling heights of the Chancellor's rural estate.

Money, power, glory, revenge, patriotism: each man in the room, listening to Kanus, had his reason for following the Chancellor.

And my reasons? Odal asked himself. *Why do I follow? Can I see into my own mind as easily as I see into theirs?*

There was duty, of course. Odal was a soldier, and Kanus was the duly elected Leader of the government. Once elected, though, he had dissolved the government

and solidified his powers as absolute dictator of the Kerak
Worlds.

There was gain to be had by performing well under
Kanus. Regardless of his political ambitions and personal
tyrannies, Kanus rewarded well when pleased. The
medal—the Star of Kerak—carried with it an annual pension that would nicely accommodate a family. *If I had
one*, Odal thought sardonically.

There was a power, of sorts, also. Working the dueling
machine in his special way, hammering a man into nothingness, finding the weaknesses in his personality and
exploiting them, pitting his mind against others, turning
sneering towers of pride like Dulaq into helpless
whipped dogs—that was power. And it was a power that
did not go unnoticed in Kerak. Already Odal was easily
recognized on the streets; girls especially seemed to be
attracted to him now.

"The most important factor," Kanus was saying, "and
I cannot stress it too heavily, is to build up an aura of
invincibility. This is why your work is so important, Major
Odal. You must be invincible! Because you represent the
will of the Kerak Worlds. You are the instrument of my
will, and you must triumph at every turn. The fate of
your people and your Chancellor rests squarely on your
shoulders each time you step into a dueling machine.
You have borne that responsibility well, Major. Can you
carry it even further?"

"I can, sir," Odal answered crisply, "and I will."

Kanus beamed at him. "Excellent! Because your next
duel—and those that follow it—will be to the death."

It took the star ship two weeks to make the journey
from Carinae to the Acquataine Cluster. Dr. Leoh spent
the time checking over the Acquatainian dueling
machine, by direct tri-di communication link. The Acquatainian government gave him all the technicians and time
he needed for the task.

Leoh spent as much of his spare time as possible with the other passengers of the ship. They were all enormously wealthy, as star-ship travelers had to be, or else they were traveling on government business—and expense. He was gregarious, a fine conversationalist, and had a nicely balanced sense of humor. Particularly, he was a favorite of the younger women, since he had reached the age where he could flatter them with his attention without making them feel endangered. But still, there were long hours when he was alone in his stateroom with nothing but memories. At times like these, it was impossible not to think back over the road he had been following.

Albert Robertus Leoh, Ph.D., professor of physics, professor of electronics, master of computer technology, inventor of the interstellar tri-di communications system. And more recently, student of psychology, professor of psychophysiology, founder of Psychonics, Incorporated, inventor of the dueling machine.

During his youthful years, with enthusiasm unbridled by experience, Leoh had envisioned himself as helping mankind to spread its colonies and civilizations throughout the galaxy. The bitter century of galactic war had ended in his childhood, and now human societies were linked together across the stars into a more-or-less peaceful coalition of nations.

There were two great motivating forces at work on those human societies, and these forces worked toward opposite goals. On the one hand was the urge to explore, to reach new stars, new planets, to expand the frontiers of man's civilizations and found new colonies, new nations. Pitted against this drive to expand was an equally powerful force: the realization that technology had put an end to physical labor and almost to poverty itself on all the civilized worlds of man. The urge to move off to the frontier was penned in and buried alive under the enervating comforts of civilization.

The result was inescapable. The civilized worlds became constantly more crowded. They became jam-packed islands of humanity sprinkled thinly across a sea of space that was still studded with unpopulated islands. The expense and difficulty of interstellar travel was often cited as an excuse. The star ships *were* expensive: their power demands were frightful. They could be used for business, for the pleasure of the very rich, for government travel; but hauling whole colonies of farmers and workers was almost completely out of the question. Only the most determined (and best financed) groups of colonists could afford them. The rest of mankind accepted the ease and safety of civilization, lived in the bulging cities of the teeming planets.

Their lives were circumscribed by their neighbors and by their governments. Constantly more people crowded into a fixed living space meant constantly less freedom. The freedom to dream, to run free, to procreate, all became state-owned, state-controlled privileges.

And Leoh had contributed to this situation.

He had contributed his thoughts and his work. He had contributed often and regularly. The interstellar communications system was only one outstanding achievement in a long career of achievements.

Leoh had been nearly at the voluntary retirement age for scientists when he realized what he and his fellow scientists had done. Their efforts to make life richer and more rewarding had only made it less strenuous and more rigid. With every increase in physical comfort, Leoh discovered, came a corresponding increase in spiritual discomfort—in neuroses, in crimes of violence, in mental aberrations. Senseless wars of pride broke out between star-nations for the first time in generations. Outwardly, the peace of the galaxy was assured except for minor flare-ups; but beneath the glossy surface of man's civilization smoldered the beginnings of a volcano. Police actions fought by the Star Watch were increasing ominously. Petty wars between once-stable peoples were flaring up steadily.

Once Leoh realized the part he had played in all this, he was confronted with two emotions: a deep sense of guilt, both personal and professional; and, countering this, a determination to do something, anything, to restore at least some balance to man's collective mentality.

Leoh stepped out of physics and electronics, and entered the field of psychology. Instead of retiring, he applied for a beginner's status in his new profession. It took considerable bending and straining of the Commonwealth's rules, but for a man of Leoh's stature the rules could sometimes be flexed a little. Leoh became a student once again, then a researcher, and finally a professor of psychophysiology.

Out of this came the dueling machine. A combination of electroencephalograph and autocomputer. A dream machine that amplified a man's imagination until he could engulf himself in a world of his own making. Leoh envisioned it as a device to enable men to rid themselves of hostility and tension, safely. Certainly psychiatrists and psychotechnicians used the machines to treat their patients. But Leoh saw further, saw that—as a *dueling* machine—the psychonic device could be used to prevent mental tensions and disorders. And he convinced many governments to install dueling machines for that purpose.

When two men had a severe difference of opinion, deep enough to warrant legal action, they could go to the dueling machine instead of the courts. Instead of passively watching the machinations of the law grind impersonally through their differences, they could allow their imaginations free rein in the dueling machine. They could settle the argument as violently as they wished, without hurting themselves or anyone else. On most civilized worlds, the results of properly monitored duels were accepted as legally binding.

The tensions of civilized life could be escaped—temporarily—in the dueling machine. This was a powerful tool, much too powerful to allow it to be used indiscriminately. Therefore Leoh safeguarded his invention by forming a private company, Psychonics, Incorporated, and securing an exclusive license from the Terran Commonwealth to manufacture, sell, install, and maintain the machines. His customers were government health and legal agencies. His responsibilities were: legally, to the Commonwealth; morally, to all mankind; and finally to his own restless conscience.

The dueling machines succeeded. They worked as well, and often better, than Leoh had anticipated. But he knew that they were only a stopgap, only a temporary shoring of a constantly eroding dam. What was needed, really needed, was some method of exploding the status quo, some means of convincing people to reach out for those unoccupied, unexplored stars that filled the galaxy, some way of convincing men that they should leave the comforts of civilization for the excitement and freedom of new lands.

Leoh had been searching for that method when the news of Dulaq's duel had reached him. Now he was speeding across light-years of space, praying to himself that the dueling machine had not failed.

The two-week flight ended. The star ship took up a parking orbit around the capital planet of the Acquataine Cluster. The passengers trans-shipped to the surface.

Dr. Leoh was met at the landing disk by an official delegation, headed by Massan, the Acting Prime Minister. They exchanged formal greetings at the base of the ship while the other passengers hurried by, curious, puzzled. As they rode the slideway toward a private entrance to the spaceport's administration building, Leoh commented:

"As you probably know, I have checked your dueling machine quite thoroughly via tri-di for the past two weeks. I can find nothing wrong with it."

Massan shrugged. "Perhaps you should have checked the machine on Szarno instead."

"The Szarno Confederation? Their dueling machine?"

"Yes. This morning, Kanus' assassin killed a man in it."

"He won another duel," Leoh said.

"You do not understand," Massan said grimly. "Major Odal's opponent—an industrialist who had spoken out against Kanus—was actually killed in the dueling machine. The man is dead!"

One of the advantages of being Commander in Chief of the Star Watch, the old man thought to himself, is that you can visit any planet in the Commonwealth.

He stood at the top of the hill and looked out over the grassy tableland of Kenya. This was the land of his birth, Earth was his home world. The Star Watch's official headquarters was in the heart of a star cluster much closer to the center of the Commonwealth, but Earth was the place the Commander wanted most to see as he grew older and wearier.

An aide, who had been following the Commander at a respectful distance, suddenly intruded himself in the old man's reverie.

"Sir, a message for you."

The Commander scowled at the young officer. "Didn't I give express orders that I was not to be disturbed?"

The officer, slim and stiff in his black-and-silver uniform, replied, "Your chief of staff passed the message on to you, sir. It's from Dr. Leoh of Carinae University. Personal and urgent, sir."

The old man grumbled to himself, but nodded. The

aide placed a small crystalline sphere on the grass before the Commander. The air above the sphere started to vibrate and glow.

"Sir Harold Spencer here," the Commander said.

The bubbling air seemed to draw in on itself and take solid form. Dr. Leoh sat at a desk chair and looked up at the standing Commander.

"Harold, it's a pleasure to see you again," Leoh said, getting up from the chair.

Spencer's stern eyes softened and his beefy face broke into a well-creased smile. "Albert, you ancient sorcerer. What do you mean by interrupting my first visit home in fifteen years?"

"It won't be a long interruption," Leoh said. "I merely want to inform you of something. . . ."

"You told my chief of staff that it was urgent," Sir Harold groused.

"It is. But it's not the sort of problem that requires much action on your part. Yet. Are you familiar with recent political developments on the Kerak Worlds?"

Spencer snorted. "I know that a barbarian named Kanus has taken over as dictator. He's a troublemaker. I've been trying to get the Commonwealth Council to let us quash him before he causes grief, but you know the Council . . . first wait until the flames have sprung up, then wail at the Star Watch to do something!"

Grinning, Leoh said, "You're as irascible as ever."

"My personality is not the subject of this rather expensive discussion. What about Kanus? And what are you doing, getting yourself involved in politics? About to change your profession again?"

"No, not at all," Leoh answered with a laugh. Then, more seriously, "It seems that Kanus has discovered a method of using the dueling machine to achieve political advantages over his neighbors."

Leoh explained the circumstances of Odal's duels with Dulaq and the Szarno industrialist.

"Dulaq is completely incapacitated and the other poor fellow is dead?" Spencer's face darkened into a thundercloud. "You were right to call me. This is a situation that could quickly become intolerable."

"I agree," said Leoh. "But evidently Kanus hasn't broken any laws or interstellar agreements. All that meets the eye is a disturbing pair of accidents, both of them accruing to Kanus' benefit."

"Do *you* believe they were accidents?"

"Certainly not. The dueling machine can't cause physical or mental harm ... unless someone's tampered with it in some way."

Spencer was silent for a moment, weighing the matter in his mind. "Very well. The Star Watch cannot act officially, but there's nothing to prevent me from dispatching an officer to the Acquataine Cluster on detached duty, to serve as liaison between us."

"Good. I think that will be the most effective way of handling the situation, at present."

"It will be done."

Sir Harold's aide made a mental note of it.

"Thanks very much," Leoh said. "Now go back to enjoying your vacation."

"Vacation? This is no vacation. I happen to be celebrating my birthday."

"So? Well, congratulations. I try not to remember mine," said Leoh.

"Then you must be older than I," Spencer replied, allowing only the faintest hint of a smile to appear.

"I suppose it's possible."

"But not very likely, eh?"

They laughed together and said goodbye. The Star Watch Commander tramped through the grassland until sunset, enjoying the sight of the greenery and the distant purple mountains he had known from childhood. As dusk closed in, he told the aide he was ready to leave.

The aide pressed a stud on his belt and a two-place

air car skimmed silently from the far side of the hills and hovered beside them. Spencer climbed in laboriously while the aide stayed discreetly at his side. As the Commander settled his bulk into his seat the aide hurried around the car and hopped into his place. The car glided off toward Spencer's planet ship, waiting for him at a nearby field.

"Don't forget to assign an officer to Dr. Leoh," Spencer muttered to his aide. Then he turned to watch the unmatchable beauty of an Earthly sunset.

The aide did not forget the assignment. That night, as Sir Harold's ship spiraled out to a rendezvous with a star ship, the aide dictated the necessary order to an autodispatcher that immediately beamed it to the Star Watch's nearest communications center, on Mars.

The order was scanned and routed automatically and finally beamed to the Star Watch unit commandant in charge of the area closest to the Acquataine Cluster, on the sixth planet circling the star Perseus Alpha. Here again the order was processed automatically and routed through the local headquarters to the personnel files. The automated files selected three microcard dossiers that matched the requirements of the order.

The three microcards and the order itself appeared simultaneously on the desk-top viewer of the Star Watch personnel officer at Perseus Alpha VI. He looked at the order, then read the dossiers. He flicked a button that gave him an updated status report on each of the three men in question. One was due for leave after an extended period of duty. The second was the son of a personal friend of the local commandant. The third had just arrived a few weeks ago, fresh from the Star Watch Academy.

The personnel officer selected the third man, routed his dossier and Sir Harold's order back into the automatic processing system, and returned to the film of primitive dancing girls that he had been watching before this matter of decision had arrived at his desk.

The space station that orbited Acquatainia's capital planet served simultaneously as a transfer point from star ships to planet ships, a tourist resort, meteorological station, scientific laboratory, communications center, astronomical observatory, medical haven for allergy and cardiac patients, and military base. It was, in reality, a good-sized city with its own markets, government, and way of life.

Dr. Leoh had just stepped off the debarking ramp of the star ship from Szarno. The trip there had been pointless and fruitless. But he had gone anyway, in the slim hope that he might find something wrong with the dueling machine that had been used to murder a man. A shudder went through him as he edged through the automated customs scanners and identification checkers. What kind of people could these men of Kerak be? To actually kill a human being deliberately. To purposely plan the death of a fellow man. Worse than barbaric. Savage.

He felt tired as he left customs and took the slideway to the planetary shuttle ships. Even the civilized hubbub of travelers and tourists was bothering him, despite the sound-deadening plastics of the slideway corridor. He decided to check at the communications desk for messages. That Star Watch officer that Sir Harold had promised him a week ago should have arrived by now.

The communications desk consisted of a small booth that contained the output printer of a computer and an attractive dark-haired girl. Automation or not, Leoh decided, no machine can replace a girl's smile.

A lanky, thin-faced youth was half-leaning on the booth's counter, his legs crossed nervously. He was trying to talk to the girl. He had curly blond hair and crystal blue eyes; his clothes consisted of an ill-fitting pair of slacks and a tunic. A small traveler's kit rested on the floor by his feet.

"So, I was sort of, well, thinking ... maybe somebody might, uh, show me around ... a little," he was stammering to the girl. "I've never been, uh here ... I mean, on Acquatainia, that is ... before...."

"It's the most beautiful planet in the galaxy," said the girl. "Its cities are the finest."

"Yes ... well, I was sort of thinking ... that is, maybe you ... eh...."

She smiled coolly. "I very seldom leave the station. There's so much to see and do here."

"Oh...."

"You're making a mistake," Leoh interrupted. "If you have such a beautiful planet for your home world, why in the name of the gods of intellect don't you go down there and enjoy it? I'll wager you haven't been out in the natural beauty and fine cities you spoke of since you started working here at the station."

"Why, you're right," she said, surprised.

"You see? You youngsters are all alike. You never think further than the ends of your noses. You should return to the planet, young lady, and see the sunshine again. Why don't you visit the university at the capital city? Plenty of open space and greenery, lots of sunshine and available young men!"

Leoh was grinning broadly and the girl smiled back at him. "Perhaps I will," she said.

"Ask for me when you get to the university. I'm Dr. Leoh. I'll see to it that you're introduced to some of the students."

"Why ... thank you, Doctor. I'll do it this weekend."

"Good. Now then, any messages for me? Anyone aboard the station looking for me?"

The girl turned and tapped a few keys on the computer's control desk. A row of lights flicked briefly across the console's face. She turned back to Leoh:

"No, sir, I'm sorry. Nothing."

"Hmp. That's strange. Well, thank you. . . . And I'll expect to see you this weekend."

The girl smiled a farewell. Leoh started to walk away from the booth, back toward the slideway. The young man took a step toward him, stumbled on his own travel kit, and staggered across the floor for a half-dozen steps before regaining his balance. Leoh turned and saw that the youth's face bore a somewhat ridiculous expression of mixed indecision and curiosity.

"Can I help you?" Leoh asked, stopping at the edge of the slideway.

"How . . . how did you do that, sir?"

"Do what?"

"Get that girl to agree to visit the university. I've been, well, sort of talking to her for half an hour and she . . . uh, she wouldn't even look straight at me."

Leoh broke into a chuckle. "Well, young man, to begin with, you were much too flustered. It made you appear overanxious. On the other hand, I'm at an age where I can be fatherly. She was on guard against you, but not against me."

"I see . . . I think."

"Yes." Leoh gestured toward the slideway. "I suppose this is where we go our separate ways."

"Oh no, sir. I'm going with you. That is, I mean . . . you *are* Dr. Leoh, aren't you?"

"Yes, I am. And you must be. . . ." Leoh hesitated. *Can this be a Star Watch officer?* he wondered.

The youth stiffened to attention and for an absurd flash of a second Leoh thought he was going to salute. "Junior Lieutenant Hector, sir; on special detached duty from cruiser SW4–J188, home base Perseus Alpha VI."

"I see," Leoh replied. "Hmm . . . Is Hector your first name or your last?"

"Both, sir."

I should have guessed, Leoh told himself. Aloud, he

said, "All right, Lieutenant, we'd better get to the shuttle before it leaves without us."

They took to the slideway. Half a second later, Hector jumped off and dashed back to the communications booth for his travel kit. He hurried back to Leoh, bumping into seven bewildered citizens of various descriptions and nearly breaking both his legs when he tripped as he ran back onto the moving slideway. He went down on his face, sprawled across two lanes moving at different speeds, and needed the assistance of an elderly lady before he was again on his feet and standing beside Leoh.

"I . . . I'm sorry to cause all that, uh, commotion, sir."

"That's all right. You weren't hurt, were you?"

"Uh, no. . . . I don't think so. Just embarrassed."

Leoh said nothing. They rode the slideway in silence through the busy station and out to the enclosed berths where the planetary shuttles were docked. They boarded one of the ships and found a pair of seats.

"Just how long have you been with the Star Watch, Lieutenant?"

"Six weeks, sir. Three weeks aboard a star ship bringing me out to Perseus Alpha VI, a week at the planetary base there, and two weeks aboard the cruiser . . . um, SW4–J188, that is. The crew called her *Old Lardbucket* . . . after the captain, I think. Oh, I mean, six weeks since I received my commission. . . . I've been at the, uh, academy for four years."

"You got through the academy in four years?"

"That's the regulation time, sir."

"Yes, I know."

The ship eased out of its berth. There was a moment of free fall, then the drive engine came on and weight returned to the passenger cabin.

"Tell me, Lieutenant, how did you get picked for this assignment?"

"I wish I knew, sir," Hector said, his lean face wrinkling

into a puzzled frown. "I was working out a program for the navigation officer ... aboard the cruiser. I'm pretty good at that ... I can work out computer programs in my head, pretty much. Mathematics was my best subject at the academy."

"Interesting."

"Yes, well, anyway, I was working out this program when the captain himself came on deck and started shaking my hand and telling me that I was being sent on special duty at Acquatainia by direct orders of the Commander in Chief. He seemed very happy ... the captain, that is."

"He was probably pleased to see you get such an unusual assignment," said Leoh, tactfully.

"I'm not so sure," Hector answered truthfully. "I think he regarded me as ... well, some sort of a, um, problem. He had me on a different duty berth practically every day I was aboard the ship."

"Well now," Leoh changed the subject, "what do you know about psychonics?"

"About what, sir?"

"Er ... electroencephalography?"

Hector looked blank.

"Psychology, perhaps?" Leoh suggested hopefully. "Physiology? Computer molectronics?"

"I'm pretty good at mathematics!"

"Yes, I know. Did you, by any chance, receive any training in diplomatic affairs?"

"At the Star Watch Academy? No, sir."

Leoh ran a hand through his thinning hair. "Then why did the Star Watch select you for this job? I must confess, Lieutenant, that I can't understand the workings of a military organization."

Hector shook his head ruefully. "Neither do I, sir."

The next week was an enervatingly slow one for Leoh, evenly divided between a tedious checking of each component of the dueling machine, and shameless ruses to keep Hector as far away from the machine as possible.

The Star Watchman certainly wanted to help, and he actually was little short of brilliant in handling intricate mathematics completely in his head. But he was also, Leoh found, a clumsy, chattering, whistling, scatter-brained, inexperienced bundle of noise and nerves. It was impossible to do constructive work with him nearby.

Perhaps you're judging him too harshly, Leoh warned himself. *You might be letting your frustrations with the machine get the better of your sense of balance.*

The professor was sitting in the office that the Acquatainians had given him in one end of the former lecture hall that now held the dueling machine. Leoh could see its impassive metal hulk through the open office door. The room he was sitting in had been one of a suite of offices used by the permanent staff of the machine. But they had moved out of the building completely, in deference (or was it jealousy) to Leoh, and the Acquatainian government had turned the cubbyhole offices into living quarters for Leoh and the Star Watchman.

Leoh slouched back in his desk chair and cast a weary eye on the stack of papers that recorded the latest performance of the machine. Earlier that day he had taken the electroencephalographic records of clinical cases of catatonia and run them through the machine's input circuits. The machine immediately rejected them, refused to process them through the amplification units and association circuits. In other words, the machine had recognized the EEG traces as something harmful to human beings.

Then how did it happen to Dulaq? Leoh asked himself for the thousandth time. It couldn't have been the machine's fault; it must have been something in Odal's mind that overpowered Dulaq's.

"Overpowered?" *That's a terribly unscientific term,* Leoh argued against himself.

Before he could carry the debate any further, he heard the main door of the big chamber slide open and bang shut, and Hector's off-key whistle shrilled and echoed through the high-vaulted room.

Leoh sighed and put his self-contained argument off to the back of his mind. Trying to think logically near Hector was a hopeless prospect.

"Are you in, Professor?" the Star Watchman's voice rang out.

"In here."

Hector ducked in through the doorway and plopped his rangy frame on the couch.

"Everything going well, sir?"

Leoh shrugged. "Not very well, I'm afraid. I can't find anything wrong with the dueling machine. I can't even *force* it to malfunction."

"Well, that's good, isn't it?" Hector chirped happily.

"In a sense," Leoh admitted, feeling slightly nettled at the youth's boundless, pointless optimism. "But, you see, it means that Kanus' people can do things with the machine that I can't."

Hector considered the problem. "Hmm . . . yes, I guess that's right too, isn't it?"

"Did you see the girl back to her ship safely?" Leoh asked.

"Yessir," Hector replied, bobbing his head vigorously. "She's on her way back to the communications booth at the space station. She said to tell you thanks and she enjoyed the visit a lot."

"Good. It was very good of you to escort her around the campus. It kept her out of my hair . . . what's left of it, that is."

Hector grinned. "Oh, I liked taking her around and all that . . . and, well, it sort of kept *me* out of your hair too, didn't it?"

Leoh's eyebrows shot up in surprise.

Laughing, Hector said, "Professor, I may be clumsy,

and I'm sure no scientist ... but I'm not completely brainless."

"I'm sorry if I gave you that impression."

"Oh no ... don't be sorry. I didn't mean that to sound ... well, the way it sounded. . . . That is, I know I'm just in your way. . . ." He started to get up.

Leoh waved him back to the couch. "Relax, my boy, relax. You know, I've been sitting here all afternoon wondering what to do next. Somehow, just now, I've come to a conclusion."

"Yes?"

"I'm going to leave the Acquataine Cluster and return to Carinae."

"What? But you can't! I mean. . . ."

"Why not? I'm not accomplishing anything here. Whatever it is that this Odal and Kanus have been doing, it's basically a political problem, not a scientific one. The professional staff of the machine here will catch up to their tricks, sooner or later."

"But, sir, if you can't find the answer, how can they?"

"Frankly, I don't know. But, as I said, this is a political problem more than a scientific one. I'm tired and frustrated and I'm feeling my years. I want to return to Carinae and spend the next few months considering beautifully abstract problems such as instantaneous transportation devices. Let Massan and the Star Watch worry about Kanus."

"Oh! That's what I came to tell you. Massan has been challenged to a duel by Odal."

"What?"

"This afternoon. Odal went to the Capital building and picked an argument with Massan right in the main corridor and challenged him."

"Massan accepted?" Leoh asked.

Hector nodded.

Leoh leaned across his desk and reached for the phone. It took a few minutes and a few levels of secretaries and assistants, but finally Massan's dark, bearded face appeared on the screen above the desk.

"You've accepted Odal's challenge?" Leoh asked, without preliminaries.

"We meet next week," Massan replied gravely.

"You should have refused."

"On what pretext?"

"No pretext. A flat refusal, based on the certainty that Odal or someone else from Kerak is tampering with the dueling machine."

Massan shook his head sadly. "My dear learned sir, you do not comprehend the political situation. The government of Acquatainia is much closer to dissolution than I dare to admit publicly. The coalition of star-nations that Dulaq had constructed to keep Kerak neutralized has broken apart completely. Kerak is already arming. This morning, Kanus announced he would annex Szarno, with its enormous armaments industry. This afternoon, Odal challenges me."

"I think I see. . . ."

"Of course. The Acquataine government is paralyzed now, until the outcome of the duel is known. We cannot effectively intervene in the Szarno crisis until we know who will be heading the government next week. And, frankly, more than a few members of the Cabinet are now openly favoring Kanus and arguing that we should establish friendly relations with him before it is too late."

"But that's all the more reason for refusing the duel," Leoh insisted.

"And be accused of cowardice in my own Cabinet meetings?" Massan shook his head. "In politics, my dear sir, the *appearance* of a man means much—sometimes more than his substance. As a coward, I would soon be out of office. But, perhaps, as the winner of a duel against the invincible Odal . . . or even as a martyr . . . I may accomplish something useful."

Leoh said nothing.

Massan continued, "I put off the duel for a week, which is the longest time I dare to postpone. I hope that in that time you can discover Odal's secret. As it is, the political situation may collapse about our heads at any moment."

"I'll take the machine apart and rebuild it again, molecule by molecule," Leoh promised.

As Massan's image faded from the screen, Leoh turned to Hector. "We have one week to save his life."

"And, uh, maybe prevent a war," Hector added.

"Yes." Leoh leaned back in his chair and stared off into infinity.

Hector shuffled his feet, rubbed his nose, whistled a few bars of off-key tunes, and finally blurted, "How can you take apart the dueling machine?"

"Hmm?" Leoh snapped out of his reverie.

"How can you take apart the dueling machine?" Hector repeated. "I mean . . . well, it's a big job to do in a week."

"Yes, it is. But, my boy, perhaps we—the two of us—can do it."

Hector scratched his head. "Well, uh, sir . . . I'm not very . . . that is, my mechanical aptitude scores at the academy. . . ."

Leoh smiled at him. "No need for mechanical aptitude, my boy. You were trained to fight, weren't you? We can do this job mentally."

It was the strangest week of their lives.

Leoh's plan was straightforward: to test the dueling machine, push it to the limits of its performance, by actually operating it—by fighting duels.

They started off easily enough, tentatively probing and flexing their mental muscles. Leoh had used the machines himself many times in the past, but only in tests of the system's routine performance. Never in actual combat against another human being. To Hector, of course, the machine was a totally new and different experience.

The Acquatainian staff plunged into the project without question, providing Leoh with invaluable help in monitoring and analyzing the duels.

At first, Leoh and Hector did nothing more than play hide-and-seek, with one of them picking an environment and the other trying to find him. They wandered through jungles and cities, over glaciers and interplanetary voids, all without ever leaving the dueling machine booths.

Then, when Leoh was satisfied that the machine could reproduce and amplify thought patterns with strict fidelity, they began to fight light duels. They fenced with blunted foils. Leoh did poorly, because he knew nothing about fencing, and his reflexes were much slower than Hector's. The dueling machine did not change a man's knowledge or his physical abilities; it only projected them into a dream he was sharing with another man. It matched Leoh's skills and knowledge against Hector's. Then they tried other weapons—pistols, sonic beams, grenades—but always with the precaution of imagining themselves to be wearing protective equipment. Strangely, even though Hector was trained in the use of these weapons, Leoh won almost all the bouts. He was neither faster nor more accurate when they were target-shooting. But when the two of them faced each other, somehow Leoh almost always won.

The machine projects more than thoughts, Leoh began to realize. *It projects personality.*

They worked in the dueling machine day and night now, enclosed in the booths for twelve or more hours a day, driving themselves and the machine's regular staff to near exhaustion. When they gulped their meals, between duels, they were physically ragged and sharp-tempered. They usually fell asleep in Leoh's office, discussing the results of the day's work.

The duels slowly grew more serious. Leoh was pushing

the machine to its limits now, carefully extending the rigors of each bout. Even though he knew exactly what and how much he intended to do in each fight, it often took a conscious effort to remind himself that the battles he was fighting were actually imaginary.

As the duels became more dangerous, and the artificially amplified hallucinations began to end in blood and death, Leoh found himself winning more and more frequently. With one part of his mind he was driving to analyze the cause of his consistent success. But another part of him was beginning to enjoy his prowess.

The strain was telling on Hector. The physical exertion of constant work and practically no relief was considerable in itself. But the emotional effects of being "hurt" and "killed" repeatedly were infinitely worse.

"Perhaps we should stop for a while," Leoh suggested after the fourth day of tests.

"No, I'm all right."

Leoh looked at him. Hector's face was haggard, his eyes bleary.

"You've had enough," Leoh said quietly.

"Please don't make me stop," Hector begged. "I . . . I can't stop now. Please give me a chance to do better. I'm improving . . . I lasted twice as long in this afternoon's duels as I did this morning. Please, don't end it now . . . not while I'm completely lost. . . ."

Leoh stared at him. "You want to go on?"

"Yes, sir."

"And if I say no?"

Hector hesitated. Leoh sensed he was struggling with himself. "If you say no," he answered dully, "then it'll be no. I can't argue against you any more."

Leoh was silent for a long moment. Finally he opened a desk drawer and took a small bottle from it. "Here, take a sleep capsule. When you wake up we'll try again."

It was dawn when they began again. Leoh entered the dueling machine determined to let Hector win. He gave the youthful Star Watchman his choice of weapons and environment. Hector picked one-man scout ships in planetary orbits. Their weapons were conventional laser beams.

But despite his own conscious desire, Leoh found himself winning! The ships spiraled around an unnamed planet, their paths intersecting at least once in every orbit. The problem was to estimate your opponent's orbital position, and then program your own ship so that you would arrive at that position either behind or to one side of him. Then you could train your guns on him before he could turn on you.

The problem should have been an easy one for Hector, with his knack for intuitive mental calculation. But Leoh scored the first hit. Hector had piloted his ship into an excellent firing position, but his shot went wide. Leoh maneuvered clumsily, but he managed to register a trifling hit on the side of Hector's ship.

In the next three passes, Leoh scored two more hits. Hector's ship was badly damaged now. In return, the Star Watchman had landed one glancing shot on Leoh's ship. They came around again, and once more Leoh had outguessed his young opponent. He trained his guns on Hector's ship, then hesitated with his hand poised above the firing button.

Don't kill him again, he warned himself. *His mind can't take another defeat.*

But Leoh's hand, almost of its own will, reached the button and touched it lightly; another gram of pressure and the guns would fire.

In that instant's hesitation, Hector pulled his crippled ship around and aimed at Leoh. The Watchman fired a searing blast that jarred Leoh's ship from end to end. Leoh's hand slammed down on the firing button; whether he intended to do it or not, he didn't know.

Leoh's shot raked Hector's ship but didn't stop it. The two vehicles were hurtling directly at each other. Leoh tried desperately to avert a collision, but Hector bore in grimly, matching Leoh's maneuvers with his own.

The two ships smashed together and exploded.

Abruptly, Leoh found himself in the cramped booth of the dueling machine, his body cold and damp with perspiration, his hands trembling.

He squeezed out of the booth and took a deep breath. Warm sunlight was streaming into the high-vaulted room. The white walls gleamed brilliantly. Through the tall windows he could see trees and early students and clouds in the sky.

Hector walked up to him. For the first time in several days, the Watchman was smiling. Not much, but smiling. "Well, we . . . uh, broke even on that one."

Leoh smiled back, somewhat shakily. "Yes. It was . . . quite an experience. I've never died before."

Hector fidgeted. "It's not so bad, I guess. It . . . sort of, well, it sort of shatters you, though."

"Yes. I can see that now."

"Try another duel?" Hector asked, nodding toward the machine.

"No. Not now. Let's get out of this place for a few hours. Are you hungry?"

"Starved."

They fought several more duels over the next day and a half. Hector won three of them. It was late afternoon when Leoh called a halt.

"We can get in another couple," the Watchman said.

"No need," said Leoh. "I have all the data I require. Tomorrow Massan meets Odal, unless we can put a stop to it. We've got much to do before tomorrow morning."

Hector sagged into the couch. "Just as well. I think I've aged seven years in the past seven days."

"No, my boy," Leoh said gently, "you haven't aged. You've matured."

It was deep twilight when the ground car slid to a

halt on its cushion of compressed air before the Kerak embassy.

"I still think it's a mistake to go in there," Hector said. "I mean, you could've called him on the tri-di, couldn't you?"

Leoh shook his head. "Never give an agency of any government the opportunity to say, 'Hold the line a moment.' They huddle together and consider what to do with you. Nineteen times out of twenty, they'll end by passing you to another department or transferring your call to a taped, 'So sorry,' message."

"Still," Hector insisted, "you're sort of, well, stepping into enemy territory."

"They wouldn't dare harm us."

Hector didn't reply, but he looked unconvinced.

"Look," Leoh said, "there are only two men alive who can shed light on this matter. One of them is Dulaq, and his mind is closed to us for an indefinite time. Odal is the only other man who knows what happened in those duels."

Hector shook his head skeptically. Leoh shrugged, and opened the door of the ground car. Hector had no choice but to get out and follow him as he walked up the pathway to the main entrance of the embassy building. The building stood gaunt and gray in the dusk, surrounded by a precisely clipped hedge. The entrance was flanked by a pair of evergreen trees, straight and spare as sentries.

Leoh and Hector were met just inside the entrance by a female receptionist. She looked just a trifle disheveled, as though she'd been rushed to her desk at a moment's notice. They asked for Odal, were ushered into a sitting room, and within a few minutes—to Hector's surprise—were informed by the girl that Major Odal would be with them shortly.

"You see," Leoh pointed out jovially, "when you come

in person they haven't as much of a chance to consider how to get rid of you."

Hector glanced around the windowless room and contemplated the thick, solidly closed door. "There's a lot of scurrying going on behind that door, I'll bet. I mean ... they might be figuring out how to get rid of us ... uh, permanently."

Leoh was about to reply when the door opened and Odal came into the room. He wore a military uniform of light blue, with his insignia of rank on the shoulders and the Star of Kerak on his breast.

"Dr. Leoh, I'm flattered," he said with a slight bow. "And Mr. Hector ... or is it Lieutenant Hector?"

"Junior Lieutenant Hector," the Watchman answered, with a curtness that surprised Leoh.

"Lieutenant Hector is assisting me," the Professor said, "and acting as liaison for Commander Spencer."

"So," Odal commented. He gestured them to be seated. Hector and Leoh placed themselves on a plush couch while Odal drew up a stiff chair, facing them. "Now, why have you come to see me?"

"I want you to postpone your duel against Minister Massan tomorrow," Leoh said.

Odal's lean face broke into a tight smile. "Has Massan agreed to a postponement?"

"No."

"Then why should I?"

"To be perfectly frank, Major, I suspect that someone is tampering with the machine used in your duels. For the moment, let's say that you have no knowledge of this. I am asking you to forgo any further duels until we get to the bottom of this. The dueling machines are not to be used for political assassinations."

Odal's smile faded. "I regret, Professor, that I cannot postpone the duel. As for tampering with the machines, I can assure you that neither I nor anyone of the Kerak

Worlds has touched the machines in any unauthorized manner."

"Perhaps you don't fully understand the situation," Leoh said. "In the past week we've tested the dueling machine here on Acquatainia exhaustively. We've learned that its performance can be greatly influenced by a man's personality and his attitude. You've fought many duels in the machines. Your background of experience, both as a professional soldier and in the machines, gives you a decided advantage over your opponents.

"However, even with all this considered, I'm still convinced that no one can kill a man in the machine—under normal circumstances. We've demonstrated that fact in our tests. An unsabotaged machine cannot cause actual physical harm.

"Yet you've already killed one man and incapacitated another. Where will it stop?"

Odal's face remained calm, except for the faintest glitter of fire deep in his eyes. His voice was quiet, but it had the edge of a well-honed blade to it. "I cannot be blamed for my background and experience. And I have not tampered with your machine."

The door to the room opened, and a short, thickset, bullet-headed man entered. He was dressed in a dark street suit, so that it was impossible to guess his station at the embassy.

"Would the gentlemen care for some refreshments?" he asked in a low-pitched voice.

"No thank you," Leoh said.

"Some Kerak wine, perhaps?"

"Well. . . ."

"I, uh, don't think we'd better, sir," Hector said. "Thanks all the same."

The man shrugged and sat at a chair next to the door. Odal turned back to Leoh. "Sir, I have my duty. Massan and I duel tomorrow. There is no possibility of postponing it."

"Very well," Leoh said. "Will you at least allow me to place some special instrumentation into the booth with you, so that we can monitor the duel more fully? We can do the same thing with Massan. I know that duels are normally private and you'd be within your legal rights to refuse the request, but morally. . . ."

The smile returned to Odal's face. "You wish to monitor my thoughts. To record them and see how I perform during the duel. Interesting. Very interesting. . . ."

The man at the door rose and said, "If you have no desire for refreshments, gentlemen. . . ."

Odal turned to him. "Thank you for your attention."

Their eyes met for an instant. The man gave a barely perceptible shake of his head, then left.

Odal returned his attention to Leoh. "I'm sorry, Professor, but I can't allow you to monitor my thoughts during the duel."

"But. . . ."

"I regret having to refuse you. But, as you yourself pointed out, there is no legal requirement for such a course of action. I must refuse. I hope you understand."

Leoh rose slowly from the couch. "No, I do not understand. You sit here and discuss legal points when we both know full well that you're planning to murder Massan tomorrow." His voice burning with anger, Leoh went on, "You've turned my invention into a murder weapon. But you've turned me into an enemy. I'll find out how you're doing it, and I won't rest until you and your kind are put away where you belong . . . on a planet for the criminally insane!"

Hector reached for the door and opened it. He and Leoh went out, leaving Odal alone in the room. In a few minutes, the dark-suited man returned.

"I have just spoken with the Leader on the tri-di and obtained permission to make a slight adjustment in our plans."

"An adjustment, Minister Kor?"

"After your duel tomorrow, your next opponent will be Dr. Leoh," said Kor. "He is the next man to die."

The mists swirled deep and impenetrable around Fernd Massan. He stared blindly through the useless view plate in his helmet, then reached up slowly and carefully placed the infrared detector before his eyes.

I never realized a hallucination could seem so real, Massan thought.

Since the challenge by Odal, the actual world had seemed quite unreal. For a week, he had gone through the motions of life, but felt as though he were standing aside, a spectator mind watching its own body from a distance. The gathering of his friends and associates last night, the night before the duel—that silent, funereal group of people—it had all seemed completely unreal to him.

But now, in this manufactured dream, he seemed vibrantly alive. Every sensation was solid, stimulating. He could feel his pulse throbbing through him. Somewhere out in those mists, he knew, was Odal. And the thought of coming to grips with the assassin filled him with a strange satisfaction.

Massan had spent many years serving his government on the rich but inhospitable high-gravity planets of the Acquataine Cluster. This was the environment he had chosen: crushing gravity; killing pressures; atmosphere of ammonia and hydrogen, laced with free radicals of sulphur and other valuable but deadly chemicals; oceans of liquid methane and ammonia; "solid ground" consisting of quickly crumbling, eroding ice; howling, superpowerful winds that could pick up a mountain of ice and hurl it halfway around the planet; darkness; danger; death.

He was encased in a one-man protective outfit that was half armored suit, half vehicle. An internal liquid suspension system kept him tolerably comfortable at four times normal gravity, but still the suit was cumbersome, and a man could move only very slowly in it, even with the aid of servomotors.

The weapon he had chosen was simplicity itself: a hand-held capsule of oxygen. But in a hydrogen/ammonia atmosphere, oxygen could be a deadly explosive. Massan carried several of these "bombs" hooked to his suit. So did Odal. *But the trick,* Massan thought to himself, *is to throw them accurately under these conditions; the proper range, the proper trajectory. Not an easy thing to learn, without years of experience.*

The terms of the duel were simple: Massan and Odal were situated on a rough-topped iceberg that was being swirled along one of the methane/ammonia ocean's vicious currents. The ice was rapidly crumbling. The duel was to end when the iceberg was completely broken up.

Massan edged along the ragged terrain. His suit's grippers and rollers automatically adjusted to the roughness of the topography. He concentrated his attention on the infrared detector that hung before his view plate.

A chunk of ice the size of a man's head sailed through the murky atmosphere in the steep glide peculiar to heavy gravity and banged into the shoulder of Massan's suit. The force was enough to rock him slightly off balance before the servos readjusted. Massan withdrew his arm from the sleeve and felt inside the shoulder seam. Dented, but not penetrated. A leak would have been disastrous, fatal. Then he remembered: *Of course, I cannot be killed except by the direct action of my antagonist. That is one of the rules of the game.*

Still, he carefully fingered the shoulder seam to make certain it was not leaking. The dueling machine and its rules seemed so very remote and unsubstantial, compared to this freezing, howling inferno.

He diligently set about combing the iceberg, determined to find Odal and kill him before their floating island disintegrated. He thoroughly explored every projection, every crevice, every slope, working his way slowly from one end of the berg toward the other. Back and forth, cross and recross, with the infrared sensors scanning 360 degrees around him.

It was time-consuming. Even with the suit's servomotors and propulsion units, motion across the ice, against the buffeting wind, was a cumbersome business. But Massan continued to work his way across the iceberg, fighting down a gnawing, growing fear that Odal was not there at all.

And then he caught just the barest flicker of a shadow on his detector. Something, or someone, had darted behind a jutting rise of ice, off by the edge of the berg.

Slowly and carefully, Massan made his way across to the base of the rise. He picked one of the oxygen bombs from his belt and held it in his right-hand claw. Edging around the base of the ice cliff, he stood on a narrow ledge between the cliff and the churning sea. He saw no one. He extended the detector's range to maximum and worked the scanners up the sheer face of the cliff toward the top.

There he was! The shadowy outline of a man etched itself on his detector screen. And at the same time, Massan heard a muffled roar, then a rumbling, crashing noise, growing quickly louder and more menacing. He looked down the face of the ice cliff and saw a small avalanche of ice tumbling, sliding, growling toward him. *That devil set off a bomb at the top of the cliff!*

Massan tried to back out of the way, but it was too late. The first chunk of ice bounced harmlessly off his helmet, but the others knocked him off balance so repeatedly that the servos had no chance to recover. He staggered blindly for a few moments, as more and more ice cascaded down on him, and then toppled off the ledge into the boiling sea.

Relax! he ordered himself. *Do not panic! The suit will float you. The servos will keep you right side up. You cannot be killed accidentally; Odal must perform the* coup de grace *himself.*

There were emergency rockets on the back of the suit. If he could orient himself properly, a touch of the control stud on his belt would set them off and he would be boosted back onto the iceberg. He turned slightly inside the suit and tried to judge the iceberg's distance through the infrared detector. It was difficult, since the suit was bobbing madly in the churning currents.

Finally he decided to fire the rockets and make final adjustments of distance and landing site while he was in the air.

But he could not move his hand.

He tried, but his entire right arm was locked fast. He could not budge it a millimeter. And the same for the left. Something, or someone, was clamping his arms tight. He could not even pull them out of their sleeves.

Massan thrashed about, trying to shake off whatever it was. No use.

Then his detector screen was slowly lifted from the view plate. He felt something vibrating on his helmet. The oxygen tubes! They were being disconnected.

He screamed and tried to fight free. No use. With a hiss, the oxygen tubes pulled free of helmet. Massan could feel the blood pounding through his veins as he fought desperately to free himself.

Now he was being pushed down into the sea. He screamed again and tried to wrench his body away. The frothing sea filled his view plate. He was under. He was being held under. And now . . . now the view plate itself was being loosened.

No! Don't! The scalding cold methane/ammonia sea seeped through the opening view plate.

"It's only a dream!" Massan shouted to himself. "Only a dream! A dream! A. . . ."

*   *   *

Dr. Leoh stared at the dinner table without really seeing it. Coming to the restaurant had been Hector's idea. Three hours earlier Massan had been removed from the dueling machine—dead.

Leoh sat stolidly, hands in lap, his mind racing in many different directions at once. Hector was off at the phone, getting the latest information from the meditechs. Odal had expressed his regrets perfunctorily, and then left for the Kerak embassy, under a heavy escort of his own plainclothes guards. The government of the Acquataine Cluster was quite literally falling apart, with no man willing to assume the responsibility of leadership . . . and thereby expose himself. One hour after the duel, Kanus' troops had landed on all the major planets of Szarno; the annexation was complete.

And what have I done since I arrived here? Leoh demanded of himself. *Nothing. Absolutely nothing. I have sat back like a doddering old professor and played academic games with the machine, while younger, more vigorous men have USED the machine to suit their own purposes.*

Used the machine. There was a fragment of an idea there. Something nebulous that must be approached carefully or it will fade away. Used the machine . . . used it. . . . Leoh toyed with the phrase for a few moments, then gave it up with a sigh of resignation. *Lord, I'm too tired even to think.*

He focused his attention on his surroundings and scanned the busy dining room. It was a beautiful place, really, decorated with crystal and genuine woods and fabric draperies. Not a synthetic in sight. The odors of delicious food, the hushed murmur of polite conversation. The waiters and cooks and bus boys were humans, not the autocookers and servers that most restaurants employed. Leoh suddenly felt touched at Hector's attempt to restore his spirits—and at a junior lieutenant's salary.

He saw the young Watchman approaching the table, coming back from the phone. Hector bumped two waiters and stumbled over a chair before reaching the relative safety of his own seat.

"What's the verdict?" Leoh asked.

Hector's lean face was bleak. "They couldn't revive him. Cerebral hemorrhage, the meditechs said . . . brought on by shock."

"Shock?"

"That's what they said. Something must've, um, overloaded his nervous system . . . I guess."

Leoh shook his head. "I just don't understand any of this. I might as well admit it. I'm no closer to an answer now than when I arrived here. Perhaps I should have retired years ago, before the dueling machine was invented."

"No. . . ."

"I mean it," said Leoh. "This is the first real intellectual problem I've had to contend with in years. Tinkering with machinery, that's easy. You know what you want and all you need is to make the machinery perform properly. But this . . . I'm afraid I'm too old to handle a puzzle like this."

Hector scratched his nose thoughtfully. Then he answered, "If you can't handle the problem, sir, then we're going to have a war on our hands in a matter of months . . . or maybe just weeks. I mean, Kanus won't be satisfied with swallowing the Szarno group. The Acquataine Cluster is next . . . and he'll have to fight to get it."

"Then the Star Watch will step in," Leoh said.

Hunching forward in his chair in eagerness to make his point, Hector said, "But . . . look, it'll take time to mobilize the Star Watch. Kanus can move a lot faster than we can. Sure, we could throw in a task force, I mean, a token group. Kerak's army will chew them up pretty quick, though. I . . . I'm no politician, but I think what'll happen is ... well, Kerak will gobble up the Acquataine Cluster and wipe out a Star Watch force in the process. Then we'll end up with the Commonwealth at war with Kerak. And that'll be a big war, because Kanus'll have Acquatainia's, uh, resources to draw on."

Leoh began to answer, then stopped. His eyes were fixed on the far entrance of the dining room. Suddenly every murmur in the busy restaurant stopped dead. Waiters stood frozen between tables. Eating, drinking, conversation hung suspended.

Hector turned in his chair and saw at the far entrance the slim, stiff, blue-uniformed figure of Odal.

The moment of silence passed. Everyone turned to his own business and avoided looking at the Kerak major. Odal, with a faint smile on his thin face, made his way slowly to the table where Hector and Leoh were sitting.

They rose to greet him and exchanged perfunctory salutations. Odal pulled up a chair and sat with them, unasked.

"What do you want?" Leoh asked curtly.

Before Odal could reply, the waiter assigned to the table walked up, took a position where his back would be to the Kerak major, and asked firmly, "Your dinner is ready, gentlemen. Shall I serve it now?"

"Yes," Hector said before Leoh could speak. "The major will be leaving shortly."

Again the tight grin pulled across Odal's face. The waiter bowed and left.

"I've been thinking about our conversation of last night," Odal said to Leoh.

"Yes?"

"You accused me of cheating in my duels."

Leoh's eyebrows arched. "I said someone was cheating. . . ."

"An accusation is an accusation."

Leoh said nothing.

"Do you withdraw your words, or do you still accuse

me of deliberate murder? I'm willing to allow you to apologize and leave Acquatainia in peace."

Hector cleared his throat noisily. "This is no place for an argument ... besides, here comes our dinner."

Odal ignored the Watchman, kept his ice-blue eyes fastened on Leoh. "You heard me, Professor. Will you leave? Or do you. . . ."

Hector banged his fist on the table and jerked up out of his chair—just as the waiter arrived with a heavy tray of appetizers and soups. There was a loud crash. A tureen of soup, two bowls of salad, glasses, assorted rolls, cheeses, and other delicacies cascaded over Odal.

The Kerak major leaped to his feet, swearing violently in his own language. The restaurant exploded with laughter.

Sputtering back into basic Terran, Odal shouted, "You clumsy, stupid oaf! You maggot-brained misbegotten peasant-faced. . . ."

Hector calmly picked a salad leaf from the sleeve of his tunic, while Odal's voice choked with rage.

"I guess I am clumsy," Hector said, grinning. "As for being stupid, and the rest of it, I resent that. In fact, I'm highly insulted."

A flash of recognition lighted Odal's eyes. "I see. Of course. My quarrel is not with you. I apologize." He turned back to Leoh, who was also standing now.

"Not good enough," Hector said. "I don't, uh, like the tone of your apology ... I mean. . . ."

Leoh raised a hand as if to warn Hector to be silent.

"I apologized," Odal said, his face red with anger. "That is enough."

Hector took a step toward Odal. "I guess I could call you names, or insult your glorious Leader, or something like that ... but this seems more direct." He took the water pitcher from the table and carefully poured it over Odal's head.

The people in the restaurant roared. Odal went

absolutely white. "You are determined to die." He wiped the dripping water from his eyes. "I'll meet you before the week is out. And you've saved no one." He turned and stalked out.

Everyone else in the room stood up and applauded. Hector bobbed his head and grinned.

Aghast, Leoh asked, "Do you realize what you've done?"

"He was going to challenge you. . . ."

"He'll still challenge me, after you're dead."

Shrugging, Hector said, "Well, yes, maybe so. I guess you're right. But at least we've gained a little more time."

"Four days." Leoh shook his head. "Four days to the end of this week. All right, come on, we have work to do."

Hector was grinning broadly as they left the restaurant. He began to whistle.

"What are you so happy about?" Leoh grumbled.

"About you, sir. When we came in here, you were, well . . . almost beaten. Now you're right back in the game again."

Leoh stared at him. "In your own odd way, my boy, you're quite something . . . I think."

Their ground car glided from the parking building to the restaurant's entrance ramp, at the radio call of the doorman. Within minutes, Hector and Leoh were cruising through the city in the deepening shadows of night.

"There's only one man," Leoh mused, "who's faced Odal and lived through it."

"Dulaq," Hector said. "But . . . he might as well be dead, for all the information anybody can get from him."

"He's still completely withdrawn?"

Hector nodded. "The medicos think that . . . well, maybe with drugs and therapy and all that . . . maybe in a few months or so they might be able to bring him back."

"Not soon enough. We've only got four days."

"I know."

Leoh was silent for several minutes. Then, "Who is Dulaq's closest living relative? Does he have a wife?"

"Umm, I think his wife's dead. Has a daughter, though. Pretty girl. I bumped into her in the hospital once or twice. . . ."

Leoh smiled in the darkness. Hector's term, "bumped into," was probably completely literal.

"There might be a way to make Dulaq tell us what happened during his duel," Leoh said. "But it's a very dangerous way. Perhaps a fatal way."

Hector didn't reply.

"Come on, my boy," Leoh said. "Let's find that daughter and talk to her."

"Tonight?"

"Now."

She certainly is a pretty girl, Leoh thought as he explained very carefully to Geri Dulaq what he proposed to do. She sat quietly and politely in the spacious living room of the Dulaq residence. The glittering chandelier cast touches of fire on her chestnut hair. Her slim body was slightly rigid with tension, her hands were clasped tightly in her lap. Her face, which looked as though it could be very expressive, was completely serious now.

"And that's the sum of it," Leoh concluded. "I believe that it will be possible to use the dueling machine itself to examine your father's thoughts and determine what took place during his duel against Major Odal. It might even help to break him out of his coma."

She asked softly, "But it might also be such a shock to him that he could die?"

Leoh nodded wordlessly.

"Then I'm very sorry, Professor, but I must say no." Firmly.

"I understand your feelings," Leoh replied, "but I

hope you realize that unless we can stop Odal immediately, we may very well be faced with war, and millions will die."

She nodded. "I know. But we're speaking of my father's life. Kanus will have his war in any event, no matter what I do."

"Perhaps," Leoh admitted. "Perhaps."

Hector and Leoh drove back to the university campus and their quarters in the dueling machine building. Neither of them slept well that night.

The next morning, after an unenthusiastic breakfast, they found themselves in the antiseptic-white chamber, before the looming impersonal intricacy of the machine.

"Would you like to practice with it?" Leoh asked.

Hector shook his head gloomily. "Maybe later."

The phone chimed in Leoh's office. They both went in. Geri Dulaq's face took form on the viewscreen.

"I just heard the news," she said a little breathlessly. "I didn't know, last night, that Lieutenant Hector had challenged Odal."

"He challenged Odal," Leoh answered, "to prevent the assassin from challenging me."

"Oh." Her face was a mixture of concern and reluctance. "You're a brave man, Lieutenant."

Hector's expression went through a dozen contortions, all of them speechless.

"Won't you reconsider your decision?" Leoh asked. "Hector's life may depend on it."

She closed her eyes briefly, then said, "I can't. My father's life is my first responsibility. I'm sorry." There was real torment in her voice.

They exchanged a few meaningless trivialities—with Hector still thoroughly tongue-tied—and ended the conversation on a polite but strained note.

Leoh rubbed his thumb across the phone switch for a moment, then turned to Hector. "My boy, I think it would be a good idea for you to go straight to the hospital and check on Dulaq's condition."

"But ... why...."

"Don't argue, son. This could be vitally important. Check on Dulaq. In person, no phone calls."

Hector shrugged and left the office. Leoh sat down at his desk and waited. There was nothing else he could do. After a while he got up and paced out to the big chamber, through the main doors, and out onto the campus. He walked past a dozen buildings, turned and strode as far as the decorative fence that marked the end of the main campus, ignoring students and faculty alike. He walked all around the campus, like a picket, trading nervous energy for time.

As he approached the dueling machine building again he spotted Hector walking dazedly toward him. For once, the Watchmam was not whistling. Leoh cut across some lawn to get to him.

"Well?" he asked.

Hector shook his head, as if to clear away an inner fog. "How did you know she'd be at the hospital?"

"The wisdom of age. What happened?"

"She kissed me. Right there in the hallway of the...."

"Spare me the geography," Leoh cut in. "What did she say?"

"I bumped into her in the hallway. We, uh, started talking ... sort of. She seemed, well ... worried about me. She got upset. Emotional. You know? I guess I looked pretty down ... I mean, I'm not that brave ... I'm scared and it must have shown."

"You aroused her maternal instinct."

"I ... I don't think it was that ... exactly. Well, anyway, she said that if I'm willing to risk my life to save yours, she couldn't protect her father any more. Said she was doing it out of selfishness, really, since he's her only living relative.... I don't believe she meant it, but she said it anyway."

They had reached the building by now. Leoh grabbed Hector's arm and steered him clear of a collision with the half-open door.

"She's agreed to let us put Dulaq in the dueling machine?"

"Sort of."

"Eh?"

"The medical staff doesn't want him moved . . . especially not back here. She agrees with them."

Leoh snorted. "All right. In fact, so much the better. I'd rather not have the Kerak people see us bring Dulaq to the dueling machine. Instead, we'll smuggle the dueling machine into the hospital!"

They plunged to work immediately. Leoh preferred not to inform the regular staff of the dueling machine about their plan, so he and Hector had to work through the night and most of the next morning. Hector barely understood what he was doing, but with Leoh's supervision he managed to dismantle part of the machine's central network, insert a few additional black electronics boxes that the Professor had conjured up from the spare-parts bins in the basement, and then reconstruct the machine so that it looked exactly the same as before they had started.

In between his frequent trips to oversee Hector's work, Leoh had jury-rigged a rather bulky headset and a hand-sized override control circuit. The late morning sun was streaming through the hall when Leoh finally explained it all to Hector.

"A simple matter of technological improvisation," he told the puzzled Watchman. "You've installed a short-range transceiver into the machine, and this headset is a portable transceiver for Dulaq. Now he can sit in his hospital bed and still be 'in' the dueling machine."

Only the three most trusted members of the hospital

staff were taken into Leoh's confidence, and they were hardly enthusiastic about the plan.

"It is a waste of time," said the chief psychotechnician, shaking his white-maned head vigorously. "You cannot expect a patient who has shown no positive response to drugs and therapy to respond to your machine."

Leoh argued, and Geri Dulaq firmly insisted that they go through with it. Finally the doctors agreed. With only two days remaining before Hector's duel with Odal, they began to probe Dulaq's mind. Geri remained by her father's bedside while the three doctors fitted the cumbersome transceiver to his head and attached the electrodes for the hospital equipment that monitored his physical condition. Hector and Leoh remained at the dueling machine, communicating with the hospital by phone.

Leoh made a final check of the controls and circuitry, then put in the last call to the tense little group in Dulaq's room. All was ready.

He walked out to the machine with Hector beside him. Their footsteps echoed hollowly in the sepulchral chamber. Leoh stopped at the nearer booth.

"Now remember," he said carefully, "I'll be holding the emergency control unit in my hand. It will stop the duel the instant I set it off. However, if something goes wrong, you must be prepared to act quickly. Keep a close watch on my physical condition; I've shown you which instruments to check on the control board."

"Yes, sir."

Leoh nodded and took a deep breath. "Very well, then."

He stepped into the booth and sat down. Hector helped to attach the neurocontacts, and then left him alone. Leoh leaned back and waited for the semihypnotic effect to take hold. Dulaq's choice of the city and the stat-wand were known. But beyond that, everything was sealed in his uncommunicating mind. Could the machine reach past that seal?

Slowly, lullingly, the dueling machine's imaginary yet very real mists enveloped Leoh. When they cleared, he was standing on the upper pedestrian level of the main commercial street of the city. For a long moment, everything was still.

Have I made contact? Whose eyes am I seeing with, my own or Duaq's?

And then he sensed it—an amused, somewhat astonished marveling at the reality of the illusion. Dulaq's thoughts!

Make your mind a blank, Leoh told himself. *Watch. Listen. Be passive.*

He became a spectator, seeing and hearing the world through Dulaq's eyes and ears as the Acquatainian Prime Minister advanced through his nightmarish ordeal. He felt the confusion, frustration, apprehension, and growing terror as, time and again, Odal appeared in the crowd—only to melt into someone else and escape.

The first part of the duel ended, and Leoh was suddenly buffeted by a jumble of thoughts and impressions. Then the thoughts slowly cleared and steadied.

Leoh saw an immense and totally barren plain. Not a tree, not a blade of grass, nothing but bare, rocky ground stretching in all directions to the horizon and a disturbingly harsh yellow sky. At his feet was the weapon Odal had chosen. A primitive club.

He shared Dulaq's sense of dread as he picked up the club and hefted it. Off on the horizon he could see the tall lithe figure holding a similar club and walking toward him.

Despite himself, Leoh could feel his own excitement. He had broken through the shock-created armor that Dulaq's mind had erected! Dulaq was reliving the part of the duel that had caused the shock.

Reluctantly, he advanced to meet Odal. But as they

drew closer together, the one figure of his opponent seemed to split apart. Now there were two, four, six of them. Six Odals, six mirror images, all armed with massive, evil clubs, advancing steadily on him. Six tall, lean, blond assassins with six cold smiles on their intent faces.

Horrified, completely panicked, he scrambled away, trying to evade the six opponents with the half-dozen clubs raised and poised to strike.

Their young legs easily outdistanced him. A smash on his back sent him sprawling. One of them kicked his weapon away.

They stood over him for a malevolent, gloating second. Then six strong arms flashed down, again and again, mercilessly. Pain and blood, screaming agony, punctuated by the awful thudding of solid clubs hitting fragile flesh and bone, over and over again, endlessly, endlessly. . . .

Everything went blank.

Leoh opened his eyes and saw Hector bending over him.

"Are you all right, sir?"

"I . . . I think so."

"The controls hit the danger mark all at once. You were . . . well, you were screaming."

"I don't doubt it," Leoh said.

They walked, with Leoh leaning on Hector's arm, from the dueling machine to the office.

"That was . . . an experience," Leoh said, easing himself onto the couch.

"What happened? What did Odal do? What made Dulaq go into shock? How does. . . ."

The old man silenced Hector with a wave of his hand. "One question at a time, please."

Leoh leaned back on the deep couch and told Hector every detail of both parts of the duel.

"Six Odals," Hector muttered soberly, leaning against the doorframe. "Six against one."

"That's what he did. It's easy to see how a man

expecting a polite, formal duel can be completely shattered by the viciousness of such an attack. And the machine amplifies every impulse, every sensation." Leoh shuddered.

"But how does he do it?" Hector's voice was suddenly demanding.

"I've been asking myself the same question. We've checked the dueling machine time and again. There's no possible way for Odal to plug in five helpers ... unless. ..."

"Unless?"

Leoh hesitated, seemingly debating with himself. Finally he nodded sharply and answered, "Unless Odal is a telepath."

"Telepath? But. ..."

"I know it sounds farfetched, but there have been well-documented cases of telepathy."

Frowning, Hector said, "Sure, everybody's heard about it ... natural telepaths, I mean ... but they're so unpredictable ... I mean, how can. ..."

Leoh leaned forward on the couch and clasped his hands in front of his chin. "The Terran races have never developed telepathy, or any extrasensory talents, beyond the occasional wild talent. They never had to, not with tri-di communications and star ships. But perhaps the Kerak people are different. ..."

"They're human, just like we are," Hector said. "Besides, if they had, uh, telepathic abilities ... well, wouldn't they use them all the time? Why just in the dueling machine?"

"Of course!" Leoh exclaimed. "Odal's shown telepathic ability only in the dueling machine!"

Hector blinked.

Excitedly, Leoh explained, "Suppose Odal's a natural telepath ... the same as dozens of Terrans have been proven to be. He has an erratic, difficult-to-control talent. A talent that doesn't really amount to much. Then he gets into the dueling machine. The machine amplifies his thoughts. It also amplifies his talents!"

"Ohhh."

"You see? Outside the machine, he's no better than any wandering fortuneteller. But the dueling machine gives his natural abilities the amplification and reproducibility that they could never attain unaided."

"I get it."

"So it's a fairly straightforward matter for him to have five associates in the Kerak embassy sit in on the duel, so to speak. Possibly they're natural telepaths, too, but they needn't be."

"They just, uh, pool their minds with his? Six men show up in the duel ... pretty nasty." Hector dropped into the desk chair. "So what do we do now?"

"Now?" Leoh blinked at the Watchman. "Why ... I suppose the first thing we do is call the hospital and see how Dulaq came through."

"Oh, yes ... I forgot about her ... I mean, him."

Leoh put the call through. Geri Dulaq's face appeared on the screen, impassive.

"How is he?" Hector blurted.

"It was too much for him," she said bleakly. "He is dead. The doctors have tried to revive him, but. . . ."

"No." Leoh groaned.

"I'm ... sorry," Hector said. "I'll be right down there. Stay where you are."

The Star Watchman dashed out of the office as Geri broke the phone connection. Leoh stared at the blank screen for a few minutes, then leaned far back in the couch and closed his eyes. He was suddenly exhausted, physically and emotionally. He fell asleep, and dreamed of men dead and dying. Sometimes it was Odal killing them, and sometimes it was Leoh himself.

Hector's nerve-shattering whistling woke him up. It was deep night outside.

"What are you so happy about?" Leoh groused as Hector popped into the office.

"Happy? Me?"

"You were whistling."

Hector shrugged. "I always whistle, sir. Doesn't mean I'm happy."

"All right." Leoh rubbed his eyes. "How did the girl take her father's death?"

"Pretty hard. She cried a lot. It . . . well, it shook us both up."

Leoh looked at the younger man. "Does she blame . . . me?"

"You? Why, no, sir. Why should she? Odal, Kanus . . . the Kerak Worlds. But not you."

The Professor sighed, relieved. "Very well. Now then, we have much work to do, and little time to do it in."

"What do you want me to do?" Hector asked.

"Phone the Star Watch Commander. . . ."

"My commanding officer, all the way back at Perseus Alpha VI? That's a hundred light-years from here."

"No, no, no," Leoh shook his head. "The Commander-in-Chief, Sir Harold Spencer. At Star Watch Central Headquarters, or wherever he may be, no matter how far. Get through to him as quickly as possible. And reverse the charges."

With a low whistle of astonishment, Hector began punching buttons on the phone.

The morning of the duel arrived, and precisely at the specified hour, Odal and a small retinue of Kerak seconds stepped through the double doors of the dueling machine chamber.

Hector and Leoh were already there, waiting. With them stood another man, dressed in the black-and-silver of the Star Watch. He was a blocky, broad-faced veteran with iron-gray hair and hard, unsmiling eyes.

The two little groups of men knotted together in the

center of the room, before the machine's main control board. The white-uniformed staff meditechs emerged from a far doorway and stood off to one side.

Odal went through the formality of shaking hands with Hector. The Kerak major nodded toward the older Watchman. "Your replacement?" he asked mischievously.

The chief meditech stepped between them. "Since you are the challenged party, Major Odal, you have the first choice of weapon and environment. Are there any instructions or comments necessary before the duel begins?"

"I think not," Odal replied. "The situation will be self-explanatory. I assume, of course, that Star Watchmen are trained to be warriors and not merely technicians. The situation I have chosen is one in which many warriors have won glory."

Hector said nothing.

"I intend," Leoh said firmly, "to assist the staff in monitoring this duel. Your aides may, of course, sit at the control board with me."

Odal nodded.

"If you are ready to begin, gentlemen," the chief meditech said.

Hector and Odal went to their booths. Leoh sat at the control console, and one of the Kerak men sat down next to him. The others found places on the long curving bench that faced the machine.

Hector felt every nerve and muscle tensed as he sat in the booth, despite his efforts to relax. Slowly the tension eased and he began to feel slightly drowsy. The booth seemed to be melting away. . . .

Hector heard a snuffling noise behind him and wheeled around. He blinked, then stared.

It had four legs, and was evidently a beast of burden. At least, it carried a saddle on its back. Piled atop the saddle was a conglomeration of what looked to Hector—

at first glance—like a pile of junk. He went over to the animal and examined it carefully. The "junk" turned out to be a long spear, various pieces of armor, a helmet, sword, shield, battle-ax, and dagger.

The situation I have chosen is one in which many warriors have won glory.

Hector puzzled over the assortment of weapons. They came straight out of Kerak's Dark Age. Probably Odal had been practicing with them for months, even years. *He may not need five helpers,* Hector thought.

Warily, he put on the armor. The breastplate seemed too big, and he was somehow unable to tighten the greaves on his shins properly. The helmet fit over his head like an ancient oil can, flattening his ears and nose and forcing him to squint to see through the narrow eye slit. Finally he buckled on the sword and found attachments on the saddle for the other weapons. The shield was almost too heavy to lift, and he barely struggled into the saddle with all the weight he was carrying.

And then he just sat. He began to feel a little ridiculous. *Suppose it rains?* But of course it wouldn't.

After an interminable wait, Odal appeared on a powerful trotting charger. His armor was black as space, and so was his mount. *Naturally,* thought Hector.

Odal saluted gravely with his great spear from across the meadow. Hector returned the salute, nearly dropping his spear in the process.

Then Odal lowered his spear and aimed it—so it seemed to Hector—directly at the Watchman's ribs. He pricked his mount into a canter. Hector did the same, and his steed jogged into a bumping, jolting gallop. The two warriors hurtled toward each other from opposite ends of the meadow, with Hector barely hanging on to his mount.

And suddenly there were six black figures roaring down on Hector!

The Watchman's stomach wrenched within him.

Automatically he tried to turn his mount aside. But the beast had no intention of going anywhere except straight ahead. The Kerak warriors bore in, six abreast, with six spears aimed menacingly.

Abruptly, Hector heard the pounding of other hoof-beats right beside him. Through a corner of his helmet slit he glimpsed at least two other warriors charging with him into Odal's crew.

Leoh's gamble had worked. The transceiver that had allowed Dulaq to make contact with the dueling machine from his hospital bed was now allowing five Star Watch officers to join Hector, even though they were physically sitting in a star ship orbiting high above the planet.

The odds were even now. The five additional Watchmen were the roughest, hardiest, most aggressive man-to-man fighters that the Star Watch could provide on one day's notice.

Twelve powerful chargers met head-on, and twelve strong men smashed together with an ear-splitting CLANG! Shattered spears showered splinters everywhere. Men and animals went down.

Hector was rocked back in his saddle, but somehow managed to avoid falling off. On the other hand, he couldn't really regain his balance, either. Dust and weapons filled the air. A sword hissed near his head and rattled off his shield.

With a supreme effort, Hector pulled out his own sword and thrashed at the nearest rider. It turned out to be a fellow Watchman, but the stroke bounced harm-lessly off his helmet.

It was so confusing. The wheeling, snorting animals. Clouds of dust. Screaming, raging men. A black-armored rider charged into Hector, waving a battle-ax over his head. He chopped savagely, and the Watchman's shield split apart. Another frightening swing—Heetor tried to duck and slid completely out of the saddle, thumping painfully on the ground, while the ax cleaved the air where his head had been a split second earlier.

Somehow his helmet was turned around. Hector tried to decide whether to grope around blindly or lay down his sword and straighten out the helmet. The problem was solved for him by the *crang!* of a sword against the back of his head. The blow flipped him into a somersault, and knocked the helmet off completely.

Hector climbed painfully to his feet, his head spinning. It took him several moments to realize that the battle had stopped.

The dust drifted away, and he saw that all the Kerak fighters were down—except one. The black-armored warrior took off his helmet and tossed it aside. It was Odal. Or was it? They all looked alike. *What difference does it make?* Hector wondered. *Odal's mind is the dominant one.*

Odal stood, legs braced apart, sword in hand, and looked uncertainly at the other Star Watchmen. Three of them were afoot and two still mounted. The Kerak major seemed as confused as Hector felt. The shock of facing equal numbers had sapped much of his confidence.

Cautiously he advanced toward Hector, holding his sword out before him. The other Watchmen stood aside while Hector slowly backpedaled, stumbling slightly on the uneven ground.

Odal feinted and cut at Hector's arm. The Watchman barely parried in time. Another feint, at the head, and a slash to the chest; Hector missed the parry but his armor saved him. Odal kept advancing. Feint, feint, crack! Hector's sword went flying from his hand.

For the barest instant everyone froze. Then Hector leaped desperately straight at Odal, caught him completely by surprise, and wrestled him to the ground. The Watchman pulled the sword from Odal's hand and tossed it away. But with his free hand Odal clouted Hector on the side of the head and knocked him on his back. Both men scrambled up and ran for the nearest weapons.

Odal picked up a wicked-looking double-bladed ax. One of the mounted Star Watchmen handed Hector a huge broadsword. He gripped it with both hands, but still staggered off balance as he swung it up over his shoulder.

Holding the broadsword aloft, Hector charged toward Odal, who stood dogged, short-breathed, sweat-streaked, waiting for him. The broadsword was quite heavy, even for a two-handed grip. And Hector never noticed his own battered helmet lying on the ground between them.

Odal, for his part, had Hector's charge and swing timed perfectly in his own mind. He would duck under the swing and bury his ax in the Watchman's chest. Then he would face the others. Probably, with their leader gone, the duel would automatically end. But, of course, Hector would not really be dead; the best Odal could hope for now was to win the duel.

Hector charged directly into Odal's plan, but the Watchman's timing was much poorer than anticipated. Just as he began the downswing of a mighty broadsword stroke, he stumbled on the helmet. Odal started to duck, then saw the Watchman was diving face-first into the ground, legs flailing, and that heavy broadsword was cleaving through the air with a will of its own.

Odal pulled back in confusion, only to have the wildswinging broadsword strike him just above the wrist with bone-shattering impact. The ax dropped out of his hand and Odal involuntarily grasped the wounded forearm with his left hand. Blood seeped through his fingers.

Shaking his head in bitter resignation, Odal turned his back on the prostrate Hector and began walking away.

Slowly the scene faded, and Hector found himself sitting in the booth of the dueling machine.

The door opened and Leoh squeezed into the booth. "You're all right?"

Hector blinked and refocused his eyes on reality. "I think so. . . ."

"Everything went well? The Watchmen got through to you?"

"Good thing they did. I was nearly killed anyway."

"But you survived."

"So far."

Across the room, Odal stood massaging his forearm while Kor demanded, "How could they possibly have discovered the secret? Where was the leak? Who spoke to them?"

"That's not important now," Odal said quietly. "The primary fact is that they've not only discovered our trick, but they've found a way to duplicate it."

The glistening dome of Kor's bullet-shaped head—which barely rose to the level of Odal's chin—was glowing with rage.

"The sanctimonious hypocrites," Kor snarled, "accusing us of cheating, and then they do the very same thing."

"Regardless of the moral values of our mutual behavior," Odal said dryly, "it's evident that there's no longer any use in calling on telepathically guided assistants. I'll face the Watchman alone during the second half of the duel."

"Can you trust them to do the same?"

"Yes. They easily defeated my aides, then stood aside and allowed the two of us to fight by ourselves."

"And you failed to defeat him?"

Odal frowned. "I was wounded by a fluke. He's a very . . . unusual opponent. I can't decide whether he's actually as clumsy as he appears, or whether he's shamming and trying to confuse me. Either way, it's impossible to predict what he's going to do." To himself he added, *Could he be telepathic, also?*

Kor's gray eyes became flat and emotionless. "You know, of course, how the Leader will react if you fail to kill this Watchman. Not merely defeat him. He must be killed. The aura of invincibility must be maintained."

"I'll do my best," Odal said.

"He must be killed."

The chime that marked the end of the rest period sounded. Odal and Hector returned to their booths. Now it was Hector's choice of environment and weapons.

Odal found himself enveloped in darkness. Only gradually did his eyes adjust. He was in a spacesuit. For several minutes he stood motionless, peering into the darkness, every sense alert, every muscle coiled for instant action. Dimly he could see the outlines of jagged rock against a background of innumerable stars. Experimentally, he lifted one foot. It stuck, tacky, to the surface. *Magnetized boots. This must be a planetoid.*

As his eyes grew accustomed to the dimness he saw that he was right. It was a small planetoid, perhaps a mile or so in diameter, he judged. Almost zero gravity. Airless.

Odal swiveled his head inside the fish-bowl helmet of his suit and saw, over his right shoulder, the figure of Hector—lank and ungainly even with the bulky suit. For a moment, Odal puzzled over the weapon to be used. Then Hector bent down, picked up a loose stone, straightened, and tossed it softly past Odal's head. He watched it sail by and off into the darkness of space, never to return. A warning shot.

Pebbles? Odal thought to himself. *Pebbles for a weapon? He must be insane.* Then he remembered that inertial mass was unaffected by gravity, or the lack of it. On this planetoid a fifty-kilogram rock might be easier to carry, but it would be just as hard to throw—and it would do just as much damage when it hit, regardless of its gravitational "weight."

Odal crouched down and selected a stone the size of

his fist. He rose carefully, sighted Hector standing a hundred meters or so away, and threw as hard as he could.

The effort of his throw sent him tumbling off balance and the stone was far off target. He fell to his hands and knees, bounced lightly, and skipped to a stop. Immediately he drew his feet up under his body and planted the magnetized soles of his boots firmly on the iron-rich surface.

But before he could stand again, a small stone *pinged* lightly off his oxygen tank. The Star Watchman had his range already! Probably he had spent some time on planetoids. Odal scrambled to the nearest upjutting rocks and crouched behind them. *Lucky I didn't rip open the suit,* he told himself. Three stones, evidently hurled in salvo, ticked off the top of the rock he was hunched behind. One of the stones bounced off his fish-bowl helmet.

Odal scooped up a handful of pebbles and tossed them in Hector's general direction. *That should make him duck. Perhaps he'll stumble and crack his helmet open.*

He grinned at that. *That's it. Kor wants him dead, and that's the way to do it. Pin him under a big rock, then bury him alive under more rocks. A few at a time, stretched out nicely. Break some of his bones in the process, and let him sweat while his oxygen supply runs out. That should put enough strain on his nervous system to hospitalize him, at least. Then he can be assassinated by more conventional means. Perhaps he'll even be as obliging as Massan, and have a fatal stroke.*

A large rock. One that's light enough to lift and throw, yet also big enough to pin him for a few moments. Once he's down, it will be easy enough to bury him under more rocks.

Odal spotted a boulder of the proper size, a few meters away. He backed toward it, throwing small stones in Hector's direction to keep the Watchman busy. In return, a barrage of stones began striking all around him. Several hit him, one hard enough to knock him slightly off balance.

Slowly, patiently, Odal reached his chosen weapon: an oblong boulder, about the size of a small chair. He crouched behind it and tugged at it experimentally. It moved slightly. Another stone zinged off his arm, hard enough to hurt. Odal could see Hector clearly now, standing atop a small rise, calmly firing stones at him. He smiled as he coiled, cat-like, and tensed himself. He gripped the boulder with his outstretched arms and hands.

Then in one vicious uncoiling motion he snatched it up, whirled around, and hurled it at Hector. The violence of the action sent him tottering awkwardly as he released the boulder. He fell to the ground, but kept his eyes fixed on the boulder as it tumbled end over end, directly at the Watchman.

For an eternally long instant Hector stood motionless, seemingly entranced. Then he leaped sideways, floating dream-like in the low gravity as the stone bore inexorably past him.

Odal pounded his fist on the ground in fury. He started up, only to have a good-sized stone slam against his shoulder and knock him flat again. He looked up in time to see Hector fire again. A stone puffed into the ground inches from Odal's helmet. The Kerak major flattened himself. Several more stones clattered on his helmet and oxygen tank. Then nothing.

Odal looked up and saw Hector squatting, reaching for more ammunition. The Kerak warrior stood up quickly, his own fists filled with stones. He cocked his arm to throw. . . .

Something made him turn around and look behind him. The boulder loomed before his eyes, still tumbling slowly as it had when he'd thrown it. It was too big and too close to avoid. It smashed into Odal, picked him off his feet, and slammed him against the upjutting rocks a few meters away.

Even before he began to feel the pain inside him, Odal began trying to push the boulder off. But he couldn't get enough leverage. Then he saw the Star Watchman's form standing over him.

"I didn't really think you'd fall for it," Hector's voice said in his earphones. "I mean . . . didn't you realize that the boulder was too massive to escape completely after it missed me? You just threw it into orbit . . . uh, a two-minute orbit, roughly. It *had* to come back . . . all I had to do was keep you in the same spot for a few minutes."

Odal said nothing, but strained every cell in his pain-racked body to get the boulder off him. Hector reached over his shoulder and began fumbling with the valves that were pressed against the rocks.

"Sorry to do this . . . but I'm not killing you . . . just defeating you. Let's see, one of these is the oxygen valve, and the other, I think, is the emergency rocket pack. Now, which is which?"

Hector's hand tightened on a valve and turned it sharply. A rocket roared to life and Odal was hurtled free of the boulder, shot completely off the planetoid. Hector was bowled over by the blast and rolled halfway around the tiny chunk of rock and metal.

Odal tried to reach the rocket throttle, but the pain was too great. He was slipping into unconsciousness. He fought against it. He knew he must return to the planetoid and somehow kill his opponent. But gradually the pain overpowered him. His eyes were closing, closing. . . .

And quite abruptly he found himself sitting in the booth of the dueling machine. It took a moment for him to realize that he was back in the real world. Then his thoughts cleared. He had failed to kill Hector. He hadn't even defeated him.

And at the door of the booth stood Kor, his face a grim mask of anger.

For the moment, Leoh's office behind the dueling machine looked like a great double room. One wall had been replaced by a full-sized viewscreen, which now seemed to be dissolved, so that he was looking directly into the austere metallic utility of a star-ship compartment.

Spencer was saying, "So this hired assassin, after killing four men and nearly wrecking a government, has returned to his native worlds."

Leoh nodded. "He returned under guard. I suppose he's in disgrace, or perhaps even under arrest."

"Servants of a dictator never know when they'll be the ones who are served—on a platter." Spencer chuckled. "And the Watchman who assisted you, this Junior Lieutenant Hector, where is he?"

"The Dulaq girl has him in tow, somewhere. Evidently it's the first time he's been a hero."

Spencer shifted his weight in his chair. "I've long prided myself on the conviction that any Star Watch officer can handle almost any kind of emergency. From your description of the past few weeks' happenings, I was beginning to have my doubts. However, Junior Lieutenant Hector seems to have scraped through."

"He turned out to be an extremely valuable man," Leoh said, smiling. "I think he'll make a fine officer."

Spencer grunted an affirmative.

"Well," Leoh said, "that's the story, to date. I believe that Odal is finished. But the Kerak Worlds have annexed the Szarno Confederacy and are rearming in earnest now. And the Acquatainian government is still very wobbly. There will be elections for a new Prime Minister in a few days, with half a dozen men running and no one in a clear majority. We haven't heard the last of Kanus, either, not by a long shot."

Spencer lifted a shaggy eyebrow. "Neither," he rumbled, "has *he* heard the last from *us*."

II

The Force of Pride

Odal sat alone in the waiting room. It was a bare cubicle, with rough stone walls and a single slit window set high above the floor, close to the ceiling. For furniture, there was only one wooden bench and a viewscreen set into the wall opposite it. The room was quiet as death.

The Kerak major sat stiff-backed and unmoving. But his mind was racing:

Kor uses this type of room to awe his visitors. He knows how much like an ancient dungeon this room looks. He likes to terrify people.

Odal also knew that the interrogation rooms, deep in the sub-basements, were also built like this. Except that they had no windows, and the walls were often blood-spattered.

"The Minister will see you now," said a feminine voice from the viewscreen. But the screen remained blank. Odal realized that he had probably been under observation every minute since he had entered Kor's headquarters.

He stood up as the room's only door opened automatically. With a measured military briskness, Odal strode down the hallway toward the other door at its end, his boots clicking on the stone flooring. He knocked once at the heavy wooden door. No answer. He knocked again, and the door opened by itself.

Kor was sitting at the far end of the office, behind a mammoth desk. The room was dimly lit, except for a single lamp over the desk that made the Intelligence Minister's bald head glisten. Odal carefully shut the door, took a few steps into the carpeted room, and waited for Kor to look up. The Intelligence chief was busily signing papers, ignoring his visitor.

Finally Kor glanced up. "Sit," he commanded.

Odal walked to the desk and sat at the single straight-backed chair before it. Kor signed a few more documents, then pushed the stack of papers off to the side of his desk.

"I spent the morning with the Leader," he said in his irritatingly shrill voice. "Needless to say, he was unhappy about your duel with the Watchman."

Odal could picture Kanus' angry tirade. "My only desire is to meet the Watchman again and rectify that error."

Kor's emotionless eyes fixed on Odal's. "Personal motives are of no interest. The Watchman is only a bumbling fool, but he has succeeded in destroying our primary plan for the defeat of Acquatainia. He succeeded because of this meddler, Leoh. *He* is our target. He is the one who must be put out of the way."

"I see. . . ."

"No, you do not see," Kor snapped. "You have no concept of the plan I have in mind, because I have told it to no one except the Leader himself. And I will tell it to no one, until it is necessary."

Odal didn't move a muscle. He refused to show any emotion, any fear, any weakness to his superior.

"For the time being you are assigned to my personal staff. You will remain at this headquarters building at all times. Your duties will be given to you daily by my assistants."

"Very well."

"And consider this," Kor said, hunching forward in his chair. "Your failure with the Watchman made the Leader accuse me of failure. He will not tolerate excuses. If you fail the next time I call on you, it will be necessary to destroy you."

"I understand perfectly."

"Good. Return to your quarters until summoned. And remember, either we destroy Leoh, or he destroys us."

Odal nodded, rose from his chair, and walked out of the office. *Us*, he thought. *Kor is beginning to feel the terror he uses on others.* If he could have been sure that he wasn't being watched by hidden cameras, Odal would have smiled.

Professor Leoh eased his bulky body into the softness of an air couch. It looked as though he was sitting on nothingness, with the glistening metal curve of the couch several centimeters from his body.

"This is what I've needed for a long time," he said to Hector. "A real vacation, with all the luxuries. It makes an old man happy."

The Star Watchman was standing by the window wall across the room from Leoh, anxiously peering down at the bustling city far below. "It's a nice apartment they've given you, all right."

The room was long and spacious, with one whole side devoted to the window wall. The decorations were color- and scent-coded to change slowly through the day. At the moment the walls were in shades of brown and gold, and the air hinted faintly of spices.

"The best part of it," Leoh said, stretching slowly on the couch, "is that the dueling machine is fixed so that a telepath can't bring in outside helpers without setting off a warning alarm, and I've got nothing to do until the new school year begins at Carinae. I might not even go back then; as long as the Acquatainians want to treat me so royally, why shouldn't I spend a year or so here? There's plenty of research I can do . . . perhaps even lecture occasionally at the university here. . . ."

Hector tried to smile at the old man's musings, but looked worried instead. "Maybe you shouldn't stay in Acquatainia too long. I mean, well . . . the Kerak people might still be after you. Odal was going to challenge you before I . . . that is. . . ."

"Before you saved me."

The Watchman's face colored. "Well, I didn't really mean . . . that is, it wasn't. . . ."

Leoh chuckled. "Don't be so flustered, my boy. You're a hero. Surely Geri regards you as such."

"Um, yes, I guess so."

Changing the subject, Leoh asked, "And how are your quarters? Comfortable, I hope."

"Sure." Hector nodded. "The Terran embassy's almost as plush as this apartment."

"Not bad for a junior lieutenant."

Hector fidgeted from the window wall to the couch, then sat on the edge of a web chair.

"Are you nervous about Sir Harold's visit?" Leoh asked.

"N . . . nervous? No, sir. Terrified!"

Laughing, Leoh said, "Don't worry. Harold's a pleasant enough old grouse . . . although he tries his best to hide it."

Nodding without looking convinced, Hector got to his feet again and went back to the window wall. Then he gasped, "He . . . he's here!"

Leoh heaved himself up from the couch and hurried to see. A sleek ground car with Star Watch markings was pulled up at the building's entrance. Official Acquatai-nian escort cars flanked it.

"He must be on his way up," Leoh said. "Now try to relax and act, . . ."

The simple-minded door computer announced in a tinny monotone, "Your expected guests are here."

"Then open up," Leoh commanded.

The door slid open to reveal a pair of sturdy, steel-eyed Watchmen, a half-dozen Acquatainian honor guards, and—in their midst—the paunchy, jowly figure of Sir Harold Spencer, dressed in a shapeless gray jumpsuit.

The Star Watch Commander in Chief broke into one of his rare smiles. "Albert, you old scoundrel, how are you?"

Leoh rushed to the doorway and grasped Spencer's outstretched hand. "Harold . . . I thought we'd never see each other again, in the flesh."

"Considering the amount of flesh between the two of us, perhaps we're violating some basic law of the universe by being in the same room together."

They laughed and walked into the room. The door slid shut, leaving the guards outside. Hector stood transfixed beside the window wall.

"Harold, you look wonderful. . . ."

"Nonsense. I'm a walking geriatrics experiment. But you, you ancient schemer, you must have transferred to another body since I saw you last."

"No, merely careful living. . . ."

"Ahah. My downfall. Too many worries and too much wine. It must be pleasant to live the university life, free of care. . . ."

"Of course. Of course. Oh . . . Harold, I'd like to intro-duce Junior Lieutenant Hector."

Hector snapped to attention and saluted.

"Stand easy, Lieutenant. No need for formality. So, you're the man who beat Kerak's assassin, are you?"

"No, sir. I mean yessir ... I mean, Professor Leoh is the one. ..."

"Nonsense. Albert told me all about it. You're the one who faced the danger."

Hector's mouth twitched once or twice, as though he was trying to say something, but no sounds came out.

Spencer stuck a massive hand into his pocket and pulled out a small ebony box. "This is for you, Lieutenant." He handed the box to Hector.

The Watchman opened it and saw inside, against a jet-black setting, two small silver pins in the shape of comets. The insignia of a full lieutenant. His jaw dropped open.

"The official notification is grinding through Star Watch processing, Lieutenant," Spencer said. "I thought there was no sense letting you wait until the computers straightened out all the records. Congratulations on a well-earned promotion."

Hector managed a half-strangled, "Thank you, sir."

Turning to Leoh, Spencer said, "Now then, Albert, let us recount old times. I assume you have some refreshments on the premises?"

Several hours later the two old men were sitting on the air couch, while Hector listened from the web chair. The room's color had shifted to reds and yellows now, and the scent was of desert flowers.

"And what do you intend to do now?" Sir Harold was asking the Professor. "Surely you don't expect me to believe that you're going to luxuriate here and then return to Carinae, in the midst of the deepest political crisis of the century."

Leoh shrugged and hiked his eyebrows, an expression that sent a network of creases across his fleshy face. "I'm not sure what I'm going to do. I'd still like to take a good look at some ideas for better interstellar transportation. And I'd want to be on hand here if those savages from Kerak try to use the dueling machine for their own purposes again."

Nodding, Spencer rumbled, "I knew it. You're getting yourself involved in politics. Sooner or later you'll be after my job."

Even Hector laughed at that.

More seriously, Spencer went on, "You know, of course, that I'm here officially to attend the inauguration of General Martine as the new Prime Minister."

"Yes," said Leoh. "And your *real* reason for coming?"

Lowering his voice slightly, Spencer answered, "I hope to persuade Martine to join the Commonwealth. Or at least to sign a treaty of alliance with us. It's the only way that Acquatainia can avoid a war with Kerak. All of Acquatainia's former allies have been taken over by Kerak or frightened off. Alone, the Acquatainians are in grave danger. As a Commonwealth member, or an ally, I doubt that even Kanus would be foolish enough to attack them right now."

"But Acquatainia has always refused Commonwealth membership . . . or even an alliance."

"Yes, but General Martine might see things differently now that Kanus is obviously preparing for war," Spencer said.

"But the General . . ." Hector began, then stopped.

"Go on, my boy. What were you going to say?"

"Well, it might not be anything important . . . just something that Geri told me about the General . . . er, the Prime Minister. She, eh, well, she said he's a stubborn, shortsighted, proud old clod. Those were her words, sir."

Spencer huffed. "The Terran embassy here used slightly different terms, but they painted the same picture of him."

"And, uh, she said he's also very brave and patriotic . . . but short-tempered."

Leoh turned a worried expression toward Spencer. "It

doesn't sound as though he'd be willing to admit that he needs Commonwealth protection, does it?"

Shrugging, Sir Harold replied, "The plain fact is that an alliance with the Commonwealth is the only way to avert a war. I've had our computer simulators study the situation. Now that Kerak has absorbed Szarno and has neutralized Acquatainia's other former allies, the computer predicts that Kerak will defeat Acquatainia in a war. Ninety-three percent probability."

Leoh's look of gloom sank deeper.

"And once Kanus has Acquatainia under his grasp, he'll attack the Commonwealth."

"What? But that's suicide! Why should he do that?"

"I'd say it's because he's a lunatic," Spencer answered, with real anger edging his voice. "The sociodynamicists tell me that Kanus' sort of dictatorship must continually seek to expand, or it will fall apart from internal dissensions and pressures."

"But he can't beat the Commonwealth," Hector said.

"Correct," Spencer agreed. "Every computer simulation we've run shows that the Commonwealth would crush Kerak, even if Kanus has Acquatainia's resources in his hands."

The Star Watch Commander paused a moment, then added, "But the computers also predict that the war will cost millions of lives on both sides. And it will trigger off other wars, elsewhere, that could eventually destroy the Commonwealth entirely."

Leoh leaned back with the shock. "Then—Martine simply *must* accept Commonwealth alliance."

Spencer nodded. But his face showed that he didn't expect it.

Leoh and Hector watched General Martine's inauguration on tri-di, in the professor's apartment. That evening, they joined the throngs of politicians, businessmen, military leaders, ambassadors, artists, visitors, and other VIP's who were congregating at the city's main spaceport for the new Prime Minister's inaugural ball. The party was to be held aboard a satellite orbiting the planet.

"Do you think Geri will be there?" Hector asked Leoh as they pushed along with the crowd into a jammed shuttle craft.

The Watchman was wearing his dress black-and-silver uniform, with the comet insignias on his collar. Leoh wore a simple coverall, as advised in the invitation to the party. It was a splendid crimson with gold trim.

"You said she's been invited," Leoh answered over the hubbub of the hundreds of other conversations.

They found a pair of seats together and strapped themselves in.

"But she wasn't certain that she ought to go . . . what with her father's death only a few weeks ago."

Leaning back in the padded chair, Leoh said, "Well, if she's not there, you can spend hours telling her all about the party."

The Watchman's lean face broke into a toothy grin. "I hadn't thought of that. . . ."

The shuttle filled quickly with noisy party goers and then took off. It flew like a normal rocket plane to the top of the atmosphere, then boosted swiftly to the satellite. The party was well under way when Hector and Leoh stepped from the shuttle's air lock into the satellite.

It was a huge globular satellite, with all the interior decks and bulkheads removed so that it was as hollow as an enormous soap bubble. The shell of the "bubble" was transparent, except for small disks around the various air locks.

There must have been more than a thousand people present already, Leoh guessed as he took a first look at the milling throng floating weightlessly through the vast globe. They seemed to be suspended over his head, many of them upside down, others hanging sideways or calmly drifting along and gesturing, deep in conversation. Most of them held drinks in sealed plastic squeeze containers with straws poking out from their tops. The crowd formed a dizzying kaleidoscope overhead: brilliant costumes, flashing jewelry, buzzing voices, crackling laughter, all mixing and gliding effortlessly in mid-air.

Leoh put a hand out to Hector, to steady himself.

"Must be some sort of grav field along the shell," the Watchman said, pulling one boot tackily from the floor.

"For the fainthearted, I suppose," Leoh said.

The other shuttle passengers were streaming past them and launching themselves like swimmers away from the air lock, coasting gracefully up into the huge chamber.

Looking around, Leoh saw refreshment bars spotted along the shell, and more floating overhead. He turned back to Hector and said, "Why don't you go look for Geri, and I'll try to find Harold."

"I sort of think I should stay close to you, Professor. After all, my job is to, uh, that is. . . ."

"Nonsense! There are no Kerak assassins in this crowd. Go find Geri."

Grinning, Hector said, "All right. But I'll be keeping one eye on you."

With that, Hector jumped off the floor to join the weightless throng. But he jumped a bit too hard, banged into a rainbow-clad Acquatainian who was floating past with a drink in his hand, and knocked the drink, the man, and himself spinning. The drink's cover popped open and globules of liquid spattered through the air, hitting other members of the crowd and breaking into constantly smaller droplets. A woman screamed.

The Acquatainian righted himself immediately, but Hector couldn't stop. He went tumbling head over heels, cleaving through the crowd like a runaway chariot, emitting a string of, "Wh . . . whoops . . . look out . . . gosh . . . pardon me . . . watch it. . . ."

Leoh stood rooted to his spot beside the air lock, staring unbelievingly as Hector barreled through the crowd.

The weightless guests scattered before him, some yelling angrily, a few women screaming, most of them laughing. Then they closed in again, and Leoh could no longer see the Watchman. A trio of servants took off after him, chasing across the gigantic globe to intercept him.

Only then did Leoh notice a servant standing beside him, with a slim belt in his hands. "A stabilizer, sir. Most of the guests have their own. It is very difficult to maneuver weightlessly without one . . . as the Star Watchman is demonstrating."

Leoh accepted the belt, decided there wasn't much he could do about Hector except add to the confusion, so he floated easily up into the heart of the party. The sensation of weightlessness was pleasant, like floating in a pool of water. He got himself a drink in one of the special covered cups and sucked on the straw as he drifted toward a large knot of people near the center of the globe.

Suddenly Hector pinwheeled past him, looking helpless and red-faced, as a couple of servants swam after him as hard as they could. The party goers laughed as Hector buzzed by, then returned to their conversations. Leoh put out a hand, but the Watchman was past and disappeared into the crowd again.

Leoh frowned. He loathed big parties. Too many people, too little activity. People talked incessantly at parties, but said nothing. They ate and drank despite the fact that they weren't hungry. They spent hours listening to total strangers whom they would never see again. It was a mammoth waste of time.

Or are you merely bored, he asked himself, *because no one here recognizes you? They seem to be having a fine time without the famous inventor of the dueling machine.*

Leoh drifted toward the transparent wall of the satellite and watched the glowing surface of the planet outside, a huge solid sphere bathed in golden sunlight. Then he turned and floated effortlessly until he got a good view of the stars. The Acquataine Cluster was a jewel box of gleaming red and gold and orange stars, packed together so thickly that you could barely see the black background of space.

So much beauty in the universe, Leoh thought.

"Professor Leoh?"

Startled out of his reverie, Leoh turned to see a small, moon-faced, balding man floating beside him and extending his hand in greeting.

"I am Lal Ponte," he said as Leoh shook his hand. "It is an honor to meet you."

"An honor for me," Leoh replied with the standard Acquatainian formality.

"You are probably looking for Sir Harold, and I know the Prime Minister would like to see you. Since they're both in the same place, may I take you to them?" Ponte's voice was a squeaky tenor.

Leoh nodded. "Thanks. Lead the way."

Ponte took off across the satellite, worming his way around knots of people—many of them upside down. Leoh followed. *Like a freighter being towed by a tug,* he thought of the sight of his bulky self tagging along after the mousy-looking Acquatainian.

Leoh searched his memory. Lal Ponte: the new Secretary of Interior Affairs. Until a few weeks ago, Ponte had been an insignificant member of the legislature. But in the hectic voting for a new Prime Minister, with four possible candidates splitting the legislature almost evenly, Ponte had risen from obscurity to bring a critical dozen votes to General Martine's side. His reward was the Cabinet position.

Ponte glided straight into an immense clot of people near the very center of the satellite. Leoh followed him ponderously, bumping shoulders and elbows, getting frowns and mutterings, apologizing like a latecomer to

the theater who must step on many toes to reach his
seat.

"Who's the old one?" he heard a feminine voice
whisper.

"Ah, Albert, there you are!" Spencer called as they got
to the center of the crowd. With that, the crowd flowed
back slightly to make room for Leoh. The mutterings
took on a different tone.

"General Martine," Spencer said to the new Prime
Minister, "you of course know Albert Leoh, the inventor
of the dueling machine and one of the Commonwealth's
leading scientists."

A buzz of recognition went through the crowd.

Martine was tall and slim, wearing a military uniform
of white and gold that accentuated his lean frame. His
face was long, serious, with sad hound's eyes and a prominent patrician nose. He nodded and put on a measured
smile. "Of course. The man who defeated Kerak's assassin. It is good to see you again, Professor."

"Thank you for inviting me," Leoh responded. "And
congratulations on your election."

Martine nodded gravely.

"I have been trying to convince the Prime Minister,"
Spencer said in his heavy public-address voice, "that
Acquatainia would benefit greatly from joining the Com-
monwealth. But he seems to have reservations."

Martine raised his eyes to look beyond the crowd, out
toward the satellite's transparent shell and the golden
planet beyond.

"Acquatainia has traditionally remained independent of
the Commonwealth," Martine said. "We have no need
of special trade advantages or political alliances. We are
a rich and strong and happy people."

"But you are threatened by Kerak," Leoh said.

"My dear Professor," Martine said, raising himself
slightly and looking down on Leoh, "I have been a military man all my adult life. I had the honor of helping to

defeat Kerak a generation ago. I know how to deal with
military threats."

Far across the satellite, at one of the air lock entrances,
Hector—wearing a stabilizer belt now—hovered above a
crowd of latecomers as they came through the air lock,
searching their faces. And there she was!

He mushed down into them, accidentally pushing
three jeweled and cloaked businessmen into an equal
number of mini-gowned wives, stepping on the foot of a
burly Acquatainian colonel, and jostling through the new
arrivals to get to Geri Dulaq.

"You came," he said, taking both her hands in his.

Her smile made his knees flutter. "I hoped you'd be
here, Hector."

"I . . . well," he was grinning like an idiot, "I'm here."

"I'm glad."

They stood there at the air lock entrance, looking at
each other, while people elbowed their way around them
to get into the party.

"Hector, shouldn't we move away from the air lock?"
Geri suggested gently.

"Huh? Oh, sure. . . ." He walked her toward a slightly
sweaty servant (one of the posse who had chased Hector
across the satellite) and then took a stabilizer belt from
him.

"You'll need one of these belts before you try to float.
Otherwise it's, eh, kind of tricky trying to maneuver."

The servant gritted his teeth and glared.

Geri blinked her large brown eyes at Hector. "Will
you show me how it works? I'm terribly poor at things
like this."

Restraining an impulse to leap off the floor and do a
triple somersault, Hector said simply, "Oh, there's really
nothing to it . . ." He glanced at the sweaty-faced servant,
then added, "Once you get the hang of it."

*   *   *

Spencer was saying, with some edge to his voice, "But when you defeated Kerak, you had the Szarno Confederacy and several other star-nations on your side. Now your old alliances are gone. You are alone against Kerak."

Martine sighed like a man being forced to exert great patience. "I repeat, Sir Harold, that Acquatainia is strong enough to defeat any Kerak attack without Star Watch assistance."

Leoh shook his head, but said nothing.

Lal Ponte, floating beside his Prime Minister and looking like a small satellite near a large planet, said, "The Prime Minister is making plans for an impenetrable defense system, a network of fortified planets and starship fleets so strong that Kerak would never dare to attack it."

"And suppose," Spencer countered, "Kerak attacks before this defense line is completed? Or attacks from a different direction?"

"We will fight and win," Martine said.

Spencer ran a hand through his shaggy hair. "Don't you realize that an alliance with the Commonwealth—even a token alliance—will force Kanus to pause before he dares to attack? Your objective, it seems to me, should be to prevent a war from starting. Instead, you're concentrating on plans to win the war, once it begins."

"If Kanus wants war," Martine said, "we will defeat him."

"But he can be defeated without war," Spencer insisted.

Leoh added, "No dictator can last long without the threat of war to keep his people frightened enough to serve him. And if it becomes clear that Acquatainia cannot be attacked successfully. . . ."

"Kanus wants war," Martine said.

"And so do you, apparently," Spencer added.

The Prime Minister glared at Spencer for a long

moment, then turned and said, "Excuse me, I am neglecting my other guests."

He pushed away, accompanied by a half-dozen followers, leaving Spencer, Leoh, and Lal Ponte in the middle of a suddenly dissipating crowd.

Geri and Hector floated close to the transparent shell, looking out at the stars, barely aware of the music and voices from the party.

"Hector."

"Yes?"

"Will you promise me something?"

"Sure. What is it?"

Her face was so serious, so beautiful, he could feel his pulse throbbing through his body.

"Do you think Odal will ever return to Acquatainia?"

The question surprised him. "Uh ... I don't know. Maybe. I sort of doubt it. I mean, well...."

"If he ever does ..." Geri's voice trailed off.

"Don't worry," Hector said, holding her close to him. "I won't let him hurt you ... or anybody else."

Her smile was overpowering. "Hector, dearest Hector. If Odal should ever return here, would you kill him for me?"

Without a microsecond's thought, he replied, "I'd challenge him as soon as I saw him."

Her face grew serious again. "No. I don't mean in the dueling machine. I mean really. Kill him."

"I don't understand the Prime Minister's attitude," Leoh said to Spencer and Lal Ponte.

"He has great pride," Ponte answered, "the pride of a military man. And we have great pride in him. He is the man who can lead Acquatainia back to glory. Dulaq and Massan ... they were good men, but civilians, too weak to deal with Kanus of Kerak."

"They were political leaders," Spencer rumbled. "They

realized that war is an admission of failure. War is the last resort, when all else fails."

"We are not afraid of war!" Ponte snapped.

"You should be," Leoh said.

"Why? Do you doubt that we could defeat Kerak?"

"Why run the risk when you could avoid the war altogether?"

The little politician waved his arms agitatedly, a maneuver that caused him to bob up and down weightlessly. "We are not afraid of the Kerak Worlds! You assume that we are cowards who must run under the skirts of your Terran Commonwealth at the first sign of danger!"

"Lack of judgment is worse than cowardice," said Leoh. "Why do you insist? . . ."

"You accuse the Acquatainian government of stupidity?"

"No, I. . . ."

His voice rising higher and higher, Ponte squeaked, "Then you accuse me of stupidity . . . or the Prime Minister, perhaps?"

"I am only questioning your judgment about. . . ."

"And I accuse you of cowardice!" Ponte screeched.

People were turning to watch them now. Ponte bobbed up and down, raging. "Because *you* are afraid of this bully, Kanus, you assume that we should be!"

"Now really . . ." Spencer began.

"You are a coward!" Ponte screamed at Leoh. "And I will prove it. I challenge you to meet me in your own dueling machine!"

For the first time in years, Leoh felt his own temper flaring. "This is the most asinine argument I've ever seen."

"I challenge you!" Ponte insisted. "Do you accept the challenge, or will you slink away and prove your cowardice?"

"Accepted!" Leoh snapped.

*   *   *

The sun was a small bluish-white disk high in the sky of Meklin, one of Kerak's forced agriculture planets. Up here on the ridge, the wind felt chill to Odal, despite the heat in the valley farmlands below. The sky was cloudless, but the wind-rippled trees rustled a mosaic of gold and red against the blue.

Odal saw Runstet sitting on the grass in a patch of sunlight with his wife and three small children. The oldest, a boy, could hardly have been more than ten. They were enjoying a picnic, laughing at something that had escaped Odal's notice.

The Kerak major stepped forward. Runstet saw him and paled. He got up to face Odal.

"This is not what I want to see," Odal said quietly. "You'll have to do better."

Runstet stood there, rooted to the spot, while everything around him began to flicker, dim. The children and their mother, still laughing, grew faint and their laughter faded. The woods seemed to go misty, then disappeared altogether. Nothing was visible except Runstet and the fearful look on his face.

"You are trying to hide your memories from me by substituting other memories," Odal said. "We know that you met with certain other high-ranking army officers at your home three months ago. You claim it was a social occasion. I would like to see it."

The older man, square-jawed, his hair an iron gray, was obviously fighting for self-control. Fear was in him, Odal knew, but he also sensed something else: anger, stubbornness, and pride.

"Inferior-grade officers were not invited to the . . . to the party. It was strictly for my old classmates, Major." General Runstet accented the last word with as much venom as he could muster.

Odal felt a flash of anger, but replied calmly, "May I remind you that you are under arrest and therefore have no rank. And if you insist on refusing me access to your memories of this meeting, more stringent methods of interrogation will be used." *Fool!* he thought. *You're a dead man and yet you refuse to admit it.*

"You can do anything you want to," Runstet said. "Drugs, torture . . . you'll get nothing from me. Use this damnable dueling machine for a hundred years and I'll still tell you nothing!"

Unmoving, Odal said, "Shall I re-create the scene for you? I have visited your home in Meklin, and I have a list of the officers who attended your meeting."

"When Marshal Lugal learns how Kor and his trained assassins have treated a general officer, you'll all be exterminated!" Runstet bellowed. "And you! An officer yourself. A disgrace to the uniform you wear!"

"I have my duty," Odal said. "And I am trying to spare you some of the more unpleasant methods of interrogation."

As Odal spoke, the mist around them dissolved and they were standing in a spacious living room. Sunlight streamed through the open patio doors. Nearly a dozen men in army uniforms sat on the couches. But they were silent, unmoving.

"Now then," said Odal, "you will show me exactly what happened. Every word and gesture, every facial expression."

"Never!"

"That in itself is an admission of guilt," Odal snapped. "You have been plotting against the Leader; you and a number of others of the general staff."

"I will not incriminate other men," Runstet said stubbornly. "You can kill me, but. . . ."

"We can kill your wife and children, too," Odal said softly.

The General's mouth popped open and Odal could feel the panic flash through him. "You wouldn't dare! Not even Kanus himself would. . . ."

"Accidents happen," said Odal. "As far as the rest of

Kerak is concerned, you are hospitalized with a mental breakdown. Your despondent wife might take her own life, or your entire family could die in a crash while on their way to the hospital to see you."

Runstet seemed to crumple. He did not physically move or say a word, but his entire body seemed to soften, to sag. Behind him, one of the generals stirred to life. He leaned forward, took a cigar from the humidor on the low table before him, and said:

"When we're ready to attack the Acquatainians, just how far can we trust Kanus to allow the army to operate without political interference?"

"I simply don't understand what came over me," Leoh said to Spencer and Hector. "I never let my temper get the better of me."

They were standing in the former lecture hall that housed the grotesque bulk of the dueling machine. No one else had entered yet; the duel with Ponte was still an hour away.

"Come now, Albert," said Spencer. "If that whining little politician had spoken to me the way he did to you, I'd have been tempted to hit him there and then."

Leoh shrugged.

"These Acquatainians are an emotional lot," Spencer went on. "Frankly, I'm glad to be leaving."

"When will you go?"

"As soon as this silly duel is finished. It's quite clear that Martine is unwilling to accept any support from the Commonwealth. My presence here is merely aggravating him and his people."

Hector spoke for the first time. "That means there'll be war between Acquatainia and Kerak." He said it quietly, his eyes gazing off into space, as though he were talking to himself.

"Both sides want war," Spencer said.

"Stupidity," muttered Leoh.

"Pride," Spencer corrected. "The same kind of pride that makes men fight duels."

Startled, Leoh was about to answer until he saw the grin on Spencer's leathery face.

The chamber filled slowly. The meditechs who operated the dueling machine came in, a few at a time, and started checking out the machine. There was a new man on the team, sitting at a new console. His equipment monitored the duels and made certain that neither of the duelists was getting telepathic help from outside.

Ponte and his group arrived precisely at the appointed time for the duel. Four newsmen appeared in the press gallery, high above. Leoh suppressed a frown. *Surely a duel involving the machine's inventor should warrant more attention from the networks.*

They went through the medical checks, the instructions on using the machine (which Leoh had written), and the agreement that the challenged party would have the first choice of weapons.

"My weapon will be the elementary laws of physics," Leoh said. "No special instructions will be necessary."

Ponte's eyes widened slightly with puzzlement. His seconds glanced at each other. Even the dueling machine's meditechs looked uncertain. After a heartbeat's silence, the chief meditech shrugged.

"If there are no objections," he said, "let us proceed."

Leoh sat patiently in his booth while the meditechs attached the neurocontacts to his head and torso. *Strange,* he thought. *I've operated dueling machines hundreds of times. But this is the first time the other man in the machine is really angry at me. He wants to kill me.*

The meditechs left and shut the booth. Leoh was alone now, staring into the screen and its subtly shifting colors. He tried to close his eyes, found that he couldn't, tried again and succeeded.

When he opened them he was standing in the middle

of a large, gymnasium-like room. There were windows high up near the lofty ceiling. Instead of being filled with athletic apparatus, this room was crammed with rope pulleys, inclined ramps, metal spheres of all sizes from a few centimeters to twice the height of a man. Leoh was standing on a slightly raised, circular platform, holding a small control box in his hand.

Lal Ponte stood across the room, his back to a wall, frowning at the jungle of unfamiliar equipment.

"This is a sort of elementary physics lab," Leoh called out to him. "While none of the objects here are really weapons, many of them can be dangerous if you know how to use them. Or if you don't know."

Ponte began to object, "This is unreasonable. . . ."

"Not really," Leoh said pleasantly. "You'll find that the equipment is spread around the room to form a sort of maze. Your job is to get through the maze to this platform, and to find something to use as a weapon on me. Now, there are traps in the maze. You'll have to avoid them. And this platform is really a turntable . . . but we'll talk about that later."

Ponte looked around. "You are foolish."

"Perhaps."

The Acquatainian took a few steps to his right and lifted a slender metal rod. Hefting it in his hand, he started toward Leoh.

"That's a lever," the Professor said. "Of course, you can use it as a club if you wish."

A tangle of ropes stood in Ponte's way. Instead of detouring around them, he pushed his way through.

Leoh shook his head and touched a button on his control box. "A mistake, I'm afraid."

The ropes—a pulley, actually—jerked into motion and heaved the flooring under Ponte's feet upward. The Acquatainian toppled to his hands and knees and found himself on a platform suddenly ten meters in the air. Dropping the lever, he began grabbing at the ropes. One

of them swung free and he jumped at it, curling his arms
and legs around it.

"Pendulum," Leoh called to him. "Watch your. . . ."

Ponte's rope, with him on it, swung out a little way,
then swung back again toward the mid-air platform. He
cracked his head nastily on the platform's edge, let go of
the rope, and thudded to the floor.

"The floor's padded," Leoh said, "but I forgot to pad
the edge of the platform. Hope it didn't hurt you too
badly."

Ponte sat up groggily, his head rolling. It took him
three tries to stand up again. He staggered forward.

"On your right is an inclined plane of the sort Galileo
used, only much larger. You'll have to hurry to get past
the ball. . . ."

At a touch of Leoh's finger on the control box, an
immense metal ball began rolling down the gangway-
sized plane. Ponte heard its rumbling, turned to stare at
it goggle-eyed, and barely managed to jump out of its
way. The ball rolled across the floor, ponderously smashing everything in its way until it crashed against the far
wall.

"Perhaps you'd better sit down for a few moments and
gather your wits," Leoh suggested.

Ponte was puffing hard. "You . . . you're a devil . . . a
smiling devil."

He reached down for a small sphere at his feet. As he
raised his hand to throw it, Leoh touched the control
box again and the turntable platform began to rotate
slowly. Ponte's awkward toss missed him by a meter.

"I can adjust the turntable's speed," Leoh explained
as Ponte threw several more spheres. All missed.

The Acquatainian, his once-bland face furiously red
now, rushed toward the spinning platform and jumped
onto it, on the side opposite Leoh. He still had two small
spheres in his hand.

"Be careful," Leoh warned as Ponte swayed and nearly fell off. "Centrifugal force can be tricky. . . ."

The two men stood unmoving for a moment: Leo alertly watching, Ponte glaring. The room appeared to be swinging around them.

Ponte threw one of the spheres as hard as he could. It seemed to curve away from Leoh.

"The Coriolis force," said Leoh, in a slightly lecturing tone, "is a natural phenomenon on rotating systems. It's what makes the winds curve across a planet's rotating surface."

The second sphere whistled by, no closer than the first.

"I should also warn you that this platform is made of alternate sections of magnetic and nonmagnetic materials." Leoh gestured toward the mosaic-colored floor. "Your shoes have metal in them. If you remain on the magnetized sections, the red ones, you should be able to move about without too much difficulty."

He touched the control box again and the turntable speeded up considerably. The room seemed to whirl wildly around them now. Leoh hunched down and leaned inward.

"Of course," he went on, "at the speed we're going now, if you should step onto a nonmagnetized section. . . ."

Ponte started doggedly across the turntable, heading for Leoh, his eyes on the colored flooring. Leoh stepped carefully away from him, keeping as much distance between them as possible. Ponte was moving faster now, trying to keep one eye on Leoh and one on his feet. He stopped abruptly, started to move directly toward Leoh, cutting in toward the center of the turntable.

"Be careful!"

Ponte's feet slipped out from under him. He fell painfully on his back, skidded across the turntable out to the edge, and shot across the floor to slam feet first into a big metal block.

"My leg ..." He groaned. "My leg is broken. ..."

Leoh stopped the turntable and stepped off. He walked over to the Acquatainian, whose face was twisted with pain.

"I could kill you fairly easily now," he said softly. "But I really have no desire to. You've had enough, I think."

The room began to fade out. Leoh found himself sitting in the dueling machine's booth, blinking at the now dead screen in front of him.

The door popped open and Hector's grinning face appeared. "You beat him!"

"Yes," Leoh said, suddenly tired. "But I didn't kill him. He can try again with his own choice of weapons, if he chooses to."

Ponte was white-faced and trembling as they walked toward him. His followers were huddled around him, asking questions. The chief meditech was saying:

"You may continue, if you wish, or postpone the second half of the duel until tomorrow."

Looking up at Leoh, Ponte shook his head. "No ... no. I was defeated. I can't ... fight again."

The chief meditech nodded. "The duel is concluded, then. Professor Leoh has won."

Leoh extended his hand to the Acquatainian. Ponte's grasp was soft and sweaty.

"I hope we can be friends now," Leoh said.

Looking thoroughly miserable, Ponte mumbled, "Yes, of course. Thank you."

Long after everyone else had left the dueling machine chamber, Leoh, Spencer, and Hector remained behind, pacing slowly across the tiled floor, speaking in low voices that echoed gloomily in the vast room.

"I must go now, Albert," Spencer said. "My ship was scheduled to leave half an hour ago. My adjutant, outside, is probably eating tranquilizers by now. He's a good man, but extremely nervous."

"And there's nothing you can do to convince Martine?" Leoh asked.

"Apparently not. But if you're going to remain on the scene here, perhaps you can try."

Leoh nodded. "I can speak to the scientists here at the university. Their voices should carry some weight with the government."

Spencer looked skeptical. "What else will you be tinkering with? I know you won't be content without some sort of research problem to puzzle over."

"I'm trying to find a way of improving on the star ships. We've got to make interstellar travel easier. . . ."

"The star ships are highly efficient already."

"I know. I mean a fundamental improvement. Perhaps a completely different way to travel through space . . . as different as the star ships are from the ancient rockets."

Spencer held up a beefy hand. "Enough! In another minute you'll start spouting metadimensional physics at me. Politics is hard enough for me to understand."

Leoh chuckled.

Turning to Hector, Sir Harold said, "Lieutenant, keep a close eye on him as long as he's in Acquatainia. Professor Leoh is a valuable man—and my friend. Understood?"

"Yessir."

Odal stood rigidly at attention before Kor. The Intelligence Minister was leaning back in his padded desk chair, his hands playing over an ornate dagger that he used as a pointer.

"You don't enjoy your duties here?" Kor was smiling coldly.

"I am an army officer," Odal said carefully. "I find that interrogation work is . . . unpleasant."

Kor tapped the dagger against his fingernails. "But you are one of the few men who can use the dueling machine for interrogation. And you are by far the best man we have for the purpose. The others are amateurs compared to you. You have talent!"

"It is difficult for me to interrogate fellow army officers."

"I suppose so," Kor admitted. "But you have done quite well. We now know exactly who in the army we can trust, and who is plotting against the Leader."

"Then my work here is finished."

"The plotting involves more than the army, Major. It goes far wider and deeper. The enemies of the Leader infest every part of our government. Marshal Lugal is involved, I'm sure. . . ."

"But there's no evidence. . . ."

"I'm convinced he's involved," Kor snapped. "And Romis, too!"

Kanus wants control of the army, Odal knew, *and you want to eliminate anyone who can compete with you for Kanus' favor.*

"Don't look so sour, Major," said Kor, his smile broader and somehow more chilling. "You have served your Leader—and me—very well in these weeks. Now then . . . how would you like to return to Acquatainia?"

Odal felt a shock of surprise and strange elation.

"Spencer has left Acquatainia," Kor explained, "and our plans are going well. But Leoh still remains there. He is still dangerous. You will destroy him."

"And the Watchman too," Odal said.

Kor jabbed the dagger toward Odal. "Not so fast. Leoh will be destroyed by his own dueling machine, but in a very special way. In fact, he has already taken the first step toward his own destruction, in a duel with a simple little man who thinks he will be Prime Minister of Acquatainia, once Kerak conquers the Cluster."

Frowning, Odal said, "I don't understand."

"You will, Major. You probably won't enjoy what you must do, any more than Lal Ponte did. But you will do your duty to Kerak and to the Leader, just as Ponte did what we told him to. You won't become Prime Minister of Acquatainia, of course—but then, neither will Lal Ponte."

Kor's laugh was like a knife scraping on bone.

The night sky of Acquatainia was a blaze of stars twinkling, shimmering, dazzling so brightly that there was no real darkness in the city, only a silvery twilight brighter than full moonlight on Earth.

Hector sat at the controls of the skimmer and raced it down the river that cut through the city, heading toward the harbor and the open ocean. He could smell the salt air already. He glanced across the skimmer's tiny cockpit at Geri, sitting in the swivel seat beside him and hunched slightly forward to keep the spray off her face. The sight of her almost made it impossible for him to concentrate on steering the high-speed skimmer.

He snaked the little vessel through the other pleasure boats on the river, trailing a plume of slightly luminous spray. Out in the harbor there were huge freighters anchored massively in the main channel. Hector ran the skimmer over to shallower water, between the channel and the docks, as Geri stared up at the vast ocean-going ships.

Finally they were out on the deep swells of the sea. Hector cut the engine and the skimmer slowed, dug its prow into an oncoming billow, and settled its hull in the water.

"The rocking isn't going to . . . uh, bother you, is it?" he asked, turning to Geri.

Shaking her head, she said, "Oh no, I love it here on the sea." Now that they were resting easily on the water, Geri reached up and unpinned her hair. It fell around her shoulders with a softness that made Hector quiver.

"The cooker should be finished by now," she said. "Are you hungry?"

He nodded. They got up together, bumped slightly as they squeezed between the two swivel seats to get to the padded bench at the rear of the cockpit. Geri smiled at him and Hector plopped back in the pilot's seat, content to savor her perfume and watch her. She sat on the bench and opened the cooker's hatch. Out came steaming trays of food.

Hector came over to the bench, stumbling slightly, and sat beside her.

"The drinks are in the cooler," she said, pointing to the other side of the bench.

After dinner they sat together on the bench, heads back to gaze at the stars, while the skimmer's autopilot kept them from drifting too far from the harbor.

"This, uh . . . thing about Odal," Hector said, very reluctantly. "It's not . . . well, it's not the kind of thing that. . . ."

"I know. It's a terrible thing to ask you to do." She put her hand in his. "But what else can I do? I'm only a girl; I can't go out and kill him myself. I need a protector, a champion, someone who will avenge my father's murder. You're the only one I can turn to, Hector."

"Yes, but . . . um . . . killing him, that's. . . ."

"It'll be dangerous, I realize that. But you're so brave. You're not afraid of Odal, are you?"

"No, but. . . ."

"And it won't be anything more than a justifiable execution. He's a murderer. You'll be the sword of justice. *My* sword of justice."

"Yes, but. . . ."

She pulled away slightly. "Of course, Odal will probably never return to Acquatainia. But if he does, you can be sure it's for one thing only."

Hector blinked. "What's that?"

"To murder Professor Leoh," she said.

The Star Watchman slumped back on the bench.

"You're right. And I guess I've got to stop him from doing that."

Geri turned and grabbed him by the ears and kissed him. Hector felt his feet come off the deck. He held onto her and kissed back. Then she slid away from him. He reached for her, but she took his hand in hers.

"Let me catch my breath," she said.

He eased over toward her, feeling his heart thumping louder than the slap of the waves against the skimmer's hull.

"Of course," Geri said coolly, "it seems that Professor Leoh can take care of himself in the dueling machine."

"Uh-huh." Hector edged closer to her.

"It was very surprising to hear that Lal Ponte had challenged the Professor," she said, backing into the corner of the bench. "Ponte is such a . . . a *nothing* type of person. I never thought he'd have the courage to fight a duel."

Leaning close to Geri and sliding an arm across the bench's backrest and around her shoulders, Hector said nothing.

"I remember my father saying that if anyone in the legislature was working for Kerak, it would be Ponte."

"Huh?"

Geri was frowning with the memory. "Yes, Father was concerned that Ponte was allied with Kerak. 'If Kerak ever conquers us,' Father said to me once, 'that little coward will be our Prime Minister.'"

Hector sat upright. "But now he's serving Martine . . . and Martine sure isn't pro-Kerak."

"I know," Geri said, nodding. "Perhaps Father was wrong. Or Ponte may have changed his mind. Or. . . ."

"Or he could still be working for Kerak."

Geri smiled. "Even if he is, Professor Leoh took care of him."

"Umm." Hector leaned back again and saw that he

and Geri had somehow moved slightly apart. He pushed over toward her.

"My foot!" Geri leaped up from the bench.

"Oh, I'm sorry. Did I step on . . ." Hector jumped up too.

Geri was hopping on one foot in the tiny cockpit, making the skimmer rock with each bounce. Hector reached out to hold her, but she pushed him away. The effort toppled her over backward. The cockpit gunwale caught her behind the knees and she flipped backward, howling, into the water with a good-sized splash.

Hector, appalled, never hesitated a second. He leaped right into the sea from the point where he stood, narrowly missing Geri as he hit the water, head first, arms and legs flailing.

He came up spouting, blurry-eyed, gasping. Geri was treading water beside him.

"I . . . I . . . I. . . ."

She laughed. "It's all right, Hector. It's my own fault. I lost my temper when you stepped on my foot."

"But . . . I . . . are you . . . ?"

"It's a lovely night," she said. "As long as we're in the water anyway, why don't we have a swim?"

"Uh . . . fine, except, well, that is . . . I can't swim," Hector said, and slowly he sank under.

As he stepped from the ramp of the spaceship to the slideway that led into the terminal building, Odal felt a strange sense of exhilaration.

He was in Acquatainia again! The warm sunlight, the bustling throngs of people, the gleaming towers of the city—he almost felt Dulaq's sense of joy about being here. Of course, Odal told himself, it's probably just a reaction to being free of Kor's dreary Ministry of Intelligence. But the Kerak major had to admit to himself—as he moved toward the spaceport terminal, escorted by four of Kor's men—that Acquatainia had a rhythm, a freshness, a sense of freedom and gaiety that he had never found on Kerak.

Inside the terminal building, he had fifty meters of automated inspectors to walk through before he could get into the ground car that would take him to the Kerak embassy. If there was going to be trouble, it would be here.

Two of his escorts got into the inspection line ahead of him, two behind.

Odal walked slowly between the two full-length X-ray screens and then stopped before the radiation detector. He inserted his passport and embassy identification cards into the correct slot in the computer's registration processor.

Then he heard someone in the next line, a woman's voice, saying, "It *is* him! I recognize the uniform from the tri-di news."

"Couldn't be," a man's voice answered. "They wouldn't dare send him back here."

Odal purposely turned their way and smiled gravely at them. The woman said, "I *told* you it was him!" Her husband glared at Odal.

Kor had arranged for a few newsmen to be on hand. As Odal collected his cards and travel kit at the end of the inspection line, a small knot of cameramen began grinding their tapers at him. He walked briskly toward the nearest doors, and the ground car that he could see waiting outside. His four escorts kept the newsmen at arm's length.

"Major Odal, don't you consider it risky to return to Acquatainia?"

"Do you think diplomatic immunity covers assassination?"

"Aren't you afraid someone might take a shot at you?"

The newsmen yelped after him like a pack of puppies following a man with an armful of bones. But Odal could feel the hatred now. Not so much from the newsmen, but from the rest of the people in the crowded terminal lobby. They stared at him, hating him. Before, when he was Kerak's invincible warrior, they feared him, even envied him. But now there was nothing in the crowd but hatred for the Kerak major, Odal knew.

He ducked into the ground car and sank into the back seat. Kor's guards filled the rest of the car. The door slammed shut, and some of the emotion and noise coming from the terminal crowd was cut off. For the first time, Odal thought about why he had returned to Acquatainia. Leoh. He frowned at the thought of what he had to do. But when he thought about Hector, about revenging himself for the Star Watchman's absurd victory in their duel, he allowed himself to smile.

Leoh sat slumped at the desk chair in the office behind the dueling machine chamber. He had some thinking to do, and his apartment was too comfortable for creative thought.

Through the closed door of the office he heard an outer door bang, hard fast-moving footsteps, and a piercing off-key whistle. With a reluctant smile, he told the door-control to open. Hector was standing there with a fist raised, ready to knock.

"How'd you know . . . ?"

"I'm partly telepathic," Leoh said.

"Really? I didn't know. Do you think that helped you in your duel with . . . oh, that's what I wanted to talk to you about. . . ."

Leoh raised a hand for silence. "Come in, my boy, and sit down. Tell me, have you seen the tri-di newscasts this morning?"

Taking a chair next to the Professor, Hector said, "No, sir, I, uh, got in kind of late last night and sort of late getting up this morning. . . . Got some water in my left ear . . . it gurgles every time I move my head. . . ."

With an effort, Leoh stayed on the subject. "The

newscasts showed Odal landing at the main spaceport. He's returned."

Hector jerked as though someone had stuck him with a pin. "He . . . he's back?"

"Now don't get rattled," Leoh said as calmly as he could. "No one's going to come in here with pistols blazing to assassinate me."

"Maybe . . . but, well, I mean . . . there's a chance that Odal—or somebody—will try something."

"Nonsense," Leoh grumbled.

Hector didn't reply. He seemed to be lost in an inner debate; his face was flashing through a series of expressions: worried, puzzled, determined.

"What's the matter?" Leoh asked.

"Huh? Oh, nothing . . . just thinking."

"This news about Odal has upset you more than I thought it would."

"No, no . . . I'm not upset . . . just, uh, thinking." Hector shook his head, as if trying to clear his mind. Leoh thought he could hear the gurgling of water.

"It's my duty," Hector said, "to, uh, protect you. So I'll have to stay, well, very close to you at all times. I think I should move into your apartment and stay with you wherever you go."

Now Leoh found himself upset more than he thought he would be. But he knew that if he didn't let the Watchman stay close to him openly, Hector would try to do it secretly, which would merely be more agonizing for both of them.

"All right, my boy, if you insist; although I think you're being overly dramatic about this."

Hector said, "No, I've got to be there when Odal shows up. . . . And anyway, I think the Terran ambassador was getting a little tired of having me around the embassy. He, uh, he seemed to be avoiding me as much as he could."

Leoh barely suppressed a smile. "Very well. Get your things together and you can move in with me today."

"Good," Hector said. And to himself he added, *I won't leave him for a minute. Then when Odal shows up I can protect him . . . and do what Geri wants me to.*

There was no escaping Hector. He moved into Leoh's apartment and stood within ten meters of the old scientist, day and night. When Leoh awoke, Hector was already whistling shrilly in the autokitchen, punching buttons, and somehow managing to make the automatic equipment burn at least one part of breakfast. Hector drove him wherever he wanted to go, and stayed with him when he got there. Leoh went to sleep with Hector's cheerful jabbering still in his ears.

Increasingly, they ate dinner at Geri Dulaq's sumptuous home on the outskirts of the city. Hector waggled like an overanxious puppy whenever Geri was in sight. And Leoh saw that she was coolly able to keep him at arm's length. There was something that she wanted Hector to do for her, the old man quickly realized, something Hector wouldn't talk about. Which—for Hector—was completely unusual.

About a week after the news of Odal's return, the Kerak major still hadn't been seen outside of his embassy's building. But an enterprising newsman, expecting new duels, asked for an interview with Leoh. The Professor met him at the dueling machine. Hector was at his side.

The newsman turned out to be Hector's age and Leoh's girth, florid in complexion, sloppy in dress, and slightly obnoxious in attitude.

"I know all about the basic principles of its operation," he told Leoh airily when the Professor began to explain how the dueling machine worked.

"Oh? Have you had courses in psychonics?"

The newsman laughed. "No, but I understand all about this dream-machine business."

Pacing slowly by the empty control desk and peering up at the dueling machine's bulky consoles and power conditioners, he asked, "How can you be sure that people can't be killed in this rig again? Major Odal actually killed people. . . ."

"I understand the question," Leoh said. "I've added three new circuits to the machine. The first psychonically isolates the duelists inside the machine; it's now impossible for Odal or anyone else to contact the outside world while the machine is in operation."

The newsman turned up the volume control on his wrist recorder. "Go on."

"The second circuit," Leoh continued, "monitors the entire duel. If either side requests, the dueling machine's chief meditech can review the tape and determine if any rules were broken. Thus, even if there is foul play of some sort, we can at least catch it."

"After the fact," the newsman pointed out.

"Yes."

"That wouldn't have helped Dulaq or Massan, or the others that were killed."

Leoh could feel irritation growing inside him. "After one duel, we could have found out what Odal was doing and stopped him."

The newsman said nothing.

"Finally, we have added an automatic override to the medical monitoring equipment, so that if one of the duelists shows the slightest sign of actual medical danger, the duel is automatically stopped."

The newsman thought it over for half a second. "Suppose a man gets a sudden heart attack? He might be dead before you can get the door to his booth open, even though you've stopped the duel immediately."

Leoh fumed. "And if there's an earthquake, both duelists and much of the city may be destroyed. Young man, there is no way to make the world absolutely safe."

"Maybe not." But his round, puffed face showed he didn't believe it absolutely.

They talked for a quarter-hour more. Leoh showed him the equipment involved in the three new safety circuits and tried to explain how they worked. The newsman looked professionally skeptical and unimpressed. Leoh's exasperation mounted.

"Frankly, Professor, all you've told me is a lot of scientific mumbo jumbo. There's no guarantee that the machine won't kill people again."

Reddening, Leoh snapped back, "The *machine* didn't kill anyone! A man murdered his opponents, deliberately."

"In the machine."

"Yes, but it can't happen again!"

Shrugging, the newsman said, "All I've got to go on is your word."

"My reputation as a scientist means something, I should think."

Hector interrupted. "If the Acquatainian government is satisfied that the dueling machine's safe. . . ."

The newsman laughed. "Both the government and the Professor claimed the machine was absolutely safe when it was first installed here. Two men died in this gadget, and who knows how many others have been killed in Szarno and other places?"

"But that. . . ."

Turning back to Leoh, he asked, "How many people have been killed in dueling machines in the Commonwealth?"

"None!"

"You sure? I can check, you know."

"Are you calling me a liar?"

"Look, it boils down to this: you told us the machine was safe, and two very important men were killed. Now you're saying it's safe again. . . ." He let the implication dangle.

"Out!" Leoh snapped. "Get out of here, or by all the ancient gods, old as I am. . . ."

The newsman backed off a step. Then, "Suppose I *am* doubting you. Not your veracity, but your optimism about the machine's being safe. Suppose I said you don't really know that it's safe, you're just hoping that it is."

Hector stepped between them. "Now wait . . . if you can't. . . ."

"Suppose," the newsman went on, ducking past Hector, "suppose I challenged you to a duel."

"I've used this machine many times," Leoh said.

"Okay, but I still challenge you."

Suddenly Leoh felt absolutely calm. "Very well. I accept your challenge. And you can do whatever you want to during our duel to try to prove your point. But I insist on one condition: the tape of the duel must be made public knowledge immediately after the duel is finished."

The newsman grinned. "Perfect."

Leoh realized that this was what he had been after all along.

Odal sat in his cell-like room in the Kerak embassy, waiting for the phone message. The room was narrow and severe, with strictly functional furniture—a bed, a desk and chair, a viewscreen. No decorations, plain military gray walls, no window.

Kor had explained the plan for Leoh's destruction before Odal had boarded the ship for Acquatainia. Odal did not like the plan, but it seemed workable and it would surely remove Leoh from the scene.

The phone buzzed.

Odal leaned across the desk and touched the ON button. The newsman's chubby face took form on the small screen.

"Well?" Odal demanded.

"He accepted the challenge. We duel in three days.

And he wants the tape shown publicly, just as you thought he would."

Odal smiled tightly. "Excellent."

"Look, if I'm going to be made to look foolish on that tape," the newsman said, "I think I ought to get more money."

"I don't handle the financial matters," Odal said. "You'll have to speak to the embassy accountant . . . *after* we see how well you play your part in the duel."

Pouting, the newsman replied, "All right. But I'm going to be finished for life when that tape is shown."

"We'll take care of you," Odal promised. *Indeed, we'll provide for you for the rest of your life.*

Geri Dulaq walked briskly out of the sunlight of the university's campus into the shadows of the dueling machine's high-vaulted chamber.

"Hector, you sounded so worried on the phone. . . ."

He took her hands in his. "I am. That's why I wanted to talk to you. It's . . . well, it's happened again. First Ponte argues the Professor into a duel, and now this newsman. You think Ponte might be working for Kerak, so . . . I mean. . . ."

"Perhaps the newsman is too," Geri finished for him.

Hector nodded. "And with Odal back . . . well, they're brewing up something. . . ."

"Where is the Professor now?" Geri asked.

Pointing to the office behind the dueling machine chamber, Hector said, "In there. He doesn't want to be disturbed . . . working on equations or something . . . about interstellar ships, I think."

Geri looked surprised.

"Oh, he's not worried about the duel," Hector explained. "I told him all about Ponte . . . what you said, I mean. But he thinks the machine can't be tampered with, so he's not, uh, worried. And he beat Ponte pretty easily."

Geri turned toward the massive, looming machine. "I've never been here before. It's a little frightening."

Hector put on a smile. "There's nothing to be frightened about . . . that is, I mean, well, it's only a machine. It can't hurt you."

"I know. It was Odal and Kanus' hired monsters that killed father, not the machine itself."

She walked along the long, curving, main control desk, looked over its banks of gauges and switches, ran a finger lightly across its plastisteel edge.

"Could you show me what it's like?"

Hector blinked. "Huh?"

"In the dueling machine," she said. "Can it be used for something else, other than duels? I'd like to see what it's like to have your imagination made real."

"Oh, but . . . well, you're not . . . I mean, nobody's supposed to run it without . . . that is. . . ."

"You do know how to run the machine, don't you?" She looked right up into his eyes.

With a gulp, Hector managed a weak, "Oh sure. . . ."

"Then can't we use it together? Perhaps we can share a dream."

Looking around, his hands suddenly clammy, Hector mumbled, "Well, uh, somebody's supposed to be at the controls to, er, monitor the duel . . . I mean. . . ."

"Just for a few little minutes?" Geri smiled her prettiest.

Hector melted. "Okay . . . I guess it'll be all right. Just for a few minutes, that is."

He walked with her to the farther booth and helped her put on the neurocontacts. Then he went back to the main desk and with shaky hands set the machine into action. He checked and double-checked all the controls, pushed the final switches, and dashed to the other booth, tripping as he entered it and banging noisily into the seat. He sat down, fumbled with the neurocontacts hastily, and then stared into the screen.

Nothing happened.

For a moment he was panic-stricken. Then the screen began to glow softly, colors shifted, green mostly, soft cool green with a hint of blue in it.... And he found himself floating dreamily next to Geri in a world of green, with greenish light filtering down ever so softly from far above them.

"Hello," Geri said.

He grinned at her. "Hi."

"I've always wondered what it would be like to be able to live underwater, without any equipment, like a mermaid."

Hector noticed, when she said that, hundreds of fish swimming lazily about them. As his eyes adjusted to the subdued lighting, he saw sculptured shapes of coral about them, colors that he had never seen before.

"Our castle," Geri said, and she swam slowly toward one of the coral pinnacles and disappeared behind it.

Hector found himself sliding easily after her. The water seemed to offer no resistance to his movement. He was completely relaxed, completely at home. He saw her up ahead, gliding gracefully along, and pulled up beside her. A great silver fish crossed in front of them, and brilliantly hued plants swayed gently in the currents.

"Isn't it beautiful?" Geri murmured. "Our own world, without troubles, without dangers."

Hector nodded. It was hard to believe that they were actually sitting in a pair of booths some thirty meters apart. Hard to admit that there was another world where a war was brewing, where Odal was waiting to commit another murder.

A dark shape slid out from behind the rocks ahead. Geri screamed.

It was Odal. Slim, dressed in black, his lean face a mask of death.

"Hector, don't let him! Hector, help me!"

Everything went black.

Hector snapped his eyes open. He was sitting in the booth beside Geri, his arms around her protectively. She was shuddering.

"How did. . . ."

"It was my fault," she gasped. "I thought about Odal. . . ."

The door to the booth was yanked open. Leoh stood there, his face a mixture of surprise and puzzlement.

"What are you two doing? All the lights and power in the building are off!"

"I'm sorry . . ." Hector began.

"It's my fault," Geri said. She explained what happened.

Leoh still looked puzzled. "But why are you both in the same booth?"

Hector started to answer, then it hit him. "I . . . I was in the other booth!"

"It's empty," Leoh said. "I looked in there first, when the power went off. The door was closed."

Hector looked at Geri, then back at the Professor. "I must've jumped out of the booth and ran over here . . . but, I mean . . . I don't remember doing it."

The chief meditech came striding into the room, his steps clicking angrily against the hard flooring. "What's going on here? Who blew out the power?"

Turning, Leoh said, "It's all right, just a little experiment that didn't work out."

The chief meditech looked over the control console in the fading sunlight of the afternoon as Geri and Hector got out of the booth. He muttered and glared at them.

"No permanent damage, I'm sure," Leoh said as soothingly as he could.

The lights on the control panels sprang back to life, as did the room's main illumination lights. "Hmp," grunted the chief meditech. "I guess it's all right. The power's on again."

"I don't understand it," Hector said.

"Neither do I," Leoh answered. "But it's something to think about."

"What is?"

"How Hector got from one booth to the other." To the chief meditech he called out, "I'm going to take the tape of this, er, experiment. Do you mind?"

The chief meditech was still inspecting the machine with the aggressive solicitude of a worried father. He nodded curtly to Leoh. "I don't think you should do any more such experiments until we have back-up power units installed. The entire building was blacked out."

Leoh sat in his office behind the dueling machine room, staring at the now blank viewscreen. In three days he had run the tape at least a hundred times. He had timed it down to the picosecond. He had seen Geri and Hector swimming lazily, happily, like two humanized dolphins perfectly at ease in the sea. Then Odal's shark-like form sliced into view. Geri screamed. The scene cut off.

It was precisely at that moment (within four picoseconds, as nearly as Leoh could calculate it) that the power in the whole building went off.

How long did it take Hector to get from his booth to Geri's? Thirty seconds? Leoh was looking into Hector's booth about thirty seconds after the power went off, he estimated. Less, then. Ten seconds? Physically impossible; no one could disconnect himself from the neurocontacts and spring from one booth to the other in ten seconds. And both booth doors were closed, too.

Leoh muttered to himself, "Knowing Hector's manual dexterity, it's difficult to imagine him making the trip in less than ten minutes."

All right then, he asked himself, *how did he get into Geri's booth? Precognition? He realized ahead of time that Odal would appear and frighten Geri? Then why doesn't he remember it, or even remember going from one booth to the other? And why the enormous power drain? What happened to the machine to cause it?*

There was only one answer that Leoh could see, but it was so farfetched that he wanted to find another one. The one answer was teleportation.

The dueling machine amplifies the powers of natural telepaths. Some telepaths have been reported to be able to move small objects with no apparent physical force. Could the dueling machine amplify that talent, too? And drain all the power in the building to do it?

Leoh shook his head. Too much theorizing, not enough facts. He wished there were tape cameras in the booths; then he could have timed Hector's arrival. Did he make the trip in four picoseconds? Or was it four-trillionths of a second?

The door slid open and Hector stood there uncertainly, his lanky form framed in the doorway.

Leoh looked up at him. "Yes?"

"It's time . . . the, uh, newsman and his seconds are here for the duel."

Feeling annoyed at the interruption, Leoh pushed himself out of the chair and headed for the dueling machine. "A lot of silliness," he muttered. "Just a publicity stunt."

The chief meditech, in his professional white coverall now, introduced the duelists and their seconds. For Leoh, only Hector. For the newsman, his editor—a thin, balding, nervous type—and a network vice president, who looked comfortable and well-fed. *Probably keeps three dietitians and a biochemist busy preventing him from going overweight*, Leoh groused to himself.

They exchanged formalities and entered the booths. Hector sat at one end of the long, curving, padded bench that ran along the wall across the floor from the machine's control desk. The editor and V.P. sat at the other end. Except for the meditechs, who took their stations at the control consoles, there was no one else in the room. The press gallery was empty. The lights on the panels winked on. The silent room vibrated with the barely audible hum of electrical power.

In ten minutes, all the lights on the control panels flicked from green to amber. The duel was finished.

Hector shot up and started for Leoh's booth. The Professor came out, smiling slightly.

"Are you . . . did it go . . . all right?" Hector asked.

The newsman was getting out of the other booth. His editor put out a hand to steady him. The V.P. remained on the bench, looking half-disappointed, half-amused. The newsman seemed like a lumpy wad of dough, white-faced, shaken.

"He has terrible reflexes," Leoh said, "and no concept at all of the most elementary rules of physics."

The V.P. got up from his seat and walked over toward Leoh, his hand extended and a toothy smile on his smooth face. "Let me congratulate you, Professor," he said in a hearty baritone.

Leoh took his hand, but replied, "This has been nothing but a waste of time. I'm surprised that a man in your position indulges in such foolishness."

The V.P. bent his head slightly and answered softly, "I'm afraid I'm to blame. My staff convinced me that it would be a good idea to test the dueling machine and then make the results of the test public. You have no objection if we run the tape of your duel on our tri-di broadcasts?"

With a shrug, Leoh said, "Your man is going to look very foolish. He was run over by a bowling ball, and then overestimated his strength and popped his back trying to lift. . . ."

The V.P. put up his hands. "I don't care what the tape shows. I made up my mind to put it on the air, if you have no objections."

"No, I don't object."

"You'll become a famous man all over the planet," the

V.P. beamed. "Your name will become a household word; tri-di stardom can do that for you."

"If the tape will convince the Acquatainian people that the dueling machine is safe, fine," Leoh said. "As for fame . . . I'm already rather well known."

"Ah, but not to the general public. Certainly you're famous among your fellow scientists, and to the elite of Acquatainia and the Commonwealth. But all the general public's seen of you has been a few fleeting glimpses on news broadcasts. But now you're going to become *very* famous."

"Because of one silly duel? I doubt that."

"You'll see," the V.P. promised.

The V.P. did not exaggerate. In fact, he had been overly conservative.

Leoh's duel was broadcast over the tri-di networks all across the planet that night. Within the week, it had been shown throughout the Acquataine Cluster and was in demand in the Commonwealth.

It was the first time a duel had ever been seen by the general public, and the fact that the inventor of the dueling machine was involved made it doubly fascinating. The sight of the chubby newsman bumbling into obvious traps and getting tangled in pulleys and inclined planes with bowling balls atop them, while Leoh solicitously urged him to be careful every step of the way, struck most people as funny. The Acquatainians, living for months now with the fear of war hanging over them, found a sudden and immense relief in Leoh's duel. Here was the inventor of the dueling machine, the man who had stopped the Kerak assassinations, appearing on tri-di, showing how clever he is, proving that Kerak is up against a mastermind.

The real facts of the matter—that Leoh had no influence with Martine's government, that Odal was now back in Acquatainia, that Kerak war fleets were quietly

deploying along the Acquatainian frontier—these facts
the average Acquatainian submerged in his joy over
Leoh's duel.

Leoh became an instant public figure. He was invited
to speak at every university in the Cluster. Tri-di shows
vied for his appearance and newsmen followed his every
move.

The old scientist tried to resist the pressure, at first.
For the week after the original showing of his duel on
tri-di, he refused to make any public statement.

"Tell them I'm busy," he said to Hector, and he tried
to barricade himself behind his equations and computer
tapes in the office behind the dueling machine.

When the universities began calling on him, though,
he bowed to their wishes. Before he knew it, he was
swept away in a giddy tide of personal appearances, tri-
di shows, and parties.

"Perhaps," he told Hector, "this is the way to meet
the people who influence Martine's government. Perhaps
I can convince them to consider the Commonwealth alliance, and they can put pressure on Martine."

At parties, at private meetings, at press conferences,
Leoh stressed the point. But there was no apparent
affect. The students, the professors, the newsmen, the
businessmen, the tri-di audience—they wanted entertain-
ment, not politics. They wanted to be assured that all
was well, not forced to think about how to protect
themselves.

The university lectures were huge successes, as lectures. Leoh expected to be speaking mainly to the psychonics students, but each vast auditorium was filled to
overflowing with students and faculty from political science, physics, mathematics, sociology, psychiatry . . .
thousands at each campus.

And at each university there were the local newsmen,
tri-di appearances, discussion clubs. And the faculty parties in the evenings. And the informal student seminars

in the late afternoons. And the newsman who just "dropped in for a few words" at breakfast time.

It took more than two months to make the rounds of each university in the Cluster. At first, Leoh tried to steal a few moments each day to work on the problem of Hector's "jump." But each day he woke up more tired, each day was filled with still more people to talk to, people who listened respectfully, admiringly. Each night he retired later; happy, exhausted, with a small nagging grumble in the back of his mind that he should really stop this show-business routine and get back to science.

Hector grew more and more worried as he shepherded Leoh from one campus to the next. The old man was obviously enjoying himself hugely, and just as obviously spending too much of his strength on the traveling and personal appearances and parties. What's more, Geri was in the capital city, and all the eager smiling girls on all the campuses in the Cluster couldn't replace her in his eyes.

In the midst of all this, Leoh even fought two more duels.

The first one was with a university physics student who had bet his friends that he could beat the Professor. Leoh agreed good-naturedly to the duel, provided the boy was willing to let the tape be shown on tri-di. The boy agreed.

Instead of the simple physics arena, Leoh chose a more difficult battleground: the intensely warped space in the powerful gravitational field of a collapsed star. The duelists fought in one-man spacecraft, using laser beams for weapons. The problem was to control the ship in a gravitational field so tenacious that one slip meant an inevitable spiral into the star's seething surface; *and* to aim the laser weapons properly, where the relativistic warp of space drove straight-line physics out the window.

The boy tried bravely as the two ships circled the dying star. The tape showed the view from each ship, alternately. Now the viewer could see the black depths of space, empty except for a few distant pinpoints of stars, and the curving crescent of the other duelist's ship streaking by, a pencil beam of laser light flicking out, bending weirdly in that crazy gravity field, seeking its target. Then the bluish inferno of the star would slide into view, blazing, brilliant, drowning out everything else from sight.

The boy fought well, but finally maneuvered himself too close to the star. He could have escaped if he had controlled the ship a little better. Instead, he power-dived straight into its flaming surface. The tri-di executives decided to erase his final screams from the tape before they showed it to the public.

The second challenge came from an Acquatainian merchant, one of the richest men in the Cluster, who had drunk too much at a party and picked a quarrel with Leoh. The Professor went back to the simple physics arena and disposed of him easily.

By the time Leoh (and Hector) returned to the capital, he was the darling of Acquatainian society. They feasted him, they toasted him, they took him to the ballet and opera, they did everything except let him alone to work. Geri was part of Acquatainia's social leadership, so Hector at least got to see her—but only in crowded, noisy rooms.

Odal sat tensely in his room's only chair and watched Kor's bullet-shaped head on the viewscreen as the Intelligence Minister said:

"So far the plan has gone extremely well. Leoh has not only been of no trouble to us, but his exploits have distracted most of the soft-headed Acquatainians. Meanwhile our preparations are exactly on schedule."

"The invasion," Odal murmured.

Kor smiled. "We have—let us say, persuaded—the government of the Etra Domain to allow us to station a battle fleet in their territory. Etra stands between the Acquatainian Cluster and the nearest Star Watch bases. If the Commonwealth tries to intervene, we can hold up their forces long enough to allow us to conquer Acquatainia."

Odal nodded curtly; he had heard the plan before.

"Now is the time," Kor went on, "for you to supply the final step. The destruction of Leoh, and the complete lulling of the Acquatainians."

Odal said nothing.

"You still do not like the role you are required to play," Kor said. "No, don't bother to deny it, I can see it in your face. Let me remind you that your duty may not always be pleasant, but if you succeed your rewards will be high."

"I will do my duty, unpleasant or not," Odal said stiffly. *And I know the penalties for failure*, he added silently.

Leoh looked bone-weary to Hector as they returned from the party. That morning, a new psychonics building had been dedicated at the university. It was named the Albert Robertus Leoh Center for Psychonics Studies.

The day had been spent in speeches on an outdoor platform in the morning, a tour of the new building in the afternoon, dinner with the president and trustees of the university, and the inevitable party that night.

"I've simply got to find time," Leoh was saying as they stepped out of the lift tube into the hallway in front of their apartment, "to run some experiments on your 'jump.' We can use the tape of. . . ."

But Hector was staring quizzically at the apartment door. It was open and the lights inside were on.

"Another newsman, I'll bet," Leoh said wearily.

"I'll tell him to come back some other time," said Hector. He moved ahead of Leoh and entered the apartment.

Sitting on the air couch in the middle of the living room was Odal.

"You!"

The Kerak major rose to his feet slowly, a tight smile on his face, as first Hector and then Leoh came in, saw him, and stopped.

"Good evening," Odal said, getting to his feet. "Come right in. After all, this is your place."

"How did you get into . . . ?"

"That's of no real concern. I'm here to settle some unfinished business. Professor Leoh, some time ago you accused me of cheating in the dueling machine. I was about to challenge you when the Watchman intervened. I challenge you now."

"Now wait," Hector began, "you can't. . . ."

"I already have. Professor, do you accept my challenge?"

Leoh stood three steps inside the door, unmoving, silent.

"Let me remind you," Odal said calmly, "that you have gone to great lengths to prove to the people of Acquatainia that the dueling machine is safe and harmless. If I may quote one of your many tri-di speeches, 'Tampering with the dueling machine is a thing of the past.' If you refuse to meet me in a duel, it will seem that you're afraid that the machine is not so safe . . . when I am the opponent."

Leoh said, "And you would, of course, see to it that my refusal became public knowledge."

Smiling again, Odal nodded. "You are a great celebrity. I'm sure the news media would learn about it one way or another."

"Don't do it," Hector said to Leoh. "It's a trap. Don't agree to duel with him. I'll. . . ."

"You, Watchman, have already beaten me in a duel," Odal said, his smile vanishing. "You can't ask me to face you again. It would be unfair."

"I'll agree to the duel," Leoh answered, "if you'll agree to have the tape shown publicly."

"Very well," Odal said. "We will meet in three days, as is customary?"

"Make it a week," Hector said. "Give us a chance to . . . uh, inspect the machine and make sure, that is. . . ."

"Make certain that the monsters from Kerak haven't tampered with it?" Odal laughed. "Very well, a week from today."

Odal walked toward the door, stepped between Hector and Leoh, and left. The door clicked shut behind him.

Hector turned his eyes from the closed door to Leoh. "You shouldn't have accepted . . . I mean, well, it's a trick of some kind, I know it is."

The Professor looked thoughtful. "Is it? Or is Odal—or Kanus, or whoever—getting desperate? I've been able to show the Acquatainian people that they have nothing to fear from the dueling machine, you know. They might be trying to restore the machine to its symbol of terror."

Hector shook his head.

"But I can beat Odal in a fair duel," Leoh said. "After all, I've won every duel I've fought, haven't I? And you beat Odal. The only duels he won were when he had outside help. I think I can beat him, I honestly do."

Hector didn't answer, but merely stared in disbelief at the old man.

The building that housed the dueling machine was surrounded with throngs of people. Their restless, anxious murmuring could be heard even inside the normally quiet room. The press gallery, high above the machine itself, was packed with reporters.

For a solid week every tri-di outlet in the Acquataine Cluster had drummed continuously on the coming duel between Leoh and Odal. Good against evil, with the issue seriously in doubt. The old, overweight, shaggy professor against the blade-slim professional killer.

Hector and Leoh stood before the machine. The medi-techs were bustling about making final checks on the controls. On the other side of the room, tiers of temporary seats had been put in. They were filled with government and social leaders, military men, policemen, and a small contingent from the Kerak embassy. Geri Dulaq sat in the front row, next to the empty chair that would be Hector's.

"I still don't like it," Hector said in a near whisper to Leoh.

With his eyes sweeping the room, watching the restless onlookers and the busy meditechs, Leoh answered, "Relax, my boy. We've turned the machine inside out. The worst he can do is to defeat me. At the slightest medical irregularity, the machine will automatically stop us. And besides, I still think I can beat him. I'll be using the neutron star environment again, the same one I used against that college student. He'll have no advantage over me there."

A roar went up from the crowd outside.

"Here he comes," Hector said.

The main doors opened. Flanked by two rows of uniformed policemen, in walked Odal and his two seconds, all in the light blue uniforms of Kerak. Odal was annoyedly brushing something from his tunic.

"Evidently," Leoh said, "diplomatic immunity didn't protect Odal entirely from the crowd."

The introductions, the medical checks, the instructions, the choice of weapon and environment—all seemed to take hours instead of minutes. Until suddenly they were over, and Hector found himself walking alone to his spectator's seat.

He sat beside Geri and watched Leoh and Odal enter their booths, watched the meditechs take their stations at the control desks, watched the panel lights turn from amber to green. The duel was on.

The crowd stirred uncertainly. A buzzing murmur filled the room. There was nothing to do now but wait.

Geri leaned close to Hector and asked sweetly, "Did you bring a gun?"

"Huh? A . . . what for? I mean. . . ."

She whispered, "For Odal. I have a small one in my handbag."

"But . . . but. . . ."

"You promised me!" Still in a whisper, but harsher now.

"I know, but not here. There're . . . well, there're too many people here. Someone might get hurt . . . if shooting starts. . . ."

Geri thought a moment. "Maybe you're right. Of course, if he kills Professor Leoh in there, he'll walk right out of here and board a Kerak star ship and we'll never see him again."

Hector couldn't think of a reply, so he just sat there feeling thoroughly miserable.

The two of them remained silent for the rest of the half-hour. At the end of the time limit for the duel, all the lights on the machine went amber. The crowd let out a gust of disappointed-yet-relieved sighs. Hector sprinted to Leoh's booth while Odal's seconds marched in time to his.

Leoh came out of the booth looking very thoughtful.

"You're all right?" Hector asked.

"What? Oh yes, fine. He played exactly by the rules," Leoh said. He looked toward Odal, who was smiling icily, calm and confident. "He played extremely well . . . extremely well. There were a couple of times when I thought he'd really finish me off. And I never really put him into much trouble at all."

The chief meditech was motioning for the two duelists to come to him at the main control desk. Hector accompanied Leoh.

"The first part of the duel has been a draw," the chief

meditech said. "You—both of you—now have the option of withdrawing for a day, or continuing the duel now."

"I will continue," Odal said unhesitatingly.

Leoh nodded, "Continue."

"Very well," said the chief meditech. Turning to Odal, "Yours is the choice of environment and weapon. Are there any special instructions necessary?"

Odal shook his head. "The Professor knows how to drive a ground car?" At Leoh's affirming nod he said, "Then that is all the skill that is necessary."

Leoh found himself sitting at the wheel of a sleek blue ground car: plastic-bubble canopy, two bucket seats, engine throbbing under an aerodynamically sculptured hood.

Ahead of him stretched a highway, arrow-straight to the horizon, where jagged bluish mountains rose against the harsh yellow sky. The car was pulled off to the side of the road, in neutral gear. The landscape around the highway was bleak desert—flat, featureless, cloudless, and hot.

Odal's voice came from the radio in the dashboard. "I am parked about five kilometers behind you, Professor. You will pull out onto the highway and I will follow you. These cars have wheels, not air cushions; there are no magnetic bumpers, no electronic controls to lock you onto the highway. A few kilometers ahead, as we enter the mountains, the road becomes quite interesting. The object of the game, of course, is to make the other fellow crash. But if you can outrun me for a half hour, I will acknowledge you as the winner."

Leoh glanced at the controls, touched the drive button, and nudged the throttle. The turbine purred smoothly. He swung onto the highway and ran up to a hundred kilometers per hour. The rear viewscreen showed a blood-red car, exactly like his own except for its color, pulling up precisely ten car lengths behind him.

"I'll let you get the feel of the car while we're on the straightaway," Odal's voice came through the radio. "We won't begin to play in earnest until we get into the mountains."

The road was rising now, Leoh realized. A gentle grade, but at their speed they were soon well above the desert floor. The mountains were no longer distant blue wrinkles; they loomed close, high, and bareboned, with scraggy bushes and sparse patches of grass on them.

Leoh nearly missed the first curve, it came on him so quickly. He cut to the inside, slammed on the brakes, and skidded around.

"Not very good," Odal laughed.

The red car was just off his left rear fender now, crowding him against the shoulder of the mountain rise that jutted up from the right side of the road. Leoh could hear pebbles clattering against the floorboards, over the whine of their two turbines. On the other side of the road, the cliff dropped away to the desert floor. And they were still climbing.

Leoh hugged the right side of the road, with Odal practically beside him. Suddenly the mountains fell away and a bridge, threaded dizzily between two cliffs, stood before them. It seemed to Leoh that the bridge was leaping toward him. He tried to get back toward the center of the road, but Odal rammed his side. The wheel ripped out of his hands, spinning wildly. The car skidded toward the road's shoulder. Leoh grabbed at the wheel, steered out of the skid, and found himself on the bridge, the supporting suspension cables whizzing past. He was sweating hard and hunched, white-knuckled, over the wheel.

Odal was in front of him now. *He must've passed me when I skidded*, Leoh told himself. The red car was running smoothly, easily; Odal waved one hand back to his opponent.

On the other side of the bridge the road became a

tortuous series of curves, climbs, and drops. The grades
were steep, the turns murderous, and at times the road
narrowed so much that two cars could barely squeeze
by. Sometimes they were flanked on both sides by looming masses of rock, rising up out of sight. Mostly, though,
one side of the road was a sheer drop of a thousand
meters or more.

Odal braked, swerved, pulled up alongside Leoh and
slammed the two cars together with bone-rattling force.
He was trying to force Leoh off the edge of the cliff.
Leoh clung to the wheel, fighting for control. His one
defense was that he could set the speed for the battle;
but to his horror he found that not even this was under his
real control. The car refused to slow much past seventy-
five.

"You wish to stop and enjoy the scenery?" Odal called
to him, banging the two cars together again, pushing
Leoh dangerously close to the cliff's edge.

Desperately, Leoh leaned on the throttle with all his
weight. The car spurted ahead, leaving Odal momentarily
in a cloud of wheel-churned dirt.

"Ah-hah, now the turtle becomes a rabbit!" The red
car streaked after him.

There was a tunnel ahead. Leoh raced for it, praying
that it was long enough and narrow enough for him to
stay ahead of Odal. *The time must be running out. It's
got to be!* It was hard for Leoh to keep his sweaty hands
firm on the wheel. His back and head were hurting, his
heart racing dangerously.

The tunnel was long and straight—and narrow! Hopefully, Leoh planted his car in the middle of the roadway
and throttled down as much as he could. Still, the tunnel
walls were a blur as he roared by, the turbine echoing
shrilly against the encasing rock.

The red car was pulling close and now it was trying
to pass him. Leoh swerved slightly to the left, to block

it. The red car moved right. Leoh edged that way. Odal cut left again.

Got to keep ahead of him. Time must be almost over. Odal was insisting on his left. Leoh pushed farther to the left, staying ahead of him. But Odal kept coming, up off the roadway and onto the curving tunnel wall with his left wheels. Leoh stayed on the left of the road and Odal swung even farther up the wall just behind Leoh's fender.

Glancing at the rear viewscreen, Leoh could see Odal's face clenched grimly, determined to pass him. The red car seemed to climb halfway up the curving tunnel wall and. . . .

And then fell over, out of control, smashing over upside down onto the roadway, exploding in a shower of sparks and fuel with a concussion that slammed Leoh so hard he nearly lost control of his car.

He found himself sitting in the dueling machine booth, the screen before him a calm flat gray, his body soaking wet, his hands pressed into aching fists in front of him, as though he were still gripping the car's steering wheel.

The door jerked open and Hector ducked into the booth, his face anxious.

"You're all right?"

Leoh's arms dropped and his whole body relaxed.

"I beat him," he said. "I beat Odal!"

They stepped outside the booth, Leoh smiling broadly now. Across the way, Odal's thin face was deathly grim. The crowd was absolutely still, not daring to believe what it saw.

The chief meditech cleared his throat and announced loudly, "Professor Leoh is the victor!"

The crowd's sudden roar burst through the room. They rose from their seats, swarmed down upon the machine and lifted Leoh and Hector to their shoulders. Jumping up and down on the main control desk, yelling louder than anyone, was the white-coated chief meditech. Outside, the much larger throng was cheering even harder.

Within a few minutes no one was left in the chamber except a few of the uniformed policemen, Odal, and his seconds.

"Are you able to go outside now?" asked one of the soldiers, also a major.

The taut expression on Odal's face relaxed a little. "Of course."

The three men walked from the building to a waiting ground car. The other soldier, a colonel, said to Odal, "You have taken your death rather well."

"Thank you." Odal managed a thin smile. "But after all, it's not as though I was killed by the enemy. I engaged in a suicide mission, and my mission has been accomplished."

"I . . . well . . . you saw what happened," Hector said to Geri. "How could anybody do anything in that mob?"

They were sitting together in a restaurant near the tri-di studio where Leoh was being lionized by a panel of Acquatainia's leading citizens.

She poked at her food with a fork and said, "You might never get the chance to kill him again. He's probably on his way back to Kerak right now."

"Well, maybe that's . . . I mean . . . murder just isn't right. . . ."

"It wouldn't be murder," Geri said coldly, staring at her plate. "It would be an execution. Odal deserves to die! And if you won't do it, I'll find someone who can!"

"Geri . . . I . . . ."

"If you really loved me, you'd have done it already." She looked as though she was going to cry.

"But it's. . . ."

"You promised me!"

Hector sagged, defeated. "All right, don't cry. I'll . . . I'll think of something."

·   ·   ·

Odal sat now in the office of the Kerak ambassador. The ambassador had left discreetly when Kor's call came through.

The Kerak major sat at a huge desk, leaning back comfortably in the soft padding of the luxurious leather swivel chair. The wall-sized viewscreen across the room seemed to dissolve into another room: Kor's dimly lit office. The Intelligence Minister eyed Odal for a long moment before speaking.

"You seem relieved."

"I have performed an unpleasant duty, and done it successfully," Odal said.

"Yes, I know. Leoh is now serving us to his full capacity. The Acquatainians will look up to him now as their savior. The fear they felt of Major Par Odal is now dissolved, and with it, their fear of Kerak is also purged. They associate Leoh with safety and victory. And while they are toasting him and listening to his pompous speeches, we will strike!"

Even though his presence in the room was only an image, Odal saw clearly what was in Kor's mind: bigger prisons, more prisoners, more interrogation rooms filled with terrified, helpless people who would cringe at the mention of Kor's name.

"Now then," Kor said, "new duties await you, Major. Not quite so unpleasant as committing suicide. And these duties will be performed here in Kerak."

Odal said evenly, "I would not wish to interrogate other army officers again."

"I realize that," Kor replied, frowning. "That phase of our investigation is finished. But there are other groups that must be examined. You would have no objection, I trust, to interrogating diplomats . . . members of the Foreign Ministry?"

Romis' people? Odal thought. *Kor must be insane. Romis won't stand for having his people arrested.*

"Yes, Romis," Kor answered the major's unspoken question. "Who else would have the pigheaded pride to lead the plotting against the Leader?"

Or the intelligence, Odal found himself thinking. Aloud he asked, "When do I return to Kerak?"

"Tomorrow morning a ship will be ready for you."

Odal nodded. *Then I have only tonight to find the Watchman and crush him.*

Hector paced nervously along the narrow control booth of the tri-di studio. Technicians and managers bent over the monitors and electronic gear. Behind them, shadowed in the dimly lit booth, were a host of visitors whom Hector elbowed and jostled as he fidgeted up and down.

Beyond the booth's window wall was the well-lit studio where Leoh sat flanked by a full dozen of Acquatainia's leading newsmen and political philosophers.

The old man looked very tired but very pleased. The show had started by running the tape of the duel against Odal. Then the panel members began questioning Leoh about the duel, the machine itself, his career in science, his whole life.

Hector turned from the studio to peer into the crowd of onlookers in the dimly lit control booth. Geri was still there, off by the far corner, squeezed between an old politician and a slickly dressed female advertising executive. Geri was still pouting. Hector turned away before she saw him watching her.

"It seems clear," one of the political pundits was saying out in the studio, "that Kanus can't use the dueling machine to frighten us any more. And without fear, Kanus isn't half the threat we thought he was."

"I disagree," Leoh said, shifting his bulk in the frail-looking web chair. "Kerak has made great strides in isolating Acquatainia diplomatically. . . ."

"But we never depended on our neighbors for our own

defense," a newsman said. "Those so-called allies of ours were more of a drain on our treasury than a help to us."

"But Kerak now has the industrial base of Szarno and outposts that flank Prime Minister Martine's new defense line."

"Kerak would never dare attack us, and if they did, we'd beat them just as we did the last time."

"But an alliance with the Commonwealth. . . ."

"We don't need it. Kanus is a paper tiger, believe me. All bluff, all dueling machine trickery, but no real strength. He'll probably be deposed by his own people in another year or two."

Something made Hector shift his gaze from the semi-circle of sonorous solons to the technical crews working the cameras and laser lights. Something made him squint into the pooled shadows far in the back of the studio, where a single tall, slim man stood. Hector couldn't see his face, or what he was wearing, or the color of his hair. Only the knife-like outline of a figure that radiated danger: Odal.

Without thinking twice about it, Hector pushed past the crowd in the control booth toward the door. He stepped on toes and elbowed technicians in the backs of their heads in his haste to get out into the studio, leaving a wake of muttering, sore-rubbing people behind him. He went right past Geri, who stepped back out of his way but refused to say anything to him or even look directly into his eyes.

The door from the control booth led into a small entryway that had two more doors in it: one to the out-side hallway and one to the studio. A uniformed guard stood before the studio door.

"I'm sorry, sir, you can't go in while the show's in progress."

"But . . . I saw someone come in the back way . . . into the studio. . . ."

Shrugging, the guard said, "Must be a member of the camera crew. No one else allowed in."

Hector blinked once, then went to the hall door. The corridor outside circled the studio. At least, he thought it did. He followed it around. Sure enough, there was another door with a blinking red light atop it, labeled STUDIO C. Hector pushed the door open. Inside, in the focus of a circle of lights and cameras, a man and woman were locked in a wild embrace.

"Hey, who opened the door?"

"Cut! CUT! Get that clown out of here! Can't even tape a simple scene without tourists wandering into the studio! Of all the...."

Hector quickly shut the door, closing off a string of invective that would have made his old drillmaster back at the Star Watch Academy grin with appreciation.

Which studio are they in?

As if in answer, farther down the hall a door opened and Odal stepped out. He was not in uniform; instead he wore a simple dark tunic and slacks. But it was unmistakably Odal. He glanced directly at Hector, a sardonic smile on his lips, then started walking the other way. Hector chased after him, but Odal disappeared around a bend in the almost featureless corridor.

A door was closing farther down the hall. Hector sprinted to it and yanked it open. The room was dark. He stepped in.

In the faint light from the hallway, Hector saw row after row of life-sized tri-di viewscreens, each flanked by a desk of control and monitoring equipment. *A tape viewing room*, he reasoned. *Or maybe an editing room.* He walked hesitantly toward the center of the room. It was big, filled with the bulky screens and desks. Plenty of room to hide in. The door snapped shut behind him, plunging the room into total darkness.

Hector froze rock-still. Odal was in here. He could feel it. Gradually his eyes grew accustomed to the darkness.

He turned slowly and began retracing his steps toward the door, only to bump into a chair and send it clattering into its desk.

"You defeated me in the dueling machine," Odal's voice echoed calmly through the room. "Now let's see if you can defeat me in real life. This room is soundproof. We are alone. No one will disturb us."

"Uh ... I'm unarmed," Hector said. It was hard to trace the source of Odal's voice. The echoes spoiled any chance of locating him in the darkness.

"I'm also unarmed. But we are both trained fighting men. You have no doubt had standard Star Watch hand-to-hand combat training."

The painful memory of fumbling through the rough-and-tumble courses at the Star Watch Academy surged through Hector's mind. What he remembered most vividly was lying flat on his back with his instructor screaming, "No, no, *no!*" at him.

Odal stepped out from behind a full-length viewscreen. "You seem less than eager to do battle with me. Perhaps you're afraid that you'll hurt me. Let me demonstrate my qualifications."

Odal's foot lashed into one of the desk chairs, smashing its fragile frame against the tough plastic of the viewscreen. The chair disintegrated. Then he swung an edge-of-the-hand chop at the top of the nearby desk: the metal dented with a loud *crunk!*

Hector backed away until he felt another desk pressing against his legs. He glanced behind him and saw that it was some sort of master control unit, long and filled with complicated switches and monitor screens. Several roller chairs lined its length.

Odal was advancing on him. Something in the back of Hector's mind was telling him to run away and hide, but then he heard the barking voice of his old instructor insisting, "The best defense is a fast, aggressive attack."

Hector took a deep breath, planted his feet solidly, and launched himself at Odal.

Only to find himself twisted around, lifted off his feet, and thrown back against the desk, banging painfully against the switches.

"LOOKING FOR THE IDEAL VACATION PARADISE?" a voice boomed at them. From behind Odal's shoulder a girl in a see-through spacesuit did a free-fall somersault. Hector blinked at her, and Odal looked over his shoulder, momentarily amazed. The voice blared on, "JOIN THE FUN CROWD AT ORBIT HOUSE, ACQUATAINIA'S   NEWEST   ZERO-GRAVITY RESORT. . . ."

Through his mind flashed another maxim from his old instructor: "Whenever possible, divert your opponent's attention. Create confusion. Feint, maneuver!"

Hector rolled off the desk top and ran along the master control unit, pounding every switch in sight.

"TIRED OF BEING CALLED SHORTY?" A disgruntled young man, standing on tiptoes next to a gorgeous, statuesque redhead, appeared beside Odal. The Kerak major involuntarily stepped back.

"THE IRRESISTIBLE PERFUME," a seductive blonde materialized before his eyes, speaking smokily.

"MODERN SCIENCE CAN CURE ANY DISEASE, BUT WHEN EMBARRASSING . . ." said a medic, radiating sincerity and concern.

Odal was surrounded by solid-looking, life-sized, tri-di advertising pitches.

"WHEN YOU'VE EATEN MORE THAN YOU SHOULD. . . ."

"THE NORMAL TENSIONS OF MODERN LIFE. . . ."

"FOR THE ULTIMATE IN FEMININE. . . ."

Eyes goggling, Odal saw himself being pressed backward by a teenage dancer, an "average family" mother, a worried young husband, a nervous businessman, a smiling teen couple, a crowd of surfers, a chorus of animated vegetables. Suddenly bellowing with rage, Odal dived through the pleading, cajoling, urgent figures and threw himself at the long control desk.

"You can't hide from me!" he roared, and he started punching at the control switches, banging the desk panels with both fists.

"Who's hiding?" Hector yelled from behind him.

Odal turned and swung heavily at the voice. Startled, he saw his fist whisk through the impalpable jaw of a lovely girl in a skimpy bathing suit. She smiled at him and continued selling. "... AND WHEN YOU'RE IN THE MOOD FOR SOMETHING REALLY REFRESHING...."

Hector had ducked away. Odal turned and chased after the Watchman, trying to follow him as he flickered in and out among the dozens of tri-di images that were dancing, urging, laughing, drinking, eating, taking pills, worrying....

"You coward!" Odal screamed over the babble of sales talk.

"Why should I fight you?" Hector hollered back from somewhere across the room.

Odal squinted, trying to see through the gyrating tri-di figures. "You tricked me in the dueling machine but now there'll be no tricks. I'll find you, and when I do, I'll kill you!"

The flash of a black-and-silver uniform among the fashion models, overweight women, underweight men, scientific demonstrations and new, new, new products. Odal headed in that direction.

"And what about Leoh?" Hector's voice cut through the taped noise. "He killed you without any tricks. But you're afraid to go after him now, aren't you?"

Odal laughed. "Do you really believe that old man beat me? I could have destroyed him at any time I wished."

He ducked under the arm of a well-preserved matron

who was saying, "WHY LET ADVANCING AGE
WORRY YOU, WHEN A REJUVE. . . ." There was Hector, edging slowly toward the door.

"You deliberately lost to Leoh?" Hector's face, in the
reflections of the tri-di images, looked more puzzled than
frightened. "To make it seem. . . ."

"To make it seem that Leoh is a great hero, and that
Kerak is populated by weaklings and cowards. All his duels
were designed for that purpose. And while he lulls the
Acquatainians with his tales of victory, we prepare to
strike."

On the final word Odal leaped at Hector, hit him with
satisfying solidity, shoulder in mid-section, and they both
went down.

A tangle of arms and legs, knees and elbows, gasps, two
strong young bodies grappling. Somehow they rolled into
one of the desk chairs, which toppled down on them. Odal
felt Hector slipping out of his grasp. As the Kerak major
started to get back to his feet, the chair slid into him again
and he slipped against it and hit the floor face first.

Swearing, he started to get up. But Hector was already
on his feet. And then the door swung open, stabbing
light from the hallway into the room. A girl stood there,
with a gun in her trembling hand.

"Hector! Here!" Geri said, and she tossed the gun to
the Watchman.

Hector grabbed it and pointed it at Odal. The Kerak
major froze, on one knee, hands on the floor, head
upturned, face a mask of rage turned to sudden fear.
Hector stood equally immobile, arm outstretched with
the gun aimed at Odal's head.

"Kill him!" Geri whispered harshly. "Quickly, they're
coming!"

Hector let his arm relax. The gun dropped slightly
away from Odal. "Get up," he said. "And . . . don't give
me any excuses for using this thing."

Odal got slowly to his feet.

"Kill him! You promised!" Geri insisted, half in tears.
"I can't . . . not like this. . . ."

"You mean you *won't!*"

Nodding without taking his eyes off Odal, Hector said,
"That's right, I won't. Not even for you."

Odal's voice was like a knife. "You'd better kill me,
Watchman, while you have the chance. I'll spend the rest
of my life hunting you."

A trio of uniformed guards puffed up to the doorway;
behind them were a half-dozen people from the tri-di
show, and Leoh.

"What's going on? Who's this? Are you. . . ."

"This is Major Odal," Hector said, pointing with the
gun. "He's . . . uh, under the protection of diplomatic
immunity. Please escort him back to the Kerak embassy."

His face expressionless, Odal nodded to the Star
Watchman and went with the guards.

"You mean it all went out on the tri-di network? Every
word?" asked Hector.

He, Leoh, and Geri were sitting in the back of an
automated Dulaq ground car as it threaded its way
through the darkened city, heading for Geri's home. The
midnight rain was falling for its programed half-hour, so
the car's bubble top was up.

Geri had not said a word since Odal was taken from
the tri-di studio.

But Leoh was chuckling. "When you hit all those
switches and turned on the commercial tapes, you also
turned on the sound system for every studio. We heard
the bedlam, with you and Odal shouting at each other
over it all. It came over the speakers right in the middle
of our show. You should have seen the look on everyone's
face! And I understand that you ruined at least six other
shows that were being taped at the time."

"Really?" Hector squirmed. "I . . . that is, I didn't
mean . . . well, I'm sorry about that. . . ."

Waving a hand at him, Leoh said, "Relax, my boy. Your fight with Odal—the audio portion of it—was beamed into nearly every home on the planet. Everyone in Acquatainia knows what a fool I've been, and that Kerak is still as much of a threat as ever."

"You're not a fool," Hector said.

"Yes, I've been one," insisted Leoh. "Worse, I've been a dupe, letting my own glory get in the way of my judgment. But that's over now. My place is in science, not politics, and certainly not show business! I'm going to concentrate on your 'jump' in the dueling machine. If that was a sample of teleportation, then the machine can amplify that talent, just as it amplified Odal's telepathic abilities. Now, if we put enough power into the machine. . . ."

The car glided to a stop under the roofed driveway in front of the entrance to Geri's house. Leoh stayed in the car while Hector walked her to her door. In the shadows, he couldn't see her face too well. They stopped at the door.

"Um . . . Geri, I . . . well, I just couldn't kill him. Not . . . not like that. I wanted to please you . . . but, well, if you want an assassin . . . I guess it's just not me that you're interested in."

She said nothing. A gentle warm breeze brought the odor of wet leaves to them.

Hector fidgeted.

Finally he said, "Well, good night. . . ."

"Good-by, Hector," Geri said flatly.

Leoh was studiously looking the other way, watching the final few drops of rain splatter on the statuary alongside the driveway, when Hector returned to the car. The old scientist looked at the Watchman as he ducked into the car and slumped in the seat.

"Why so glum, my boy? What's the matter?"

Shrugging, Hector said, "It's a long story. . . ."

"Oh, I see. Well then. To get back to the teleportation idea. If we can boost the power of the machine. . . ."

III

The Farthest Dream

It was ironic, thought Odal, that they were using the dueling machine to torture him. For it was torture, no matter what they called it or how they smiled when they were doing it.

He sat there in the cramped cubicle, staring at its featureless walls, the blank viewscreen, waiting for them to begin.

The price of failure was heavy, too heavy. Kanus had made Odal the glory of Kerak while he was a success, while he was killing the enemies of Kerak.

Now they were killing him.

Not that they caused him any physical harm. He was not even under arrest, technically. Merely assigned to experimentation at Kor's headquarters, the Ministry of Intelligence: a huge, stone, hilltop castle, ancient and brooding from the outside; inside, a maze of pain and terror and Kor's swelling lust for victims.

In the dueling machine, the illusion of pain was no

364

less agonizing than the real thing. Odal smiled sardonically. The men he had killed died first in their imaginations. But soon enough their hearts stopped beating.

Now then, are you ready? It was a voice in his mind, put there by the machine's circuitry through the neuro-contacts circling his head.

We are going to probe a bit deeper today, in an effort to find the source of your extrasensory talents. I advise you to relax and cooperate.

There had been three of them working on him yesterday, from the other side of the machine. Today, Odal could tell, there were more. Six? Eight? A dozen, possibly.

He felt them: foreign thoughts, alien personalities, in his own mind. His hands twitched uncontrollably and his body began to ache and heave.

They were seizing his control centers, battering at sensory complexes. Muscles cramped spasmodically, nerves screamed in anguish, body temperature soared, ears shrilled, eyes flashed flaming reds and unbearable star bursts. Now they were going deeper, beyond the physical effects, digging, clawing away through a lifetime of self-protective neural patterns, reaching down with a searing, white-hot, twelfth-power probe into the personality itself.

Odal heard a terrified voice howling, *They're after ME. They're trying to get ME. Hide! Hide!*

The voice was his own.

Despite its spaciousness, Leoh thought, the Prime Minister's office was a stuffy antique of a room, decorated in blue and gold, with the weight of outmoded traditions and useless memories hanging more heavily than the gilt draperies that bordered each door and window.

The meeting had been small and unspectacular. Martine had invited Leoh for an informal chat; Hector was pointedly not invited. A dozen or so aides, politicians, and administrators clustered around the Prime Minister's desk as he officially thanked Leoh for uncovering Kerak's attempt to use the dueling machine as a smoke screen for their war preparations.

"It was Star Watch Lieutenant Hector who actually uncovered the plot, not me," Leoh insisted.

Martine waved away the words impatiently. "The Watchman is merely your aide; you are the man that Kanus fears."

After about ten minutes of talking, Martine nodded to one of his aides, who went to a door and admitted a covey of news photographers. The Prime Minister stood up and walked around his desk to stand beside Leoh, towering proudly over the old man, while the newsmen took their pictures. Then the meeting broke up. The newsmen left and everyone else began to drift out of the office.

"Professor Leoh."

He was nearly at the doorway when Martine called. Leoh turned back and saw the Prime Minister sitting at his tall desk chair. But instead of his usual icy aloofness, there was a warm, almost friendly smile on Martine's face.

"Please close the door and sit down with me for a few minutes more," Martine said.

Puzzled, Leoh did as the Prime Minister asked. As he took an armchair off to one side of the desk, he watched Martine carefully run a hand over the communications panel set into his desk top. Then the Prime Minister opened a drawer in the desk and Leoh heard the tiny click of a switch being turned.

"There. Now I'm sure that we're alone. That switch isolates the room completely. Not even my private secretary can listen to us now."

Leoh felt his eyebrows rising toward his scalp.

"You have every right to look surprised, Professor. And I should look apologetic and humble. That's why I had to make certain that this meeting is strictly private."

"*This* meeting?" Leoh echoed. "Then the meeting we just had, with the others and the newsmen. . . ."

Martine smiled broadly. "Kanus is not the only one who can put up a smoke screen."

"I see. Well, what did you want to tell me?"

"First, please convey my apologies to Lieutenant Hector. He was not invited here for reasons that will be obvious in a moment. I realize that he wormed the truth out of Odal, although I'm not convinced that he knew what he was doing when he did it."

Leoh suppressed a chuckle. "Hector has his own way of doing things."

Nodding, Martine went on more soberly. "Now then, the real reason for my wanting to speak to you privately: I have been something of a stubborn fool. I realize that now. Kanus has not only outwitted me, but has actually penetrated deeply into my government. When I realized that Lal Ponte is a Kerak agent. . . ." The Prime Minister's face was grim.

"What are you going to do with him?"

A shrug. "There's nothing I can do. He has been implicated indirectly by Odal. There's no evidence, despite a thorough investigation. But I'm sure that if Kanus conquered the Acquataine Cluster, Ponte would expect to be named Prime Minister of the puppet government."

Leoh said nothing.

"Ponte is not that much of a problem. He can be isolated. Anything that I want from his office I can get from men I know I can trust. Ponte can sit alone at his desk until the ceiling caves in on him."

"But he's not your only problem."

"No. It's the military problem that threatens us most directly. You and Spencer have been right all along. Kerak is building swiftly for an attack, and our defensive buildup is too far behind them to be of much use."

"Then the alliance with the Commonwealth. . . ."

Shaking his head unhappily, Martine explained, "No,

that's still impossible. The political situation here is too unstable. I was voted into office by the barest margin . . . thanks to Ponte. To think that I was elected because Kanus wanted me to be! We've both been pawns, Professor."

"I know."

"But, you see, if Dulaq and Massan and all their predecessors never allied Acquatainia with the Commonwealth, then for me to attempt it would be an admission of weakness. There are strong pro-Kerak forces in the legislature, and many others who are still as blind and stubborn as I've been. I would be voted out of office in a week if I tried to make an alliance with the Terrans."

Leoh asked, "Then what can you do?"

"I can do very little. But you can do much. I cannot call the Star Watch for help. But you can contact your friend, Sir Harold, and suggest that he ask me for permission to bring a Star Watch fleet through the Cluster. Any excuse will do . . . battle maneuvers, exploration, cultural exchange, anything."

Leoh shifted uneasily in his chair. "You want me to ask Harold to ask you. . . ."

"Yes, that's it." Martine nodded briskly. "And it must be a small Star Watch fleet, quite small. To the rest of Acquatainia, it must appear obvious that the Terran ships are not being sent here to help defend us against Kerak. But to Kanus, it must be equally obvious that he cannot attack Acquatainia without the risk of killing Watchmen and immediately involving the Commonwealth."

"I think I understand," said Leoh, with a rueful smile. "Einstein was right: nuclear physics *is* much simpler than politics."

Martine laughed, but there was bitterness in it.

Kanus sat in brooding silence behind his immense desk, his thin, sallow face dark with displeasure. Sitting with him in the oversized office, either looking up at him at his cunningly elevated desk, or avoiding his sullen stare, were most of the members of his Inner Cabinet.

At length, the Leader spoke. "We had the Acquataine Cluster in our grasp, and we allowed an old refugee from a university and a half-wit Watchman to snatch it away from us. Kor! You told me the plan was foolproof!"

The Minister of Intelligence remained calm, except for a telltale glistening of perspiration on his bullet-shaped dome. "It *was* foolproof, until. . . ."

"Until? Until? I want the Acquataine Cluster, not excuses!"

"And you shall have it," Marshal Lugal promised. "As soon as the army is re-equipped and. . . ."

"As soon as! Until!" Kanus' voice rose to a scream. "We had a plan of conquest and it failed. I should have the lot of you thrown to the dogs! And you, Kor; this was your operation, your plan. You picked this mind reader . . . Odal. He was to be the express instrument of my will. And he *failed!* You both failed. Twice! Can you give me any reason for allowing you to continue to pollute the air with your presence?"

Kor replied evenly, "The Acquataine government is still very shaky and ripe for plucking. Men sympathetic to you, my Leader, have gained important posts in that government. Moreover, despite the failures of Major Odal, we are now on the verge of perfecting a new secret weapon, a weapon so powerful that. . . ."

"A secret weapon?" Kanus' eyes lit up.

Kor lowered his voice a notch. "It may be possible, our scientists believe, to use a telepath such as Odal and the dueling machine to transport objects from one place to another—over any distance, almost instantaneously."

Kanus sat silent for a moment, digesting the information. Then he asked:

"Whole armies?"

"Yes."

"Anywhere in the galaxy?"

"Wherever there is a dueling machine."

Kanus rose slowly, dramatically, from his chair and stepped over to the huge star map that spanned one entire wall of the spacious room. He swept the whole map with an all-inclusive gesture and shouted:

"Anywhere! I can strike anywhere. And they will never know what hit them!"

He literally danced for joy, prancing back and forth before the map. "Nothing can stand in our way now! The Terran Commonwealth will fall before us. The galaxy is ours. We will make them tremble at the thought of us. We will make them cower at the mention of my name!"

The men of the Inner Cabinet nodded and murmured agreement.

Suddenly Kanus' face hardened again and he whirled around to Kor. "Is this really a secret, or is someone else working on it too? What of this Leoh?"

"It is possible," Kor replied as blandly as he could, "that Professor Leoh is also working along the same lines. After all, the dueling machine is his invention. But he does not have the services of a trained telepath, such as Odal."

Kanus said, "I do not like the fact that you are depending on this failure, Odal."

Kor allowed a vicious smile to crack his face. "We are not depending on him, my Leader. We are using his brain. He is an experimental animal, nothing more."

Kanus smiled back at the Minister. "He is not enjoying his new duties, I trust."

"Hardly," Kor said.

"Good. Let me see tapes of his . . . ah, experiments."

"With pleasure, my Leader."

The door to the far end of the room opened and Romis, Minister of Foreign Affairs, stepped in. The room fell into a tense silence as his shoes clicked across the marble floor. Tall, spare, utterly precise, Romis walked straight to the Leader, holding a lengthy report in his hand. His patrician face was graven.

"I have unpleasant news, Chancellor."

They stood confronting each other, and everyone in the room could see their mutual hatred. Kanus—short, spare, dark—glared up at the silver-haired aristocrat.

"Our embassy in Acquatainia," Romis continued icily, "reports that Sir Harold Spencer has requested permission to base a Star Watch survey expedition temporarily on one of the frontier stars of the Acquataine Cluster. A star near our border, of course. Martine has agreed to it."

Kanus went white, then his face slowly turned red. He snatched the report from Romis' hand, scanned it, crumpled it, and threw it to the floor. For a few moments he could not even speak. Then the tirade began.

An hour and a half later, when the Leader was once again coherent enough to speak rationally, his ministers were assuring him:

"The Terrans will only be there temporarily."

"It's only a small fleet . . . no military value at all."

"It's a feeble attempt by Martine and Spencer. . . ."

At the mention of Spencer's name, Kanus broke into another half-hour of screaming tantrum. Finally, he abruptly stopped.

"Romis! Stop staring out the window and give me your assessment of this situation."

The Foreign Minister turned slowly from the window and answered, "You must assume that the Terrans will remain in Acquatainia indefinitely. If they do not, all to the good. But your plans must be based on the assumption that they will. That means you cannot attack Acquatainia by military force. . . ."

"Why not?" Kanus demanded.

Romis explained, "Because the Terrans will immediately become involved in the fighting. The entire Star Watch will be mobilized, under the pretext of saving their survey fleet from danger, as soon as we attack. The fleet is simply an excuse for the Terrans to step in against us."

But Kanus' eyes began to glow. "I have the plan," he announced. Turning to Kor:

"You must push the development of this instantaneous transporter to the ultimate. I want a working device *immediately*. Do you understand?"

"Yes, my Leader."

Rubbing his hands together joyfully, Kanus said, "We will have our army appear in the Acquatainian capital. We'll conquer the Cluster from within! Wherever they have a dueling machine, we'll appear and conquer with the swiftness of lightning! Let the Star Watch plant their hostages on the frontier . . . they'll gather cobwebs there! We'll have the whole Cluster in our fist before Spencer even realizes we've moved!"

Kanus laughed uproariously, and all his aides laughed with him.

All except Romis.

Professor Leoh slouched unhappily in a chair at the dueling machine's main control desk. Hector sat uneasily on the first few centimeters of the desk edge.

"We have adequate power," Leoh said, "the circuits are correct, everything seems normal." He looked up, puzzled, at Hector.

The Watchman stammered, "I know . . . I just . . . well, I just can't do it."

Shaking his head, Leoh said, "We've duplicated the conditions of your first jump. But now it doesn't work. If the machine is exactly the same, then there must be something different about you."

Hector wormed his shoulders uncomfortably.

"What is it, my boy? What's bothering you? You haven't been yourself since the night you caught Odal."

Hector didn't reply.

"Listen," said Leoh. "Psychic phenomena are very difficult to pin down. For centuries men have known cases where people have apparently teleported, or used telepathy. There are thousands of cases on record of poltergeists—they were actually thought to be ghosts, ages ago. Now I'm sure that they're really cases of telekinesis: the poltergeist was actually a fairly normal human being, under extraordinary stress, who threw objects around his house mentally without even knowing it himself."

"Just like when I jumped without knowing it," Hector said.

"Exactly. Now, it was my hope that the dueling machine would amplify the pyschic talent in you. It did once, but it's not doing it now."

"Maybe I don't really have it."

"Maybe," Leoh admitted. Then, leaning forward in his chair and pointing a stubby finger at the Watchman, he added, "Or maybe something's upsetting you so much that your talent is buried, dormant, switched off."

"Yes ... well, uh, that is. . . ."

"Is it Geri? I haven't seen her around here lately. Perhaps if she could come ... after all, she was one of the conditions of your original jump, wasn't she?"

"She won't come here," Hector said miserably.

"Eh? Why not?"

The Watchman blurted, "Because she wanted me to murder Odal and I wouldn't, so she's sore at me and won't even talk to me on the view phone."

"What? What's this? Take it slower, son."

Hector explained the whole story of Geri's insistence that Odal be killed.

Leaning back in the chair, fingers steepled on his broad girth, Leoh said, "Hmm. Natural enough, I suppose. The Acquatainians have that sort of outlook. But somehow I expected better of her."

"She won't even talk to me," Hector repeated.

"But you did the right thing," said Leoh. "At least,

you were true to your upbringing and your Star Watch training. Vengeance is a paltry motive, and nothing except self-defense can possibly justify killing a man."

"Tell it to her."

"No, my boy," Leoh said, pulling himself up and out of the chair. "*You* must tell her. And in no uncertain terms."

"But she won't even see me. . . ."

"Nonsense. If you love her, you'll get to her. Tell her where you stand and why. If she loves you, she'll accept you for what you are, and be proud of you for it."

Hector looked uncertain. "And if she doesn't love me?"

"Well . . . knowing the Acquatainian temperament, she might start throwing things at you."

The Watchman remained sitting on the desk top and stared down at the floor.

Leoh grasped his shoulder. "Listen to me, son. What you did took courage, real courage. It would have been easy to kill Odal and win her approval . . . everyone's approval, as a matter of fact. But you did what you thought was right. Now, if you had the courage to do that, surely you have the courage to face an unarmed girl."

Hector looked up at him, his long face somber. "But suppose . . . suppose she never loved me. Suppose she was just . . . well, *using* me . . . until I killed Odal?"

Then you're well rid of her, Leoh thought. But he couldn't say that to Hector.

"I don't think that's the case at all," he said softly.

And he added to himself, *At least I hope not.*

In his exhausted sleep, Odal did not hear the door opening. The sergeant stepped into the bare windowless cell and shined his lamp in Odal's eyes. The Kerak major stirred and turned his face away from the light. The sergeant grabbed his shoulder and shook him sternly.

Odal snapped awake, knocked the guard's hand from his shoulder, and seized him by the throat. The guard dropped his lamp and tried to pry Odal's single hand from his windpipe. For a second or two they remained locked in soundless fury, in the weird glow from the lamp on the floor—Odal sitting up on the cot, the sergeant slowly sinking to his knees.

Then Odal released him. The sergeant fell to all fours, coughing. Odal swung his legs out of the cot and stood up.

"When you rouse me, you will do it with courtesy," he said. "I am not a common criminal, and I will not be treated as one by such as you. And even though my door is locked from the outside, you will knock on it before entering. Is that clear?"

The sergeant climbed to his feet, rubbing his throat, his eyes a mixture of anger and fear.

"I'm just following orders. Nobody told me to treat you special. . . ."

"*I* am telling you," Odal snapped. "And as long as I still have my rank, you will address me as *sir!*"

"Yes, sir," the sergeant muttered sullenly.

Odal relaxed slightly, flexed his fingers.

"You're wanted at the dueling machine . . . sir."

"In the middle of the night? By whose orders?"

The guard shrugged. "They didn't say. Sir."

Odal smiled. "Very well. Step outside while I put on my 'uniform.'" He gestured to the shapeless fatigues draped over the end of the cot.

A single meditech stood waiting for Odal beside the dueling machine, which bulked ominously in the dim night lighting. Odal recognized him as one of the inquisitors he had been facing for the past several weeks. Wordlessly, the man gestured Odal to his booth. The sergeant took up a post at the doorway to the large room as the meditech fitted Odal's head and torso with the necessary neurocontacts. Then he stepped out of the compartment and firmly shut the door.

For a few moments nothing happened. Then Odal felt a voice in his mind:

"Major Odal?"

"Of course," he replied silently.

"Yes . . . of course."

There was something puzzling. Something wrong. "You . . . you are not the. . . ."

"I am not the man who put you into the dueling machine. That is correct." The voice seemed both pleased and worried. "That man is at the controls of the machine, while I am halfway across the planet. He has a miniature transceiver with him, and I am communicating with you through it. This means of communication is unorthodox, but it probably cannot be intercepted by Kor or his henchmen."

"But I know you," Odal thought. "I have met you before."

"That is true."

"Romis! You are Minister Romis."

"Yes."

"What do you want with me?"

"I learned only this morning of your situation. I was shocked at such treatment for a loyal soldier of Kerak."

Odal felt the words forming in his mind, yet he knew that Romis' words were only a glossy surface, hiding a deeper meaning. He communicated nothing, and waited for the Minister to continue.

"Are you being mistreated?"

Odal smiled mirthlessly. "No more so than any laboratory animal. I suppose it's no worse than having one's intestines sliced open without anesthetics."

Romis' mind recoiled. Then he recovered and said, "There might be some way in which I can help you. . . ."

Odal lost his patience. "You haven't contacted me in the middle of the night, using this elaborate procedure, to ask about my comfort. Something is troubling you greatly and you believe I can be useful to you."

"Can you actually read my thoughts?"

"Not in the manner one reads a tape. But I can sense things . . . and the dueling machine amplifies this talent."

Romis hesitated a moment, then asked, "Can you . . . sense . . . what is in my mind?"

Now it was Odal's turn to hesitate. Was this a trap? He glanced around the confining walls of the tiny booth, and at the door that he knew was locked from the outside. *What more can they do? Kill me?*

"I can feel in your thoughts," Odal replied, "a hatred for Kanus. A hatred that is matched only by your fear of him. If you had it in your power you would. . . ."

"I would what?"

Odal finally saw the picture clearly. "You would have the Leader assassinated."

"How?"

"By a disgraced army officer who would have good cause to hate Kanus."

"*You* have cause to hate him," Romis emphasized.

"Perhaps."

"Perhaps? Can you fail to hate him?"

Odal shook his head. "I've never considered the question. He is the Leader. I have neither loved nor hated, only followed his commands."

"Duty above self," Romis' thought returned. "You speak like a member of the nobility."

"Such as you are. And yet you wish to assassinate the Leader."

"Yes! Because a true member of the nobility puts his duty to the Kerak Worlds before his allegiance to this madman—this usurper of power who will destroy us all, nobleman and commoner alike."

"I am only a commoner," Odal replied, very deliberately. "Perhaps I'm not equipped to decide where my duty lies. Certainly, I have no choice in my duties at present."

Romis recovered his composure. "Listen to me. If you agree to join us, we can help you escape from this beastly experimentation. As you can see, certain members of Kor's staff are with us; so too are groups in the army and space fleet. If you will help us, you can once again be a hero of Kerak."

If I murder Kanus and survive the deed, Odal thought to himself. *And if I am not then assassinated in turn by your friends.*

To Romis he asked, "And if I don't agree to join you?" The Minister remained silent.

"I see," Odal answered for himself. "I know too much now to be allowed the risk of living."

"Unfortunately, the stakes are too high to let personal feelings intervene. If you do not agree to help us before leaving the dueling machine, the medical technician and sergeant are waiting outside for you. They have their orders."

"To murder me," Odal said bluntly, "and make it seem as though I tried to escape."

"Yes. I am sorry to be brutal, but that is your choice. Join or die."

While Odal deliberated his choice in the midnight darkness of Kerak, it was sunset in the capital city of Acquatainia.

High above the city, Hector circled warily in a rented air car that had been ready for the junk heap long ago. He kept his eyes riveted to the viewscreens on the control panel in front of him, sitting tensely in the pilot's seat; the four-place cabin was otherwise empty.

Part of his circle carried him through one of the city's busier traffic patterns, but he ignored other air cars and kept the autopilot locked on its circle while homeward-bound commuters shrieked into their radios at him and dodged around the Watchman's vehicle. Hector had his radio off; every nerve in his body was concentrating on the viewscreens.

The car's tri-di scanners were centered on Geri Dulaq's house, on the outskirts of the city. As far as Hector was concerned, nothing else existed. Cars buzzed by his bubble-topped canopy and apoplectic-faced drivers shook their fists at him. He never saw them. Wind whistled suspiciously through what should have been a sealed cabin; the air car groaned and rattled when it should have hummed and soared. He never noticed.

There she is! He felt a charge of electricity flash through him as he saw her at last, walking through the garden next to the house.

For an instant he wondered if he had the nerve to go through with it, but his hands had already nudged the controls and the air car, shuddering, started a long whining descent toward the house.

The reddish sun of Acquatainia was shining straight into Hector's eyes, through the ancient photochromic canopy that was supposed to screen out the glare. Squinting hard, Hector barely made out the menacing bulk of the house as it rose to meet him. He pulled back on the controls, jammed the brake flaps full open, flipped the screeching engine pods to their landing angle, and bounced the car in a shower of dust and noise and wind squarely into Geri's flower bed.

"*You!*" she screamed as he popped the canopy open.

She turned and ran to the house. He went to leap out after her, but the seat harness yanked cuttingly at his middle and shoulders.

By the time Hector had unbuckled the harness and jumped, stumbling, to the ground, she was inside the house. But the door was still open, he saw. Hector sprinted toward it.

A servant, rather elderly, appeared on the walk before the door. Hector ducked under his feebly waving arms and launched himself toward the door, which was now swinging shut. He got halfway through before the door slammed against him, wedging him firmly against the jamb.

Hector could hear someone panting behind the door, struggling to get it closed despite the fact that one of his arms and a leg were flailing inside the doorway. Hoping it wasn't Geri, he pushed hard against the door. It hardly budged. *It's not her,* he realized. Setting himself as solidly as he could on his outside leg, he pushed with all his might. The door gave slowly, then suddenly burst open. Hector sailed off balance into the husky servant who had been pushing against him. They both sprawled onto the hard plastiwood floor of the entryway.

Hector groped to all fours and caught a glimpse of Geri at the top of the wide, curving stairway that dominated the main hall of the house. Then the servant fell on him and tried to pin him down. He rolled over on top of the servant, broke loose from his clumsy grip, and got to his feet.

"I don't want to hurt you!" he said shakily, holding his hands out in what he hoped was a menacing position. Another pair of arms grappled at him from behind, but weakly. The old servant. Hector shrugged him off and took a few more steps into the house, his eyes still on the husky one, who was now crouched on the floor and looking up questioningly at Geri.

All she has to do is nod, Hector knew, *and they'll both jump me.*

"I told you I never wanted to see you again!" she screamed at him. "Never!"

"I've got to talk to you," he shouted back. "Just for five minutes. . . . Uh, alone."

"I don't . . . your nose is bleeding."

He touched his upper lip with a finger. It came away red and sticky.

"Oh . . . the door . . . I must've banged it on the door."

Geri took a few steps down the stairway, hesitated, then seemed to take a deep breath and came slowly down the rest of the way.

"It's all right," she said calmly to the servants. "You may leave."

The brawny one looked uncertain. The old one piped, "But if he. . . ."

"I'll be all right," Geri insisted firmly. "You can stay in the next room, if you like. The lieutenant will only be here for five minutes. No longer," she added, turning to Hector.

They withdrew reluctantly.

"You ruined my flowers," she said to Hector. But softly, and the corners of her mouth looked as though they wanted to turn up. "And your nose is still bleeding."

Hector fumbled through his pockets. She produced a tissue from a pocket in her dress.

"Here. Now clean yourself up and leave."

"Not until I've said what I came to say," Hector replied nasally, holding the tissue against his nose.

"Keep your head up, don't bleed on the floor."

"It's hard to talk like this."

Despite herself, Geri smiled. "Well, it's your own fault. You can't come swooping into people's gardens like . . . like. . . ."

"You wouldn't see me. And I had to tell you."

"Tell me what?"

Putting his head down, his neck cracking painfully as he did, Hector said:

"Well . . . blast it, Geri, I love you. But I'm not going to be your hired assassin. And if you loved me, you wouldn't want me to be. A man's not supposed to be a trained pet . . . to do whatever his girl wants him to. I'm not. . . ."

Her expression hardened. "I only asked you to do what I would have done myself, if I could have."

"You would've killed Odal?"

"Yes."

"Because he murdered your father."

"That's right."

Hector took the tissue away from his face. "But Odal was just following orders. Kanus is the one who ordered your father killed."

"Then I'd kill Kanus, too, if I had the chance," she snapped angrily.

"You'd kill anybody who had a hand in your father's death?"

"Of course."

"The other soldiers, the ones who helped Odal during the duel, you'd kill them too?"

"Certainly!"

"Anybody who helped Odal? Anybody at all? The starship crew that brought him here?"

"Yes! All of them! Anybody!"

Hector put his hand out slowly and took her by the shoulder. "Then you'd have to kill me, too, because I let him go. I helped him to escape from you."

She started to answer. Her mouth opened. Then her eyes filled with tears and she leaned against Hector and began crying.

He put his arms around her. "It's all right, Geri. It's all right. I know how much it hurts. But . . . you can't expect me to be just as much of a murderer as he is . . . I mean, well, it's just not the way to. . . ."

"I know," she said, still sobbing. "I know, Hector. I know."

For a few moments they remained there, holding each other. Then she looked up at him, and he kissed her.

"I've missed you," she said, very softly.

He felt himself grinning like a circus clown. "I . . . well, I've missed you, too."

They laughed together, and she pulled out another tissue and dabbed at his nose with it.

"I'm sorry about the flowers."

"That's all right, they'll. . . ." She stopped and stared toward the doorway.

Turning, Hector saw a blue-anodized robot, about the size and shape of an upended cargo crate, buzzing officiously at the open doorway. Its single photoeye seemed to brighten at the sight of his face.

"You are Star Watch Lieutenant Hector H. Hector, the operator of the vehicle parked in the flower bed?" it inquired tinnily.

Hector nodded dumbly.

"Charges have been lodged against you, sir: violations of flight safety regulation regarding use of traffic lanes, failure to acknowledge radio intercept, unauthorized flight patterns, failure to maintain minimum altitude over a residential zone, landing in an unauthorized area, trespass, illegal and violent entry into a private domicile, assault and battery. You are advised to refrain from making any statement until you obtain counsel. You will come with me, or additional charges of resisting arrest will be lodged against you. Thank you."

The Watchman sagged; his shoulders slumped dejectedly.

Geri barely suppressed a giggle. "It's all right, Hector. I'll get a lawyer. If they send you to jail, I'll visit you. It'll be very romantic."

Odal sat in the darkness of the dueling machine booth, turning thoughts over and over in his mind. To remain as Kor's experimental animal meant disgrace and the torture of ceaseless mind-probing. Ultimately an utterly unpleasant death. To join Romis meant an attempt to assassinate the Leader; an attempt that would end, successful or not, in death at the hands of Kanus' guards. To refuse to join Romis led again—and this time immediately—to death.

Every avenue of choice came to the same end. Odal sat there calmly and examined his alternatives with a cool detachment, almost as though this was happening to someone else. It was even amusing, almost, that events could arrange themselves so overwhelmingly against a lone man.

Romis' voice in his mind was imperative. "I cannot keep this link open much longer without risking detection. What is your decision?"

To stay alive as long as possible, Odal realized. Hoping that thought didn't get across to Romis, he said, "I'll join you."

"You do this willingly?"

A picture of the armed guard waiting for him outside flashed through Odal's mind. "Yes, willingly," he said. "Of course."

"Very well, then. Remain where you are, act as though nothing has happened. Within the next few days, a week at most, we'll get you out of Kor's hands."

Only when he was certain that contact was broken, that Romis and the relay man at the machine's controls could no longer hear him, did Odal allow himself to think: *If I round up Romis and all the plotters against the Leader, that should make me a hero of Kerak again.*

Hector was all smiles as he strode into the dueling machine chamber. Geri was on his arm, also smiling.

Leoh said pleasantly, "Well, now that you're together again and you've paid all your traffic fines, I hope you're emotionally prepared to go to work."

"Just watch me," said Hector.

They began slowly. First Hector merely teleported himself from one booth of the dueling machine to the other. He did it a dozen times the first day. Leoh measured the transit time and the power drain each time. It took four picoseconds, on the average, to make the jump. And—according to the desk-top calculator Leoh had set up alongside the control panels—the power drain was approximately equal to that of a star ship's drive engines pushing a mass equal to Hector's weight.

"Do you realize what this means?" he asked of them.

Hector was perched on the desk top again, with Geri sitting in a chair she had pulled up beside Leoh's. Drumming his fingers thoughtfully on the control panel for a moment, Hector replied, "Well . . . it means we can move things about as efficiently as a star ship. . . ."

"Not quite," Leoh corrected. "We can move things or people as efficiently as a star ship moves its *payload*. We needn't lift a star ship's structure or power drive. Our drive—the dueling machine—can remain on the ground. Only the payload is transported."

"Can you go as fast as a star ship?" Geri asked.

"Seemingly faster, if these tests mean anything," Leoh answered.

"Am I traveling in subspace," Hector wanted to know, "like a star ship does? Or what?"

"Probably 'what,' I'd guess," said Leoh. "But it's only a guess. We have no idea of how this works, how fast you can really go, how far you can teleport, or any of the limits of the phenomenon. There's a mountain of work to do."

For the next few days, Hector moved inanimate objects while he sat in one booth of the dueling machine. He lifted weights without touching them, and then even transported Geri from one booth to the other. But he could only move things inside the dueling machine.

"We may have an interstellar transport mechanism here," Leoh said at the end of a week, tired but enormously happy. "There'd have to be a dueling machine, or somethimg like it, at the other end, though."

The pain was unbearable. Odal screamed soundlessly, in his mind, as a dozen lances of fire drilled through him. His body jerked spasmodically, arms and legs twitching uncontrolled, innards cramping and coiling, heart pounding dangerously fast. He couldn't see, couldn't hear, could only taste blood in his mouth.

Romis! Where is Romis? Why doesn't he come? He would have told his inquisitors everything, anything, just to make them stop. But they weren't even asking him questions. They weren't interested in his memories or his confessions.

Jump!

Transport yourself to the next booth.

You are a trained telepath, you must have latent teleportation powers, as well.

We will not ease up on this pressure until you teleport to the next booth. Indeed, the pressure will be increased until you do as you are told.

JUMP!

Hector sat in the dueling machine in Acquatainia and concentrated on his job. A drawerful of papers, tapes, and holograms was in the other booth. Hector was going to transport it to a dueling machine on the other side of the planet. This would be the first long-distance jump.

It wasn't easy to concentrate. Geri was waiting for him outside. Leoh had been working him all day. A stray thought of Odal crossed his mind: *I wonder what he's up to now? Is he working on teleportation too?*

He felt a brief tingling sensation, like a mild electric shock.

"Funny," he muttered.

Puzzled, he removed the neurocontacts from his head and body, got up, and opened the booth door.

The technicians at the control desk gaped at him. It took Hector a full five seconds to realize that they were wearing Kerak uniforms. A pair of guards, looking equally startled, reached for their side arms as soon as they recognized the Star Watch emblem on Hector's coveralls.

He had time to say, "Oh-oh," before the guards shot him down.

On Acquatainia, Leoh was shaking his head unhappily as he inspected the pile of materials that Hector was supposed to teleport.

"Nothing," he muttered. "It didn't work at all."

His puzzled musing was shattered by Geri's scream. Looking up, he saw her cowering against the control desk, screaming in uncontrolled hysteria. Framed in the doorway of the farther booth stood the tall, lithe figure of Odal.

"This is absolutely fantastic," said Sir Harold Spencer.

Leoh nodded agreement. The old scientist was at his desk in the office behind the dueling machine chamber. Spencer seemed to be on a star ship, from the looks of the austere, metal-walled cabin that was visible behind his tri-di image.

"He actually jumped from Kerak to Acquatainia?" Spencer still looked unconvinced.

"In something less than a second," Leoh repeated. "Four hundred and fifty light-years in less than a second."

Spencer's brow darkened. "Do you realize what you've done, Albert? The military potential of this . . . teleportation. And Kanus must know all about it, too."

"Yes. And he's holding Hector somewhere in Kerak. We've got to get him out . . . if he's still alive."

"I know," Spencer said, absolutely glowering now. "And what about this Kerak assassin? I suppose the Acquatainians have him safely filed away?"

Nodding again, Leoh answered, "They're not quite sure what to do with him. Technically, he's not charged with any crimes. Actually, the last thing in the world anyone wants is to send him back to Kerak."

"Why did he leave? Why come back to Acquatainia?"

"Don't know. Odal won't tell us anything, except to claim asylum on Acquatainia. Most people here think it's another sort of trick."

Spencer drummed his fingers on his thigh impatiently. "So Odal is imprisoned in Acquatainia, Hector is presumably jailed in Kerak—or worse. And I have a survey fleet heading for the Acquataine-Kerak frontier on a mission that's now obviously hopeless. Kanus needn't fight his way into Acquatainia. He can pop into the midst of the Cluster, wherever there are dueling machines."

"We could shut them down, or guard them," Leoh suggested.

Frowning again, Spencer pointed out, "There's nothing to prevent Kanus from building machines inside every Kerak embassy or consulate building in the Cluster . . . or in the Commonwealth, for that matter. Nothing short of war can stop him from doing that."

"And war is exactly what we're trying to prevent."

"We've got to prevent it," Spencer rumbled, "if we want to keep the Commonwealth intact."

Now Leoh was starting to feel as gloomy as Sir Harold. "And Hector? What about him? We can't abandon him . . . Kanus could kill him."

"I know. I'll call Romis, the Foreign Minister. Of that whole lot around Kanus, he's the only one who seems capable of telling the truth."

"What can you do if they refuse to return Hector?"

"They'll probably offer to trade him for Odal."

"But Odal doesn't want to go," Leoh said. "And the Acquatainians might not surrender him. If they hold Odal and Kanus keeps Hector, then the Commonwealth will be forced into. . . ."

"Into threatening Kerak with armed force if they don't release Hector. Good Lord, this lieutenant could trigger off the war we're trying to avert!"

Spencer looked as appalled as Leoh felt.

Minister Romis left his country villa punctually at dawn for his usual morning ride. He proceeded along the bridle path, however, only until he was out of sight of the villa and any possible spies of Kor's. Then he turned his mount off the path and into the thick woods. After a hard climb upslope, he came to a little clearing atop a knoll.

Standing in the clearing was a small shuttle craft, its hatch flanked by a pair of armed guards. Wordlessly, Romis dismounted and went into the craft. A man dressed identically, and about the same height and build as the Foreign Minister, came out and mounted the animal and continued the ride.

Within moments, the shuttle craft rose on muffled jets and hurtled up and out of Kerak's atmosphere. Romis entered the control compartment and sat beside the pilot.

"This is a risky business, sir," the pilot said. "We could be spotted from the ground."

"The nearest tracking station is manned by friends of ours," Romis said tiredly. "At least, they were friends the last time I talked with them. One must take some risks in an enterprise of this sort, and the chief risk seems to be friends who change sides."

The pilot nodded unhappily. Twelve minutes after lift-off, the shuttle craft made rendezvous with an orbiting star ship that bore the insignia of the Kerak space fleet. A craggy-faced captain met Romis at the air lock and guided him down a narrow passageway to a small, guarded compartment. They stepped in. Lying on the bunk built into the compartment's curving outer bulkhead was the inert form of Star Watch Lieutenant Hector. Nearby sat one of the guards and a meditech who had been at the dueling machine. They rose and stood at attention.

"None of Kor's people know about him?" Romis' voice was quiet, but urgent.

"No, sir," said the meditech. "The interrogators were all knocked unconscious by the power surge when Major Odal and the Watchman transferred with each other. We were able to get the Watchman here without being detected."

"Hopefully," Romis added. Then he asked, "How is he?"

The meditech replied, "Sleeping like a child, sir. We thought it best to keep him drugged."

Romis nodded.

"At my order," the captain said, "they've given the Watchman several doses of truth drugs. We've been questioning him. No sense allowing an opportunity like this to go to waste."

"Quite right," said Romis. "What have you learned?"

The captain's face darkened. "Absolutely nothing. Either he knows nothing ... which is hard to believe, or," he went on, shifting his gaze to the meditech, "he can overcome the effects of the drug."

Shrugging, Romis turned back to the meditech. "You are certain that you got away from Kor undetected."

"Yes, sir. We went by the usual route, using only those men we know are loyal to our cause."

"Good. Now let us pray that none of our loyal friends decide to change loyalties."

The captain asked, "How are you going to explain Odal's disappearance? The Leader will be told about it this morning, won't he?"

"That is correct. And I do not intend to say a word. Kor assumes that Odal, and this meditech and guard, all escaped in the dueling machine. Let him continue to assume that; no suspicion will fall on us."

The captain murmured approval.

There was a rap at the door. The captain opened it, and the guard outside handed him a written message. The captain scanned it, then handed it to Romis, saying, "Your tri-di link has been set up."

Romis crumpled the message in his hand. "I had better hurry, then, before the beam leaks enough to be traceable. Here," he handed the rolled-up paper to the meditech, "destroy this. Personally."

Romis quickly made his way to another compartment, farther down the passageway, that served as a communications center. When he and the captain entered the compartment, the communications tech rose, saluted, and discreetly stepped out into the passageway.

Romis sat down before the screen and touched a button on the panel at his side. Instantly the screen showed the bulky form of Sir Harold Spencer, sitting at a metal desk, obviously aboard his own star ship.

Spencer's face was a thundercloud. "Minister Romis. I was going to call you when your call arrived here."

Romis smiled easily and replied, "From the expression on your face, Commander, I believe you already know the reason for my calling."

Sir Harold did not return the smile. "You are a well-trained diplomat, sir. I am only a soldier. Let's come directly to the point."

"Of course. A major in the Kerak army has disappeared, and I have reason to believe he is on Acquatainia."

Spencer huffed. "And a Star Watch lieutenant has disappeared, and I have reason to believe he is on Kerak."

"Your suspicions are not without foundation," Romis fenced coolly. "And mine?"

The Star Watch Commander rubbed a hand across his massive jaw before answering. "You have been using the words 'I' and 'mine' instead of the usual diplomatic plurals. Could it be that you are not speaking on behalf of the Kerak government?"

Romis glanced up at the captain, standing by the door out of camera range; he gave only a worried frown and a gesture to indicate that time was racing.

"It happens," Romis said to Sir Harold, "that I am not speaking for the government at this moment. If you have custody of the missing Kerak major, you can probably learn the details of my position from him."

"I see," Spencer said. "And should I assume that you —and not Kanus and his gang of hoodlums—have custody of Lieutenant Hector?"

Romis nodded.

"You wish to exchange him for Major Odal?"

"No, not at all. The Major is ... safer ... where he is, for the time being. We have no desire for his return to Kerak at the moment. Perhaps later. However, we do want to assure you that no harm will come to Lieutenant Hector—no matter what happens here on Kerak."

Spencer sat wordlessly for several seconds. At length he said, "You seem to be saying that there will be an upheaval in Kerak's government shortly, and you will hold Lieutenant Hector hostage to make certain that the Star Watch does not interfere. Is that correct?"

"You put it rather bluntly," Romis said, "but, in essence, you are correct."

"Very well," said Spencer. "Go ahead and have your upheaval. But let me warn you: if, for any reason whatever, harm should befall a Star Watchman, you will have an invasion on your hands as quickly as star ships can reach your worlds. I will not wait for authorization from the Terran Council or any other formalities. I will crush you, one and all. Is that clear?"

"Quite clear," Romis replied, his face reddening. "Quite clear."

Leoh had to make his way through the length of the Acquatainian Justice Department's longest hallway, down a lift tube to a sub-sub-basement, past four checkpoints guarded by a dozen armed and uniformed men each, into an anteroom where another pair of guards sat next to a tri-di scanner, and finally—after being stopped, photographed, questioned, and made to show his special identification card and pass each step of the way— entered Odal's quarters.

It was a comfortable suite of rooms, deep underground,

originally built for the Secretary of Justice as a blast shelter during the previous Acquataine-Kerak war.

"You're certainly well guarded," the old man said to Odal as he entered.

The Kerak major had been sitting on a plush lounge, listening to a music tape. He flicked the music silent and rose as Leoh walked into the room. The outside door clicked shut behind the scientist.

"I'm being protected, they tell me," said Odal, "both from the Acquatainian populace and from the Kerak embassy."

"Are they treating you well?" Leoh asked as he sat, uninvited, on an easy chair next to the lounge.

"Well enough. I have music, tri-di, food and drink." Odal's voice had a ring of irony in it. "I'm even allowed to see the sun once a day, when I get my prison-yard exercise."

As Odal sat back in the lounge, Leoh looked closely at him. He seemed different. No more icy smile and haughty manner. There were lines in his face that had been put there by pain, but not by pain alone. Disillusionment, perhaps. The world was no longer his personal arena of triumph. Leoh thought, *He's settled down to the same business that haunts us all: survival.*

Aloud, he said, "Sir Harold Spencer has been in touch with your Foreign Minister, Romis."

Odal kept his face blank, noncommittal.

"Harold has asked me to speak with you, to find out where you stand in all of this. The situation is quite confused."

"It seems simple to me," Odal said. "You have me. Romis has Hector."

"Yes, but where do we go from here? Is Kanus going to attack Acquatainia? Is Romis going to try to overthrow Kanus? Harold has been trying to avert a war, but if anything happens to Hector, he'll swoop in with every

Star Watch ship he can muster. And where do you stand? Which side are you on?"

Odal almost smiled. "I've been asking myself that very question. So far, I haven't been able to find a clear answer."

"It's important for us to know."

"Is it?" Odal asked, leaning forward slightly in the lounge. "Why is that? I'm a prisoner here. I'm not going anywhere."

"You needn't be a prisoner. I'm sure that Harold and Prime Minister Martine would agree to have you released if you guaranteed to help us."

"Help you? How?"

"For one thing," Leoh answered, "you could help us to get Hector back to safety."

"Return to Kerak?" Odal tensed. "That would be risky."

"You'd rather sit safely here, a prisoner?"

"Why not?"

Leoh shifted his weight uncomfortably in the chair. "I should think that Romis could use you in his attempt to overthrow Kanus."

"Possibly. But not until the moment he's ready to strike directly at Kanus. Until then, I imagine he's just as happy to let me remain here. He'll call me when he wants me. Whether I'll go or not is another problem."

Leoh suddenly found that he had run out of words. It seemed clear that Odal was not going to volunteer to help anyone except himself.

Rising, he said, "I'd like you to think about these matters. There are many lives at stake, amd you could help to save them."

"And lose my own," Odal said as he politely stood up.

Leoh cocked his head to one side. "Very possibly, I must admit."

"You regard Hector's life more highly than my own. I don't."

"All right then, stalemate. But there are a few billion Kerak and Acquatainian lives at stake, you know."

Leoh started for the door. Odal remained standing in front of the lounge. Then he called:

"Professor. That girl . . . the one who was so startled when I arrived at your dueling machine. Who is she?"

Leoh turned. "Geri Dulaq. The late Prime Minister's daughter."

"Oh, I see." For an instant, Odal's nearly expressionless face seemed to show something: disappointment, regret?

"She hates me, doesn't she?" he asked.

"To use your own words," said Leoh, "why not?"

Hector scratched his head thoughtfully and said, "This sort of, well, puts me in a . . . um, funny position."

The Kerak captain shrugged. "We are all in an extremely delicate position."

"Well, I suppose so, if . . . that is, I mean . . . how do I know you're telling me the truth?"

The captain's blunt, seamed face hardened angrily for a moment. They were sitting on the bridge of the orbiting star ship to which Hector had been brought. Beyond the protective rail, on the level below, was the control center of the mammoth vessel. The captain controlled his rage and replied evenly:

"A Kerak officer does not tell lies. Under any circumstances. My—superior, let us say—has spoken to the Star Watch Commander, as I explained to you. They reached an agreement whereby you are to remain on this ship until further notice. I am willing to allow you free rein of the ship, exclusive of the control center itself, the power plant, and the air locks. I believe that this is more than fair."

Hector drummed his fingers on the chart table next to him. "Guess I've got no choice, really. I'm sort of, well, halfway between a prisoner and, um, a cultural exchange tourist."

The captain smiled mechanically, trying to ignore the maddening finger-drumming.

"And I'll be staying with you," Hector went on, "until you assassinate Kanus."

"DON'T SAY THAT!" The captain almost leaped into Hector's lap and clapped a hand over the Watchman's mouth.

"Oh. Doesn't the crew know about it?"

The captain rubbed his forehead with a shaky hand. "How ... who ... whatever gave you the idea that we would ... contemplate such a thing?"

Hector frowned in puzzlement. "I don't really know. Just odds and ends. You know. A few things my guards have said. And I figure that Kanus would have pickled my brain by now. You haven't. I'm being treated almost like a guest. So you're not working for Kanus. Yet you're wearing Kerak insignia. Therefore you must be...."

"Enough! Please, it is not necessary to go into any more detail."

"Okay." Hector got to his feet. "It's all right for me to walk through the ship?"

"Yes; with the exceptions I mentioned." The captain rose also. "Oh, yes, there is one other forbidden area: the computers. I understand you were in there this morning."

Hector nodded. "The guards let me go in. I was taking my after-breakfast exercise. The guards insisted on it. The exercise, that is."

"That is irrelevant! You discussed computation methods with one of our junior programers...."

"Yes. I'm pretty good at math, you see, and...."

"Please! I don't know what you told him, but in attempting to put your so-called 'improvements' into the computer program, he blew out three banks of logic circuits and caused a shutdown of the computer for several hours."

"Oh? That's funny."

"Funny?" the captain snapped.

"I mean odd."

"I quite agree. Do not enter the computer area again."

Hector shrugged. "Okay. You're the captain."

The young Star Watchman turned and walked away, leaving the captain seething with frustration. He had not saluted; he had not waited until dismissed by the superior officer; he just slouched off like ... like a civilian! And now he was whistling! Aboard ship! The captain sank back into his chair. That computer programer was only the first casualty, he suddenly realized. *Romis had better act quickly. It is only a matter of time before this Watchman drives us all insane.*

The bridge, Hector found, connected to a series of technical stations, such as the navigation section (idle now that the ship was parked in orbit), the communications center (well guarded) and—most interesting of all— the observation center.

Here Hector found a fair-sized compartment crammed with viewscreens showing almost every section of the ship's interior, and also looking outside in various directions around the ship. Since they were orbiting Kerak's capital planet, most of the exterior views were turned on the ground below.

Hector soon struck up an acquaintance with the men on duty. Despite the Star Watch emblem on his coveralls, they seemed to accept him as a fellow-sufferer in the military system, rather than a potential enemy.

"That's the capital city," one of them pointed out.

Hector nodded, impressed. "Is that where they have the dueling machine?"

"You mean the one at the Ministry of Intelligence? That's over on the other side of the planet. I'll show it to you when we swing over that way."

"Thanks," Hector said. "I'd like to see it ... very much."

Every morning Odal was taken from his underground suite of rooms to the enclosed courtyard of the Justice

building for an hour of sunshine and exercise. Under the
cold eyes of the guards he ran endless circles around the
courtyard's manicured grass, or did push-ups, knee-
bends, sit-ups ... anything to break the monotony and
prevent the guards from seeing how miserable and lonely
he really felt.

Romis, he thought, *is no fool. He won't need me until
all his plans are finished, until the actual moment to kill
the Leader arrives. What could be better for him than
to leave me here, and then offer the Watchman—at precisely the right moment—in trade for me? Spencer will
have me shipped back to Kerak, too late to do anything
but Romis' bidding.*

There were stately, pungent trees lining the four sides
of the courtyard, and in the middle a full, wide-spreading
wonder with golden, stiff leaves that tinkled like glass
chimes whenever a breeze wafted them. As Odal got up,
puffing and hot, from a long set of push-ups, he saw
Geri Dulaq sitting on the bench under that tree.

He wiped his brow with a towel and, tossing it over
his shoulder, walked slowly to her. He hadn't noticed
before how beautiful she was. Her face looked calm, but
he could sense that she was working hard to keep control
of herself.

"Good morning," he said evenly.

She nodded but said nothing. Not even a smile or a
frown. He gestured toward the bench, and when she
nodded again, he sat down beside her.

"You're my second visitor," said Odal.

"I know," Geri replied. "Professor Leoh told me about
his visit to you. How you refused to try to help Hector."

Allowing himself a smile, Odal said, "I thought that's
what you'd be here for."

She turned to face him. "You can't leave him in Kerak!
If Kanus. . . ."

"Hector is with Romis. He's safe enough."

"For how long?"

"As long as any of us," Odal said.

"No," Geri insisted. "He's a prisoner, and he's in danger."

"You actually love him?"

Her eyes had the glint of tears in them. "Yes," she said.

Shaking his head in disbelief, Odal asked, "How can you love that bumbling, tongue-twisted. . . ."

"He's stronger than you are!" Geri flashed. "And braver. He'd never willingly kill anyone, not even you. He let you live when everyone else on the planet—including me—would have shot you down."

Odal backed away involuntarily.

"You owe your life to Hector," she said.

"And now I'm supposed to throw it away to save his."

"That's right. That would be the decent thing to do. It's what he'd do for you."

"I doubt that."

"Of course you do. You don't know what decency is."

He looked at her, carefully this time, trying to fathom the emotions in her face, her voice.

"Do you hate me?" Odal asked.

Her mouth started to form a *yes*, but she hesitated. "I should; I have every reason to. I . . . I don't know . . . I want to!"

She got up from the bench and walked rapidly, head down, to the nearest exit from the courtyard. Odal watched her for a moment, then went after her. But the guards stopped him as he neared the door. Geri went on through and disappeared from his sight without ever turning back to look at him.

"Cowards!" Romis spat. "Spineless, weak-kneed old women."

He was pacing the length of the bookshelf-lined study in his villa, slashing out words as cold and sharp as knife blades. Sitting next to the fireplace, holding an ornate glass in his hand, was the captain of the star ship in which Hector was being held.

"They plot for months on end," Romis muttered, more to himself than the captain. "They argue over the pettiest details for days. They slither around like snakes, trying to make certain that the plan is absolutely foolproof. But as soon as some danger arises, what do they do?"

The captain raised the glass to his lips.

"They back down!" Romis shouted. "They place their own rotten little lives ahead of the welfare of the Kerak Worlds. They allow that monster to live, for fear that they might die."

The captain asked, "Well, what did you expect of them? You can't force them to be brave. The army leaders, maybe. But they've all been arrested. Whole families. Your politician friends are scared out of their wits by Kor. It's a wonder he hasn't picked you up."

"He won't," Romis said, smiling strangely. "Not until he finds out where Odal is. He fears Odal's return. He knows how well the assassin's been trained."

"Well, you won't be getting Odal back from Spencer unless you give up the Watchman. And once he goes, you can expect Spencer to hover over us like a vulture."

"Then what must I do? Kill Kanus myself?"

"You can't." The captain shook his head.

"Why not? You think I lack. . . ."

"My old friend, don't lose sight of your objectives. Kanus is the monster, yes. But he's surrounded by lesser monsters. If you try to kill him, you'll be killed yourself."

"So?"

"Then who will take over leadership of the goverment? One of Kanus' underlings, of course. Would you like to see Greber in power? Or Kor?"

Romis visibly shuddered. "Of course not."

"Then put the idea of personally performing the execution out of your head. It's suicide."

"But Kanus must be stopped. I'm certain he means to

attack Acquatainia before the month is out." Romis
walked over to the fireplace and stared into the flames.
"I suppose we will have to ask for Odal's return. Even
if it means giving back the Watchman and having Spencer poised to invade us."

"Are you sure?"

"What else can we do? If we can pull off the assassina-
tion quickly enough, we can keep Spencer out of Kerak.
But if we hesitate much longer, we'll be at war with
Acquatainia."

"We can beat the Acquatainians."

"I know," Romis replied. "But once we do, Kanus will
be so popular among the people that we wouldn't dare
touch him. And then the madman will attack the Terrans.
That will pull the house down on all of us."

"Hmmm."

Romis turned to face the captain. "We must return
the Watchman and get Odal back here. At once."

"Good," said the captain. "Frankly, the Watchman has
been a royal nuisance aboard my ship. He's disrupting
everything."

"How can one man disrupt an entire star ship?"

The captain took a fast final gulp of his drink. "You
don't know this one man."

As the captain approached his star ship in his personal
shuttle craft, he could sense something was wrong.

It was nothing he could see, but the ship simply did
not seem right. His worries were confirmed when the
shuttle docked inside one of the giant star ship's air locks.
The emergency lights were on, and they were very dim
at that. The outer hatch was cranked shut by two space-
suited deck hands, and it took nearly fifteen minutes to
bring the lock up to normal air pressure, using the auxiliary air pumps.

"What in the name of all the devils has happened

here?" the captain stormed to a cringing junior officer
as he stepped out of the shuttle.

"It . . . it's the power, sir. The power . . . shut off."

"Shut off?"

The officer swallowed nervously and replied, "Yessir.
All at once . . . all through the ship . . . no power!"

The captain fumed under his breath for a moment,
then snapped, "Crank the inner hatch open and get me
to the bridge."

The deck hands jumped to it, and in a few minutes
the captain, junior officer, and lower ratings had
deserted the air lock, leaving the shuttle empty and
unguarded.

Out of the pressurized control compartment at the far
end of the lock stepped Hector, his thin face wary and
serious, but not without the flickerings of a slightly self-
satisfied smile.

*They should be finding the cause of the power failure
in a minute or two,* he said to himself. *And as soon as
the main lights go on, out I go.*

Hector tiptoed around the lock, making certain adjustments to the temporarily inert air pumps and hatch control unit. Then he climbed into the little shuttle, sealed
its hatch, and studied the control panel. *Not too tough
. . . I think.*

It had been a ridiculously easy job to cause a power
breakdown. All Hector had needed was a little time, so
that the guards would begin to allow him to roam certain
parts of the ship alone. He had spent long hours in the
observation center, learning the layout of the mammoth
ship and pinpointing his ultimate objective—the Ministry
of Intelligence, where a dueling machine was.

An hour ago, he had taken one of his customary strolls
from his quarters to the communications center. His
guards, after seeing Hector safely seated among a dozen
Kerak technicians, relaxed. Hector waited a while, then

casually sauntered over to the stairwell that led down to the switching equipment, on the deck below.

Hector nearly fouled his plan completely by missing the second rung on the metal ladder and plummeting to the deck below. For a long moment he lay on his face, trying to look invisible, or at least dead. Finally he risked a peep up the ladder. No one was coming after him; they hadn't noticed. He was safe, for a few minutes.

He quickly found what he wanted: the leads from the main power plants and the communications antennas. He pulled one of the printed circuit elements from a standby console and used it to form a bridge between the power lead connectors and the antenna circuit. While the rules of physics claimed that what he was attempting was impossible, Hector knew from a previous experience on a Star Watch ship (he still shuddered at the memory) exactly what this "accidental" misconnection would do.

It took about fifteen seconds for the power plants to pump all their energy into the short circuit. The effect was a quiet one: no sparks, no smoke, no explosion. All that happened was that all the lights and motors aboard the ship went off simultaneously. The emergency systems turned on immediately, of course. But in the dim auxiliary lighting, and the confusion of the surprised, bewildered, angry men, it was fairly simple for Hector to make his way along a carefully preplanned route to the main air lock.

Now he sat in the captain's shuttle, waiting for the power to return. The main lights flickered briefly, then turned on to full brightness. The air-lock pumps hummed to life, the outer hatch slid open. Hector nudged the throttle and the shuttle edged out of the air lock and away from the orbiting ship.

The Kerak captain needed about ten minutes to piece together all the information: the deliberate misconnection in the switching equipment; Hector's disappearance;

and, finally, the unauthorized departure of his personal
shuttle.

"He's escaped," the captain mumbled. "Escaped.
When we were just about to send him back."

"What shall we do, sir? If the planetary patrols detect
the ship, he won't be able to identify himself satisfacto-
rily. They'll blast him!"

The captain's eyes lit up at the thought. But then, "No.
If we lose him, the whole Star Watch will pour into
Kerak." He thought for a moment, then told his aides,
"Have our communications men send out a flight plan
to the planetary patrol. Tell them that my shuttle and an
auxiliary boat are bringing a contingent of men and officers to the Ministry of Intelligence. And get one of the
boats ready for immediate departure. Take your best
men. This mess is going to get worse before it gets
better."

Odal paced his windowless room endlessly: from the
wall screen, around the lounge, past the guarded door to
the outside hall, to the bedroom doorway, back again.
And again, and again, across the thick carpeting.

He was trying to use his mind as a dispassionate computer, to weigh and count and calculate a hundred different factors. But each factor was different, imponderable,
non-numerical. And any one of them could determine
the length of Odal's life span.

Kanus, Kor, Romis, Hector, and Geri.

*If I returned to Kerak, would Kanus restore me to my
full honors? I hold the key to teleportation, to a devastating new way to invade and conquer a nation. Or has
Kanus found other psychic talents? Would he regard me
as a traitor or a spy? Or worst of all, a failure?*

Kor. Odal could report everything he knew about
Romis' plot to kill the Leader. Which wasn't much. Kor
probably already had that much information and more.

What about Romis? *Is he still bent on overthrowing the Leader? Does he still want an assassin?*

And the Watchman, that bumbling fool. But a tele-porter, and probably as fully talented as Odal himself. *I can impress Leoh and Spencer by rescuing him. It would be risky, but if I do it . . . it will impress the girl, too.*

The girl. Geri Dulaq. Yes, Geri. She has every reason to hate me, and yet there is something other than hate in her eyes. Fear? Anger? They say that hate is very close to love.

The viewscreen chimed, snapping Odal from his chain of thought and pacing. He clapped his hands and the wall dissolved, revealing the bulky form of Leoh sitting at his desk in the dueling machine building. The machine itself was partially visible through the open doorway behind the Professor.

"I thought you should know," Leoh said without pre-liminaries, his wrinkled face downcast with worry, "that Hector has apparently escaped from Romis' hands. We received a message from one of Romis' friends in the Kerak embassy that he's disappeared."

Odal stood absolutely still in the middle of the room. "Disappeared? What do you mean?"

Shrugging, Leoh replied, "According to our informa-tion, Hector was being kept aboard an orbiting star ship. He somehow got off the ship in a shuttle craft, presum-ably heading for the Kerak dueling machine. The same one you escaped from. That's all we know."

"That machine is in Kor's Ministry of Intelligence," Odal heard himself saying calmly. But his mind was rac-ing: *Kor, Hector, Romis, Geri.* "He's walking straight into the fire."

"You're the only one who can help him now," Leoh said.

Geri. The look on her face. Her voice: "You wouldn't know what decency is."

"Very well," said Odal. "I'll try."

He had expected to feel either an excitement at the thought of pleasing Geri, or a new burden of fear at the prospect of returning to Kor's hands. Instead he felt neither. Nothing. His emotions seemed turned off—or, perhaps, they were merely waiting for something to happen.

It was late at night when Odal, closely guarded, arrived at the dueling machine. He was wearing black from his throat to his boots, and looked like a grim shadow against the antiseptic white of the chamber.

Leoh met him at the control desk. The Acquatainian guards stood back.

"I'm sorry it took so long to get you here. Every minute's delay could mean Hector's life. And yours."

Odal smiled tightly at the afterthought.

The old man continued, "I had to talk to Martine for two whole hours before he'd permit your release. And I roused Sir Harold from his sleep. He was less than happy."

"If I recall the time differential correctly," Odal said, "it's nearly dawn at Kor's headquarters. An ideal time to arrive."

"But is their dueling machine on?" Leoh asked. "We can't make the jump unless the machine on the receiving end is under power."

Odal thought a moment. "It might be. When Kor was ... experimenting with me, they used the machine early each morning. It was always turned up to full power when I arrived for the day's testing. They probably turn it on at dawn as a matter of routine."

"There's one way to find out," said Leoh, gesturing to the dueling machine.

Odal nodded. The moment had come. He was returning to Kerak. *To what fate? Death or glory? To which allegiance? Kor or Romis? Kill Hector or save him?*

And the picture he held in his mind as they adjusted the neurocontacts and left him in the dueling machine's booth was the picture of Geri's face. He tried to imagine how she would look smiling.

It was late at night, dark and wind swept, when Hector skidded the stolen shuttle craft to a bone-rattling stop deep in a ravine a few kilometers from the Intelligence Ministry.

He had come in low and fast, hoping to avoid detection by Kerak scanners. Now, as he stood atop the dented shuttle craft, feeling the wind, hearing its keening through the dark trees in the ravine, he focused his gaze on the beetling towers of the Intelligence building, silhouetted darkly atop a hill against the star-bright sky.

Looks like an ancient castle, Hector thought, without knowing that it was.

He ducked back through the hatch into the equipment storage racks, pulled out a jet belt, and squirmed into it. Then he went forward to the pilot's compartment and turned off all the power on the ship.

Might need her again, in case I can't get to the dueling machine.

It took him ten minutes to grope his way back to the hatch in darkness. Ten minutes, three shin-barkings, and one head-banging of near concussion magnitude. But finally Hector stood outside the hatch once more. He took a deep breath, faced the Intelligence building, and touched the control stud of the jet belt.

In the quiet night, the noise was shattering. Hector's ears rang as he flew, squinting into the stinging wind, toward the castle. *Maybe this isn't the best way to sneak up on them,* he suspected. But now the battlements were looming before him, racing up fast. Cutting power, he tumbled down and hit hard, sprawling on the squared-off top of the tallest tower.

Shaking his head to clear it and get rid of the ear-ringing, Hector got to his feet. He was unhurt. The platform was about ten meters square, with a stairway leading down from one corner. *Did they hear me coming?*

As if in answer, he heard footsteps ticking up the stone stairway. Shrugging off the jet belt, he hefted its weight in his hands, then hurried over to the top of the stairs. A man's head came into view. He turned as he ran up the last few steps and started to whisper hoarsely, "Are you here, Watchman? I. . . ."

Hector knocked him unconscious with the jet belt before he could say any more. As he struggled into the Kerak guard's uniform, pulling it over his own coveralls, Hector suddenly wondered: *How did he know it was a Watchman? Maybe he's been alerted by the star-ship captain. If that's the case, then these people are against Kanus.*

Once inside the guard uniform, Hector started down the steps. Three more guards were waiting for him at the bottom of the flight, in a stone-faced hallway that curved off into darkness. The lighting wasn't very good, but Hector could see that these men were big, tough-looking, and armed with pistols. He hoped they wouldn't notice that he wasn't the same man who had gone up the stairs a few minutes earlier.

Hector grinned at them and fluttered a wave. He kept walking, trying to get past them and down the corridor.

"Hey, you're the . . ." one of the guards started to say, in the Kerak language.

Hector suddenly felt sick. He could barely understand the Kerak tongue, much less speak it. He kept his grin, weak though it was, and walked a bit faster.

The second guard grabbed the first one's arm and cut him short. "Let him through," he whispered. "We'll try to get the word to our people downstairs and get him into the dueling machine and out of here. But don't get caught near him by Kor's people! Understand?"

"All right, but somebody better cut off the scanners that watch the halls."

"Can't do that without running the risk of alerting Kor himself!"

"We'll have to chance it . . . otherwise they'll spot him in a minute, in a guard uniform four sizes too small for him."

Hector was past them now, wondering what the whispering was about, but still moving. As he rounded the corner of the corridor, he saw an open lift tube, looking raw and new in the warm polished stone of the wall. The tube was lit and operating. Hector stepped in, said, "Dueling machine level" in basic Terran to the simple-minded computer that ran the tube, and closed his eyes.

The computer's squeaky voice echoed back, "Dueling machine level; turn left, then right." Hector opened his eyes and stepped out of the tube. The corridor here was much brighter, better lit. But there was still no one in sight.

It was almost like magic. Hector made his way through the long corridors of the castle without seeing another soul. He passed guard stations where steaming mugs sat alone on desk tops, passed open doors to spacious rooms, passed blank viewscreens. He saw scanning cameras set high up on the corridor wall every few meters, but they seemed to be off. Once or twice he thought he might have heard scuffling and the muffled sounds of men struggling, but he never saw a single person.

Then the big green double doors of the dueling machine chamber came into view. One of them was open, and he could see the machine itself, dimly lit inside.

Still no one in sight!

Hector sprinted into the big, arched-ceiling room and ran straight to the main control desk of the machine. He started setting the power when all the lights in the chamber blazed on blindingly.

From all the doors around the chamber, white-helmeted guards burst in, guns in their hands. A viewscreen high above flashed into life and a furious man with a bald, bullet-shaped head shouted:

"There he is! Get him!"

Before Hector could move, he felt the flaming pain of a stun bolt smash him against the control desk. As he sank to the floor, consciousness spiraling away from him, he heard Kor ordering:

"Now arrest all the traitors who were helping him. If they resist, kill them!"

Hector's head was buzzing. He couldn't get his eyes open all the way. He seemed to be in a tiny unlit cubicle, metal-walled, with a blank viewscreen staring at him. Something was on his head, something else strapped around his chest. He couldn't see his hands; they were down on his lap and his head wouldn't move far enough to look at them. Nor would his hands move, despite his will.

He heard voices. Whether they were outside the cubicle or inside his head, he couldn't tell.

"What do you mean, nothing? He must have *some* thoughts in his head!"

"Yes, Minister Kor, there are. But they are so random, so patternless ... I've never examined a brain like his. I don't see how he can walk straight, let alone think."

"He is a natural telepath," Kor's harsh voice countered. "Perhaps he's hiding his true thought patterns from you."

"Under the influence of the massive drug doses we've given him? Impossible."

"The drugs might not affect him."

"No, that couldn't be. His physical condition shows that the drugs have stupefied him almost completely."

A new voice piped up. "The monitor shows that the drugs are wearing off; he's beginning to regain consciousness."

"Dose him again," Kor ordered.

"More drugs? The effect could be dangerous ... even fatal."

"Must I repeat myself? The Watchman is a natural telepath. If he regains full consciousness inside the dueling machine, he can disappear at will. The consequences of *that* will be fatal ... to you!"

Hector tried to open his eyes fully, but the lids felt gummy, as though they'd been glued together. *Inside the dueling machine! If I can get myself together before they put me under again....* His hands weighed two hundred kilos apiece, and he still couldn't move his head. But through his half-open eyes he could see that the viewscreen was softly glowing, even though blank. The machine was on. *They've been trying to pick my brain,* he realized.

"Here's the syringe, Doctor," another voice said. "It's fully loaded."

Frantically, Hector tried to brush the cobwebs from his mind. *Concentrate on Acquatainia,* he told himself. *Concentrate!* But he could hear the footsteps approaching his booth.

And then his mind seemed to explode. His whole body wrenched violently with a flood of alien thought pouring through him.

One moment Odal was sitting in the Acquatainian dueling machine, thinking about Geri Dulaq. An instant later he *knew* he was in Kerak, and someone else was in the dueling machine with him. Hector! His mind was open and Odal could look deep.... A flash like a supernova explosion rocked Odal's every fiber. Two minds exposed to each other, fully, amplified and cross-linked by the circuits of the machine, fused together inescapably. Every nerve and muscle in both their bodies arched as though a hundred thousand volts of electricity were shooting through them.

Odal! Hector realized. He could see into Odal's mind

as if it were his own. In a strange, double-visioned sort of way, he *was* Odal ... himself and Odal, both at the same time. *And Odal, sharing Hector's mind, became Hector.*

Hector saw long files of cadets marching wearily in heavy gray uniforms, felt the weight of the lumpy field packs on their backs, sweated under the scorching sun.

Odal felt the thrill of a boy's first sight of a star ship as it floated magnificently in orbit.

Now Hector was running through the narrow streets of an ancient town, running with a dozen other teenagers in brown uniforms, wielding clubs, shouting in the night shadows, smashing windows on certain shops and homes where a special symbol had been crudely painted only a few minutes earlier. And if anyone came outside to protest, they smashed him, too.

Odal saw a Star Watch instructor sadly shaking his head at his/Hector's attempts to command the bridge of a training ship.

Standing at attention, face frozen in a grim scowl, while the Leader harangued an assembly of a half-million troops and citizens on the anniversary of his ascent to power.

Running after the older boys, trying to get them to let you into the game; but they say you're too small, too dumb, and above all too clumsy.

Holding back the tears of anger and fright while the captain slowly explained why your parents had been taken away. He was almost using baby talk. He didn't like this task, didn't like sending grown-ups to wherever it was that they put bad people. But Mother and Father were bad. They had said bad things about the Leader. And now he would become a soldier and help the Leader and kill all the bad people.

Playing ball in zero gee with four other cadets, floating in the huge, metal-ribbed, spheroidal gym, laughing, trying to toss the ball without flipping yourself into a weightless tumble.

Smashing the smug face of the upperclassman who called his parents traitor. His bloody, surprised face. Kneeing, clubbing, kicking him into silence. No one will mention that subject again.

Standing, shaking with exertion and fear, gun in hand, wanting to kill, wanting to please the girl who screamed for death, but looking into the face of the downed man and realizing that nothing, NOTHING, warrants taking a human life.

Clubbing the moon-faced Dulaq, smashing him down into shrieking blood as the six of you hammered him to death, telling yourself he's an enemy, an enemy, if I don't kill him he'll kill me, if I don't kill him the Leader will find someone else who will.

Half-thoughts, emotions, snatches of memory. A mother's face, the special smell of your own room, the sound of laughter. The forgotten past, the buried past, the warmth of the fireplace at home after a day in the snow, the fragrance of Father's pipe, the satisfied purring of the soft-furred kitten in your arms.

Leaving home saying goodbye, Dad still unconvinced that you belonged in the Star Watch. Driving off with the captain, away from the house that was empty now. *Fumbling, faltering through training, somehow passing, but always by the barest margin.* Being the best, first in the ranks: best student, best athlete, best soldier. Always the best. *Learning the real mission of the Star Watch: protect the peace.* Learning how to hate, how to kill, and above all, how to revenge yourself against Acquatainia.

Meeting and merging, spiraling together, memories of a lifetime intertwining, interlinking, brain synapses flashing, chemical balances subtly changing, two lives, two histories, two personalities melting together more completely than any two minds had ever known before. Hector and Odal, Odal/Hector—in the flash of that instant when they met in the dueling machine they became briefly one and the same.

And when one of the Kerak meditechs noted the power surging through the machine and turned it off, each of the two young men became an individual again. But a different individual than before. Neither of them could be the same as before. They were linked, irrevocably.

"What is it?" Kor snapped. "What caused the machine to use power like that?"

The meditech shrugged inside his white lab coat. "The Watchman is in there alone. I don't understand. . . ."

Furious, Kor bustled toward Hector's booth. "If he's recovered and escaped, I'll. . . ."

Both doors opened simultaneously. From one booth stepped Hector, clear-eyed, straight-backed, tall and lean and blond. His face was curiously calm, almost smiling. He glanced across to the other booth.

Odal stood there. Just as tall and lean and blond as Hector, with almost exactly the same expression on his face: a *knowing* expression, a satisfaction that nothing would ever be able to damage.

"You!" Kor shouted. "You've returned."

For half an instant they all stood there frozen: Hector and Odal at opposite ends of the dueling machine, Kor stopped in mid-stride about halfway between them, four meditechs at the control panels, a pair of armed guards slightly behind Kor. Kerak's wan bluish sun was throwing a cold early-morning light through the stone-ribbed chamber's only window.

"You are under arrest," Kor said to Odal. "And as for you, Watchman, we're not finished with you."

"Yes you are," Hector said evenly as he walked slowly and deliberately toward the Intelligence Minister.

Kor frowned. Then he saw Odal advancing toward him

too. He took a step backward, then turned to the two guards. "Stop them. . . ."

Too late. Like a perfectly synchronized machine, Odal and Hector launched themselves at the guards and knocked them both unconscious before Kor could say another word. Picking up a fallen guard's pistol, Odal pointed it at Kor. Hector retrieved the other gun and covered the cowering meditechs.

"Into the prisoners' cells, all of you," Odal commanded.

"You'll die for this!" Kor screamed.

Odal jabbed him in the ribs with the pistol. "Everyone dies sooner or later. Do you want to do it here and now?"

Kor went white. Trembling, he marched out of the chamber and toward the cell block.

There were guards on duty at the cells. One of them Odal recognized as a member of Romis' followers. They locked up the rest, then hurried back upstairs toward Kor's office.

"You take this pistol," Odal said to the guard as they hurried up a flight of stone steps. "If we see anyone, tell them you're taking us to be questioned by the Minister."

The guard nodded. Hector tucked his pistol out of sight inside his coveralls.

"We've only got a few minutes before someone discovers Kor in the cells," Odal said to Hector. "We must reach Romis and get out of here."

Twice they were stopped by guards along the corridors, but both times were permitted to pass. Kor's outer office was empty; it was still too early for his staff to have shown up.

The guard used Kor's desktop communicator to reach Romis, his fingers shaking slightly at the thought of exposing himself to the Minister's personal equipment.

Romis' face, still sleepy-looking, took shape on the

desk-top viewscreen. His eyes widened when he recognized Odal.

"What? . . ."

Hector stepped into view. "I escaped from your ship," he explained swiftly, "but got caught by Kor when I tried to get to the dueling machine here. Odal jumped back from Acquatainia. We've got Kor locked up temporarily. If you're going to move against Kanus, this is the morning for it. You've only got a few minutes to act."

Romis blinked. "You . . . you've locked up Kor? You're at the Intelligence Ministry?"

"Yes," Odal said. "If you have any troops you can rely on, get them here immediately. We're going to release as many of Kor's prisoners as we can, but we'll need more troops and weapons to hold this building against Kor's private army. If we can hang on here and get to Kanus, I think most of the army will go over to your side. We can win without bloodshed, perhaps. But we must act quickly!"

Sitting on the edge of his bed, staring at the two young blond faces on his bedside viewscreen, Romis struggled to put his thoughts in order.

"Very well. I'll send every unit I can count on to hold the Intelligence Ministry. Major Odal, perhaps you can contact some of the people you know in the army."

"Yes," said Odal. "Many of their officers are right here, under arrest."

Romis nodded. "I'll call Marshal Lugal immediately. I think he'll join us."

"But we've got to get Kanus before he can bring the main force of the army into action," Hector said.

"Yes, yes of course. Kanus is at his retreat in the mountains. It's not quite dawn there. Probably he's still asleep."

"Is there a dueling machine there?" Odal asked.

"I don't know. There might be. I've heard rumors

about his having one installed for his own use recently. . . ."

"All right," Hector said. "Maybe we can jump there."

"Not until we've freed the prisoners and made certain this building is well defended," said Odal.

"Right," Hector agreed.

"There's much to do," Odal said to the Foreign Minister. "And not a second to waste."

"Yes," Romis agreed.

The tri-di image snapped off, leaving him looking at a dead-gray screen set into the side of his bed table. Romis shook his head, as though trying to clear it of the memory of a dream.

It could be a trap, he told himself. *One of Kor's insidious maneuvers.* But the Star Watchman was there; he wouldn't help Kor. Or was it the Watchman? Might it have been an impersonator?

"Trap or not," Romis said aloud, "we'll never have another opportunity like this . . . if it's real."

He made up his mind. In three minutes he placed three tri-di calls. The deed was done. He was either going to free Kerak of its monster, or kill several hundred good men—including himself.

He got up from bed, dressed swiftly, and called for an air car. Then he opened the bed-table drawer and took out a palm-sized pistol.

His butler appeared at the door. "Sir, your air car is ready. Will you require a pilot?"

"No," said Romis, tucking the gun into his belt. "I'll go alone. If I don't call you by noon, then . . . open the vault behind the bed, read the instructions there, and try to save yourself and the other servants. Goodbye."

Before the stunned butler could say another word, Romis strode past him and out toward the air car.

Kanus was abruptly awakened by a terrified servant. "What is it?" the Leader grumbled, sitting up slowly in the immense circular bed. The sun had barely started to touch the distant snow-capped peaks that were visible through the giant room's floor-to-ceiling windows.

"A . . . a call from the Minister of Intelligence, sir."

"Don't stand there, put him through!"

The servant touched an ornamented dial next to the doorway. Part of the wall seemed to dissolve into a very grainy, shadowy image of Kor. He appeared to be sitting on a hard bench in a dimly lit, stone-walled cell.

"What's going on?" Kanus demanded. "Why have you awakened me?"

"It has happened, my Leader," Kor said quietly, unemotionally. "The traitors are making their move. I've been locked in one of my own cells. . . ."

"*What?*" Kanus sat rigidly upright in the bed.

Kor smiled. "The fools think they can win by capturing me and holding the Intelligence Ministry. They overlooked a few details. For one, I have my pocket communicator. I've monitored their calls. Romis is no doubt on his way to your palace right now, intent on killing you."

"Romis! And you're locked up!"

Raising his hands in a gesture of calm, Kor went on, "No need to be overly alarmed, my Leader. They are merely exposing themselves, at last. We can crush them."

"I'll call out the army," Kanus said, his voice rising.

"Some parts of the army may turn out to be disloyal to you," Kor answered. "Your personal guards should be sufficient, however, to stop these traitors. If you could detach a division or so to recapture the Ministry building, and have your own dueling machine there guarded, that should take care of most of it. Romis is flying into your hands, so it should be a simple matter to deal with him when he arrives."

"My dueling machine? They're coming through my dueling machine?"

"Only two of them: the traitor Odal, and the Watchman."

"I'll have them killed by inches!" Kanus roared. "And Romis too!"

"Yes, of course. But it will be important to recapture the Intelligence Ministry and free me. And also, you should be ready to deal with any elements of the army and space fleet that refuse to follow your orders."

"Traitors! Traitors everywhere! I'll have them all killed!"

Kanus banged the control stud over his bed and the wall screen went dark. He began screaming orders to the cringing servant, still standing by the doorway. Within minutes he was robed and hurrying down the hallway toward the room where he had his own private dueling machine.

A squad of guards met him at the door to the dueling machine room.

"Keep that machine off!" Kanus ordered. "If anyone appears inside the machine, bring him to me at once."

The guard captain saluted.

Another servant appeared at Kanus' elbow. "Foreign Minister Romis has arrived, my Leader. He. . . ."

"Bring him to my office. At once!"

Kanus strode angrily back to his office. Two guards, armed and helmeted, stood at the door. He brushed past them and stalked inside. Romis was already there, standing by the window alongside the elevated desk.

"Traitor!" Kanus screamed at the sight of the diplomat. "Assassin! Guards, cut him down!"

Startled, Romis reached for the gun at his waist. But the guards were already inside the office, guns drawn.

Romis hesitated. Then the guards took off their helmets to reveal two blond heads, two lean, grinning faces.

"We arrived at your dueling machine sooner than you thought we would," Odal said to Kanus. "It was a simple matter to overpower the guards at the door and take their uniforms."

"We left when your squad of guards arrived," Hector added, "and came here, just a few steps ahead of you."

Kanus' knees boggled.

Romis relaxed. His hands dropped to his sides. "It's all over, Chancellor. You are deposed. My men have seized the Intelligence Ministry; most of the army is against you. You can avoid a good deal of bloodshed by surrendering yourself to me and ordering your guards not to fight their countrymen."

Kanus tried to shriek, but no sounds would come from his throat. Wild-eyed, he threw himself between Odal and Hector and dashed to the door.

"Don't shoot him!" Romis shouted. "We need him alive if we're going to prevent a civil war!"

Kanus raced blindly down the halls to the dueling machine. Without a word to the startled guards standing around the machine, he punched a half-dozen buttons on the control board and bolted into one of the booths. He slapped the neurocontacts to his head and chest and took a deep, long breath. His pounding heart slowed, steadied. His eyes slid shut. His body relaxed.

He was sitting on a golden throne at the head of an enormously long hall. Throngs of people lined the richly tapestried walls, and the most beautiful women in the galaxy sat, bejeweled and leisurely, on the cushioned steps at his feet. At the bottom of the steps knelt Sir Harold Spencer, shackled, blinded, his once proud uniform grimy with blood and filth. No, not blind. Kanus wanted him to see, wanted to look into the Star Watch Commander's eyes as he described in great detail how the old man would be slowly, slowly killed.

And now he was floating through space, alone, unprotected from the vacuum and radiation but perfectly comfortable, perfectly at ease. Suns passed by him as he sailed majestically through the galaxy, his galaxy, his personal conquest. He saw a planet below him. It displeased him. He extended a hand toward it. Its cities burst into flames. He could hear the screams of their inhabitants, hear them begging him for mercy. Smiling, he let them roast.

Mountains were chiseled away to become statues of Kanus the Conqueror, Kanus the All-Powerful. Throughout the galaxy men knelt in worship before him.

They feared him. Yet more, they loved him. He was their Leader, and they loved him because he was all-powerful. His word was the law of nature. He could suspend gravity, eclipse stars, bestow life or take it.

He stood before the kneeling multitudes, smiling at some, frowning at those who displeased him. They curled and writhed like leaves in flame. But there was one who was not kneeling. One tall, silver-haired man, straight and slim, walking purposively toward him.

"You must give yourself up," said Romis gravely.

"Die!" Kanus shouted.

But Romis kept advancing toward him. "Your guards have surrendered. You've been in the dueling machine for two hours now. Most of the army has refused to obey you. The Kerak Worlds have repudiated you. Kor has committed suicide. There is some fighting going on, however. You can end it by surrendering to me."

"I am the master of the universe! No one can stand before me!"

"You are sick," Romis said stiffly. "You need help."

"I'll kill you!"

"You cannot kill me. You are helpless...."

Everything began to fade, shrink away, dim into darkness. There was nothing now but grayness, and Romis' grave, uncompromising figure standing before him.

"You need help. We will help you."

Kanus could feel tears filling his eyes. "I am alone," he whimpered. "Alone ... and afraid."

His face a mixture of distaste and pity, Romis extended his hand. "We will help you. Come with me."

Professor Leoh squinted at his wrist screen and saw

that it was four minutes before lift-off. The bright red sun of Acquatainia was near zenith. A warm breeze wafted across the spaceport.

"I hope he can get here before we leave," Geri was saying to Hector. "We owe him ... well, something."

Hector started to nod, then noticed a trim little air car circling overhead. It banked smartly against the cloud-puffed sky and glided to a landing not far from the gleaming shuttle craft that stood before them. Down from its cockpit clambered the lithe figure of Odal.

Hector trotted out to meet him. The two men shook hands, both of them smiling.

"I never realized before," Leoh said to the girl, "how much they resemble each other. They look almost like brothers."

Odal was wearing his light-blue uniform again; Hector was in civilian tunic and shorts.

"I'm sorry to be so late," Odal said to Geri as he came toward her. "I wanted to bring you a wedding present, and had to hunt all over Kerak for one of these...."

He handed Geri a small plastic box filled with earth. A single, thin bluish leaf had pushed up above the ground.

"It's an eon tree," Odal explained to them. "They've become very rare. It will take a century to reach maturity, but once grown it will be taller than any other tree known."

Geri smiled at him and took the present.

"I wanted to give you a new life," Odal went on, "in exchange for the new life you've given me."

Hector said, "We wanted to give you something, too. But with the wedding and everything we just haven't had the time to breathe, practically. But we'll send you something from Mars."

They chatted for a few more minutes, then the loud-speaker summoned Hector and Geri to the ship.

Standing beside Leoh, watching the two of them walk

arm in arm toward the ship, Odal asked, "You're going to return to Carinae?"

"Yes." Leoh nodded. "Hector will join me there in a few months, he and Geri. We've got a lifetime of work ahead of us. It's a shame you can't work with us. Now that we know interstellar teleportation is possible, we've got to find out how it works and why. We're going to open up the stars to *real* colonization, at last."

Looking wistfully at Geri as she rode the lift up to the shuttle's hatch, Odal said, "I think it would be best for me to stay away from them. Besides, I have my own duties in Kerak. Romis is teaching me the arts of government . . . peaceful, law-abiding government, just as you have in the Commonwealth."

"That's a big job," Leoh admitted, "cleaning up after the mess Kanus made."

"You'd be interested to know that Kanus is being treated psychonically, in the dueling machine. Your invention is being turned into a therapeutic device."

"So I've heard," the old man said. "Its use as a dueling machine is only one possible application for the machine. Look what it did to you and Hector. I never realized that two men could be so dramatically drawn together."

It was Odal's turn to smile. "I learned a lot in that moment with Hector in the machine."

"So did he. And yet," Leoh's voice took on a hint of regret, "I almost wish he were the old Hector again. He's so . . . so mature now. No more scatterbrain. He doesn't even whistle any more. He'll be a great man in a few years. Perhaps a Star Watch commander someday. He's completely changed."

As they watched, Hector and Geri waved from the hatch of the shuttle craft. The hatch slid shut, but somehow Hector's hand got caught still outside. A crewman had to reopen the hatch, glaring at the red-faced Watchman.

Leoh began laughing. "Well, perhaps not *completely* changed after all," he said with some relief.

PRAISE FOR
LOIS MCMASTER BUJOLD

What the critics say:

The Warrior's Apprentice: "Now here's a fun romp through the spaceways—not so much a space opera as space ballet.... it has all the 'right stuff.' A lot of thought and thoughtfulness stand behind the all-too-human characters. Enjoy this one, and look forward to the next." —Dean Lambe, *SF Reviews*

"The pace is breathless, the characterization thoughtful and emotionally powerful, and the author's narrative technique and command of language compelling. Highly recommended." —*Booklist*

Brothers in Arms: "... she gives it a geniune depth of character, while reveling in the wild turnings of her tale.... Bujold is as audacious as her favorite hero, and as brilliantly (if sneakily) successful." —*Locus*

"Miles Vorkosigan is such a great character that I'll read anything Lois wants to write about him.... a book to re-read on cold rainy days." —Robert Coulson, *Comics Buyer's Guide*

Borders of Infinity: "Bujold's series hero Miles Vorkosigan may be a lord by birth and an admiral by rank, but a bone disease that has left him hobbled and in frequent pain has sensitized him to the suffering of outcasts in his very hierarchical era.... Playing off Miles's reserve and cleverness, Bujold draws outrageous and outlandish foils to color her high-minded adventures." —*Publishers Weekly*

Falling Free: "In *Falling Free* Lois McMaster Bujold has written her fourth straight superb novel.... How to break down a talent like Bujold's into analyzable components? Best not to try. Best to say 'Read, or you will be missing something extraordinary.'" —Roland Green, *Chicago Sun-Times*

The Vor Game: "The chronicles of Miles Vorkosigan are far too witty to be literary junk food, but they rouse the kind of craving that makes popcorn magically vanish during a double feature." —Faren Miller, *Locus*

MORE PRAISE FOR
LOIS MCMASTER BUJOLD

What the readers say:

"My copy of *Shards of Honor* is falling apart I've reread it so often.... I'll read whatever you write. You've certainly proved yourself a grand storyteller."
— Liesl Kolbe, Colorado Springs, CO

"I experience the stories of Miles Vorkosigan as almost viscerally uplifting.... But certainly, even the weightiest theme would have less impact than a cinder on snow were it not for a rousing good story, and good storytelling with it. This is the second thing I want to thank you for.... I suppose if you boiled down all I've said to its simplest expression, it would be that I immensely enjoy and admire your work. I submit that, as literature, your work raises the overall level of the science fiction genre, and spiritually, your work cannot avoid positively influencing all who read it."
— Glen Stonebraker, Gaithersburg, MD

" 'The Mountains of Mourning' [in *Borders of Infinity*] was one of the best-crafted, and simply best, works I'd ever read. When I finished it, I immediately turned back to the beginning and read it again, and I can't remember the last time I did that."   — Betsy Bizot, Lisle, IL

"I can only hope that you will continue to write, so that I can continue to read (and of course buy) your books, for they make me laugh and cry and think ... rare indeed."   — Steven Knott, Major, USAF

What do you say?

Send me these books!

Shards of Honor 72087-2 $4.99 _____
The Warrior's Apprentice 72066-X $4.50 _____
Ethan of Athos 65604-X $4.99 _____
Falling Free 65398-9 $4.99 _____
Brothers in Arms 69799-4 $4.99 _____
Borders of Infinity 69841-9 $4.99 _____
The Vor Game 72014-7 $4.99 _____
Barrayar 72083-X $4.99 _____
The Spirit Ring (hardcover) 72142-9 $17.00 _____
The Spirit Ring (paperback) 72188-7 $5.99 _____
Mirror Dance (hardcover) (available March 1994)
   72210-7 $21.00 _____

Lois McMaster Bujold:
Only from Baen Books

If these books are not available at your local bookstore, just check your choices above, fill out this coupon and send a check or money order for the cover price to Baen Books, Dept. BA, P.O. Box 1403, Riverdale, NY 10471.

NAME: _____

ADDRESS: _____

_____

I have enclosed a check or money order in the amount of $ _____.

010141

PS 3552 .O84 W2 1994
Bova, Ben.
The watchmen

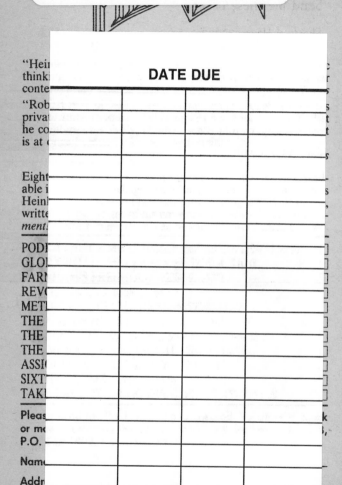

"Hei
think
conte

"Rob
privat
he co
is at

Eight
able i
Heinl
writte
ment.

PODI
GLO
FARI
REVC
METI
THE
THE
THE
ASSIC
SIXT
TAKI

Pleas
or m
P.O.

Nam

Addr

DATE DUE			
GAYLORD			PRINTED IN U.S.A.